CIAO,
BELLA

BOOKS BY RYAN M. PHILLIPS

Saving Grace

After the Fall

Fall From Grace

A NOVEL

about searching for beauty

AND *finding* LOVE

CIAO, BELLA

Ryan M. Phillips

DESTINY IMAGE® PUBLISHERS, INC.

P.O. Box 310, Shippensburg, PA 17257-0310

"Speaking to the Purposes of God for This Generation and for the Generations to Come."

This book and all other Destiny Image, Revival Press, MercyPlace, Fresh Bread, Destiny Image Fiction, and Treasure House books are available at Christian bookstores and distributors worldwide.

For a U.S. bookstore nearest you, call 1-800-722-6774.

For more information on foreign distributors, call 717-532-3040.

Reach us on the Internet: www.destinyimage.com.

ISBN 13 TP: 978-0-7684-3726-3

ISBN 13 Ebook: 978-0-7684-9008-4

For Worldwide Distribution, Printed in the U.S.A.

1 2 3 4 5 6 7 8 9 10 /15 14 13 12 11

Dedication

For you, Dad.

PART I

If Only, If Only

One

Some truths are inescapable.

Metabolisms grind to a halt, hips spread, as do stretch marks, and aging, though unavoidable, is rarely ever done without considerable angst.

On the eve of my thirtieth birthday, no one could attest to that last one more than I. It's not that I wanted to stay young forever. In fact, unlike many women who wage war against the start of a brand-new decade with shots of collagen and stockpiles of Clairol, I welcomed my stray gray hairs and my delicate crow's feet. I liked the permanent laugh lines that framed my lips and the way the veins in the back of my hands protruded ever-so-slightly.

It wasn't the thought of growing old that had me careworn with dread in the last few, rapidly depleting hours of my twenties. It was the thought of growing old alone.

I'd started planning my wedding when I was nine, after I stumbled upon my parents slow dancing in our living room one halcyon evening. Sitting on the carpeted steps, I peered intently through the balustrade, warmth consuming me as I memorized their movements; the way my father cradled my mother to his body, how she gently rested her temple against his shoulder as he softly sang the words of a love song into her ear. In that moment, I truly believed that every soul had a mate, and I quietly began to pine for mine.

But life hadn't been moved by my hopes; it hadn't seen fit to play by my rules. Twenty years later, I was still waiting to be found, still praying that someone out there was the missing piece that would make me whole.

There was a time when I used to look forward to the future—a time before doubt set in like arthritis, when adulthood felt like a far-off world of endless possibility. Back then, I could never have imagined that I would be facing the big three-o at home on my own. And yet there I was, curled up on my living room couch giving myself a pedicure in a futile attempt to soften the blow of my impending milestone.

Just as I was getting ready to apply a topcoat, there was a knock at the door.

Fanning my toes, I set aside the bottle and hobbled across the living room— my face adorned with a pore-minimizing avocado mask, my hair wrapped, Aunt Jemima style—to answer it.

Oliver was standing in the hallway, his shirt sleeves shoved past his elbows, his tie hanging loosely beneath his collar—a sure sign he'd just left the office. "This is a new look," he said, taking in my baggy red T-shirt and sagging pink and yellow flannel pajama bottoms with obvious amusement.

"How did you get up here?" I asked, dusting popcorn crumbs from my clothes and throwing my shoulders back, as though straighter posture would somehow be enough to reclaim my dignity.

"You know me and Carlos," he said, referring to the lackadaisical doorman who worked the night shift. "We have an understanding."

I shook my head. "What'd you give him this time?"

Olly grinned. "Half a hoagie and last month's issue of *Sports Illustrated*."

"Nice." I stepped aside so he could come in. "Really classy."

"Speaking of classy," he said, smirking as he grabbed a fistful of popcorn from the bowl on the coffee table and flopped onto my loveseat. "What's with the getup? I know we all have our off days, but this…." He shook his head and gave me another once-over. "This is a new kind of scary."

I snatched the towel draped over the back of the couch. "Don't you have someplace better to be?"

Slowly, he popped kernels into his mouth. "A better place to be?"

"You heard me," I said, wiping the homemade mask from my face.

"Better than here with you—my best friend in the entire world—on your birthday?" His forehead wrinkled as he feigned deep thought. "No." He shook his head. "I don't think so."

I tossed the soiled towel aside and reclaimed my spot on the sofa with a sigh. "Technically, it's not my birthday."

"Give it a few hours," he said.

I tucked my knees to my chest and groaned.

Olly chuckled softly.

Born the year before me in February, he'd made the cross into his thirties 18 months earlier. There were no complaints when his time came, no digging in of heels, no bemoaning what could have or should have been. "Come on, Mack," he said, calling me by the soubriquet my father had given me as a child, after he'd grown weary of my tearful tomboy complaints that Isabelle was too girlie, too delicate a name. "It's not that bad."

"Easy for you to say," I huffed. "You just get better with age."

Oliver and I had been best friends since college, and I'd had a front-row seat over the years as his lanky, boyish appeal had steadily matured into sinewy, rugged handsomeness. Now tall and square-shouldered, with smoldering eyes framed by thick lashes and a hint of stubble usually shadowing his chiseled jaw, he was the kind of guy who could've easily been spotted in a mall by a talent scout, cleaned up, dusted off, and turned into an underwear model.

"Can't argue with that," he said, brushing off his hands. "Now quit your bellyaching and get dressed. We're going out."

"I don't feel like it," I said, resting my chin on my knees.

"Then I guess it's a good thing I'm not giving you a choice."

"Olly, please," I whined. "Iona called in sick. I had to open and close the shop by myself. I'm tired and cranky, and all I want to do is finish painting my nails, order in, watch a movie, and grow one year older in peace."

He blinked, unmoved by the detailed account of my grueling day. Four years as a junior associate had turned him into a machine. Sleep Deprived and Caffeinated were the only two gears in which he knew how to function. "It's Friday night. I'm taking you to dinner, and there's no way you're getting out of it.

"Now, you can go dressed like that if you want," he said, straining to suppress his smile. "But as your friend, I strongly recommend you change into something that doesn't suggest you have a grocery cart of aluminum cans parked next to a cardboard box in a nearby alley. Whatever you decide, I'll be right here." He patted the arm of the chair. "And you've got twenty minutes."

Before I could open my mouth to argue, he swiped the remote control from the side table and flipped to *SportsCenter*. "Nineteen minutes, forty seconds," he said, his eyes still trained on the television.

There was no room for discussion. I could see it in the sharp slant of his brow, the rigid set of his jaw. He'd made up his mind and there would be no budging. I'd thought maybe, just maybe, he'd forget—that the date would've somehow gotten lost in his hectic schedule, the occasion buried under a mound of files and briefs.

But that wouldn't have been Olly. He was more likely to forget his own birthday than someone else's. It was one of the many reasons why I loved him. And it's why, against my better judgment and my deepest desires, I headed to my bedroom to get changed.

Two

"Where are we going?" I asked, checking my makeup in my compact's small mirror as our cabby snaked aggressively through the congested traffic heading northbound on Lake Shore Drive.

"How many times are you going to ask me that?"

I frowned at my reflection, inexplicably disappointed by the person looking back, and snapped the compact shut. "As many times as it takes for you to give me a straight answer," I said.

Olly sighed and glanced out of the window at Navy Pier, brightly lit, its gigantic Ferris wheel front and center and spinning notoriously slow. "I told you already. It's a new place. You've never been there."

"I don't understand why we have to go somewhere new," I said. "It kind of goes against the whole theme of tonight, doesn't it? I'm old now. I look old, I feel old, and old people shouldn't be trying out new places."

"You're not old," he said, placing his hand on top of mine. Our eyes locked across the shadow-strewn backseat. "And you look great."

Suddenly shy, I was the first to glance away. It was an odd sensation.

From the beginning, my friendship with Olly had been effortless, second nature even. We could predict each other's responses; understand each other's thoughts and feelings regardless as to whether they'd been expressed. We knew each other's secrets—potentially humiliating truths to which no one else was privy—and yet there I was, flustered and overly aware of our intertwined fingers resting on the blue vinyl seat between us.

We rode in silence for a while, both of us gazing out of our respective windows, as the cab exited on Randolph and made a series of turns that led us farther away from what I considered familiar territory. Ten minutes later we pulled up to SoHo, a swanky Rush Street bar, where the uniformed valet opened my door and helped me out of the cab.

"I'm impressed," I said, once Olly had paid the driver and joined me on the sidewalk. "You went all out."

"You know me," he said and shrugged, looking uncharacteristically stiff and out of his element. "I aim to please."

I studied him, eyes slanted, my curiosity balanced only by my suspicion. "I wouldn't have pegged this as your kind of place."

"Believe me, it's not," he mumbled, ushering me inside to the waiting hostess before I had a chance to question him.

He gave his name, and we were pointed across the main level—which was already packed with a twenty-something, in-the-know crowd, sporting different versions of the same look—and up to the second floor.

"No matter what," Olly said, giving my shoulders a reassuring squeeze as we reached the velvet curtain draping the entryway at the top of the stairs, "we're in this together."

"In what together?" I asked, turning just as he shoved me forward.

"SURPRISE!!!"

Rowdy cheers and clamorous applause were immediately followed by popping champagne corks and Cameron's boisterous signature laugh, which when turned on full blast, was really more of a cackle.

I stood, frozen, unpleasant shock coursing through my veins, and surveyed the room of smiling, clapping people. I didn't know half of them, and the others I hadn't seen or spoken to in years.

They swarmed me, offering their congratulations and best wishes like I'd announced my engagement or won the lottery. Really, I'd only managed to survive another year. Still, I accepted their compliments, returned their air kisses and handshakes, and offered my most convincing portrayal of a woman who believed she had something to celebrate.

"Happy thirtieth!" Cameron shrieked, elbowing through the crowd in her plunging halter and skintight Bermuda shorts. She spread her arms wide.

"You shouldn't have," I said, forcing a smile and giving her a hug, at which point I discovered that her cleavage-baring top was backless as well. "This is too much."

"There's no such thing," she said, glowing with an excitement that only the promise of a good party could bring. "Besides, you gotta make the most of this, right? You only turn thirty once."

"Thankfully," I said with a wry nod. Cam, who'd only just turned 28, had no idea what she was talking about.

"Good job, Olive Oil," she said, poking Olly's arm. "I didn't think you'd be able to pull it off."

He pursed his lips, causing the muscles in his jaw to flex with irritation the way they always did when Cameron called him Olive Oil. "Yeah, Cam, it's real brain surgery picking someone up and bringing them to a bar."

"You know what I mean," she said, ignoring the scorn in his tone. "I thought you might have to spill the beans to get her here."

"Nope, not one bean spilled," I said, looking up at Olly, my stare piercing and deliberate.

Smirking, he watched with a taunting wave as Cameron grabbed hold of my wrist and dragged me off to meet a few of the "gorgeous, single" guys she'd invited especially with me in mind.

Sometime later after everyone had mingled, the gifts had been opened, the cake had been cut, and the general preference in drink had switched from champagne to fruity, albeit, hard liquor, the music was turned up and the dancing began.

I stayed seated at a table with Joelle and Emily, once close childhood friends who had grown understandably distant after getting married a few years earlier and starting families. Like every other proud wife and mother I knew, they didn't hesitate to whip out their wallets, thick with photos, and delve into detailed anecdotes about something cute their kids had said or something charming their husbands had done. I nodded blankly, cooing at each picture without actually looking at it.

"I love this song!" Cam exclaimed loudly as the first few chords of some bass-heavy, just released remix sounded, sending her body into a sensual, writhing motion. She threw her arms over her head and churned her hips, capitalizing on the view of her exposed back, which was shimmering with what I could only assume was body glitter. "Come on, Mack," she said, waving me over to where she and a few of her PR friends, whom I'd only met in passing, had climbed onto the bar.

I declined with a shake of my head—as she knew I would—and watched along with everyone else present as the four of them improvised a rather risqué routine to the great delight of the men in attendance.

Emily, whose disdain for Cam had begun years earlier when Cameron had shown up to our church picnic wearing a micromini and an obscenely snug, "Jesus is my Homeboy" T-shirt that she'd altered to show her midriff, glared disapprovingly at the spectacle. "When is she going to grow up?"

"No time soon, I'm sure," Joelle said, sneering.

Emily shook her head. "She should be ashamed."

Joelle smirked. "It's hard to feel shame, when you don't have any."

"More cake?" I asked, admittedly eager to escape their company. Though I may not have been a wild, bar-dancing, club-hopping party girl like Cam, I wasn't a member of their car-pooling, SUV-driving wives' club either.

Joelle shook her head. "No, I'm good."

Emily smiled. "Me, too."

I crossed the crowded room in the direction of the cake, but once out of their line of vision veered left to an empty table in the back. Away from the throng and out of sight, I, along with everyone else, watched Cameron finish her performance with a provocative thrust of her pelvis.

One of the guys among the bevy who had congregated at the base of the bar swept her down from her perch and into his arms in one fluid motion.

She giggled profusely as he returned her to the floor and handed her another drink.

A tingle of envy crept down my spine.

The once-foreign feeling had become a frequent guest in my gut recently. I wasn't necessarily jealous in a way that begrudged Cameron her happiness. I didn't want to *be* her. Not per se. I just…I wanted more.

I'd spent most of my life abiding by the precepts of my faith. I loved the Lord, I lived the Word, and I trusted, by extension, that the rest would fall into place. The Bible was full of assurances, full of promises for those who made a decision for Christ. If I sought Him first, if I did not grow weary in well-doing, if I loved others, my cup would someday overflow. Joy and fulfillment unspeakable would be mine, as would the desires of my heart. The problem was, I didn't feel joy; I wasn't fulfilled.

My relationship with God was supposed to free me. But instead, over the years, it had seemingly whittled my world. Life had been reduced to a list of do's and don'ts, an index of rights and wrongs. I had structure, but no meaning; security, but no significance. I felt less complete at 29 than I did at 19. Youth had offered a sense of invincibility that had steadily worn away with age. And as a result, my unremitting trust had been replaced by fear and regret, but most of all, resentment.

It had started several months earlier as a niggling thought, a distant, but steadily pervasive feeling that I'd been duped, cheated. Suddenly, I couldn't read the Word without questioning the very promises that had once been my primary source of hope. I couldn't sing a praise song or listen to a sermon without wondering how any of it applied to me. The more I doubted, the angrier I became; until, finally, I just stopped trying to pursue God altogether. Now, after weeks of no prayer or church, no devotionals or Bible studies, I found myself wondering, more and more, if God really even existed.

Cameron's laughter pealed from across the room, where she was flirtatiously sidling up to the guy who'd helped her down from the bar. I watched as he playfully twisted a wisp of her hair around his finger before leaning forward to whisper something into her ear. Face flushed, she nodded in response; and seconds later the two of them headed, hand-in-hand, to the dance floor.

An involuntary sigh escaped my lips. If only I could learn how to be more like her. Close friends since childhood, Cameron and I were each other's polar opposites. Happy-go-lucky, she approached life with carefree abandon; while I, pensive and inquisitive by nature, made a habit of analyzing everything. In fact, it was my investigative personality that I credited, in part, with starting me down my path to the Lord.

As a teenager, when the thoughts of most other kids my age didn't roam much beyond what the cafeteria was serving for lunch, I was consumed with questions about where people went when they died. My searching ultimately led me to Christ. But Cameron, who dealt only in the immediate, couldn't be convinced to consider something as intangible as her salvation, much less be persuaded to spend her current life preparing for the one to come.

And so we learned, through the years, how to operate across the chasm of our respective beliefs, even as those beliefs led us farther and farther down diverging paths.

Mine sent me to college and then to Chicago, where I toiled miserably for three years as a freelance copyeditor before abandoning publishing altogether and eventually opening up my Christian bookstore, Au Bon Livre. Cameron's took her to Europe. Under the guise of gaining valuable world experience, she bummed around on her parents' dime until they finally cut her off. Then, with no money and no earthly idea what to do with herself, she tracked me down in the Windy City, where, after two months of sleeping on my couch and temping as an administrative assistant for Snyder & Smith, she was offered a dream entry-level PR position, for which she had never even applied.

Now, nearly seven years later, I spent my days lugging boxes, stocking shelves, cataloguing inventory, tallying receipts, and supervising fickle employees, while Cameron's days, which consisted of confirming guest lists and shopping at Saks on her two-hour lunches, rarely started before noon and ended at chic, invitation-only parties.

For most of our friendship, I'd looked at her choices—at how she readily catered to her whims instead of waiting for God to bless her according to His will—and I pitied her. I grieved the fragileness of the life she'd created, certain that it would someday come crashing down around her. But I'd been wrong. Glancing at her swaying happily on the dance floor, I frowned. Unlike me, Cameron had forged her own destiny, and she had wound up the better for it.

"Cheer up," Olly said, his stubble grazing my cheek. I flinched, startled by the scrape of his breath against my ear. "Didn't anyone tell you?" he asked, straddling the empty chair beside mine. "It's a party."

"No, come to think of it," I said, my arms folded, my brow hiked accusingly. "No one told me a thing."

He smiled. "Be mad if you want, but you wouldn't have come any other way; and believe it or not you deserve this party. You deserve to have some fun."

"Fun. Right." I rolled my eyes with a sigh. "When's that supposed to start again?"

Oliver studied me, his gaze searching. "What's going on with you?"

"What do you mean?"

"I mean something's different. You haven't been yourself lately."

"No?" I smirked. "Who have I been, then?"

"I'm serious." He tilted his head. "What is it?"

My grin faded. "Nothing," I said, looking away. "I'm just trying to figure some things out right now."

"Anything you want to talk about?"

I shook my head. "Not really." In the ten years we'd been friends, I hadn't once seen Oliver's faith falter. On the contrary, it had only steadily matured. There was no possible way he could understand what I was thinking, how I felt. And even on the off chance that he would, I didn't know that I wanted to tell him. Confessing my doubt out loud made it real; it transformed it from wavering uncertainty to acknowledged unbelief, and I wasn't sure I was ready to take that leap just yet.

"Well, whatever it is, you know God's got it, right?"

"Yes, Oliver." I sighed, automatically chafed by the assertion. He said it all the time, but I couldn't seem to recall very many instances when I'd felt like God had actually had my back. "You don't have to keep repeating it; I'm not a child."

"No, but you are human and that makes it easy to forget—especially when you're going through something."

"Well, thanks for the reminder, but I'm fine," I said, my gaze involuntarily gravitating back to Cameron.

"Don't." He laid his hand over mine. "She's not the standard, Mack. You are. You don't want to be like her."

Embarrassed, I shrugged. "I never said I did."

"You don't have to. I see the way you look at her sometimes, the admiration." He leaned in close—as if to tell me a secret. "It's the same way I look at you."

I smiled, despite my mood.

"Dance with me," he said, standing abruptly and pushing his chair aside.

I laughed. "Exactly how much champagne have you had?"

"Up, let's go." He pulled me to my feet. "I'm not taking no for an answer."

"Olly," I started to object, but he silenced me with a shake of his head.

"Save it. And no more sulking. This is it, Mack. This is the life God has blessed you with. It may not be perfect; it may not be everything you wanted or anything like you expected; but it's yours. And if you don't enjoy it, if you don't learn to appreciate it, who will?"

Grudgingly, I let him lace his fingers with mine and twirl me in the direction of the crowded dance floor.

Against its will, my body began to loosen in time with the heavy pulse of the song blasting overhead. I laughed as Oliver, who had comically appalling rhythm, attempted some sort of pop-and-lock move. He tried to get me to follow along, and when I refused, he hooked an arm around my waist, drew me close, and with his torso flush against my back, rocked us from side to side to the beat of the music.

A strange, but undeniable bolt of excitement shot through me as he rested his chin on my shoulder and cradled me tightly, his palms pressed firmly against my stomach.

The next several hours snuck by unnoticed, and before I knew it, the guests were heading home, the cleaning crew had come, and the party was officially over. "You want to share a cab?" I asked, once the last of the stragglers had left.

"Might as well," Olly said, neatly consolidating the smaller gift bags with the larger ones as we gathered my birthday presents from their designated table. "We'll have to swing by her place on the way."

Turning, we both looked at Cameron slumped over the bar, semi-conscious. I sighed. "It's OK; she can just crash with me tonight."

We headed outside into the warm September breeze and flagged a cab. I carried the bags. Oliver carried Cam.

The ride back to my condo was quiet save Cameron's drunken ramblings. Propped between us, her flaccid body fell helplessly against me or Olly depending on which way the cab turned.

Once at my building, I climbed out first and used my weight to steady Cam against the side of the car, while Oliver reminded the driver to keep the meter running and grabbed my bags from the trunk.

Instead of struggling to walk her to the elevators, Olly hoisted Cameron over his shoulder and schlepped her up the awning-covered walkway and through the glass double doors.

"You need some help there?" Carlos asked. It wasn't the first time he'd witnessed Oliver carrying Cameron past his post.

Olly politely declined his offer without missing a stride.

A short elevator ride later, we were inside my living room, where he gingerly deposited Cameron on the couch. She immediately curled into a fetal position and began snoring. "Mental snapshot," he said. "Remember this the next time you wish you were her."

I laughed. "Definitely."

"So did you have fun tonight?" he asked.

"Oddly, yes."

"Well then," he said, reaching for a hug. "Mission accomplished."

Circling my arms around his narrow waist, I squeezed him to me and, with a content sigh, breathed in the familiar scent of his cologne. "Thank you."

"Anytime," he said, gently resting his cheek against the crown of my head.

I waited, expecting that any moment he would pull away, but instead his

21

hold around me tightened. "What're you thinking?" he asked.

"About tonight?"

There was a pause. "About us," he clarified.

I peered up at him, disarmingly aware of the heat emanating from his chest. "What do you mean?"

"You and me," he said, gliding a hand down the nape of my neck and between my shoulder blades to the hollow of my back. "Do you ever wonder?"

"Ol," I whispered. "What're we doing?"

Slowly, tentatively, his lips inched forward and met mine.

We stood motionless for a moment—foreheads butted, noses brushing—until I mustered the nerve to tilt my chin upward and reciprocate with a kiss of my own. This one was deeper and less hesitant. My breath caught as his mouth parted. He tasted of vanilla icing and champagne.

When we finally separated, I was surprised to discover that we had somehow migrated to the other side of the room. Disoriented, I braced myself against a nearby wall and willed my heart, which was pounding like a jackhammer against my ribcage, to resume its normal pace. Meanwhile, Oliver, his body pressed softly against mine, cupped my jaw and skimmed a thumb across my lips; his touch was electrifying. I met his searching gaze with a small, but approving nod and watched, stomach flitting, as the corners of his mouth curved up into an apprehending grin. Gingerly, he tilted his head, leaned forward, and guided my face once more toward his.

"Mack?" Cam croaked.

I felt Oliver's muscles tense beneath my hands. Frozen, like two statues in the dark, we listened as she stirred helplessly on the couch.

"Mack," she whimpered again. "I'm cold."

Groaning, I shook my head.

Oliver stepped away with a chuckle and waited for me to retrieve a spare blanket from the hall closet. I draped it over Cameron's reedy frame.

"You have to hand it to her," he said, smiling, though his tone was thick with disappointment. "She's got impeccable timing."

"One of her many talents," I joked feebly. Stuck in muddy silence, we stood across from each other, our postures stiff with uncertainty, as the moment, now sufficiently ruined, gave way to painful awkwardness.

"I should probably go," he said, sidestepping my ottoman toward the front door.

"You don't have to." Rounding the coffee table, I quickly regained the space he'd put between us. "You could stay." I shrugged. "We could hang out, talk."

Olly smiled. "It's late." He tossed his thumb over his shoulder in the general direction of the cab still waiting outside. "And the meter's running."

I nodded. "OK."

His thoughts a mystery to me, Oliver studied me for several seconds. Despite myself, I fidgeted self-consciously beneath the intensity of his probing gaze, unable to speak or even lift my eyes from the cherry-stained slats of my wood floor. I listened, pulse racing, to the rustle of his shirt as he moved closer, tucked a strand of hair behind my ear and delivered a feather-light peck to my temple. "Happy birthday, Mack."

I stared at the door long after Oliver had let himself out, trying, unsuccessfully, to make sense of what had transpired. My first inclination was to write off the entire event as a fluke—some uncanny combination of lighting, timing, and champagne that had masterfully counterfeited romantic chemistry.

Outlandish as it was, the theory struck me as far more plausible than the notion that Oliver and I, after nearly a decade of friendship, might actually become something more.

And yet, when I replayed the kiss in my mind—when I recalled the way he'd looked at me, the way his touch had erased all sense of space and time—I could almost convince myself that we'd just ignited a spark neither of us ever knew existed.

Three

"How much do you love me right now?" Cameron asked, her voice a hoarse blend of unsettled phlegm and early-morning rasp.

My mattress bounced and bobbed as she crawled clumsily across it, brazenly inviting herself to climb under the sheets and thaw her ice-cold feet against my warm legs.

She waited a few seconds for me to acknowledge her, and when I didn't, she kneaded her pointy chin into my upper arm and impatiently demanded, in a loud whisper, for me to wake up.

My mind foggy with sleep, I ignored her and burrowed deeper beneath the covers. Undeterred, Cameron poked the small of my back until I swatted her hand away. "I think I'm officially the world's best, best friend," she said, shamelessly fishing for praise.

I mumbled my concurrence, hoping it would buy me more time. It didn't.

"You should have seen the look on your face." She tugged at my shoulder until she'd managed to roll me onto my back. I grudgingly pried one eye open to discover her smiling down at me. "It was priceless."

"It was shock," I said, slowly hoisting myself up into a sitting position.

Cameron laughed. "Hence the term *surprise* party."

I leaned back against my headboard and sighed. An innate introvert, I'd never been one for big bashes and splashy celebrations. A low-key dinner with a few close friends would have been more my style. But Cameron had obviously put a great deal of thought and effort—however misguided—into the previous night's festivities and for that, at least, I was grateful. "You did an amazing job," I said, giving her hand an appreciative squeeze. "It was far and away the nicest party anyone has ever thrown for me and I will remember it always."

Flush with accomplishment, she hugged a stray pillow to her chest and smiled. "I can't take all of the credit," she said. "Oliver was a huge help."

An automatic smirk crept across my face. Our kiss, every detail of which was irrevocably etched into my memory, had played for hours, like a looped tape in my head. "Really?" I asked, quietly marveling at how the sound of his name suddenly made my heart flutter.

"It took a little coaxing, at first," she confessed. "He kept insisting on a lame dinner instead. But eventually he came around."

"And that surprises you?" I smirked. "When don't you get your way?"

Cameron shrugged and tossed the covers aside. "Honestly, I wasn't sure he'd have the time," she said, slinging her legs over the side of the bed and standing. "He's been all work and no play these days."

I nodded. In recent months, Oliver had learned that he was one of several attorneys in his firm being considered for senior associate—a promotion that would all but guarantee him an eventual offer for partner. The news was proof that his tireless effort and complete dedication, both of which he gave at great sacrifice to his personal life, had not gone unnoticed. Determined to further distinguish himself from his well-credentialed colleagues, he'd taken on several high-profile cases. The workload had him clocking 80-hour weeks, many of which were spent sleeping and showering at the office. But he was confident that it would all be worth it in the long run.

Cameron padded her way to the mirror hanging over my dresser. "It was nice getting a glimpse of the old Olly," she said, rubbing her swollen eyes, still stained with last night's mascara.

"What do you mean?"

"I saw him holding his own on the dance floor. You too." She turned to face me, her grin mischievous. "You guys looked awfully cozy."

"Whatever," I said, heat flaming up my neck and across my cheeks. I dismissed the suggestion with a roll of my eyes. "Clearly, your imagination has run away with you again."

"If you say so." She tossed a jibing grin over her shoulder as she loped the last few feet to the bathroom. Moments later the spray of the shower sounded from behind the closed door.

Grateful for the quiet, I lay back down and pulled the duvet over my head, hoping to sneak in a few more minutes of rest. Between the party, which hadn't ended until the wee hours of the morning, and the kiss, which had kept my mind racing well past dawn, I'd barely slept. But no sooner had my limbs grown heavy and my eyelids drooped closed with exhaustion did the phone ring.

Reaching a hand out from under the cover, I blindly felt for the cordless, which was buried somewhere beneath the piles of papers and books perpetually cluttering my nightstand. "Hello?"

"Good morning, Ms. Mackenzie. This is Peter at the front desk."

"Hey, Pete," I said, tucking the receiver between the pillow and my ear with a yawn. "What's up?"

"Mr. Tate is here to see you."

My eyes fluttered open as I scrambled to sit up. Immediately, my gaze dropped to my tattered nightshirt, while my free hand traveled to my tangled mess of hair.

"Ms. Mackenzie?" Peter called.

"Yes...um...OK, great," I sputtered. "Thank you."

"My pleasure," Peter said. "I'll send him up now."

Tossing the phone aside, I tumbled out of bed and dashed to my closet. I knew, even as I was maniacally combing through clothes and clumsily tripping over shoes, that the effort was unnecessary. Oliver, who just last night had caught me in avocado and flannel, didn't care how I looked or what I wore; his acceptance of me was unconditional. At our core, we were best friends, and that single fact superseded everything, including bed-head and morning breath.

It didn't, however, stop me from stripping off my pajamas and exchanging them for a pair of jeans and a tank top or from scuttling to the bathroom, where I raced to brush my teeth, while Cameron, hidden behind the shower curtain and a thick plume of steam, unwittingly serenaded me with a dissonant compilation of show tunes.

Moving at warp speed, I managed to comb my hair into submission, slather on a coat of lip gloss and dab a little perfume behind each ear, before he knocked.

Smoothing the wrinkles from my pants, I gave myself a quick once-over in the hallway mirror on my way to let him in. I opened the door to find Oliver leaning against its frame, an easy grin on his face, a bouquet of flowers in hand.

Gone were yesterday's rumpled suit and silk tie. Instead, he wore pressed khakis, white tennis shoes, and a navy polo—collar turned up. The shirt, I couldn't help but note, was one I'd complimented him on several times before.

His hair, still damp from his shower, rested delicately against his forehead and fell in waves across his ears. He'd shaved—a rarity for Oliver, who favored the five o'clock shadow look—and the dark circles that usually sat under his eyes were gone.

"You look great," we both said simultaneously.

My nervous laugh echoed his.

"Sorry." I shook my head. "This is…"

"Different?" he offered.

I nodded. "That's one way to put it."

"Different isn't necessarily bad," he said.

"No." Shyly, I looked away. "Just unbearably awkward."

He handed me the flowers he'd brought. "Maybe these will help."

"They're beautiful," I said, taking in their sweet fragrance before glancing back up at him. My eyes narrowed teasingly. "I hope this isn't your way of letting me down easy."

Slowly, his smile faded. My stomach responded by twisting into a painful knot. While I'd hoped he wouldn't wake in the morning regretting the impulse that had compelled him to kiss me, I had, of course, considered the possibility. The threat seemed far-fetched, the chances minuscule, as I'd lain in bed blissfully rehearsing it in my mind. But in the light of a new day, with his strangely solemn expression bearing down on me, I wasn't so sure.

"We should talk," he said. "Can I take you to breakfast?"

I shook my head. "It's OK. You don't have to."

"Mack," he called softly.

"Listen, I get it," I said, feigning composure, despite the lump forming at the back of my throat. "Last night was a mistake and you just want to be friends." I shrugged. "It's fine, really. Let's not turn it into a major production."

"Hey," he hooked his finger through my belt loop and tugged me toward him. "Look at me."

I couldn't. Instead, I combed my hand through my hair and silently wished to disappear.

"Hey," he called again. "I have never regretted anything that's involved you." When I didn't respond, he cradled my neck in his massive palm and raised my head until our gazes met. "Especially not last night."

I searched his face for signs of doubt, but all I saw was his brow, knitted with sincerity, and the warming reassurance of his broad smile. As if to affirm his veracity, he leaned forward and kissed me. It was tender and lingering and deceptively explosive.

"Come to breakfast with me," he said, running his lips along the curve of my earlobe. I grinned.

"Olly!" Cameron exclaimed.

We sprang apart, foiled, yet again, by Cam's atrocious timing. "To what do we owe this unfortunate intrusion?" she jibed.

I turned to see her standing inside the living room clad in nothing but a towel, her hair clinging in wet strands against her damp shoulders.

Oliver, who'd inched his way back into the front hall, nodded at the bouquet in my hand. "Just delivering a little birthday cheer."

Cameron's eyes darted suspiciously between the two of us. "Did I interrupt something?" she asked, her smirk suggestive.

"Not at all," Oliver said. His tone possessed an easiness that I didn't feel. "Actually, I was just heading out."

I looked over at him, my mouth turned down disappointedly. "What about breakfast?"

"Another time," he said, his shrug small and helpless. "I'll call you."

"Oh, come on," Cameron prodded, stealthily inviting herself along to what was supposed to be a private outing for two. "It'll be fun."

"By the time you get ready, it'll be lunch," Olly said with a knowing frown. "And I'm not in the mood to sit around all day while you primp."

"I can be dressed in ten minutes," Cam said, her brow hiked daringly, as if he'd just issued her a challenge. "And besides," she lowered her voice and cut her eyes furtively in my direction, "we still have some unfinished business."

It was my turn to be suspicious. "Should I be worried?"

Cameron grinned impishly. "Let's just say we saved the best birthday surprise for last."

The news might have excited me, had it not so clearly ruffled Oliver. He folded his arms across his chest and quietly studied the two of us, debating, I could tell, whether or not he would acquiesce. Finally, he sighed. "Ten minutes?"

Cam's squeal was triumphant. "Thirty, tops," she said, scampering around the corner toward the bedroom before he could object.

"We could just leave her," I joked.

He laughed. "Don't tempt me."

"Are you sure you're OK with this?" I asked. "You seem a little tense."

"I'm fine," he said, closing the distance Cameron's intrusion had put between us in one easy stride. "Better than fine, actually. I get to spend today with my favorite person in the entire world."

"Well, when you put it that way," I said, tilting my face away bashfully.

He smiled. "But you want to know what the best part is?"

"What's that?" I asked.

He rested his hands low on my hips and pulled me to him. "We have a whole thirty minutes with which to occupy ourselves."

I laughed. "What'd you have in mind?"

Abandoning words, he lowered his lips to mine and answered me with a kiss.

Four

For a Saturday morning, Leona's wasn't as crowded as we'd expected. Many a weekend brunch had taught us that only the early birds got the good tables outdoors beside the cobbled walkway lined with colorful buds and gently bristling trees. The less time-conscious birds got the next best seating. Granted it was inside, but it was beside the floor-to-ceiling picture windows; a spot where the sun's warmth shone with ample supply and the ambiance wasn't spoiled by the smoke from the patrons puffing on cigarettes in their designated section in the back, which, incidentally, was exactly where the tardy birds landed on a regular basis.

Though we arrived around eleven—well into tardy bird territory—Oliver, Cameron, and I were fortunate enough to get one of the coveted window booths.

Olly scooted in beside me. Inching closer than usual, he slid his hand under the table and rested it atop my knee, while Cameron settled across from us, kicking off her shoes and crossing her legs Indian-style.

Just as eager to be near him, I angled my body toward his, but in the interest of discretion, resisted the urge to lay my head against his shoulder.

"So." Cameron smiled and yanked a plain, white envelope from her purse.

"Let's get down to business."

"Now?" Olly asked.

She shrugged, her gaze questioning. "Why not?"

Oliver shifted stiffly in his seat. "We should at least order first."

"Is this the big surprise?" I asked, admittedly curious as to what in that sealed envelope kept turning Oliver squirrelly.

Nodding, Cameron slid it across the table.

"Is it from both of you?"

"Yes," she said at the same time he answered, "No."

Cameron waved her hand, indicating that the details were unimportant. "Just open it already."

"You guys didn't have to do this," I said, watching from the corner of my eye for Olly's reaction. Sinking against the cushioned back of the booth, he fiddled idly with his sweating glass of water, but said nothing.

Spurred on by Cameron's impatient sighs, I tore open the envelope and retrieved two tickets to *The Kitty Asher Show*. "Wow." I smirked.

Kitty Asher was a retired supermodel, one of those Amazonian knockouts who'd spent the past 15 years dominating the runway on every continent and raking in the equivalent of a small nation's gross national product, only to decide at the pinnacle of her career that she'd grown bored of strutting her stuff in the name of fashion. No sooner were her designer gowns hung and her four-inch Manolos shelved, did her face pop up on every bus and billboard in the city, advertising her newest endeavor: talk show queen.

I studied Cameron's expectant face. "Thank you?" I said, the words involuntarily escaping as a question.

She smiled, eyes twinkling. "They're for this Monday's taping."

"Yes, they are," I said, scanning the tickets before returning them to their envelope and sliding them back across the table. "And I'd love to go," I said, not nearly as sorry as I sounded. "But I have to work."

"Got it covered," she said, sliding the envelope back to me. "Olly volunteered to fill in for the day."

"Did he?" I asked, shifting my quizzical gaze to Oliver, who'd moved from fiddling with his water to rearranging the condiments.

Before either of them had the opportunity to explain further, our waitress appeared tableside. She was young, a cross between punk and goth, with piercings everywhere on her face, but in her ears. Her black-collared shirt did very little to hide the series of tattoos encircling her long neck. And her short, spiked hair, which was dyed ink black, save the tips, which were frosted bleach blonde, was a striking contrast to her fair, milky skin. Across town, she'd have a hard time getting hired, but in modish Wicker Park, where the tattoo parlors outnumbered the Starbucks, she was the norm.

Like most of the regulars to whom Leona's was a staple, we ordered without bothering to crack one of the cheap laminated menus propped between the half-empty bottle of ketchup and the napkin dispenser.

"It was a last-minute thing," Olly said, as soon as our waitress had disappeared back into the sea of chatting patrons. "The show, I mean." He glanced over at me, his eyes wide, his expression contrite.

Munching happily on an ice cube, Cameron nodded. "We really lucked out. I know people who had to wait months to score tickets."

Their starkly contrasting reactions to the exact same event made me chuckle. There was no doubt in my mind that Oliver had been bulldozed by Cameron's trademark zeal. I, too, had been reluctantly enlisted to help carry out a few of her half-baked schemes over the years.

Granted, I could think of far better ways to spend my Monday. But if going to a taping of *The Kitty Asher Show* meant that I could ease Oliver's conscience and make Cameron happy to boot, I'd play along.

"You know what?" I said, giving his thigh a reassuring pat. "I'm in."

His forehead puckered doubtfully.

"No really." I smiled. "I've never been to a live taping before. It'll be fun."

"See?" Cam said, gloatingly cocking her head. "I told you she'd love it."

I nodded. "And don't worry about the bookstore. I'll get someone to cover for me."

"Are you sure?" he asked. "I don't mind."

35

"You're busy enough as it is."

He laced his fingers with mine. "I can make the time."

Our gaze locked and I smiled.

"Do you two need some privacy?" Cam asked, watching our exchange from across the table with an amused smirk.

The first to look away, I cleared my throat and changed the subject. "So, Cameron, have you told Olly about your promotion?"

"You got promoted?" Oliver asked, sounding as shocked as I'd been when she'd first told me.

Cameron, who'd turned slacking into an art form, wasn't exactly an ideal employee. She was, however, attractive and charismatic, both of which had helped her sign two big clients within months of each other.

"I got offered one," she said with a disinterested shrug.

"She's thinking about turning it down," I explained.

Oliver shook his head. "Why?"

"Because." I smirked. "She'll actually be expected to work."

"It's just a title change," she said. "I'd be managing twice as many accounts for the same salary."

"But it could lead to something bigger. They might end up offering you a raise a few months down the line once you prove you can do the job," Olly argued. "This is a real opportunity to start focusing on the long term, Cameron. You can't coast forever."

Cameron stared silently out of the window beside us, her eyes glazing over with boredom the way they always did when Oliver lectured her.

Though I felt for her during moments like these, I also knew that Oliver's admonishments—unwanted and unheeded as they were—came from a genuine place of concern. Cameron made good money and she had no financial obligations to anyone but herself. But she was more likely to drop a grand on a designer purse than she was to put it into her savings account. Weekly outings to Neiman Marcus, a need to dine out as often as possible, and an aversion to any sort of budgeting kept her living from paycheck to paycheck. And Oliver, who had long ago stopped tallying the loans he had made her, worried about her future.

To Cameron's obvious relief, our waitress emerged from the kitchen and headed our way, heaping plates of steaming food balanced expertly in both hands. All but breakfast was forgotten as she set our dishes down on the table.

A comfortable silence settled over us after Oliver blessed the meal. We ate heartily and intently, pausing only every now and then to comment on how delicious the food was.

Cameron, the first to finish, tossed her napkin aside and turned her attention to her freshly refilled cup of coffee. "So what're you doing after this?" she asked me, stirring in two creamers and a packet of sweetener.

I glanced at Olly, whose fork had halted midway on the journey from his half-eaten French toast to his mouth. The only thing certain about either of our plans was that they involved each other. "Nothing," I said, shrugging breezily. "I'll probably just go home and relax."

Her eyes brightened, and I knew instantly that I'd given the wrong answer. "Let's go shopping," she said.

"And get what?" Olly asked. "You already own one pair of everything that's ever been made."

"I'm not really up for it today," I said, using the butt of my knife to push the cold remnants of my omelet from one side of my plate to the other. "Another time."

"But I thought we'd buy outfits for the show on Monday," she said, the stubborn pout of her mouth a telltale indication that she wasn't going to give in without a fight. "And besides, we never hang out, just the two of us, anymore."

"You should go," Olly said. He drained the last of his orange juice, before meeting my gaze with an understanding smile. "A little retail therapy might be good for the soul."

I nodded. "I guess there'll still be time to relax later." It was a question disguised as a statement. Really, I wanted to know if he and I could get together afterward, but I didn't dare ask in front of Cameron, who was anxiously hanging onto our every word.

"Plenty of time," Olly said, knocking his knee against mine in secret confirmation.

I smiled. "Shopping it is, then."

Cameron clapped, elated by the prospect of an afternoon of buying clothes. "Just let me run to the bathroom," she said, hurriedly scooting out of the booth. "Be right back."

"Good for the soul?" I asked, as soon as she'd disappeared around the corner.

He laughed. "She would've worn you down eventually, anyway."

"She always does," I said, sighing.

Oliver draped his arm around my shoulders and drew me close. "Trust me, the day will fly by before you know it," he said, his breath sweeping across my forehead in warm waves. "And then tonight, we'll enjoy some quality time of our own."

My head lingered against his chest until Cameron sauntered back around the corner several minutes later. "I think we should hit Water Tower first," she said, fishing her purse from underneath the table, while Oliver headed to the register to settle the bill.

"Whatever you want," I said, nodding distractedly as I snuck glances at him from across the room.

Turning unexpectedly, he caught me staring and grinned.

I looked away, embarrassed, and faked a sudden deep interest in the straw dispenser while he made his way back over to us.

"All set," he said, tossing down the tip.

Cameron led the way outside. "Do you guys want a ride anywhere?" Olly asked.

"No, we're good," she said, her arm already waving overhead at several taxis in the distance.

I turned to Olly and smiled. "So I'll see you later?"

He nodded. "Absolutely."

Before we could say anything more, a yellow cab pulled up to the curb.

Cameron climbed in and beckoned impatiently for me to join her. "Michigan and Chestnut," she called to the driver from behind the Plexiglas partition.

Olly closed the door behind us. "Have fun."

I gave him a small wave as the car pulled off and then settled into my seat beside Cameron, who was already chronicling the long list of stores she wanted to visit.

Several blocks up at a red light, I turned to look out of the back window. And there, still standing on the sidewalk was Oliver, watching with a smile as we drove away.

Five

Shopping with Cameron proved far more exhausting than even I'd anticipated. Her quest for the perfect blouse turned into a search for a pair of jeans to go with it, which then led to a hunt for strappy heels.

Three hours, a half-dozen shopping bags, and a mango smoothie later, we wound up sampling makeup at a cosmetics counter in Macy's.

"This one's more of an earth tone," the saleswoman said, handing Cameron yet another tester tube of lipstick and a fresh Q-tip with which to apply it.

"What do you think?" Cam asked, turning to face me.

I thought it looked exactly the same as the other six shades she'd already tried on. "It suits you."

"I don't know." She studied her reflection. "It's not too dark?"

My patience running on fumes, I groaned. "Does it really matter? No one's going to see you in the audience."

"I'll see me," she said, puckering at herself in the mirror once more before settling on the shade she'd rejected five colors back.

I sighed as she moved on to their selection of blushes. "I'm going to go look for a place to sit."

She nodded distractedly, her attention rapt by the spinning display of color palettes. With an irritated huff, I schlepped her bags over to a cozy lounge area I'd spotted earlier near the escalators. Just as I eased into one of the armchairs, my cell phone rang. It was Oliver.

"Have they cut up her card yet?" he asked.

"Not yet, but I might, if she doesn't hurry up."

"Come on," he said. "It can't be that bad."

"Have you ever watched someone try on twenty pairs of jeans?"

"No." I could hear him smiling. "Thank God."

"Well believe me," I said over his laughter. "It's torturous—possibly even traumatizing."

"Are you too traumatized to hang out tonight?"

I grinned. "No, I'm pretty sure I'll be recovered by then."

"Good," he said. His voice was low, sweet. "Because it's only been a few hours and I already miss you."

My smile was wide. "Yeah, me too."

"So you'll come by later?" he asked.

"Sure," I said. "What time?"

"How about seven? We can order in some dinner, maybe watch a movie."

"Sounds good."

"OK," he said. "It's a date."

We lingered quietly for several seconds, neither one of us particularly eager to let the other go, before reluctantly saying good-bye.

Hoisting myself out of the chair, I gathered the collection of bags lying at my feet. Then, with my mood drastically improved from when I'd sat down only a few minutes earlier, I navigated my way back into the maze of glass displays and perfume mist to find Cameron.

Six

By the time I arrived at Oliver's later that evening, my nerves had gotten the better of me. Boundless enthusiasm had gradually disintegrated into an acute anxiety that left my knees rubbery and my hands trembling as I made my way up the steep set of brick steps that led to his townhouse and rang the doorbell.

An hour earlier, I'd been standing in my closet trying, as best I could, to piece together something to wear. Hardly a fashionista, my personal sense of style revolved around comfort, not beauty. As far back as I could remember, my wardrobe had consisted of slouchy jeans, loose T-shirts, and sensible shoes. It's not that I didn't notice trends as they came and went or that I didn't secretly wish that I had a look like Cameron's that could turn heads. But in a world where people were either exceptional or ordinary, I had long ago accepted my fate as the latter.

Over the years, I'd seen plenty of women enter and exit Olly's life. While they'd ranged in age and race, size and personality, they had all been impeccably polished and dauntingly urbane, unlike me, whose dowdy clothes and mousy brown hair others openly pitied. In time, he and his girlfriends wound up going their separate ways and each of their names inevitably faded from my mind, but their collective memory served as a very vivid reminder that Oliver was mortifyingly out of my league.

I'd attempted to replicate the pulchritude of his past loves, but two hours of trying on everything I owned and another hour of fiddling with my hair and clumsily painting on makeup had only confirmed that even on a good day, with my best efforts, I was just average.

"Look at you," Oliver said, opening the door and stepping aside so I could squeeze by.

At the last minute, I'd settled on a halter dress that Cameron had once praised as bohemian chic. The whole ride over, I'd worried that the outfit might come off as too much of an effort for a night of takeout and movies. But gauging from Oliver's sweeping gaze and approving nod, I'd made the right choice.

"You're a vision," he said.

"Thanks." I smiled and took him in with a sweeping gaze of my own. He'd traded his polo and slacks for a black V-neck and a pair of dark-rinse jeans. "You look great too."

"Dinner's not quite ready yet," he said, ushering me down the long, dimly lit corridor that led to his kitchen. "But you can keep me company while I cook."

"So much for takeout," I said, eyeing the impressive array of cookware cluttering nearly every inch of counter space.

"It's our first date." He grinned and reclaimed his post behind the cutting board next to the double ovens. "I had to pull out all of the stops."

Sliding onto one of the stools lined along the center island, I watched as he expertly diced several tomatoes into perfect cubes, before transferring them into one of the steaming pots.

"OK, I'm officially impressed," I said.

He laughed and motioned for me to come closer. "Have a taste."

Eagerly, I hopped off the stool and joined him by the stove, where he dipped a wooden spoon into the simmering sauce and held it carefully to my lips.

"Perfect," I said, my nod commending. Thick and velvety, it boasted a delicate mixture of herbs and just the right amount of spice. "It doesn't need another thing."

He returned the lid to the pot. "In that case I just have to sear the scallops."

"Anything I can do?"

"You want to make the salad?" he asked, eyeing the colander full of baby spinach leaves sitting in the sink.

I smiled. "I think I can handle that."

While he proceeded to melt butter in a cast iron pan, I grabbed a knife from the block next to the cutting board and busied myself slicing a colorful medley of carrots, bell peppers, cucumbers, and beets.

We worked in comfortable silence for some time, occasionally sidling closer than necessary to sneak playful peeks at each others' progress. It was nice, just being there with him, appreciating the ease of our natural dynamic, while at the same time enjoying the exhilarating intensity of our newfound attraction.

Though it was nascent and undefined, I couldn't stop myself from considering where our courtship could one day lead, what it might someday become. I liked the idea of a lifetime of cooking dinner with Olly, of an eon of waking up next to him. He was my best friend, and the prospect of sharing my future with him—a man whose mere presence turned every day into a treasure—excited me.

"All done," I said, admiring my handiwork.

Oliver removed the pan from the heat and turned off the burner. "I'm just about set, too," he said. I watched him transfer the scallops to a waiting bed of pasta and top the dish with an artistic drizzle of sauce.

"I'll put the salad out," I said, grabbing the bowl and a pair of tongs and heading in the direction of the dining room.

"Actually," he stopped me. "It's a nice night. I thought we'd eat on the deck."

I smiled. "Good idea." Changing course, I made my way toward the set of French doors that led outside and down a narrow staircase to his backyard.

The air was mild, the sky a transfixing spectrum of pinks and orange. Stopping briefly, I closed my eyes and turned my face to the gentle breeze, before rounding the corner to discover a strikingly beautiful scene.

Dozens of rice paper lanterns swung ethereally from the gangly branches of a white elm that hovered over us like a gentle giant. Illuminating the deck were an enchanting assortment of glass bauble lights that had been strung with great care along its balusters and railing. And in the center of it all was a candle-bedecked table elegantly set for two.

"You did this?" I asked.

Oliver looked boyish and timid, his sharp features softened by the warm blanket of hazy light. "I told you I was pulling out all the stops."

I smiled, unable to tear my eyes away from the stunning backdrop. "It's like our own little slice of Heaven."

"That was the idea," he said, guiding me to the table. Seated across from each other, I served the salad, while he spooned generous portions of scallops and pasta onto our plates.

Grace was followed by eager silence as he watched me savor my first bite. "This is incredible," I said, reaching for a piece of bread from the sliced boule swathed in the basket between us.

He smiled. "I'm glad you like it."

I tore the crust off and used the soft center to sop up the sauce on my plate. "It's been so long since you've cooked for me, I almost forgot how good you are at it."

"Come on." He speared a tomato with his fork. "It hasn't been that long."

"At least a year."

"What about Thanksgiving?" he asked. "I threw that huge dinner."

"Which I missed because I went home to see my family."

"That's right." He chewed thoughtfully. "Well, what about Cameron's birthday? I always cook for Cam's birthday."

"We went out this year, remember?" I asked. "She invited half her office, showed up two hours late, ordered way too much sake, and then stuck you with the bill when her credit card was declined."

He shook his head. "How could I forget? I think I'm still making payments on that sushi."

"So that would mean," I said, smirking, "I haven't enjoyed the pleasure of your culinary genius since last year's Super Bowl."

He laughed. "You had to bring it up, didn't you?"

Giving in to our incessant pleas, Oliver had agreed to let Cameron and me throw a Super Bowl party at his house, which was considerably bigger than both our places combined. He'd also agreed to brave below-zero temperatures for the greater good of our guests, most of whom were just as interested in getting their hands on his slow-smoked barbecue ribs as they were in watching the game.

But in the frenzy of the afternoon, someone had prepped the grill without Oliver's knowledge. And as soon as he'd doused the smoldering coals with lighter fluid, a sudden combustion of flames caught his gloves on fire.

Panicking, he managed to claw them off, but in the process, ignited his coat, which he then flailed into the nearby shrubbery that neatly lined the perimeter of his property. By the time we heard his calls for help, half of his privacy fence was alight.

Forty-five minutes, two fire trucks, and a battery of squad cars later, the blaze was extinguished; and with the exception of his charred backyard and bruised ego, Oliver had escaped unscathed. We banned any further attempts at grilling that day and settled, instead, for pizza and the immensely satisfying entertainment of ribbing Olly for nearly recreating the Great Fire of Chicago.

"Thanks to you and Cameron, people called me Mr. O'Leary for weeks," he said.

I laughed. "We've had some good times."

Reaching across the table for my hand, he smiled. "And a great friendship."

"The best," I said, entwining our fingers. "Which is why I can't help but wonder what's going on; what suddenly changed?"

"It's not as sudden as you might think," he said with a small shrug. "It just took me some time—and a lot of prayer—to work up the courage to tell you."

"Well, when did you know?" I asked.

He smiled. "It was a few months ago, after a long, horrible day. You know, the kind of day when everything goes wrong and nothing you do is right and everyone is looking to you to make miracles happen?"

I nodded.

"We were all packing it in, and everybody was talking about their plans for the rest of the night. How they couldn't wait to catch the end of some game or have dinner with their kids. And I realized that I couldn't wait to get home and talk to you. It hit me, right then and there, that you're my favorite part of every day." His gaze met mine over the soft flame of the candles flickering between us. "There's no one, at any given moment, I'd rather be with more, no one who means as much, no one who matters the same way.

"And it's not just because we're best friends or because we've known each other for such a long time," he rushed to add. "It's because you're you. It's the way your eyes light up when you tell a story and how you hide your face behind your hair when you laugh. It's the feeling I get when I see your car pull up or I hear your voice on the other end of the phone. It's your willingness to give of yourself as much as you can to everyone you can. It's your passion for Christ, the way you live the Word and inspire others to do the same. It's the way, even now after ten years, you still surprise me, how every day, I find something new in you to admire, something different to love."

I sat stunned and I stared at him, mouth ajar—my thoughts tangled, my words lodged at the back of my throat which had grown thick with emotion.

"Too much, too fast," he said, drawing his hand away with an embarrassed simper. "You're freaked out."

"No." I shook my head. "I'm not, I swear. I'm just processing."

"I get it if you need time to think things over," he said. "We don't have to figure it all out tonight; I'm not going anywhere."

"Neither am I." Reaching across the table, I re-laced our fingers. "And it's not that I can't see us together that way, because I can. I want to. But there's a lot at stake, you know? Our friendship means more to me than anything, and the idea of changing who we are makes me nervous. I don't want to gamble what we have on the chance at something more and wind up losing both."

"I don't think it's possible," he said, caressing the back of my hand with his thumb. "You and I are one of the few things in life that make uncondi-tional sense. And that sort of destiny is not easily thwarted. But what do you say, in the interest of prudence, that we agree just to take it slow and see what happens?"

I smiled. "I think I can handle that."

We finished dinner on the deck and then moved inside for dessert. Con-versation came easily as we sat in his kitchen sipping coffee and feeding each other tiramisu. Our plates empty and our stomachs full, I got up to take care of the dirty dishes, but Oliver stopped me. "Leave it," he said. "I'll deal with the mess tomorrow."

Taking hold of my wrist, he led me into the living room, where we perused his extensive movie collection until we settled on one neither of us had seen. Dimming the lights, Oliver made his way to the loveseat situated in front of the television and kicked off his shoes. Smiling, he propped his feet on the ot-toman and beckoned me over with a pat of the cushion. I crossed the room in three easy strides and nestled into the small space beside him.

"Comfy?" he asked, draping his arm around my shoulders and hugging me close.

I nodded, a contented sigh escaping my lips, and rested my head against his chest.

Just as I'd suspected. We were a perfect fit.

Seven

"Two lines, folks! Two lines!" the stoop-shouldered security guard shouted above the clamoring ruckus being made by the 300-person throng eagerly waiting to enter the television studio.

Cameron and I shuffled forward, our arms linked so we wouldn't get separated. *What was it about the words "two lines" that these people didn't understand?*

"Aren't you glad we got here early?" Cam asked, bouncing her brows proudly. It wasn't something I'd brag to my grandchildren about, but I had to admit, we were looking pretty good in our spot, fourth from the front in Line A.

"Have your tickets out!" the guard's booming voice instructed. "Once you're through the main doors, Line A heads to the left, Line B to the right. Ushers will assist you from there."

The crowd, Cam included, responded with a vociferous round of cheers and applause. I closed my eyes to keep from rolling them.

"OK, ladies," he said, speaking to the trio in front of us as he unhooked the velvet rope blocking the doorway and waved them through. "Welcome to *The Kitty Asher Show.*"

We followed the sprightly young women down a long corridor to another set of double doors, where just as we'd been promised, an usher clad in black jeans, and a black T-shirt with *The Kitty Asher Show* logo emblazoned brightly across his chest, was waiting to collect our tickets.

"All the way down," he said, plucking our two passes to talk-show torture from Cam's hand.

The studio looked nothing like it was portrayed on television. I quickly deduced that was because cameras spent the hour bouncing between the captivating host, who was backdropped by a nattily dressed stage, and the mesmerized audience. The strategic shots gave viewers at home the impression of perpetual warmth and intimacy.

Really, the room was cavernous and chilly. Beams supporting an assortment of massive lights aiming in different directions sat where a ceiling should have been. And along the edges of the room, rows of blinking cameras, some on cranes, some on mounts, towered in lieu of walls. Behind the cameras, staff members wearing headsets and clipboards scurried around in a frenetic dance of hyperactivity.

Stadium bleacher seating formed a large ascending crescent around the elevated platform from which Kitty dazzled her adoring fans daily. The set, flanked by JumboTrons, was nothing more than an elaborate prop festooned with homey, butterscotch sofas, ornate tables, intricate oriental rugs, and a smattering of huge flower arrangements. It looked foreign sitting there, as though a tornado had ripped it from someone's house in the suburbs and planted it downtown, amid a mass of steel rafters and heavy-duty recording equipment.

"Keep going. All the way down to the front," another usher instructed. There was one stationed every few feet, urging us forward by winding his arms in a circular propeller motion.

I smirked. A reflective jumpsuit, a pair of headphones, and a couple of orange batons and they could work at O'Hare Airport, landing Boeing 747s.

Cameron and I took our leads from the well-oiled crew, stepping lively all the way down to the first row where we slid in beside the three girls who'd beat us to the front of the line. I assessed our proximity to the stage. The only way we could've gotten closer to it was if we were on it.

"Can you believe it?" the middle one squealed to the friend, who was sitting next to me. They gripped one another's hands, elation seeping from every pore.

The masses filed in behind us, filling up seats to the very back wall. Within minutes, the studio was bursting with the same excited buzz that had permeated the air outside.

Feeling like a nervous spectator amongst a pack of whooping orangutans, I prayed for the show to start. The sooner Kitty came out and the lights went up, the sooner I could go home. But before we could get to that point, I discovered, we had to endure a half an hour of fun and games as the caffeinated staff riled up the audience members with dares and trivia questions that scored them caps, tote bags, and other promotional freebies.

Next to follow, ten minutes of prepping for what was to come.

We were to take our cues from Dan and Ricky, two production assistants stationed on either side of the stage. When they waved their hands, we were told, that was our signal to jump out of our seats and cheer with as much enthusiasm as we could muster until they dropped them again, which was code for us to sit back down.

Then, as if being commissioned as Kitty Asher's personal cheer squad wasn't degrading enough, they had the audacity to make us practice standing, clapping, and sitting on cue.

Dan raised his arms over his head and waved his hands. Everyone jumped up and screamed. He dropped them, and the applause lulled as we retook our seats.

Ricky carried out the same drill, and then they performed it together, each time garnering the same response from the audience.

Finally, almost an hour after I'd expected the wretched event to begin, the studio lights dimmed, save for the cluster of bright beams aimed at the sliding wall behind the sofas, where I knew from previous episodes that Kitty would emerge, microphone in hand, and strike a pose.

The show's theme song began blaring at a decibel level that made my eardrums throb. In the blink of an eye, Dan and Ricky were up, arms overhead, hands waving. We all flew out of our seats applauding with vigor and screaming at the tops of our lungs the way we'd been trained minutes earlier in talk-show boot camp.

The music trembled into a suspenseful crescendo, the wall parted in two and...(gasp!)...there she was, Kitty Asher—in the flesh.

Light flooded the studio as if Heaven itself had opened at her grand arrival. She flicked her cascading hair over her shoulder and sashayed a few steps forward, spinning so that we could appreciate her from every angle, preened and then sashayed the rest of the way to the front of the stage.

"How are you all doing today?" she shouted over our cheers. I looked at Dan and Ricky. Their hands were still waving. We continued to scream.

Kitty flashed her perfectly capped teeth and shook her head as if to say, "Stop. Really, it's too much." Her expression may have translated as sincere through the camera lenses, but from where I was sitting, I could tell she was eating it up.

"Thank you, thank you," she said, motioning for us to sit down once she'd basked in the glory of our admiration a few seconds longer. "Please. Have a seat."

Dan and Ricky lowered their hands.

We knew what to do.

"We have a great show in store for you all today," she said. Only she wasn't speaking to us. She was speaking into the camera directly to her right. That didn't stop the audience members around me from offering another, brief round of applause.

"How many of you have that one friend or relative who's got no fashion sense whatsoever?" Nearly everyone raised their hands.

Kitty laughed, nodding as she surveyed the collective response. "Bless their hearts, right? They can't help it if they're clueless. You've got the ones stuck in the '80s, who still wear shoulder pads. Others cake on foundation that's two shades too light or go overboard with their eyeliner. And then there are those with the bushy eyebrows and outdated bangs. Do any of you know someone like that?"

The audience confirmed that they did by clapping.

"Me too," Kitty said. "In fact, I used to be one of them." There was an abrupt intake of air as the room of 300 gasped in simultaneous disbelief.

Sitting mere feet away from her, I could attest to the fact that Kitty was just as flawless in person as she was on television. Dressed in a short-sleeved, shrunken velvet blazer, a lacy camisole, cropped dark-rinse jeans, and fire engine red sling-backs, she was the epitome of chic. It was hard to imagine that someone like her, someone who'd become synonymous with cosmopolitan style, was once a walking fashion faux pas.

"Believe it," she said, her timing eerily on cue. "It's true. Before I got into the modeling industry, I didn't know what I was doing. But I've spent years learning from the best and now..." she paused for dramatic effect, "I'm going to pass my secrets on to a few lucky, deserving women."

You're too kind, I thought wryly while everyone else applauded.

"Our guests today are the worst of the worst when it comes to bad fashion. And their frumpy looks have done a number on their self-esteem. So I called in some favors and put together a panel of premiere beauty experts who've agreed to team up with the show to give our ugly ducklings...KITTY. ASHER. EXTREME. MAKEOVERS!"

Dan and Ricky were up and waving. *Why did that deserve a standing ovation?* I wondered as I rose to my feet with everyone else.

"The catch is," Kitty continued, once we'd all sat back down and the cheers had died to a dull roar. "They don't know they've been picked to be on our show."

Poor suckers, I thought shaking my head. *Poor, poor suckers.* The audience *ooooed*, rapt by the dark delight of witnessing a real, live coup.

"With the help of their closest friends and a few hidden cameras, we've spent the past two weeks following their every move, interviewing their co-workers, talking with their families, even rummaging through their closets for a firsthand, inside look at their wardrobes. I've seen the footage," she warned, her tone, closely related, I suspected, to the way a crime scene investigator would caution a novice before entering the scene of a gruesome homicide. "We've got our work cut out for us, but I think we're up for the challenge.

"So let's not waste any more time," she said, her smile wide and plastic. "Please give a warm welcome to Aisha Walton, Bridgette Patterson, and Isabelle Mackenzie!"

Sweet Jesus.

My jaw dropped as my mind scrambled frantically to make sense of what everyone else already knew.

I'd been had.

Eight

A group of scientists at a well-respected institute outside of Maryland decided to study the effect of shock on the human body. How did it influence our senses—sight, smell, taste; our vitals—blood pressure, temperature, heart rate? How did it alter our mindsets, our ability to reason and react?

They enlisted a slew of subjects, all different races and ages from different walks of life with different beliefs and fears, different habits and preferences, different diets and routines and histories—different everything. And for the next three years they subjected them to a sometimes-grueling series of tests. They monitored them as they watched what most would consider disturbing films, analyzing their immediate and delayed reactions to personal and world-wide tragedies, studying them in different stages of sleep deprivation, even, at times, secretly tweaking and altering their environments in order to analyze their physiological responses. One scientist went so far as to put a dead rat in the coat pocket of one of his subjects.

I remembered being offended when I read that, thinking with disgust that even science had grown base, pulling pranks on the innocent in the name of medical research.

Their findings didn't impress me enough to forgive their questionable antics. But one conclusion did stick in my mind.

Among other things, shock, they'd deduced, was a degenerative emotion. It traumatized, paralyzed, suffocated, and deadened, eroding its victim's mental and physical health and establishing distorted associations that worked to stunt essential maturation as well as one's ability to rely on or trust in the most basic of human bonds.

That was me—traumatized, paralyzed, suffocated, deadened, my faith in friendship stunted—as I saw my mega-sized face flash on the behemoth monitors alongside the other two blindsided guests, their horrified expressions mirroring mine.

The scene that followed dragged on in slow motion. What I knew cognitively couldn't have been more than 20 seconds, felt like 20 minutes.

Warped sense of time—that wasn't one of the researcher's scientific findings. But it was happening. The audience was on its feet, their claps clashing like cymbals against my ears as those nearest to me smiled down, reveling in my obvious torture, and urged me to get up. I couldn't.

Delayed reaction—that *was* concluded to be a side effect of shock, as well as suppressed senses and high blood pressure, both of which I could attest to as I shrugged off the hands of pushy strangers who were trying to force me out of my seat and onto the stage.

Nedra, a portly brunette, who'd introduced herself to the crowd as one of the producers during the pre-show hoopla, walked over and offered me her hand. "This way," she said, her words sluggish, her voice registering octaves lower than it had earlier, thanks to my frazzled state.

I took her hand, and the cheers around me grew even louder, serenading us as we climbed the shallow set of stairs leading to the stage where Kitty and the other two ugly ducklings were already waiting.

Kitty wrapped her arm around my shoulder and squeezed me close. "There's lots more to come. Don't go away," she said to the camera hovering in front of us. "We'll be right back."

We held that unnatural pose until a man squatting to the side in the shadows stood. "And we're clear," he said.

Kitty released me, and a brigade of makeup artists, hairstylists, and assistants descended upon the set out of nowhere to powder her T-zone, fluff her tresses, and review for the next segment.

"Great energy, everyone!" One of the black-clad personnel shouted, stroking and distracting the hyper audience while two other staff members gathered me, Aisha, and Bridgette to the side.

"Hold still," one said, clipping something onto my collar and reaching under my shirt to string through a wire. "We've just got to mic you real quick."

Gradually emerging from my stupor, I pushed her hand away. "No."

"Hon, without a microphone we won't be able to hear you."

"I said, no!" I snapped, snatching off the wire and brushing by her. I had no idea where I was going, which way was out, and which way would lead me deeper into Kitty Asher's perverse lair; I just knew that the farther away I got from that set and its audience, the safer everyone would be.

"How do I get out of here?" I asked, blowing by flustered employees as I stomped my way past the loaded craft-service table and through the first open door I saw.

"Isabelle! Isabelle!" someone called after me. I didn't slow my pace. "You don't have to do anything you don't want to do," the voice said.

Darn skippy, I thought, still breezing through the maze of corridors like I owned the place.

"Please," the voice begged. "Just stop and talk to me for a sec."

I turned to see Nedra running behind me, her headset dangling from her neck.

"I am *not* going back out there," I barked before she'd even come to a full stop.

"Fair enough," she nodded, winded from her short jog.

"And you do *not* have my permission to air that footage," I shouted, my finger wagging inches from her face. "How dare you! Who do you people think you are? Throwing me on national television without my consent?"

"I understand you're upset," she said, her tone soothing. "We won't air anything you're uncomfortable with. You have my word. Now let's just calm down——take a few deep breaths."

"Don't do that!" I said, my chest heaving with fury. "Don't try to handle me. I'm not a puppet and I'm not interested in anything else you have to tell me unless it's how to get to the nearest exit. Do you understand?" My glare was scathing. "We're done here!"

"Mack?" Cam called, her voice tentative and feeble.

"Go away," I said, my words chopped with anger.

She inched toward me in the gold stilettos I'd helped her pick out. "Are you OK?"

"Just back off!" I ordered, motioning for her not to come any closer, as I paced in front of her like a caged animal.

"We were only trying to help," she said, maintaining her distance.

"We!" I shrieked. "We who?"

Cameron shrugged as though the answer was obvious. "Me and Olly."

My eyes stung. "Oliver?"

Our first date had ended at dawn with another knee-buckling kiss and our second had commenced only a few hours later at church. It'd been months since I'd stepped into a sanctuary, but I couldn't resist the urge to accompany Oliver when he'd invited me to attend Sunday service with him. While I went mostly to be near him, there was a small part of me that was curious to see if my old spiritual verve would miraculously return. It didn't. I spent two hours mechanically singing, clapping, and praying. But my efforts were rewarded afterward when Oliver drove us to North Beach. Barefoot, we strolled for hours along the Lake Michigan shore until a light drizzle persuaded us to retreat to my place. There, we lazed away the rest of the day on my living room floor talking, eating Indian food, and listening to my prized collection of 33s.

We covered every topic imaginable that afternoon. From the silly to the mundane to the intensely personal, nothing had been off-limits.

Except this, apparently.

My stomach instantly curdled with regret at the realization that I'd spent the past two days trustingly peeling back layers of myself, while Oliver had spent them tiptoeing around the truth.

"We thought maybe this would bring you out of your shell," Cameron explained.

"How?" I asked, my voice quivering. "By humiliating me?"

She shook her head, a pained expression on her face. "Of course not."

"Why don't you ladies let me show you to the green room?" Nedra offered. "Give you a chance to work this out privately."

I looked around to discover a cast of dozens watching our heated exchange. "Fine," I said, avoiding Cameron's pleading stare.

Nedra escorted us through the studio offices to a small corner niche between the vending machines and the restrooms. "Let me know if you need anything," she said, bowing out with a sympathetic tilt of her head.

Cam and I stood on opposite ends of the sparsely furnished room, swallowed by deafening silence as I watched her stare at her feet.

"So talk already," I snapped.

"We never meant to embarrass you," she said, her chin trembling. "This was supposed to be a once-in-a-lifetime experience—a good one, a gift."

Glaring, I folded my arms across my chest.

"You always used to talk about the things you were going to do, the person you would someday be," she said. Her stare was penetrating. "You don't do that anymore."

I held my tongue in tenuous check and waited for her to go on.

"It's like you've given up, like you've stopped believing in yourself," she said slowly, her tone cautious. "And we thought a new look would be a great way to jumpstart the old you."

There was a measure of truth in what she was saying. I *had* quit; I *was* adrift. But calling me out on national television in front of millions of people had not been the right way to address it. I sighed. "This was completely out of line."

Cameron nodded. "Clearly, it was a mistake. If we had known it was going to upset you like this, we never would have done it."

My chest tightened every time she said "we." I'd long since resigned myself to this sort of behavior from Cameron. Impulsive and unmindful of most basic social boundaries, she occasionally made victims of those she tried to help—herself notwithstanding. But Oliver was different. His actions were preceded by thought, his choices by careful consideration. If he had consented to this makeover, if he had helped orchestrate it or even passively watched it turn from thought to reality, it was because he'd wanted it to happen.

I stood across from Cameron for what seemed like an eternity, neither of us daring to utter another word for fear of further injuring our wounded friendship.

"Knock, knock," Nedra sang, cracking open the door and popping her head in. "Everything OK?" she asked, surveying the two of us for any signs of assault.

"I'd like to go home now," I said. My tone was decidedly calmer than it had been during our first encounter, but no less adamant.

"Is there any way we can convince you to stay?" Nedra asked, her hands pressed together under her chin in praying formation. "I think you'd be pleasantly surprised by the amount of support you've got."

Frustrated, I sighed and shook my head.

"We understand and accept that you don't want to participate in the makeover," she persisted. "Kitty would just like to talk to you. Believe it or not, everyone out there is on your side."

"I know no one in here is," I said, cutting my eyes accusingly in Cameron's direction.

"So is that a yes?" Nedra asked, her tone hopeful.

Something told me Kitty Asher's system wasn't one that could be easily bucked. The sooner I submitted, it seemed, the better chance I had of being sent on my way.

"How long will this take?" I asked.

Nedra's smile was triumphant. "Ten minutes."

"Fine." I shrugged. "Whatever."

"You don't have to." Cameron planted herself between me and Nedra. "We can leave now and forget this ever happened."

"Why don't we find someone to show you back to your seat?" Nedra said, hastily ushering Cameron out of the room. "And Isabelle, you follow me."

Cam, escorted by a rather burly security guard, turned down one hallway and Nedra and I turned down another that led backstage. There, I was wired for a microphone by the same woman whose hand I'd slapped away earlier. She showed no signs of resentment as she chattily explained the equipment and clipped it into place.

"You're going to stand here," Nedra said, leading me forward a few yards. "You'll hear the music start after which point you'll be introduced."

I realized then that I was standing behind the infamous separating wall—the one from which Kitty herself emerged at the beginning of every show. "Head straight for the couch," Nedra instructed. "Kitty will meet you halfway."

I had no idea what had happened since I'd stormed off the set. But from the familiar sound of the show's theme song, I knew I was about to find out.

Once she'd delivered a brief recap, I heard Kitty's muffled voice say, "Please help me welcome back Isabelle."

The wall opened and I proceeded forward like I'd been instructed, squinting past the blinding studio lights. A towering Kitty greeted me with a convivial embrace, before guiding me to the waiting sofa. We sat amid a boisterous standing ovation from the audience. I might have managed to feel honored were Dan and Ricky not waving their arms overhead. Knowing that people were being signaled to celebrate my arrival automatically made the welcome disingenuous.

"Now, Isabelle," Kitty began. She looked down at the cards in her lap. "Or do you prefer to be called 'Mack'?"

I blinked. "Isabelle's fine."

She nodded. "My producers tell me you're not very happy to be here."

"Your producers are correct," I said.

"Can you explain why?" she asked, one dip of her brow morphing her from a happy-go-lucky ex-model into a serious journalist.

I shrugged. "I don't like surprises."

"Really?" she asked, leaning back, as if the possibility that someone might not appreciate being ambushed in front of a live studio audience was something that had never once crossed her mind. "What don't you like about them?"

"The surprise part," I said, my tone impatient.

She frowned, clearly chafed by my curtness.

"I, personally, was terribly saddened to learn that you were so hurt by the idea of a makeover," she said, affectedly pressing her hand to her chest. "We here at *The Kitty Asher Show* promote female empowerment, confidence, and strong self-image—nothing less."

"Does that go for everyone?" I asked, my lips pursed testily. "Or just us ugly ducklings?"

Her laugh was stiff. "That's only a figure of speech," she said, crossing her legs. "No one's ugly—especially not you." She turned to the 300 onlookers for back up. "Right audience?"

They applauded.

"I'm looking at a truly gorgeous woman," Kitty said, squeezing my knee.

I knew she was working me—knew it like I knew the sky was blue and rain was wet, but just hearing the words spoken and the idea being embraced by others made me feel better. "Thank you," I said, careful not to grin too widely.

"We all need a little help every once in a while," Kitty continued. "There's no shame in that. Earlier in the show, I even confessed to needing a push in the right direction."

I shrugged, my defenses slowly slacking. "I guess I never considered myself unfashionable," I said. "No one ever told me."

"Well we've got a clip of your loved ones expressing some of their thoughts and observations. They had some really encouraging things to say. Would you like to take a look?"

My curiosity adequately piqued, I nodded. "OK."

We all turned our attention to the JumboTrons.

"Isabelle was a beautiful baby," my mom's voice began to narrate. Background music played as a photograph of me naked in a bathtub as a toddler popped up onto the screens. The audience cooed as several other baby pictures flashed by. "From the very beginning, she was a little ball of energy. So it was no surprise when she blossomed into a tomboy."

A photograph of me and my brothers at the beach appeared. Our feet and legs were covered in sand; our skin was darkened from hours in the sun. I remembered that day well. We were so young, so blissfully unaware of everything but our own happiness.

The shot cut to my mom perched stiffly on a familiar sofa. She continued to recount my younger years, while old family pictures flickered across the screens.

"She's got a sweet spirit," a different voice interjected. Immediately, I recognized it as my brother, Gabe.

"And a wicked sense of humor," added my sister, Danielle.

"Mack's the baby of our bunch," Caleb, the younger of the two boys, said. "And the heart of this family."

The shot shifted once again from a montage of photographs to the actual speakers. Gathered around the living room in the house where we'd grown up, my mother, sister, and two brothers continued to wax fondly about the old days.

Unexpectedly, the music changed key, segueing from a light, upbeat orchestral number to something a little flatter. "I would say a huge turning point in Mack's life came when her father left," mom said, shaking her head. "One day he was her hero and the next day he was gone."

"Looking back, I'm not sure she really knew what was happening," Gabe added. "Or understood that none of it was her fault."

Caleb nodded. "I think part of her was holding out hope he'd come back. And when he didn't, she lost a pivotal piece of herself."

Ominous drums were followed by several pictures of me as a teenager, caught off guard, looking somber and awkward.

"She's always been a fighter," Danielle said. "But I don't know that she could have made it through without her friends."

An old photo of me and Cameron at a high school homecoming game flitted across the screens, followed by a snapshot of me and Oliver posing on the Quad in matching university sweatshirts.

"Mack is the best person I've ever known," Cameron announced, her brow furrowed with conviction. She was standing outside on a downtown street I couldn't place. "I wouldn't be me without her."

Oliver's voice, smooth and thoughtful, cut in. "She's a rare find," he said. My stomach knotted as the camera panned left to reveal him standing beside Cameron. "Every life she touches, she changes for the better—mine included."

Cameron nodded. "Mack's been integral in helping a lot of people realize their potential. Now it's our turn to return the favor."

"After years of putting others first, I think she's forgotten that she's important too. I want to remind her how much she means to all of us." Oliver smiled. "How much she means to me."

"Our hope is that this makeover will give Mack a fresh outlook," Cameron concluded. "And the confidence to start believing in herself again."

The screens faded to black as the accompaniment ended on a long, hopeful note. Kitty turned to me. "I see your tears," she said, handing me a tissue from the box on the end table beside her. "Tell me what you're feeling."

I dabbed at my eyes and shrugged.

"Is there any truth, you think, to what was said?"

"Probably," I conceded, my voice shaky.

"Well," Kitty turned to the camera to our left. "Armed with a couple of camcorders from my staff, Isabelle's friends, Oliver and Cameron, did a little P.I. work for us over the past couple of weeks. Take a look."

Back to the JumboTrons we went to watch raw footage of me walking down the street, grocery shopping, ordering coffee, even getting money from an ATM machine.

Abruptly, the scene changed and we were looking at the inside of my condo. "Mack's at work right now," Cam said, wringing her hands guiltily.

"Hurry up so we can get out of here," Oliver hissed from behind the camcorder.

Seconds later they were in my room, rummaging through my stuff and putting everything I wore on display for the world to see. I made a mental note to confiscate the emergency keys I'd given them.

"This, I've begged her to get rid of a million times," Cam said, holding up a T-shirt I'd bought at a garage sale for a buck-twenty-five. She held the tag out while Oliver zoomed in. "Extra, extra large," she said with audible bewilderment.

"Get the milkmaid dress," Oliver said.

Cam rushed back into the closet and emerged with my favorite summer outfit. It was a loose-fitting, pale pink jumper with cargo pockets on the side. I loved the feel and the fit of it—the way the soft, flowy fabric hung past my calves, but from the audience's laughter, it was safe to assume that the dress was as ugly and unflattering as Cameron had always claimed it to be.

"She wears them with these," Cameron said, flashing my beaten up pair of Birkenstock's. This only garnered more laughter.

I winced, slinking farther into the sofa with each revealing frame.

Last to get raided was my underwear drawer. My face grew hot at the realization that Oliver had gotten to know my intimates intimately. "Please, Kitty," Cameron begged, swinging a pair of my panties in front of the lens. "Help us help our friend."

The audience applauded as the screens faded to black again.

No term could adequately describe the mortification raging through my every limb. If I'd been given the choice between watching one more clip of my shortcomings on the JumboTrons and dying a slow painful death, I would've chosen the latter. Thankfully, it didn't come to that.

"Obviously, you've got a great support system," Kitty said. "And we'd really like to be a part of it. Your friend Cameron has packed you a bag. We've booked you a luxurious suite at the marvelous Drake Hotel. And there are five beauty experts eager to release your 'inner swan'." She took my hand in hers.

"What do you say, Mack? Aisha and Bridgette have already agreed to do it so you won't have to go through this transformation alone. Just think," she leaned forward, her eyes wide and urgent. "Today could be the beginning of a whole new you."

Did I want a whole new me?

Not long ago, I was content with who I'd become. I was secure in my faith, my family loved me, as did my friends, and that was enough. It was enough because it should be—because so many others managed to be happy with so much less.

But somewhere along the way, I'd become disenchanted with the world and with my place in it. My twenties had been marked by a state of perpetual longing—longing for the woman I would one day become, for the life I would someday lead. By 30, I'd expected to have a doting husband, a couple of precocious kids, and a burgeoning editing career. But instead of family dinners and bedtime stories and a home in the suburbs bursting with laughter and teeming with memories, I'd wound up alone with only a fledgling bookstore to call my own.

Time felt like it was slipping through my fingers. I couldn't afford to waste another ten years waiting for God to bless me. I didn't want to expend any more energy hoping when I could be doing, praying when I should be acting.

Rejecting this invitation, I realized as Kitty and her audience awaited my answer with bated breath, was not an option. I couldn't go back.

The only way out was forward.

"OK," I said, nodding my consent.

Kitty smiled, her collagen-enhanced lips spreading from ear to ear, and raised our linked hands in victory, as the studio filled with deafening applause.

Nine

"OK, you're up," Bridgette said. She took a few tentative sips of her cocktail and licked the thin layer of brine and citrus from her lips before fixing her glassy eyes on me.

Aisha, who was still nursing a dimpled mug of Heineken, met my gaze with a smile and a reassuring nod. "Let's hear it."

After the show had ended, the studio had been emptied and Kitty had been whisked away by security. Aisha, Bridgette, and I were chauffeured to the Drake, where we were checked in and told that we'd be left to our own devices until the following morning.

Twenty minutes later, the three of us were tucked into a booth in the back of a nearby Irish pub shelling pistachios and chatting as though we were long-lost friends.

Over burgers and steak fries, I learned that Aisha was a residential real estate developer from Atlanta. She and I seemed to have similar styles that revolved solely around comfort and convenience. From her faded jeans and weathered loafers to her slow, laid-back demeanor, she was artlessly simple. She also possessed an intimidating confidence and a quiet wisdom that had instantly garnered my respect.

Bridgette, a proud stay-at-home mom, was compact and chubby with a husky voice and a robust laugh. Everything about her was refreshing, hearty. Wholesomely charming and easy-natured, she struck me as a woman who was destined for a blissful future; one that involved grandkids and second honeymoons and golden anniversaries.

I listened with keen interest, as they shared story after story about the many people in their lives and the experiences that had effectively molded them into the women they had become. By the time the conversation finally made its way to me, we'd long since finished eating and the bar's patronal landscape had shifted from after-work drinkers to after-hour barflies.

Sensing that none of us were ready to return to our rooms, Bridgette suggested a nightcap. We readily agreed, and she flagged down our waitress for the liquor menu; it was extensive. After mulling over our options, Bridgette eventually settled on a Matador, while Aisha ordered another beer and I opted for a cup of coffee.

Minutes later, our drinks were in hand and their attention was squared on me. At only 26, Bridgette was the archetypal power-mom-slash-super-wife. And Aisha, as brazenly independent as she was phenomenally successful, had gone on every kind of adventure and traveled to every corner of the world. My journey, a monotonous rotation of work and church, had been nowhere near as meaningful. Oliver's unexpected kiss a couple nights ago had been the first promise of something special in years. But in the wake of this afternoon, even that had turned out to be a wrenching disappointment.

Feeling suddenly self-conscious, I doctored my coffee with cream and sugar and used the extra seconds to summon the nerve to speak. "Well," I began slowly, "I'm originally from Indiana, but I moved here about ten years ago. After college, I worked as a freelance editor for a while, but it wasn't for me." Just as I was about to segue into how I came to own a bookstore, my cell phone beckoned loudly from my purse. "Sorry," I said, frowning as I retrieved it. Between my family and Cameron, my voicemail inbox had reached capacity before I'd ever left the studio.

Unprepared to sift through their explanations or apologies and wearied by their persistence, I started to turn off the phone, but a quick glance at the miniature screen revealed that this call was from Oliver.

"You should answer it," Aisha said, arching a brow at my flustered expression. She took a swig of her beer and shrugged. "Can't hide forever."

Hesitating briefly, I considered ignoring him as I had the others. But even as the thought was crossing my mind, I knew I wouldn't. His draw was undeniably stronger than my will to push him away. With a resigned sigh, I pressed my eyes shut and flipped open the phone. "Hi."

"I'm glad you picked up," he said. Despite what had happened, his voice still made my heart skip a beat.

With a wave of my hand, I excused myself from the table. "I can't talk long," I said, snaking my way through the crowd toward the front entrance.

"Where are you?" he asked.

"At a bar."

"Are you drinking?" There was a nettling edge of disapproval in his tone.

"I don't really see how that concerns you."

A long pause followed. "Can we please talk about this?" he finally asked.

"We spent all weekend talking."

He sighed. "I know and I should have told you. But I didn't know how." His sentence gave way to a loud swallow. "I made a mistake."

"No," I said, pacing anxiously up and down the desolate block. "You made a choice."

"You don't have to do this," he said. "You can walk away right now and nobody will think any less of you."

I stopped short and shook my head. "I'll think less of me."

"Why? Because some B-list talk show host, who barely knows your name, thinks you have bad taste in clothes?"

"No, because, you guys were right, OK?" I sighed. "I *am* lost—I have been for a while now. Most days I look at how my life's turned out, at who I've turned into, and it makes me want to cry. It makes me question everything I ever thought I knew, everything I ever thought I believed. All I want is to get back to the way it used to be. I want to feel like there's still something to look forward to, like I still have purpose. But I don't know how. I'm not even sure where I lost my way.

"I'm desperate," I said, the confession coming out as a whisper. "And I'm willing to try anything—even a stupid makeover. Do I think a different hairstyle and a few new outfits will actually be the solution? Not really. But it's a start, and I figure any step away from where I am now is a move in the right direction."

"Mack," he called. His voice was gentle, pleading. "You were created to do amazing things. I've known that from the first moment we met. And you know as well as I do that the bigger the call, the longer and harder the training. Look at Joseph," he said. "I'm pretty sure his life's ambitions didn't include thirteen years of slavery and false imprisonment. But both were necessary parts of his journey. He wouldn't have been able to fulfill his destiny otherwise."

I rolled my eyes. "Next you're going to start preaching about David and how he probably didn't feel much like royalty when he was ducking Saul in caves."

"Because it's true," he said. "They were both favored, both chosen by God, and because of that they both suffered. But they were also both faithful and eventually God delivered them; He restored them and used them to accomplish extraordinary things. He'll do the same with you. I know He will."

"Well that makes one of us."

Oliver sighed. "We're supposed to live by faith, not by sight. You can't be moved by your circumstances. They're hardly ever an indication of where you are and never an indication of where you're going."

"I'm not moved by just my circumstances, Olly; I'm also moved by everyone else's. I mean, look at Cameron. It's all so easy for her. Things just fall into her lap when she's not even trying, when she doesn't even deserve them."

"Kind of reminds me of Psalm 73. Do you remember what it says?"

I frowned, irritated by his relentless haranguing. "No."

"'My feet had almost slipped; I had nearly lost my foothold,'" he began quoting. "'For I envied the arrogant when I saw the prosperity of the wicked. They have no struggles; their bodies are healthy and strong. They are free from the burdens common to man; they are not plagued by human ills.'

"On and on it goes," he mused. "About how the unrighteous have everything, about how unfair it seems. But if you skip to the end, it also details their fate—their ultimate destruction. Cameron may look like she's got it made, like she's on top of the world, but you're seeing a snapshot of a point in time; it's not the whole picture.

"She doesn't have a relationship with Christ, and until she does, nothing she accomplishes in this life will be of any eternal value. Nothing will negate the fact that she is always just a breath away from hell. It's not something to envy," he admonished. "It's something to pity."

Though I heard the truth in his words, they didn't reach me; I couldn't feel them. But there was no explaining that to Oliver. It was like we suddenly spoke two different languages. He'd just recite more Bible verses or tell more stories, and while that used to work—while at one time it might have been enough to clear away the fog—it didn't anymore.

"You still there?" he asked.

"It's late," I said, glancing through the bar's plate-glass window at Aisha and Bridgette, who looked deeply engrossed in conversation. "I should probably go."

"Can I at least pray with you first?"

My sigh was impatient. "I'm tired, Oliver. It's been a long day."

"OK," he relented. "But if you change your mind, I'm here."

"Goodnight." I flicked the phone shut without bothering to wait for his response and returned to the bar. Aisha and Bridgette had just started working on a heaping platter of nachos and a couple of colorful margaritas. "We had them pour you a fresh one," Aisha said, nodding down at the steaming cup of coffee in front of me.

I slumped into my chair with a frown as Oliver's chiding tone rang provokingly in my ears. "I might need something a little stronger."

Aisha smirked and slid her salt-rimmed glass toward me. "Here. Take mine," she said, reclaiming the half-empty mug of beer still on the table.

"We should make a toast," Bridgette said, wiping her cheese-stained fingers on a stray napkin and reaching for her glass.

"To what?" I asked.

Aisha smirked. "To ugly ducklings."

We laughed. "To new friends?" I suggested.

"No," Bridgette said, raising her drink in the air. "To new beginnings."

The three of us looked at each other knowingly and nodded. For better or for worse, a fresh start was exactly what the impending days promised.

Aisha and I raised our drinks alongside Bridgette's and smiled. "To new beginnings," we echoed in a toast that was dedicated as much to embracing the future as it was to forgetting the past.

Ten

"Rise and shine!" someone sang. The sound of clapping hands caused an immediate throbbing in my temple, while the sudden assault of unbearably bright sunlight pierced my bloodshot eyes.

I sat up to see Nedra, clipboard in hand, standing by the window where she'd thrown back the blackout curtains. She was dressed in jeans and a camel blazer. Her hair was neatly pinned back, and her smile was warm, but the determined glint in her eye told me she meant business.

"You ladies must have had quite a night," she said, disappearing around the corner into the bathroom.

I heard the faucet running. Moments later, she emerged with a cup of water into which she promptly dumped two round tablets.

"Drink this," she instructed, handing me the fizzing glass. "And then get dressed. We've got to be downstairs in fifteen minutes."

I gave the drink a tentative sniff before draining it in two determined gulps. "I need to take a shower."

"No time," she said. "Besides, it's always better when the guests look a little…" she searched for a judicious adjective. "Unkempt." She smiled. "Makes the results that much more dramatic. Just throw something on and meet me in the lobby," she said, already headed for the door. "Fifteen minutes," she called over her shoulder.

I grunted my compliance and waited until she was gone to lie back down.

Margaritas had turned into boilermakers and boilermakers into a blur of throat-burning, eye-watering shots. The guilt had only lasted as long as my sobriety, after which I could hear and sense myself turning into a different person, but didn't care. The more I drank, the more I forgot, and the more I forgot, the better I felt. Anesthetized to my self-perception and impervious to others' opinions, I was indestructible. I was free.

Early in my walk, when God's presence was like a constant fire in my belly and I could see His miracles in everything and everyone, obedience for the sake of His good pleasure was an easy sacrifice. I took pride in my relationship with Jesus and how it separated me from the worldly. But those days were gone.

I was done being distinguished by my faith, done adhering to a standard that required exponentially more than it gave in return. And I was done bemoaning how short my life had fallen of my expectations. Instead, I was going to start doing something about it. I was going to start operating on my own terms. If others had created purpose solely based on personal desire, if they'd found contentment independent of duty or conviction, then so could I.

Hoisting myself out of bed, I schlepped to the bathroom where I brushed my teeth and finger-combed my unruly hair. Taking Nedra's counsel under advisement, I slipped into a baggy pair of sweat pants and threw on an oversized T-shirt, before grabbing my room key and heading downstairs.

Bridgette and Aisha were already in the lobby looking equally disheveled and sluggish. Glancing up from the finely upholstered chairs in which they were lolling, they nodded good morning. I greeted them with a nod of my own and eased into the couch across from them.

Moments later, Nedra appeared with a gaggle of people at her heels, all of whom were sporting black crew T-shirts and solicitous grins.

Glancing at her watch, Nedra checked something off on her clipboard before commencing. "OK, ladies," she flashed a row of slightly crooked, albeit impossibly white teeth. "You all have busy days ahead of you. So let's get started.

"Isabelle, this is your team." She motioned to the equipment-toting cluster to her immediate left. "That's Rashad." A mountain of a man holding a long boom offered me a courteous smile and stepped forward to shake my hand. I forced myself not to stare at his unbridled man-chest, which swayed heavily from side-to-side beneath his shirt whenever he moved.

"That's Thomas," Nedra continued. He was lanky with an auburn goatee that matched his head of unruly curls. Keeping a tight grip on the camera situated on his shoulder, he waved with his free hand. "Tom's fine."

"John," Nedra pointed to the muscular gentleman towering over the rest of the huddle. Scattered at his feet were several large black duffel bags. With his stance wide and his sculpted arms crossed in front of his bulging chest, he winked hello.

"And Spencer." Nedra pointed to the only other female member of my team. She was petite with a cropped cut and a colorful collage of tattoos running down her arm. Donning an oversized headset and carrying a clipboard identical to Nedra's, Spencer approached, hand extended, while Nedra introduced Bridgette and Aisha to their respective teams.

"Everyone just calls me Spence," she said, tugging me out of my comfortable seat and into a standing position. Her cold, uninvited hands brushed against my stomach as she set to work concealing a microphone wire beneath my clothes.

"OK, people," Nedra shouted over the chatter. "On today's agenda, we've got Isabelle at Sergio Breccoci Salon & Spa for hair." She consulted her trusty clipboard. "Bridgette, you're headed to Dr. Weiner for teeth whitening; and Aisha, you'll be spending the day shopping with Kelson, Kitty's personal stylist."

"Can't wait," Aisha muttered, her expression as bored as her tone.

"Don't be afraid to have fun with this, ladies," Nedra instructed in a voice that was too loud and too chipper for those of us who'd been up just a few hours earlier doing shots.

"Are you excited?" Spence asked, her hands still roving under my T-shirt.

I shrugged. "I guess."

"You should be." I heard the battery pack clip to the brim of my sweatpants.

"This show does the best makeovers, hands down. They spare no expense," she said, stepping away. "In three days, you are going to look and feel like a completely different person."

I nodded, a twinge of anticipation sending chills across my skin.

Completely different was exactly what I wanted.

———— • ————

Sergio Breccoci Salon & Spa was located on Chicago's über swanky Oak Street. Tucked between two large brick buildings, it sat a ways from the sidewalk above a very trendy, very expensive boutique.

Its understated exterior, however, did not carry into its interior, which boasted glossy hardwood floors, bold gold walls, lush leather styling chairs, and an indulgent number of flat-screen televisions.

Riveted, my gaze compassed the sumptuous space before finally landing on a staff of five waiting in the wings. As if on cue, they parted and out strode a short portly man, his hands extended, his chubby fingers strangled by several gaudy rings. With some alarm, I took in his comb-over, his rimless tinted glasses, and the bushel of chest hair sprouting from beneath his pale pink button-down shirt.

"Isabella!" he bellowed, in an accent I couldn't quite catch. "Welcome." He grabbed my shoulders and kissed the air on either side of my cheeks.

"Thanks for having me," I said, resisting the urge to look into the nearby camera dutifully filming our exchange.

He brushed off my attempt at formalities with an insistent shake of his head. "Today Sergio's salon is your salon."

"So what do you think?" Spence asked, edging next to him. With his eyes narrowed and the corners of his mouth turned downward into a contemplative frown, he studied me as a sculptor might scrutinize an inchoate mass of clay. Fidgeting beneath his pointed stare, I kept my gaze trained on my shoes.

"Color," he said, slowly circling me, his chin pinched between his index finger and thumb. "Something dark, dramatic." He ran his hands through my shoulder-length locks with a grimace. "And extensions."

Spence let out a telling sigh. "You've got your work cut out for you."

He nodded. "We should get started."

Sergio's course of action determined, they turned to me, their expressions purposeful. "Are you ready?"

I searched myself for any last-minute resistance, any lingering apprehension, but there was none.

Meeting their gazes with an expectant smile, I nodded. "Let's do it."

Eleven

The next two days flew by in a chaotic blur.

Sergio's salon was followed by laser teeth whitening, which was followed by a one-on-one session with a personal trainer, consultations with a nutritionist and a cosmetician, and an appointment with a very patient and determined esthetician, who bravely undertook the challenge of removing unwanted hair from places I wasn't sure hot wax was ever meant to go.

Though decorum forbade anyone from saying so, I'd inadvertently become something of a breakout star.

All conversation had ceased when I'd walked into the lobby the morning after my trip to Sergio's. Nedra, whose take-charge personality rarely seemed to leave her at a loss for words, could only stare, while Aisha and Bridgette ogled with obvious envy.

Only Spencer, who'd suffered tirelessly alongside Sergio and me long after his assistants had hung their smocks and the film crew had packed up their gear and headed home for the night, had been there when Sergio had finally unveiled his hours of work.

Tears of utter amazement had sprung to both our eyes. Gone was my mousy brown hair and pedestrian cut. They'd been replaced with cascading layers of raven waves and a sultry bang that swept across my forehead and alluringly concealed my left eye. We'd marveled, mouths agape, at how the length and thickness elongated my face, instantly sharpening my ordinarily blunt features, while the darker color contrasted dramatically with my skin, giving me a strikingly exotic appearance.

Overwhelmed, I'd barely managed to compose myself long enough to sit through Sergio's detailed tutorial on extension care, after which I'd cried with unabashed gratitude the entire ride back to the hotel. I was physically exhausted when I finally reached my room and wasted no time changing and climbing into bed. But I never slept. Instead, I'd spent the night making frequent trips to the bathroom mirror, where I searched the woman staring back at me for glimpses of my old self, to no avail.

All my life, I'd been a wallflower—ordinary and invisible in every conceivable way. Average height, with dime-a-dozen brown eyes, and a garden-variety smile, I was rarely ever acknowledged with more than a passing glance. I was the woman who couldn't catch the attention of her waiter long enough to get the check, the woman who was jounced every morning on her short walk to work by people who didn't notice her in their path.

But, as I made my way—amidst a ripple of admiring gazes—toward the hotel's restaurant, where I was meeting Bridgette and Aisha for our last dinner together, I realized that was no longer the case.

Chin up, shoulders back, I strode with novel confidence, to the waiting maître d', whose double take confirmed my suspicions that I looked ravishing in my black, tailored pantsuit. It was one of many additions to the new wardrobe I'd acquired earlier that afternoon under the expert tutelage of Kelson, Kitty's personal stylist, who, over the course of the three days, had taken each of us on an exorbitant shopping excursion, courtesy of the show.

"Good evening," said the maître d' with a welcoming grin and a small, formal bow.

I smiled, offering him a brief glimpse of my recently whitened teeth. "Mackenzie, reservation for three."

"Of course." He scanned the open ledger on his podium. "It seems the other members of your party have already arrived. Allow me to escort you to your table."

Nodding graciously, I accepted his proffered arm and together we entered the restaurant's majestic dining room. The white-gloved wait staff ingratiatingly stepped aside as we wove our way around the clusters of moneyed guests sampling the finest in haute cuisine.

Aisha and Bridgette's conversation stalled when they saw us approaching. Ignoring the stir of swiveling heads from the surrounding tables, I thanked my escort as he pulled out my chair and, mindful of my audience, took my seat in as graceful a fashion as I could.

"You put the two of us to shame," Aisha said with a smirk, once the maître d' had taken his leave.

"That's not true," I scolded. "You guys look amazing."

Bridgette, once our reliable source of optimism and cheer, raised a cynical brow. She'd been the unfortunate recipient of an unflattering pixie cut, as well as the resentful participant in a shopping trip that had limited her spree to plus-size clothing stores. "It's been interesting, I'll say that much." She reached for her glass of wine. "But I'm ready to get back home."

Aisha nodded. "Same here."

I was also looking forward to getting back, but not because I missed the life from which I'd been so conspicuously absent for the past week. I was eager to see what long-awaited changes my transformation would usher into my old world.

"Do you know who's coming to the reveal tomorrow?" Bridgette asked.

Aisha nodded. "My mom and sister. You?"

Bridgette's smile was warm with the anticipation. "My husband."

Expectantly, they turned to me.

I shrugged. I hadn't bothered to keep anyone apprised of my progress over the past several days. In fact, since the night I'd spoken to Oliver, my cell phone had remained deliberately off and buried at the bottom of my suitcase. "I guess it'll be a surprise."

"Well, ladies." Aisha smiled, but the somber slant of her eyes betrayed her sadness. "I couldn't imagine having taken this adventure with anyone else."

"Let's not lose touch," Bridgette said, reaching out to us. Aisha and I slipped our hands into hers.

"We won't," I promised with a reassuring squeeze.

Dinner was consumed amidst a bittersweet milieu of sanguine expectation and melancholy farewell. We took our time ordering, savoring each other's company as much as the food. Over dessert and then coffee, I memorized their features, their mannerisms—the way Aisha's hand waved gracefully through the air when she spoke; the comforting gurgle of Bridgette's guttural laughs—and realized with a gnawing pang that I would miss them more than words could say.

Sometime later, back in my hotel room, after I'd rinsed the carefully applied makeup from my face and had braided my new hair into loose plaits, I crawled into bed and lost myself in imaginings of what the following day would bring.

I wondered if Kitty and her studio audience would find my transformation at all impressive, if the change was as dramatic as I'd been led to believe. Or if, after everything that had happened—everything I'd endured—the rest of the world would take one look at me and see the same bedraggled woman who'd stumbled onto the stage a few days earlier. Was I prepared for their verdict? Would it matter?

Not nearly as much, I realized, as I hovered in the delicious state between dreaming and awake, as the opinion of one.

Stubbornly, I pushed Oliver's face from my mind and with the sound of his name still ringing silently in my ears, gave myself willingly over to sleep.

Twelve

"We're on in ten!" Kitty's stage manager shouted as he blew past the dressing rooms toward the studio. My pulse quickened. It seemed like only moments earlier he'd made the rounds announcing we had an hour until showtime.

Upon arriving early that morning, Aisha, Bridgette, and I had learned that we were going to unveil our makeovers while strutting down a 20-foot catwalk that stretched from the infamous sliding wall, across the stage, and into the audience. Each of us would take two trips, sporting different looks coordinated by Kelson, who had brought with her several racks of exquisite clothes from which to piece together our ensembles.

Having to walk past the cameras, through the glaring lights, and into a sea of raucous people, added unexpected pressure. But after a few trial runs, during which the complimentary crew padded our fragile egos with enthusiastic applause, and Nedra, exploiting her trademark moxie, demonstrated how to sashay with abandon and pose with attitude, our paralyzing dread grudgingly dwindled into a manageable anxiety.

What lingering butterflies I had flitting in my stomach were quelled the instant I got a peek at my first finished look. Kitty's makeup artist had expertly airbrushed my face to glowing perfection, after which her on-set hairstylist, with copious amounts of product, an industrial flatiron, and a great deal of patience, had painstakingly straightened my wavy extensions into a shiny bed of smooth wisps. Meanwhile, my outfit—a pair of dark-wash straight-leg jeans, a maroon graphic tee that hung past my hips, hugging curves I never knew I had, and simple black pumps—rendered my waist deceivingly tiny and my legs deceptively long.

I pretended not to notice the gawks from assorted staff and crew members as I strolled from the dressing room to the designated area backstage with a lissome lope.

Nedra, clipboard in hand, headset dangling from her neck, was speaking to Aisha and Bridgette in a hasty, matter-of-fact tone. A flicker of surprise lit her eyes when she glanced up to see me approaching.

"Am I late?" I asked, mostly to fill the silence that had accompanied their speechless stares.

"No." Nedra reset her expression with a shake of her head and stepped aside to make room for me in the huddle. "I was just telling Aisha and Bridgette that all of the guests have been confirmed. They'll be joining you on-set during your segments."

I swallowed audibly at this latest piece of news. "Who's here for me?" I asked, straining not to sound too curious.

She trailed her finger down the short list of names. "Cameron Sheffield and Oliver Tate."

I nodded, my self-assurance vanishing like water down a drain. Aisha took in my suddenly slumped shoulders with a curious tilt of her head. "You're going to knock them dead," she said, gently nudging my side.

I managed a tight grin.

"Last thing," Nedra said, just as the show's theme song and the sound of hundreds of screaming voices could be heard in the distance. "We've changed the order around a bit. It's not a big deal," she hastily added, taking in our panic-stricken faces. "Aisha will go first, then Bridgette, and then Isabelle."

Aisha turned to me with a smirk. "Always save the best for last, right?"

I hugged her, careful not to wrinkle her clothes, and wished her good luck as Nedra led her around the corner where she was to take her place behind the sliding wall. Bridgette and I rushed to a bank of nearby monitors to watch the rest unfold.

"Well," Kitty said, already primly perched atop her butterscotch sofa. "You folks are in for a real treat." She flashed her plastic smile. "Three days ago we sent three very deserving women off to the fabulous Drake hotel where they were given Kitty Asher Extreme Makeovers."

Kitty paused while the audience cheered.

"And they are back today to show off their new looks!"

More cheering. The cameras panned the hyper crowd.

Bridgette gasped with delight and jabbed her finger at the screen. "There's my husband. And isn't that Cameron?"

I scanned the sea of unfamiliar faces until I spotted her in the front row. Faint circles shadowed her delicate eyes, which were slanted tiredly. She combed a hand through her hair and tossed an anxious glance at Oliver, who was seated beside her. He looked irresistible in a simple gray cashmere Henley and black jeans. I watched with fading resolve as he offered several stolid claps in response to Kitty's ongoing monologue before folding his arms across his broad chest.

"It's been a tense and demanding 72 hours for our three guests," Kitty continued. "But as you're about to see, they braved the challenge with grace and determination."

A chronicle of our harrowing adventure began to play on the large screens flanking the stage. Initially, I tensed at the sight of myself looking haggard and inconvenienced in the hotel lobby the morning after my night out drinking. But as the carefully edited scenes started to unfold into an uncomfortably revealing, albeit captivating story, my self-consciousness gave way to amusement, and I found myself smiling and laughing alongside everyone else.

"How about it?" Kitty asked, once the accompaniment had ended and the screens had faded back to black. "Are you ready to see the final results?"

The audience's cheers were loud and expectant.

Kitty responded with a compliant nod. "This was Aisha three days ago," she shouted above the ruckus. A life-size photo of Aisha—presumably at work—sporting torn jeans, muddy boots, and a hard hat was projected on the parting wall from which she was about to emerge. "And *this*," she paused dramatically, "is Aisha now!"

Bridgette gripped my wrist as Aisha teetered down the runway in a pair of beige, open-toe sling-backs, a knee-length pencil skirt, and a dark brown blazer. Her reception was polite, if not a little mild. She made it to the end, offered an unnatural pose, turned, and quickly doddered her way to the couch where Kitty was waiting, arms spread wide.

"So how do you feel?" she asked, after they'd both taken their seats.

Aisha shrugged and crossed her ankles. "Pretty good."

"Well, you look great," Kitty said, rewarding her with a wooden pat on the knee.

"Tell us about your experience."

While Aisha was regaling the audience with all that had happened since she'd been ambushed several days earlier, Nedra surfaced and informed Bridgette that it was time for her to take her place behind the wall.

Bridgette blanched.

"You're going to do fine," I promised; my heartstrings tugged at the sight of her quivering lip. Flashing her two thumbs up as Nedra led her away, I watched the two of them disappear around the corner and then returned my attention to the monitors.

Aisha was now sandwiched awkwardly between her mom and sister. They'd been beckoned to the sofa for a quick chat with Kitty, who was already ordering her viewers at home to stay tuned for more unbelievable results.

Someone gave the all clear and several members of the show's crew immediately set to work stroking the restless audience, while Aisha parted ways with her family. Seconds later she was backstage. "So how'd I do?" she asked, kicking off her heels with a relieved sigh.

I smiled. "You're a natural."

She arched a skeptical brow, but smiled. "Well, if I don't see you before you head out there, good luck."

Nodding my thanks, I watched as she sauntered off, sling-backs in hand, toward the dressing rooms to change into her second outfit.

The audience received Bridgette with less enthusiasm than they had Aisha. She maintained a brave grin, but schlepped down only half of the runway before turning, without striking a pose as she'd been instructed, and double-timing it back to a waiting Kitty. While Bridgette's husband and mother attempted to soften the blow of her dowdy threads and unbecoming haircut, Nedra appeared backstage to escort me to my fate.

"Remember to smile," she whispered, inching me forward so that I was standing directly on my mark.

I shook the jitters from my icy palms and listened to Kitty's muffled voice invite Cameron and Oliver onstage. They chatted for several minutes, namely about my initial reluctance to participate, while I tried to take solace in the fact that in a matter of minutes it would all be over.

"This was Isabelle before her makeover," Kitty said. I wondered what hideous photo they'd chosen to blow up and splash across the wall for the world to see. "And this is Isabelle now!"

Blinded by the sudden onslaught of studio lights, I held my breath and placed one foot in front of the other. A collective inhale of surprise swept through the crowd before me, immediately followed by thunderous applause and several high-pitched whistles. I was both flattered and stunned when I reached the end of the catwalk and past the glare of the spotlights to see that the audience was giving me a standing ovation.

I put one hand on my jutted hip and threw my other arm in the air—a move that only seemed to garner more applause—turned and, with renewed confidence, pranced back down the runway.

My gaze immediately gravitated to Oliver, who was standing next to Cameron, eyes round as saucers. I allowed Kitty to hold me at an arms distance before twirling me around so that the still cheering audience could get one last look before we moved on to the interview.

Cameron, obviously dazed, stood just inches away. What residual resentment I harbored instantly dissipated when she drew me into a long hug. Oliver managed to slip me a lingering peck on the cheek before we were asked to sit.

"*Hellooooo* sexy!" Kitty purred once the commotion had died down. "I can only assume you feel as amazing as you look."

A stray whistle sounded from the back of the studio.

"I do," I said, my smile radiant. "This has been an unforgettable experience."

Kitty leaned forward, eyes pinched curiously. "How so?"

"It's just been really gratifying to watch my transformation take shape over the past week," I said, acutely aware of Oliver's knee gently resting against my own; his touch made my skin tingle. I crossed my leg toward Cameron to create space between him and me. "A lot of incredible people worked hard to make it happen and I'm grateful. I feel like I'm walking away with more than just a new look. I'm also taking with me the amazing new friendships I've made along the way."

"Let's take a closer look at your journey," Kitty read from the teleprompter to our left.

A montage of my week flickered across the JumboTrons. Some of it was endearing; most of it was humorous. The novelty of seeing myself on-screen still proved captivating.

Midway through, Oliver's sleeve brushed against my bare arm as he repositioned himself on the sofa. I tried to return my attention to the rolling footage, but couldn't manage to regain my focus.

"Cameron, Oliver," Kitty said once the JumboTrons had faded to black. "Anything you'd like to say to Isabelle before we go to break?"

Cameron reached for my hand. "Just that I love you," she said, her eyes searching mine for some sort of assurance that my change of heart wasn't an act for the cameras; that the experience really had proven to be a positive one; and that, most importantly, she and I were OK.

"I know," I said, giving her hand a squeeze. "I love you, too."

"Oliver?" Kitty prodded.

He cleared his throat and slowly raised his gaze until his eyes locked with mine. "You're beautiful."

"My sentiments exactly," Kitty said to the camera stationed directly in front of us. "And on that note, we'll be right back."

The world around us resumed its frenetic pace as a brigade of producers and assistants swarmed Kitty to prep for the upcoming segment; the audience, at the behest of their wranglers, gave themselves a boisterous round of applause; and several prop hands toting chairs and tables shooed Cameron into the wings in their rush to rearrange the furniture.

But Oliver and I remained frozen in time; caught in an arcane magnetism that refused to be denied. I opened my mouth to speak, but found myself helpless to express my thoughts, to identify my feelings.

He stepped closer, hesitating imperceptibly for the briefest moment, before resting his hand on my waist. "Can we talk?" he asked, his grip tightening as he guided my body toward his. "Please?"

The list of arguments I'd spent the past three days compiling promptly slipped from my memory. Reflexively, I nodded.

"When?" he asked. "Tonight?"

"Isabelle." Nedra's voice, sharp and urgent, intercepted my answer. "You're supposed to be in wardrobe," she said, taking hold of my forearm.

Hesitantly, Oliver released me and watched as Nedra tugged me backstage.

The rest of the show went smoothly. My second and final trip down the runway, during which I modeled an off-the-shoulder minidress that hugged my frame like a second skin and platform leopard-print heels that added a provocative sway to my hips when I moved, earned such persistent applause that the show eventually just cut to commercial.

Still, not even the collective validation of a studio full of strangers was as exhilarating as Oliver's expression when I reemerged. I felt his stare moving with me every step of the way. And despite my most earnest attempts to focus on the assigned task, I couldn't seem to pry my eyes from his.

"It's been an amazing day of transformations," Kitty began, our final segment underway. Bridgette, Aisha, and I sat side by side in our eveningwear, while our host waxed poetically for several minutes about the meaning of true beauty.

"You ladies are all treasures," she said, facing us once more. "And we hope that you've enjoyed your time with us as much as we've enjoyed our time with you."

We thanked her and promised to send updates on our progress, though I, for one, knew that would probably never happen.

"Well," Kitty said, her brow hiked, the ends of her mouth turned up into a devious grin. "Before you go, we have one last surprise."

Bridgette sighed—in disappointment or anticipation, I couldn't tell. Ordinarily, news of something unexpected looming would've had me wringing my sweaty palms, but surviving the week's events had girded my nerves.

"Immediately after the show," Kitty announced. "You ladies will be headed to sunny Los Angeles, California, where you will get the chance to show off your new looks at the Fight for Life gala!"

The exclusive fundraiser in support of AIDS and HIV awareness in developing nations had been covered on every newscast and in every major paper for the past couple of weeks. Starting with a sumptuous five-course meal and culminating in a star-studded benefit concert, the televised event promised to be an affair to remember.

Kitty offered a few more details—first-class flight accommodations and a penthouse suite at some infamously swanky hotel—but I had a difficult time hearing her over the roars of the studio's cheering audience.

They continued to clap wildly as Kitty bade farewell to her viewers until next time and then gave me, Bridgette, and Aisha gawky embraces before making her signature grand exit down the center aisle and through the applauding crowd.

PART II

Everything That Glitters

Thirteen

"It's official," Aisha said, tossing her suitcase onto the immaculately made bed closest to the window. "First class is the only way to fly."

"Look at this view," I said, shoving aside the heavy blackout curtains.

She smirked. "Hey, I'd be happy to trade you."

Three fortuitous rounds of Rock-Paper-Scissors had won me the only single room in the suite. Though it faced the rooftop pool and not the picturesque mountains, its king-size bed, plasma television, and en suite Jacuzzi tub more than made up for the lack of scenery.

Aisha took in my gloating smile with a roll of her eyes. "Yeah." She tossed several folded shirts onto the bed. "Didn't think so."

"What're you going to wear?" I asked, settling Indian-style into the rather regal-looking office chair stationed in front of the desk.

"I don't know." She unzipped her garment bag and pulled out a slinky red number; the tags still dangled from its spaghetti strap. "I was thinking maybe this."

She handed it to me. "Nice," I said, thumbing the silky fabric. "You'll be able to wrangle one of those hotshot producer types in this thing."

Just at that moment, the toilet flushed. "That's if we go," Aisha said.

A sallow Bridgette emerged. The nearly four-hour flight, though cushioned by unlimited cocktails, individual movie screens, and the best chicken Caesar salad I'd had—bar none—was inexplicably turbulent.

Forty-five minutes into it, Bridgette had utilized her barf bag, as well as mine. Deep breaths and a motion sickness patch provided by a fellow passenger had settled her stomach enough to get her to LAX, but as soon as we boarded the limo waiting for us outside, her nausea returned—and from the look of her waxy complexion and drooping eyelids, it had returned with a vengeance.

"How're you feeling?" Aisha asked, her words slow, her voice hushed as though noise or sudden movements might trigger more vomit.

Bridgette groaned, easing diagonally across her bed. "I don't get it." She belched. "There shouldn't be anything left to throw up."

"Do you need something?" I asked. "I can call room service—get you some broth, maybe a glass of ginger ale."

She rolled onto her side and gingerly propped her head against one of the pillows. "Don't we have to get ready?"

"We could stay here," I suggested and glanced at Aisha, who nodded.

"She's right," she said, her grin consoling. "We don't have to go. We've got everything we could possibly want right here at our fingertips."

Tucking my chin sympathetically, I smiled down at her. "I'd be perfectly happy with a hot shower and a good movie."

Bridgette sat up, her brows knitted disapprovingly. "I thought we said we were going to make this trip unforgettable. I thought we were supposed to be having fun."

In the green room, long after the audience had filed out of the studio and we'd said our all-too-brief good-byes to our loved ones, we'd passed the wait for our limo to the airport with musings about what awaited us in California.

Aisha had guessed a serendipitous run-in with a celebrity that would—as all worthwhile fantasies did—result in a whirlwind romance. Bridgette had posited the possibility of a passing introduction turned movie career. And I, my thoughts held hostage by Oliver, had theorized a surprise reunion with our friends and families.

At the time, though, we'd still been high off the accomplishment of surviving the show. The long day's events hadn't yet given birth to crippling fatigue or, in Bridgette's case, debilitating illness.

"Sweetie, you puked across six states." Aisha frowned. "I would've thought fun flew out of the window for you a while ago."

"I did not come to California to sit in a hotel room." Bridgette hoisted herself out of bed, swaying slightly before balancing a hand on either hip. "If you two want to lie around and slurp soup all night, be my guests," she said, shambling toward the bathroom. "But I've got an invitation that I plan to use."

Aisha laughed and shook her head as spraying water sounded from behind the closed door. "The woman has spoken," she said.

I smiled and handed back her red dress with a sly smirk. "So she has."

Fourteen

The venue for the Fight for Life gala was everything one would have expected from an event of that caliber. Massive and oozing chic from every securely guarded corner, the lounge area where all of the guests were being held until the grand unveiling of the much anticipated dining-slash-concert hall, boasted a stark, bold, industrial vibe with polished concrete floors, asymmetrical windows, exposed rafters, and thick, metal support beams around which dark gray circular couches had been situated for anyone who might've wanted to cool their designer heels.

It was all accented by a well-trained catering staff who made their rounds stealthily, politely offering milling guests glasses of champagne and artful-looking hors d'oeuvres before vanishing back into obscurity.

Bridgette, Aisha, and I absorbed this scene huddled timidly by the only plant in the room, where we'd spent the better part of an hour trying to convince ourselves and each other that we were still just as sexy and just as worthy as we'd been made to believe earlier that morning on *The Kitty Asher Show*.

It was working until some snobby princess, who'd bumped into Bridgette—not the other way around—and carelessly sloshed champagne onto her expensive-looking stilettos, asked us if we were getting paid to be in the way.

"Do we look like we work here?" Aisha had snapped, cementing my suspicions that she was the type of woman who'd give a purse-snatcher a run for his money.

The unfriendly woman sneered and flashed us a look of unadulterated disgust before stalking off. The encounter shouldn't have been surprising. Though we'd spent the week being treated like superstars, in actuality, we were nobodies. And in case we had forgotten—in case we'd foolishly bought into our own hype—the salvo of publicists, agents, paparazzi, reporters, and actual celebrities who'd been shoving us aside and brushing past us since we'd arrived had easily and successfully put us back in our place.

"Maybe we should just go," I said, the first to voice what all of us were thinking. "I mean, we came, we saw, we drank champagne. All things considered, I'd say mission accomplished."

"Room service and Pay-Per-View don't sound like such a bad idea," Bridgette acquiesced. What spunk she'd managed to muster earlier had been trounced by yet another round of queasiness that had returned during the short limo ride from the hotel.

"Then it's settled," Aisha said, her attention abruptly stolen by something in the distance. I followed her gaze, catching a quick glimpse of a petite blonde in a strapless chiffon dress being whisked behind the velvet ropes that led to the V.I.P. room. "Was that Sarah Jessica Parker?" she asked.

Awestruck, I nodded. "I think it was."

"She's so little," Aisha mused.

An audible gurgle sounded from Bridgette's abdomen followed by a noise that closely resembled a dull growl. "Oh, please," she begged, gripping her stomach with a grimace. "Not here."

The threat of projectile vomit was enough to snap Aisha and me out of our respective trances. "I think I saw the restrooms over there," she said, handing me her flute along with Bridgette's. "We'll be back."

I watched them maneuver through the crowded space, Aisha's arm wrapped protectively around Bridgette's waist. Only after they rounded the corner and were out of my sight did an overbearing sense of self-consciousness take hold. I tried to blend in, offering my best rendition of cool and aloof, but it was nearly impossible not to look pathetic and alone standing in the corner nursing three half-empty glasses of champagne.

"I would offer to get you a drink," an unfamiliar voice joked. "But it looks like you've already got that covered."

I turned; my senses failed the instant my mind was able to register what my eyes refused to believe. Standing in front of me with his seductive gaze and the signature come-to-bed smile that had found a home on the cover of every major magazine in the known free world, was Cooper Young.

He was Hollywood's "it" man—the silver screen's hottest new commodity. He had made some pretty big waves in the film industry, debuting in a couple of little-known, but well-received Indie flicks and then offering a show-stealing performance in a pithy dramedy opposite Robin Williams a year later. But he didn't officially earn his stripes as a bona fide movie star until recently, when he blew everyone away with his performances in not one, but two, summer blockbusters.

I responded with an embarrassingly boisterous laugh that bordered on a cackle—the best I could do under the circumstances—and silently wished to disappear.

"Here, let me help you out there." He relieved me of the glasses I was holding and unloaded them onto an empty tray being carried by one of the passing servers.

"They weren't all mine," I said, gripping my clutch with both hands. "I was just, you know, holding them for a friend—two friends actually. They went to find the lady's room, but they'll be back." I offered a quick smile. "Any minute." And then a nervous titter. "I hope."

He laughed, his brows knitted curiously as I cringed, mortified by my sudden case of verbal diarrhea. "I know," he said, leaning forward so that he could be heard above the background murmur.

His voice was almost as inveigling as his smile.

"I was watching you from over there." He motioned toward the other side of the room. "I've sort of been waiting for the right time to make my move. I saw your friends leave and figured it was now or never."

"I'm sorry," I shook my head, turning a disbelieving ear his way. "Did you say *make your move*?"

He shrugged sheepishly and glanced at the floor between us. "I just wanted to meet the most stunning woman in the room."

I froze, the situation slowly sinking in.

Cooper Young—*the* Cooper Young—was flirting with me. He had watched me, worked up the nerve to come talk to me, and was now, in an implausibly bizarre twist of fate, standing before me, a bundle of shy uncertainty, asking for my name. *My* name!

If I weren't living it, I would have accused myself of lying.

"Isabelle Mackenzie," I said, smiling through the quake in my voice. I extended my hand. In a move right out of a romantic movie, he raised it to his lips and planted a gentle kiss on the back of it.

"Cooper." He hesitated several moments before releasing my fingers. "Cooper Young."

"I know who you are," I said, unable to swipe the wide, giddy grin from my face. "I think everybody knows who you are."

He smiled, the picture of modesty, and shoved his hands in his pants pockets. There was a boyish quality about him, an innocence I realized now, seeing him in person, that wasn't readily captured behind the lens of a camera. "So what do you do?" he asked. "Are you in the biz?"

"No. Actually, I own a bookstore," I said, reeling at how insignificant my life's work suddenly seemed.

"Really?" His expression was one of genuine interest. "Where is it? Maybe I can stop by some time."

"You *could*," I said. "If you're ever in Chicago."

I waited for my answer to register.

"You don't live here?"

I shook my head. "Unfortunately."

"Then what brings you to L.A.?"

The surreal joy of having a personal, one-on-one conversation with Cooper Young had prevented me from anticipating this inevitable line of questioning. Confessing that Kitty Asher had sent me to California as a job well done for a makeover that had only come about because my friends and family were so disturbed by my appearance that they felt the need to stage a nationally televised intervention to get me professional help, was absolutely, positively, not an option.

"My friends and I needed a vacation," I said, wincing at my half-truth.

"And you find stuffy galas relaxing, do you?"

"The opportunity presented itself." I smiled. "We're not ones to pass up the chance at a new adventure."

"You *are* mysterious, Ms. Mackenzie," he said, stopping a passing server to retrieve two fresh flutes of champagne. He handed me mine, studying me closely while I took a sip. "But then again, I've always been a sucker for a good mystery."

I smiled coyly beneath his unwavering gaze.

"So," he began. But before he could go any further, Aisha and Bridgette returned from the restroom.

"I think we've contained it for the time being," Aisha said, oblivious to the tall, stalwart suitor beside me. "If we go now, we should be able to make it back to the hotel with no upsets."

"You're leaving?" Cooper asked, his voice low, his tone one of unmistakable disappointment.

Aisha glanced up and instantly halted, her lips slightly parted, her surprised eyes mirroring Bridgette's. "This is Cooper Young," I said, knowing that no introduction was needed, but feeling obligated to make one anyway.

"Yes," Aisha said, offering a hideously loud cackle similar to the one I'd belted only minutes earlier. "Yes, you are."

"These are my friends, Bridgette and Aisha."

He smiled genially, greeting each of them by name. Aisha pumped his arm, blinking up at him in stunned adoration while a seemingly paralyzed Bridgette stood by wordlessly and stared.

"Cooper was kind enough to keep me company while you guys were gone," I said, squeezing Aisha's arm. She took the hint and relinquished Cooper's hand.

Bridgette giggled nervously. "Lucky you."

"So you guys are heading out?" he asked.

I titled my head with regret. "I think so."

He nodded. "I guess there are more exciting ways to spend your vacation."

"No, it's not that," I said, casting a quick nervous glance at Aisha and Bridgette. The former arched her brow. The latter bit her lip. But fortunately for me, neither one said anything that might've compromised my little white lie. "We would stay, but Bridge has this stomach thing that—"

"Is one hundred percent better," Bridgette interjected. "It really wasn't a stomach thing so much as a touch of jetlag."

"Are you sure?" Aisha asked, her gaze prying, her tone uncertain. The trail of throw up she'd left from Chicago told an entirely different story.

Bridgette bulged her eyes at Aisha and pointed to Cooper's turned back, as if to say that for him, she'd find a way to suck it up. "Yep," she nodded, her expression wiped clean by the time he looked her way again. "All better."

Cooper smiled. "That's great," he said. "I'm at Table 2. Where are you?"

Aisha retrieved our invitations from her purse. "Table 194," she read. My face grew warm with embarrassment. Something told me that Table 194 was situated in No Man's Land between the kitchen and the restrooms.

"Let me see what I can do about that," he said, taking all three invitations from Aisha.

"It's fine, really," I objected, my pride throbbing at his charity. "Don't worry about it."

He smiled. "I'll be right back. Don't go anywhere."

I nodded and watched him until he disappeared into the crowd. Aisha and Bridgette tried unsuccessfully to mute their ecstatic shrieks. "How did you do that?" Bridgette asked. "How did you lasso a gorgeous movie star in the time it took me to throw up my lunch?"

"I have no idea," I said, emerging from a stupor I hadn't realized I was in. "This is. . .." I shook my head and placed my hand over my chest to make sure that my heart was still beating. "This sort of thing never happens—not to me."

"Never say never," Aisha said, producing a black tube from her purse. "Pucker," she ordered. I obeyed and she quickly reapplied a coat of lipstick. "Now rub." I did. She folded a cocktail napkin and held it to my lips. "Blot."

"OK," Bridgette said, patting down a stray hair and then examining my appearance at arm's length. "You're good to go."

"What about you?" I asked, glancing hurriedly in the general direction in which Cooper had strode. "Are you sure you can make it?"

She dismissed my concern with a sigh and a wave. "I'll figure something out."

"Here he comes. Here he comes," Aisha whispered through a taut smile, her lips barely moving.

"Ladies," Cooper said. "I'd like you to meet Adrienne, my manager." He stepped aside to reveal the catty snot who'd snapped at us after she'd clumsily spilled champagne on herself.

Whatever cordial greeting she'd prepared disappeared along with her fake smile the instant she laid eyes on us. "This is Isabelle," Cooper said, smoothly resting his hand against the small of my back. "That's Aisha and that's Bridgette."

Adrienne's eye twitched with irritation as she nodded, barely able to form a polite grin.

"How're the shoes?" Aisha asked, the taunting tenor in her voice lost only on Cooper.

"Damp," Adrienne said, her cold stare contrasting starkly with her jocund tone. "But otherwise OK."

"You've met?" Cooper asked.

"We ran into each other earlier," I said.

Aisha smirked. "No pun intended, of course."

"Of course," Adrienne smiled, her posture stiff with disdain.

"Well, great." Cooper nodded, pleased. "Adrienne and a couple others have offered to switch tables with you."

"Are you sure?" I asked, secretly reveling in the dark delight of Adrienne's pained expression.

Adrienne held her hands up in feigned humility. "It's no problem. Really. I'm glad to help."

"Thanks, Addy," Cooper said, giving her a rough pat on the shoulder. "I owe you."

Inhaling deeply, she motioned toward the now open doors of the main venue. "Shall we?"

We followed her through the maze of extravagantly set tables, our attention just as rapt by the elegantly appointed room as it was by the famous guests we spotted along the way.

Table 2, it turned out, was situated front and center, mere feet from the stage. Adrienne greeted a few acquaintances milling nearby while Aisha and Bridgette took their seats. Cooper gallantly pulled out my chair. I thanked him, flattered by his attentiveness.

"Looks like you've all settled in nicely," Adrienne noted once she'd said her obligatory hellos. "Is there anything I can get you? More champagne?" Her flat tone suggested that we'd be wise not to take her up on the offer.

Cooper smiled. "I think we're good."

"Well, if you need us, we'll be," she glanced down at our invitations with a frown. "Way, *way* back there."

Over the next 20 minutes, the remaining five guests assigned to Table 2 arrived. Only one, Kimberley Hogan, the lead actor in a fledgling medical drama series, was semi-famous. The others consisted of Kimberley's date, two little-known producers, and an equally obscure director. Conversation, most of which was intended for Cooper, flowed well. He expertly staved off the opportunistic director's persistent invitations and turned down pleas to collaborate on future projects, while Kimberley and Aisha carried on a lively discussion about vintage cars, a subject on which both were passionate and surprisingly knowledgeable.

Kimberley, still new to the Hollywood game, seemed genuinely grateful to have three regular nobodies at her table. And Bridgette, Aisha, and I, still woozy from the stench of snobbery left behind by Adrienne, were relieved to be surrounded by, perhaps, the only other down-to-earth people in the room.

Dinner, a parade of gourmet delicacies I'd never heard of and had no hope of pronouncing correctly, was absolutely delicious. Cooper proudly took charge, leaning in closely to introduce each plate as it arrived. He took the time to explain which sauces best complimented which meats and what wines best worked to cleanse the palate between courses.

I listened intently, soaking in his presence, more so than his knowledge, and marveled at how I, a woman who less than one week earlier had been lamenting her age and place in life, had, through a series of most unlikely circumstances, wound up halfway around the country sampling braised lamb with Cooper Young.

"You really know your stuff," I said, the unique blend of cool mint relish and warm tender meat exciting my taste buds.

He smiled. "Next to acting, food is my biggest passion."

"I wish I could say the same."

"Picky eater?" he asked.

I shook my head. "Bad cook."

He laughed and wiped his mouth with the white linen napkin he'd re-trieved from his lap.

"I *can* bake," I said, stopping to savor another bite of food. "I have sort of a sweet tooth. Desserts have always been my favorite part of every meal."

"I'll definitely have to keep that in mind," he said with a sly grin.

By the time the main course had been swept away and the final dish was getting ready to be served, our table had developed a comfortable rapport. But our full stomachs and easy banter did little to distract me from the fact that Bridgette was fading fast.

Though her attempt to weather the evening with her nausea in full throttle was noble, it was also short-lived. She'd managed to get down a few forkfuls of the first dish—an interesting fusion of fettuccine with langouste and escargot. The second course, a light salad adorned with sashimi sliced salmon and an artichoke vinaigrette, she pushed away after only a nibble. The third creation, she declined to taste altogether. And by the fourth course, she'd grown quiet, smiling and nodding when appropriate, but otherwise incoherent.

Aisha discreetly attempted to help, offering multiple times to escort her to the lady's room or to take a stroll outside where she could get some air. But Bridgette, determined to see it through to the end, insisted she was fine.

I knew she was sticking it out for me. I could tell by the wistful glances she'd cast my way whenever Cooper would inch closer or gingerly brush my hair aside so he could whisper something into my ear.

Caught between making the night last as long as it could and being as devoted a friend to Bridgette as she had been to me, I toyed with the idea of leaving early, promising her after each course that we would go soon, only to find myself unable to walk away.

"Have you ever tasted port?" Cooper asked.

I shook my head and snuck a peek at Bridgette, who was rubbing slow, deliberate circles across her belly.

"A dessert fanatic who's never had dessert wine?" He laughed.

Bridgette, whose complexion even under the soft lights of the hall was conspicuously ashen, looked miserable. It had been an incredibly long day for all of us, one that had begun in a different time zone nearly 18 hours earlier. Having spent the bulk of our trip either hurling into a paper bag or wrapped around a toilet, Bridge deserved to go back to the hotel and rest.

Though it seemed like an impossibly difficult task, I knew the time had finally come for me to thank Cooper for a wonderful evening and take my leave. But before I could scrounge up enough mettle to explain the circumstances and say good-bye, Adrienne appeared tableside and insisted that Cooper circulate. "Alone," she added, cutting her eyes daringly in my direction.

Cooper bowed his head apologetically. "Duty calls," he said, placing his napkin onto the table and standing. "Sorry."

I shook my head. "Don't be."

"Yes," Adrienne said, taking hold of his elbow. "I'm sure your guests will manage just fine without you."

"I'll only be a few minutes," he said, already being led away by Adrienne. "Don't start dessert without me."

I watched as they made a beeline to a nearby table, where Cooper flashed a charming smile and chatted warmly with several people, none of whom I recognized.

"Hey," Aisha whispered, snapping me to. "I really think we should head out soon." She nodded at Bridgette, who was seated between us, eyes closed, sweat beading on her wrinkled forehead.

I nodded and turned back to the table where Adrienne and Cooper had been visiting. They were no longer there. I searched the surrounding tables, but spotting one tuxedo-clad man in a sea of tuxedo-clad men was a fruitless hunt.

Bridgette belched into her napkin and groaned. "Isabelle," Aisha called, desperate. We both knew what was coming.

"It was really lovely meeting you all," I said, smiling at the other members of our table chatting quietly amongst themselves.

"You're leaving already?" Kimberley asked. "The concert hasn't even begun."

"We're exhausted," I explained, my tone apologetic.

Aisha helped Bridgette up, while I gathered our purses. "Is she OK?" Kimberley asked.

"Nothing a little air won't fix," I said, backing away with a smile. "Enjoy the rest of your evening." I glanced around the room one last time. The servers were starting to file from the side doors in a neat line, dessert-laden trays balancing expertly on their shoulders. "Give Cooper my best," I said, disappointment settling in my stomach like a two-ton weight. "And tell him I said thanks for everything."

Before they had the chance to question me further, I turned and trotted after Aisha and Bridgette who'd already made their way out of the main venue and past the lounge, where Bridgette burst through the doors to the parking lot just in time to throw up in a bush beside the limo-lined curb.

Fifteen

After expelling what little she'd eaten on the manicured shrubbery and sipping a bottle of seltzer water from the stocked minibar in our limousine, Bridgette swore she felt better.

"It's not too late," she insisted repeatedly, an unwarranted twinge of guilt in her voice. "We should go back."

Aisha chorused her sentiments. "You left without saying anything. You've got to at least give him a proper good-bye. Otherwise, he'll think you just bailed on him."

"I did bail on him," I said, as the driver pulled up to our hotel.

"Not because you wanted to," Bridgette argued. "Who knows." Her smile was quixotic. "He might ask for your number or something."

"It's not the sort of thing you don't see through," Aisha said, stifling a yawn. Her voice was hoarse with exhaustion.

I grinned, touched by their unfaltering allegiance. "You guys are the best," I said. "But I think we should just call it a night."

"And Cooper?" Bridgette asked.

I was strangely at peace with our mysterious parting. Our interlude, after all, had begun to expire the moment we met. Though I'd suspended disbelief for those few inviolable hours, I'd done so with the realistic expectation that once the night was over, we'd retreat back to our respective worlds.

Returning to the gala would only serve to delay the inevitable; whereas cooperating with circumstances would spare us both the unfortunate duty of a labored good-bye.

If Cooper thought of me ever again, it would be with ruminative longing for the sultry temptress who had slipped through his fingers as enigmatically as she had entered into his sights. And that was as satisfying an ending as I could have hoped for.

"Trust me," I said, surrendering to reality with an assenting shrug. "By tomorrow he won't even remember my name."

Sixteen

"Get up! Now! Come on. Up! Up! Up!"

My eyes fluttered in time with my racing heart as my mind, groggy with sleep, slowly began to focus.

The lights were on. Bridgette was clapping inches from my face and Aisha, for reasons I couldn't fathom, was brushing out the plait I'd braided.

"Is she wearing a bra?" Bridgette asked.

"I don't think so."

Bridgette rushed over to the open suitcase resting on the stand by the dresser and yanked out a white hoodie. "Here," she thrust it at me. "Put this on."

What was the big emergency, I wondered, still lost in a numb haze. Had we overslept and missed our flights? Were we being kicked out? "Is the hotel on fire?" I asked, picking from one of a dozen scenarios swirling around in my head.

"Worse," Aisha said. "Cooper Young is waiting for you outside in the hall."

"Are you serious?" I asked, suddenly alert.

"As a heart attack," she said.

"And why is that a bad thing?"

Bridgette unzipped the hoodie she'd given me to put on. "Have you seen yourself?" she asked.

Momentary stillness ensued as I swallowed back the swell of panic brought on by their worried faces. "Plug in the curling iron," I ordered, half crawling, half bouncing across the king-size mattress.

"There's no time for that," Aisha said. "Just go brush your teeth."

"I'll find those jeans you like," Bridgette called after my retreating back.

The next several minutes were filled with a corybantic dance of preparation as all three of us pooled our limited know-how to make me as presentable as possible as speedily as possible.

"Not bad," Aisha said, studying our handiwork in the closet's full-length mirror. I'd changed into a low cut, short-sleeved cardigan and a pair of black boot-cut jeans, while Bridgette had applied lip gloss, blush, and mascara and Aisha had brushed my hair back into a side-swept ponytail.

"Maybe I should–"

"No," Bridgette said, shoving me into the living room. "You look great and he's waiting."

"Don't forget this." Aisha slipped me the hotel key. "You know, just in case we're asleep by the time you get back."

"Be good," Bridgette chided, herding me toward the front door, which Aisha swung open before I had the opportunity to compose myself.

Leaning easily against the taupe wall, still festooned in his tuxedo—sans the bowtie and cummerbund—Cooper's smile met me, his features instantly brightening as I neared.

"Hey there," he said.

"Hi." I grinned and resisted the curious urge to touch his face—to prove to my staggered senses that his flawlessness was not merely a delightful figment of my imagination. "How did you find us?"

"I have my ways," he said, the corners of his mouth turned up into a rascally grin.

I laughed. "Apparently."

"Plus, Aisha told Kimberley where you were staying at dinner. So, you know," he shrugged, a jesting glint in his eyes, "that helped too."

"Listen," I began, my tone apologetic. "About this evening. I'm really sorry for disappearing on you like that. It's just—"

"Bridgette wasn't feeling well," he said.

I glanced up at him, nonplussed.

"Kimberley explained everything," he said. "Don't sweat it; I completely understand." He reached for my hand and traced my palm with the tip of his index finger. "Actually, I was kind of worried you'd be upset with me."

"What for?" I asked.

"Stopping by this late," he said, his approving gaze taking me in from coiffed head to manicured toe. "Were you headed somewhere?"

Desperate not to cast myself as the old maid who turned in early on Friday nights, I responded with a breezy shrug. "Nowhere special."

He smiled. "Then, do you want to hang out for a while? I've got something I'd like to show you."

There was a brief, reflexive moment of hesitation. Though Cooper was a bona fide movie star and, as such, had one of the most recognizable faces in the world, he was still a virtual stranger. It seemed imprudent to roam off alone with him in the wee hours of the morning. Even though I had no doubts I'd be safe or that his intentions were innocent enough, the optics were misleading. I didn't want to give anyone the wrong impression, least of all Aisha and Bridgette.

A dull thud from within the hotel suite, followed by a series of loud whispers, confirmed that we were not alone.

Cheeks aflame with embarrassment, I closed my eyes and waited for the commotion on the other side of the door to cease. "I'm sorry."

"Don't be. What are friends for, right?" He smiled and held out his hand for me to take. "So, shall we?"

I thought of the pledge I'd made to myself—my promise to live more impulsively, to act on emotion, not conscience. This was a prime opportunity. If ever there was a reason to throw caution to the wind, surely a private invitation to spend time with Cooper Young was it. The chance would probably never come along again, and I didn't want to look back with regret at one more thing I could have done, but didn't.

Brushing my reservations to the side, I nodded and slipped my hand in his. Entwining our fingers, he led me to the elevators where we made our descent to the third floor. "Do you know where you're going?" I asked, as he wordlessly escorted me around the closed cocktail lounge, past the desolate restaurant, through a set of restricted swinging doors, and into pitch blackness.

His only response was a low chuckle.

"Are you sure we're allowed to be back here?" I whispered, suddenly wary.

"Hang on a sec," he said, dropping my hand. I heard the distinct sound of retreating footsteps and then nothing.

"Cooper?" My unsteady voice was met by stillness. Inching forward with my arms feeling blindly around my immediate perimeter, I blinked and waited helplessly for my eyes to adjust. "Cooper?" I called again.

A loud click sounded, followed by an abrupt flood of overhead lights. I was in a kitchen.

"Sorry," Cooper said, emerging from a small passage way to my right. "I couldn't find the switch."

He took my hand again and led me to one of three imposing refrigerators. "Sit," he said, pointing at a pair of nearby stools.

I obeyed and watched, with some concern, as he yanked open one of the massive doors and began rummaging inside. "You're sure this is OK?" I asked.

"Positive." He poked his head out and smiled. "This place is like a second home; I'm on a first-name basis with half the staff."

Mildly reassured, I nodded. "That's good to know."

"OK, close your eyes," he said, maneuvering his body so that I couldn't see what he was carrying.

Grinning, I did as I was told, and listened with mounting curiosity to the familiar sound of silverware scraping against dishes, followed by a series of peculiar rustlings and finally Cooper's expectant voice giving me permission to look.

There, displayed before me, was a pictorial arrangement of desserts. "I figured since you couldn't stay for the fifth course," he said, handing me a spoon, "I'd bring the fifth course to you."

I blinked at the collection of tortes and mousses, ice creams and truffles, all beautifully presented, and shook my head, disarmed by the gesture. "You brought me dessert," I said, smitten, not just with his obvious charm, but with the thoughtfulness that accompanied it.

He grinned, clearly aware of his masterful play. "You did say it was your favorite part of every meal."

I nodded, my face warming several degrees beneath his steamy gaze, and glanced back down at the table. "So what've we got here?" I asked, acutely aware of my heart drumming loudly against my ribs; the force pumped the blood to my head in quick, rhythmic rushes.

He scooted his stool closer. "These two, they served at the gala." One was a rich chocolate mousse served atop a hardened dark chocolate shell. The other was a citrus torte garnished with gold leafing that looked more suitable for wearing than for eating. "And these," he said, describing the others in impressive detail. "Are a few of the hotel's specialties. My personal favorite is the homemade vanilla bean ice cream—but only when it's drizzled in just the right amount of strawberry and chocolate sauce."

I surveyed the options before me. They all looked sinfully decadent, but one in particular really caught my eye. "I think I'm going to have to go with the mousse."

He nodded, his lips bunched in mock seriousness. "Good choice, good choice. I'm gonna stick with the ice cream," he said. "It's never done me wrong."

I watched him smother the small white mound in thick syrup before picking up his spoon. "Bon appétit," he said, clinking his bowl against my plate.

The mousse was every bit as appetizing as I'd suspected. Cooper studied my face with obvious pleasure. "You look like you're in Heaven."

"This is unreal," I said, pointing at my already half-eaten dessert. "How about you? Ice cream as good as you remembered it?"

"Better," he said. "Wanna taste?"

I eyed his dish, admittedly curious. "Maybe just a little."

Scooping some into his spoon, he carefully fed it to me, taking care to hold his hand beneath my chin to ensure that nothing dripped onto my clothes.

Nodding, I closed my eyes as the understated sweetness of vanilla met with the bold burst of berries and cocoa. "That *is* good," I said, happily licking the frosty remnants from my lips, before reciprocating his generosity by sliding my plate toward him. "Here, try mine."

He hesitated, a hint of flirtation in his grin, then opened his mouth—neck craned, chin protruding—and waited, eyes flickering with amusement, for me to feed him.

Laughing, I navigated a spoonful of mousse his way. He grabbed hold of my wrist and helped guide my hand.

"Pretty good," he said, once he'd swallowed. Peering up at me from beneath the long lashes framing his piercing eyes, he smiled. "But I think I've got something even better."

"What's that?"

Placing our dishes on the stainless steel top of the island, he pulled my stool, with me still on it, so close to his that their metal legs scraped. Slowly, with deliberate strokes, he caressed my neck and traced the outline of my jaw with his thumb, before finally drawing my face toward his until our mouths met.

His lips, cool, but soft and sweetened by our desserts, molded with tender perfection against mine. A breath of hesitant wonder passed between us, quickly followed by a spark of intrigue and then a rush of feverish attraction.

Even in the fluster of the moment, I understood that Cooper and I were moving too fast for two people who'd met only a few hours earlier. The same nagging inner voice that had given me pause upstairs in the hallway returned. But with his hands pressed against my back and my fingers tangled in the soft tufts of hair at the base of his neck, it was much easier to ignore.

Time, measured only by the spastic rhythm of our flustered heartbeats, passed inconsequently and without notice.

"You're right," I said, once we'd parted. "That *was* better."

He smiled and without a word, pulled me in for another kiss.

Seventeen

"You're sure you're not cold?" Cooper asked, securing his clasp around me for the third time. I assured him I wasn't, but allowed myself to snuggle more deeply into his warm, shielding chest.

After mustering enough restraint to pry ourselves apart, we'd cleaned up the small mess we'd made in the kitchen and then headed, hand-in-hand, back up to my hotel suite. Several attempts to say goodnight in the deserted hallway had only led to more kissing, followed by dallying whispers on his part and shy laughter on mine.

It was a flashback to my younger years, when my brothers and I would crouch by the front window and watch my sister spend the last few minutes of her curfew suctioned to her boyfriend. With teasing gags, we'd roll our eyes as they'd pretend to walk away only to rush right back into each other's waiting arms. At eleven o'clock, on the dot, we'd flip on the porch light, and if by eleven-oh-one, she'd failed to heed our warnings, we'd throw open the door, hoping to catch her mid-tryst, and hector her mercilessly until she came inside.

At the time, I didn't know what to make of her explosive reactions. The tears and shouting and incensed stomps seemed so dramatic, so excessive a response to being separated from someone she would, no doubt, reunite with the very next day. Still, even then—young and inexperienced in matters of the heart—I could detect the pivotal nature of requited desire.

Two decades later, I finally understood with absolute clarity her intractable passion; I felt the impotence, the complete inability to let someone go, even if just for a little while. It was a force against which we were both utterly and willingly helpless.

We wound up cuddled on one of the double chaise lounges beside the rooftop pool talking endlessly. It was dimly lit and secluded—a perfect place to pretend that the world belonged to us and no one else.

"I used to come up here a lot when I first moved to L.A."

I peered up at him. "Why'd you stop?"

He shrugged—his gaze adrift, his mind ambling somewhere mine couldn't follow. "It was easier back then," he said. "Nobody knew me. I'd just sneak in through the service elevator after my night shift."

I pulled away a fraction. "You worked here?"

He nodded. "Three years as a bellhop."

The idea of Cooper Young, festooned in a tacky polyester uniform, toting luggage to and fro for tips, was inconceivable.

The low rumbling of his laughter vibrated soothingly against my reclined body. "It wasn't that bad," he said, taking note of my expression. "Actually, I kind of liked it. Working nights freed me up to go on auditions. Or, if I wasn't up for a part, it meant the day was mine to spend how I wanted."

"And what exactly does the great Cooper Young do on his days off?" I asked.

"To be honest, I can't remember the last time I had one. My career took flight a couple of years ago and I've been working nonstop ever since."

"Is it everything you thought it would be?" I asked. "The fame and fortune."

He shrugged. "Yes and no. It's definitely more grueling than I ever could have anticipated. Press junkets and photo shoots, five A.M. call times and transcontinental red-eyes. Trust me when I tell you that room service and hotel suites get old pretty quickly. But then I remind myself that I'm one of the lucky few who get to do what they love. I get to wake up every single day and live my dream. And I'm grateful." He smiled. "God's been good."

Despite my recent decision to minimize the role faith played in my life, I couldn't help but feel a sliver of excitement at Cooper's acknowledgment of God. "So you're a Christian?" I asked.

He gave a small, noncommittal shrug. "I don't subscribe to any one religion. But I am very spiritual."

"Spiritual," I echoed.

Cooper nodded. "You've got to believe in something bigger than yourself."

"Just not Jesus," I said.

"I believe in Jesus."

My disappointed lifted, but only briefly.

"To an extent, anyway," he amended. "I think He was a great man—a great teacher—who did great things during His time on Earth. I just don't believe He was God."

It was a conversation I'd had dozens of times before—usually on first dates that ended early with a cordial, but decisive, "So long" from both sides. Occasionally, if the guy wasn't staunchly opposed to all things Christ or he expressed an interest in knowing more, I would share my personal testimony in hopes of engaging him in conversation that would get him thinking, get him questioning his current mindset. But I couldn't bring myself to challenge Cooper that way. I didn't want to risk the chance of scaring him off. "So what *do* you believe in?"

He shrugged. "I think that if you live well, keep your nose clean, and do your best to be a good person, the universe will take care of the rest."

I smiled. "That's a little hokey, don't you think?"

"I don't know." He planted a trail of kisses down my arm. "Seems to be working so far. I'm here with you, aren't I?"

"I'm not sure the universe can take credit for this," I said. "It just sort of happened."

"Well, can it just sort of happen again tomorrow?"

"You mean today?" I asked, glancing up at the cloud-bedecked sky, pink and orange with the encroaching dawn.

"OK," he said, angling toward me with an easy swivel of his hip. "Today."

I sighed. "I wish I could, but my flight leaves in a few hours."

"What's a few?" he asked.

I glanced down at his watch. "Five."

The corners of his eyes slanted with disappointment. "I didn't think you'd be leaving so soon."

I nodded. "I didn't know it would matter."

We were still for a while as we watched the sun rise gracefully over the adumbral mountains lining the horizon. The soft light swept methodically across the encompassing canvas and colored the sleeping city beneath it with morning. "Maybe I could come see you," he said, an edge of pleading in his voice. "Or you could come back to see me. I'd fly you out. We could make a weekend of it."

"Maybe." I nuzzled my face into the warm hollow between his neck and shoulder. This was exactly the sort of somber scene we'd managed to avoid earlier when I'd unreadily slipped away from the gala. Farewells were no one's specialty. They were inherently awkward, pregnant with uncertainty and vague intentions—always threatening to unravel the best stories, to mar the most perfect of memories.

"Or maybe," I said, closing my eyes against the lulling rise and fall of his chest. "Instead of figuring out how to fight fate, we could accept it and just…"

"Breathe?" He offered in a tone that told me he understood.

I nodded.

"OK," he whispered, resting his chin on the crown of my head with a resigned sigh. "We'll just breathe."

And with our gazes turned toward the wondrous view above us, that's exactly what we did.

Eighteen

"I thought we were going to have to file a missing person's report," Aisha said, smiling, despite the soupçon of disapproval in her voice. It was just past eight in the morning and she and Bridgette were seated across from each other at a rakishly set Pembroke table situated in front of the living room window.

The scents of bacon and freshly baked bread hung in the air between us. Bridgette looked up from her plate, her mouth turned down into a reproving frown. "You could have called."

"I'm sorry," I said, heading, with labored steps, toward the couch a few feet away. Easing into the cushions, I let out an exhausted sigh. "If it makes you feel any better, I was here the whole time; we never left the hotel."

The creases lining their wrinkled brows smoothed as their displeasure was replaced by curiosity. "So how was it?" Aisha asked.

A smile, wide and automatic, crept across my face.

Abandoning her breakfast with an inquisitive grin, Bridgette joined me on the couch. "That good?"

In vivid detail, I recounted the entire night, reliving it in my mind as though it were happening for the first time. Bridgette and Aisha, who were hanging onto my every word, gasped and chirred with wistful disbelief.

"So how'd you leave it?" Aisha asked.

"With good-bye," I said, shrugging listlessly.

Bridgette's jaw unhinged. "Please tell me you're joking."

"It's not like we were ever going to develop into something more," I said, hoisting myself off of the couch and away from her glower.

The reality was I'd entertained the possibility of pursuing a relationship with Cooper since the moment his lips had grazed mine. But while the idea seemed like a no-brainer in theory, in actuality, it was far more complicated.

As winsome and attractive and successful as he was, he didn't know Christ, which, I knew from past mistakes, meant it would only be a matter of time until our differing beliefs and convictions had us tugging in opposite directions. Then there was Oliver to consider. He and I had left things messy and unsettled. I couldn't just show up with someone new. It wouldn't be fair to cast him aside like that, to simply disregard us with no explanation, no warning.

Nor could I discount how incredibly little Cooper and I knew about each other. Tempting as it was to give myself away to the fantasy, I didn't want to go back home encumbered with false expectations. I didn't want to leave believing we'd shared something truly special only to pick up a magazine a month down the road and wonder if the bosomy blonde on his arm was the reason why he never called.

But even if I could manage to overlook the glaring obstacles in our way, even if I was willing to defy logic entirely and follow my heart, nothing would change the fact that his life was in L.A. and mine was 2,000 miles away in Chicago.

"What?" Bridgette asked, trying to read my silence. "Didn't he want to see you again?"

"He offered to visit," I confessed. "Or fly me back for a weekend."

Her eyes flickered with excitement. "Then what's the problem?"

"Let's just say it wasn't meant to be," I said, my nod resolute. "And leave it at that."

Arms folded, Bridgette shook her head. But before she had the chance to argue further, I veered around the couch and into the safety of my bedroom, where I focused the last of my depleted energy on packing.

Wearily emptying the drawers and closet, I tried not to consider Bridgette's objections or to harp on the increasingly weighty realization that I—regardless of my reasoning and irrespective of my motives—had turned down Cooper Young.

I also tried my best to ignore how much I already missed him. Though in total we'd only spent a matter of hours together, his presence was imbued in my memory, so much so that when I closed my eyes, I could still hear the raspy softness of his voice and the allaying rhythm of his laughter. I could still feel the weight of his hand on my back, still smell his musky scent permeating the air around me.

Absently, I picked up the pajamas that had been left in a rumpled heap on the floor the night before and stuffed them into my suitcase with a sigh. What if Bridgette was right? What if I'd made a mistake? Maybe Cooper and I could have figured out how to make it work. Maybe the only real obstacle in our way was me.

For all my talk of living in the moment and operating on my own terms, all my promises to stop playing it safe and start taking chances, I'd wimped out. I had tucked tail and run from my first opportunity to act like the person I claimed I wanted to be.

"They say after depression comes acceptance."

I turned to see Bridgette—eyes keen, arms akimbo—watching me from the door. "I'm not grieving," I said, dumping an armful of toiletries on top of my wrinkled heap of clothes. "You can't grieve the loss of someone you hardly know."

"You don't have to know someone to feel a connection with them," she said, a matronly wisdom attending her tone. "Look at us. A week ago, I didn't know you and Aisha existed. Now we're like sisters."

"It's not the same," I said, discreetly swiping a rogue tear from my cheek as I tossed several pairs of shoes on top of the toiletries. "And besides, it doesn't even matter. He already left."

Her gaze was soft, compassionate. "I'm sure we can find him."

"He's Cooper Young," I said. My voice cracked slightly. "Tracking him down is probably next to impossible."

"How do you know unless you try?"

Abandoning the mass of tangled clothes with a defeated sigh, I slumped to the floor and rested my back against the bed's footboard. Bridgette joined me. "I wouldn't even know where to start," I whispered.

"Did he happen to mention where he was staying?"

Eyes closed, I shook my head.

"Do you know how long he'll be in town?"

I shook my head again.

"Well, what about the Internet?" she suggested. "He's got to have a Website with a fan mail address or a tour schedule—something that could point you in the right direction."

And then what? I wondered. *Was I supposed to write him a letter professing my feelings and send it on the off chance that he would someday respond? Was I really going to follow him around the country hoping to get close enough to him to tell him that I'd changed my mind—that I wanted to give it a shot after all?* Bridgette's suggestions, while sweet and earnest, were merely wishful means to an unlikely end.

Cooper was gone, and I was the one who'd sent him packing.

"What are we talking about?" Aisha asked, taking note of me and Bridgette on the floor with a curious arch of her brow. She commandeered a nearby ottoman and joined us.

"Ways to track down Cooper," Bridgette said.

Aisha looked at me, my lashes dampened with tears. "What happened to leaving it at good-bye?"

Bridgette grunted. "We decided that it's as dumb of a plan now as it was twenty minutes ago."

"OK, then." Aisha grinned. "Well have you thought about trying to get a hold of his agent or a publicist? I'm sure if you explained the situation, someone in his camp would be willing to help you get in touch with him."

Bridgette laughed. "Something tells me the Wicked Witch of West

Hollywood wouldn't be all that helpful."

A chill swept the room at the mention of Adrienne. "She was a piece of work, wasn't she?" I asked, recalling her permanent scowl and frosty eyes with an involuntary shiver.

Bridgette frowned. "I just wish I knew what her problem was."

"Beats me," Aisha said. "But if I could get five minutes alone with her in a dark alley, she'd be a changed woman."

We laughed.

Huddled in a circle at the foot of my bed, the three of us began to reminisce about our week together. There were no complaints or compunctions as we tallied the sum total of the experience, only gratitude—not just for the opportunity, but also for the chance to have braved it with each other.

All too soon, the front desk rang to inform us that our car was waiting. There was no more mention of Cooper Young as we rolled our luggage down the hall and onto the elevator. He'd become a small part of a greater loss in the wake of our rapidly dwindling time together. Unlike the false farewell we'd encountered the day before in Chicago, this time around our separation would be actual and indefinite. We had reached the end of our incredible journey and that recognition was sobering.

The ride to the airport was quiet, bracing. Captives of our own thoughts, we gazed out of the windows at the passing city, none of us daring to speak.

Once our bags had been checked and our boarding passes were in hand, we wove our way through the labyrinth of lingering travelers to the stalled security line, where Bridgette, who had the earliest scheduled departure, was the first to crack. "This is not good-bye," she said.

Aisha shook her head. "Of course it isn't."

"We'll keep in touch." I smiled.

"And we'll visit," Aisha said. "I'll see you both again before you know it."

We carried on like that—tempering the sting of our present separation with the assurance of a future reunion—until we'd passed through the metal detector and into the airport's main terminal.

"This is me," I said, motioning to my left.

Aisha tilted her head in the opposite direction. "My gate's down there."

"And I'm headed that way," Bridgette said, pointing across the crowded hub.

I shrugged and bit my lip, determined not to cry. "So this is it," I said.

Aisha drew Bridgette, whose round face had gone flush with emotion, into a hug. "I'll call you when I get in."

"Me too," I said, taking her into my arms as soon as Aisha let her go.

"Take care of yourself," I said, slipping my hand into Aisha's.

She nodded.

With one last look at the two of them, I slung my carry-on over my shoulder and headed for my gate. The knot in my stomach tightened with each step, but I kept moving, despite the tears dripping from my trembling chin and the sob gathering at the back of my throat.

I kept moving—one foot in front of the other—and rounded the corner toward home without so much as a backward glance.

Nineteen

"Mack!" Cameron shouted across the congested baggage claim. "Over here!"

I followed the sound of her voice until I spotted her waving fervidly beside an empty bank of payphones. Aglow with excitement, she bounded the short distance between us and threw her arms around my neck.

I smiled, relieved by the immediate comfort that accompanied her face and returned her hug with one of my own.

"It's so weird." She stepped back, her wide stare sweeping me from head to toe. "I'm still not used to seeing you like this."

"Me either," I confessed as we strolled toward my assigned carousel, already rotating with the varied pieces of luggage from my flight. "So, what did I miss while I was gone? How's the bookstore?"

"Burned to the ground," she deadpanned. "Nothing left but ashes."

I rolled my eyes. "A simple 'fine' would have sufficed."

"It's better than fine; it's perfect." She smirked. "Oliver's made sure of it."

My chest tightened at the sound of his name. "How is he?" I asked, masking my unease behind what I hoped was a casual tone.

I'd seen him only a couple of days ago in the green room after the show, right before I had been scuttled to the airport. Seizing the opportunity when Cameron had excused herself to take a call, he'd pulled me away from Aisha and Bridgette and their gathering of chattering family and friends to a secluded corner.

Drawing me close, he'd asked if there was any way we could pick up where we'd left off before the makeover, before he'd made the unforgiveable mistake of disappointing me.

I'd thought back to our first kiss in my living room—how vivid it had been, how visceral—how every second we'd shared afterward had only intensified the charge between us—and I'd surrendered. Standing there, with his arms around me, all missteps had been forgiven, all resentments forgotten. I couldn't imagine forfeiting our chance to be together, couldn't fathom anything jeopardizing my feelings for him.

"Moping, I think." Cameron shook her head reprovingly. "That boy has no idea what to do with himself when you're not around."

"I'm sure he managed," I said. Scanning the approaching luggage more intently than necessary, I spotted my bag with a grateful sigh.

Cameron stepped aside as I heaved my suitcase from the slowly revolving conveyor belt with a grunt. "The way his lip was dragging the ground yesterday, you'd a thought Kitty had sent you off to war instead of some posh Hollywood gala. Speaking of which..." She smiled and hiked her brows expectantly. "I want all of the details."

"It was amazing," I said as we made our way through a set of automatic glass doors and across a covered walkway to the parking garage. "I had a great time."

"Define amazing," she demanded. "Were there celebrities? Did you get to meet any of them?"

I smirked.

"What?" she asked, studying me, her expression eager.

Turning my face, which had gone hot at the thought of Cooper, I shook my head. "Nothing," I said, my steps quickening.

She kept pace easily. "Did something happen in California?"

"No," I said, dismissing the implication with a vehement guffaw. But my resolve quickly began to buckle beneath the weight of her badgering stare. "Well, sort of," I backpedaled. "It was a weird...I don't know. Chance encounter—if you can even call it that."

Her eyes sprang wide at the sudden realization. "Oh my gosh, Mack." She squealed. "You met someone!"

"It's not a big deal." I waited while she disarmed her alarm and popped the trunk. "We hung out for a while; that's all," I said, hoisting my bag inside.

"Well, what's he like?" she asked, sliding in behind the steering wheel.

I climbed in on the passenger's side and fastened my seatbelt. "Gorgeous," I conceded with another involuntary smirk. "And sweet."

She laughed. "Always an excellent combination. So does this mysterious Prince Charming have a name?"

I was fairly certain that Cameron was the one person I could tell about Cooper who wouldn't accuse me of lying or check my head for signs of blunt force trauma. But I was also pretty positive that she wouldn't be able to understand just how special our time together had been. I didn't want to have to explain myself or feel pressured to define it in a way that would make sense to someone else. Though it would have undoubtedly made for a jaw-dropping story, I decided then and there to keep my brush with Cooper Young a secret—one perfect memento just for me.

"It's not important." I shrugged and relaxed against my seat with a sigh. "Odds are we'll never see each other again anyway."

"That's depressing," she said, scrunching her nose disappointedly.

"So then let's talk about you." I smiled. "How's life?"

Navigating us out of the airport and onto the Dan Ryan, Cameron launched into a detailed briefing on her latest interoffice feud. As with most of the drama that unfolded across the ergonomic cubicles of Snyder & Smith, it was mindless drivel—another petty rivalry resulting between trivial women with too much time on their hands. Still, I nodded dutifully as she detailed, with palpable affront, how Tessa Ulrich—co-worker and long-time arch-nemesis—had conspired to wear the same dress as her to a client's book release party.

While she methodically outlined an argument for why she'd looked better, I gazed out of the window at the passing scenery and let my thoughts meander.

The last week, though mildly torturous at certain junctures, had been incredibly exhilarating. No two days had followed the same pattern; no one outcome had presupposed the next. The hectic pace had been refreshing, the uncertainty thrilling.

I couldn't help but wonder how I would implant that new sense of excitement into my old predictable life. For years I'd viewed the monotonous repetition of my daily schedule as security, but now, faced with returning to it after an unprecedented reprieve, I found myself staving off dread. Waking indefinitely to the same uneventful routine seemed less like the comforting consistency I'd once considered it and more like mind-numbing drudgery.

"Home sweet home," Cameron announced, tactically maneuvering her car into an empty parking space.

"That was fast," I said, surprised to see my building across the street.

"Happy to be back?"

I nodded, but took in the familiar mid-rise with an unenthusiastic shrug. It seemed smaller than when I'd last seen it—duller and generally less appealing.

Luggage in tow, Cameron and I made our way up the awning-covered sidewalk that led to the large glass double doors of the main entrance. We were halfway across the stately lobby when Peter, duteously attending his doorman's post, intercepted us with a pleasant, but formal, "How may I help you, Ms. Sheffield?"

Cameron stopped abruptly and cast me an unsure glance. "We were just heading upstairs," she said.

He offered a polite nod, but held his position. "I'm afraid Ms. Mackenzie is still out of town."

"I'm right here, Pete," I said, my wave small and sheepish.

His eyes narrowed as they searched my face, only to bulge seconds later with delayed recognition. "Of course!" he said, tripping over his own foot as he rushed to step aside. "Welcome back! You look…I hardly…that's just…

Wow!" he sputtered, tripping again, this time over one of the imposing decorative pots situated at either end of his station.

I blushed. Cameron snickered.

"Here, let me get that for you," he said, scurrying to the elevator and jabbing the button on the upholstered wall beside it. The doors swung open, and he ushered us inside with a gallant sweep of his arm.

Cameron grinned, clearly entertained. "Thanks."

"I'm here until nine," he said, his regardful smile aimed at me. He tossed a backward glance at his vacant desk. "If you happen to need anything—anything at all—just give me a buzz."

"Will do," I said, nodding bewilderedly just as the mirrored panels closed between us. In the many years he'd watched me come and go, Peter had never before felt obliged to apprise me of his availability. "That was bizarre."

Cameron chuckled. "I think you have a new admirer."

"Just what I need," I said, grimacing at the idea of passing his post every morning on my way to work.

"Oh, don't be such a grouch," Cameron tsked, her eyes twinkling with amusement. "It'll wear off eventually."

"You're enjoying this just a little too much," I said as we reached my floor.

Smirking, she debarked and led the way to my unit at the farthest end of the main corridor. I dug the keys out of my travel-worn carryall dangling from her shoulder and let us in.

Everything was exactly as I had left it—neat, wonted, stiflingly familiar. I tugged my suitcase down the narrow hallway to my room, where I discovered my robe hanging from its usual peg beside the closet and my nightstand still cluttered with the same stack of books and papers and my plain white bedding arranged in its usual fashion. The scene was strangely disheartening.

"So don't be mad," Cameron called from the living room.

Sighing, I abandoned my bag by the door and retraced my steps to find her leaning against my antique armoire with a guilty grin. "Should I be worried?"

She bit her lip. "I might have arranged a small homecoming party. Nothing big or fancy," she quickly added. "Just your family and a few friends."

"Where?" I asked, folding my arms. "When?"

She pointed her index finger at my floor with a squint. "Here, tomorrow night."

"Cam," I grumbled.

"Come on, Mack." She tilted her head. "What was I supposed to do? People have spent the last few weeks secretly digging up old photos and giving on-camera interviews. They're curious. They want to see the finished product."

It didn't happen often, but Cameron made a valid point. I was going to have to debut my new look to everyone eventually. At least this way, I could get it over with in one fell swoop.

"Small?" I confirmed.

"Tiny," she promised. "I've already taken care of everything. All you have to do is show up."

"OK." I acquiesced after a few hesitant moments. "I'm in."

Cameron's smile was broad, triumphant. "Then, I will see you tomorrow," she said, heading for the front door. "Oh—and the caterer will be here at five."

"Caterer?" I asked, my concern audible. That didn't exactly sound like the workings of a casual get-together.

"Don't forget to wear something dazzling," she said, ignoring me completely as she crossed my short foyer in three sprightly steps. "It's semi-formal attire."

"But I thought you said—"

It was no use. She was gone, the door already closed behind her.

Groaning knowingly, I shook my head and with a defeated sigh returned to my room to unpack.

Twenty

I was grateful, when I woke Sunday—not necessarily for the party, but for the inherent distractions that came with it.

Bypassing my Bible, which was laying saliently on the armchair beside the window, I padded to my closet, changed into an old pair of sweatpants and a T-shirt and then migrated to the kitchen.

There, I nibbled on a piece of toast and flipped aimlessly through a magazine, while doing my best to ignore the message indicator flashing red from the base of the phone next to the pantry. Oliver's calls had started yesterday afternoon, not long after Cameron had dropped me off, and had continued in regular intervals throughout the rest of the day and halfway into the night.

I should have answered, if for no other reason than to let him know that I'd gotten home safely. But what if he'd asked to come over? Or worse yet, what if I hadn't found the strength to say no? It's not that I didn't want to see Olly; it's not that I wasn't always aware of his absence. I just wasn't sure what to say to him after what had happened in California. I hadn't yet figured out how to reconcile the woman I was before my transformation with the woman I'd become afterward.

Draining the last bit of my coffee in two easy swallows, I grudgingly set to work unloading the dishwasher, scrubbing down the countertops and emptying my cupboards and refrigerator of anything that had expired or looked remotely questionable. They weren't grueling chores, but a small part of a larger preemptive effort to appease my mother, who would undoubtedly nitpick when she arrived along with the rest of my family later that evening.

Eventually my cleaning frenzy progressed to the living room, where I dusted the bookcases, vacuumed the floors, and tried, without much success, not to think of Cooper.

I realized that in all likelihood, he'd already put me soundly out of his mind. Pining over me, when he could have practically any woman he wanted, would have been a colossal waste of his energy. Still, I couldn't help but wonder where he was, what he was doing, and if, at any given moment, there was even the slightest chance that he was thinking of me too.

Nor could I seem to stop myself from getting swept up in embarrassingly detailed daydreams about what things might have been like had I accepted his offer to meet again. I imagined a whirlwind of movie premieres and red carpets, private jets and five-star restaurants, paparazzi and screaming fans. In my head, it was glamorous and glittery—a world far removed from anything I knew, but closely related to everything I was starting to want. I played and replayed my fantasies until I nearly made myself sick—until wistful wishing turned into a sense of aching loss. And then, just when the longing for Cooper became too much to bear, Oliver sprang to mind and sidetracked me with an entirely different set of anxieties.

I wasn't sure where he and I stood or if I still wanted to move forward from where we'd left off. I didn't know what to expect when I saw him or how I would explain what had happened in California. But regardless of the many uncertainties and despite all of the unanswered questions, one truth remained. We were best friends. And I could count on that to navigate us safely across the uncharted terrain on which we currently found ourselves.

Or at least that's what I told myself later that afternoon as I emerged from the shower a bundle of nerves and headed to my closet in search of something to wear. Carefully combing through my new wardrobe, I finally settled on a fitted black sheath paired with a wide woven belt. Surveying my reflection in the mirror, I smiled, pleased by how the dress's low V-neckline framed my collarbones and how my platform stilettos gave me the illusions of length and poise.

Next, I heedfully applied my makeup, taking care to spread my foundation with short brisk strokes, layer my shadows from light to dark and sweep my blush from cheekbone to hairline as I'd been taught by the experts. Then, with Sergio's instructions committed to memory, I began the unnerving task of styling my extensions into soft, tumbling waves.

The caterer arrived as I finished putting on my earrings and Cameron followed only minutes after that. As she scurried about showing the small staff of three where to set up, I skimmed my extensive CD collection for ambiance music and braced myself for the onslaught of guests to begin.

I didn't have to wait long. By eight o'clock, my place was packed and the party was well underway. I split my time chatting hospitably and refilling empty platters with spring rolls and gougeres, while Cameron circulated the room, wine and water bottles in hand, and graciously offered to refresh people's drinks. Despite her assurances that she'd only invited close friends and family, there were a suspicious number of single men from her firm in attendance. Every so often, she would corner me long enough to make a hasty introduction, and then flit away with a waggish smirk to go pour more Perrier.

Jesse was her third and most recent attempt at a setup. Average height with a lean build, he was stoop-shouldered and soft spoken, save for an energetic laugh that, when unbridled, shook his entire body. We carried on a cordial conversation, filling in the awkward pauses with random observations about the weather and work. Occasionally, I scanned the crowded space, hoping to catch Cameron's eye and signal for her to rescue me, but she had conveniently vanished.

Nodding mechanically with feigned interest as he labored through his fifth anecdote in as many minutes, I began quietly plotting a tactful way to excuse myself. Just when I'd settled on a plan that involved a fake sneeze and an urgent search for Kleenex, a familiar voice gasped my name.

Turning, I saw my mother, a gobsmacked expression on her face, staring at me from across the room. Behind her, my sister and two brothers stood frozen, gazes wide with shock. Tilting my head apologetically, I excused myself, abandoning Jesse mid-yarn, and made my way over to them. I laughed as they converged on me, dispensing hugs and compliments, as they passed me down the line to examine me one by one.

"I hardly even recognize you," Mom said, cupping my cheek in her hand. She brushed my new bangs from my face. "It would have been nice if they'd styled your hair so people could see your eyes."

"Ignore her," Danielle said, swatting mom's hand away. "You look fantastic."

"So how much trouble are we in?" Caleb asked.

I smiled. "Lucky for you I'm a forgiving person."

Gabe draped an arm around my shoulders and squeezed me close. "Well, if it's any consolation, you are absolutely gorgeous."

"I'll second that," someone said behind us. We turned to see Oliver standing just inside of the open doorway. He looked even more debonair than usual dressed in a black herringbone sport coat, grey crewneck, and double-pleated trousers.

"Olly!" Mom exclaimed, clasping her hands in delighted surprise. Gripping the lapels of his jacket, she yanked him down to her level and delivered a maternal kiss to his forehead.

"Mona," he said, his long arms engulfing her slight frame as they folded around her. "How've you been?"

"You'd know if you ever bothered to visit," she said, her tone scolding. "We haven't seen you in ages."

He nodded and gave her an apologetic grin. "It's been awhile."

"Don't be like these guys," she said, motioning at me, my sister, and my brothers with a dismissive wave. "I'll be gone and buried before they finally find the time to appreciate me. And then what?"

Gabe rolled his eyes. She'd been leveling that threat at us since we were kids. "As you can see, not much has changed," he said, offering Olly a firm handshake and a gruff pat on the back.

"Good, you guys made it," Cameron said, appearing seemingly out of thin air, an empty serving tray in hand. She welcomed my family with a quick round of pecks to the cheek before facing Oliver with a testy frown. "And you! You were supposed to get here early and help me set up."

"I know. I'm sorry. I got stuck at the office this afternoon and lost track of time," he said, sighing tiredly. "But I'm glad you were able to pull it off without me. Everything looks great."

Danielle smiled. "Everything and everyone."

On cue, their proud gazes settled over me, but my attention was occupied by the statuesque woman hovering nearby in Oliver's shadow. He followed my stare and immediately blenched at his oversight. "I'm so sorry," he said, placing a hand on the woman's back and guiding her forward so that she was part of our small gathering. "Guys, this is Claire."

"Nice to meet you," Mom said, taking the two of them in with a hopeful smile. It was no secret that she was just as eager for Oliver to get married and start a family as she was for her own children to settle down. "I'm Mona."

One by one, we went around the circle and introduced ourselves. Claire was polite, but phlegmatic—acknowledging everybody with little more than a stoic expression and a reserved nod.

"Isabelle," I said, when my turn came. Her eyes, sharp and daring, swept me from top to bottom in one appraising glance. With draining confidence, I took in her striking features and shapely build, my stare automatically lingering on Oliver's hand resting easily at her waist.

Claire took note of my gaze and closed the few inches between them with a provocative sway of her hip. No one but Cameron, who was well versed in the game of catty tactics, seemed to notice. She was by my side in one graceful step, her glare fiery. "How exactly do you know Oliver?"

Claire arched a brow and sighed, as though being asked to speak somehow offended her. "We work together."

"Claire's new to the firm," Oliver said. "She just relocated from Boston a couple of weeks ago."

"Well, welcome," Mom trilled. "You know, Isabelle's lived here forever. You two should exchange numbers. She could show you around—help you get your bearings."

"Thanks." Claire tossed me a stiff smile that could have doubled as a sneer.

"But Oliver's already got me pretty well oriented." She touched her temple to his shoulder. "He's the consummate tour guide."

"We took in a few sites yesterday," Oliver explained. "Shedd Aquarium, Sears Tower. I was going to take her to Millennium Park, but it looked like rain."

"Pity," Cameron said, sounding anything but sorry.

Claire shrugged. "There's always next weekend."

I had no right to be upset. If I could spend my time canoodling with Cooper, Oliver could certainly spend his sightseeing with Claire. I wasn't the only one who was allowed to change my mind. He was free to do what he wanted, to see who he pleased—no matter how much it stung. Swallowing back a wave of emotion, I grabbed the empty serving tray in Cameron's hand. "I think the brochettes are running low. Excuse me."

Turning, I brushed past a bewildered Gabe and wove my way through the crowded living room to the kitchen. Cameron was not far behind.

"Is it just me or does Olly's taste in women get worse with age?" she asked as soon as we were alone.

Absently transferring more hors d'oeuvres to the waiting platter, I grunted. "She's definitely one for the books."

"*There's always next weekend,*" Cameron thrummed, mimicking Claire's haughty voice with eerie accuracy. "What a harpy. And did you see how she was draped all over him. I thought we were going to need a crowbar to pry her loose."

I nodded, my chest tightening, and slumped against the cluttered counter with a shaky sigh. "I can't believe he brought her here."

"Hey," Cameron called, her forehead wrinkling with concern at my moist eyes and trembling chin. She pushed the tray aside and placed her hand over mine. "This is your night, remember that. Just ignore Claire; it'll be fine." She studied me for several moments, her eyes pinching suspiciously. "Unless I'm missing something."

"Oliver kissed me," I confessed quietly.

She didn't seem nearly as surprised as I'd expected. "When?"

"My birthday, initially." I shrugged and looked away. "I thought maybe it was turning into a thing. But then the makeover happened and after that California." I shook my head. "Clearly, I read too much into it."

"I don't know," Cameron said, sliding onto the stool beside me. "Oliver's not the sort of guy who runs around arbitrarily kissing women."

"He brought a date, Cam."

She shrugged. "Don't sell yourself short. Maybe they're just friends."

I frowned at the unlikelihood. "Yeah, maybe."

"You should talk to him. He might—" She stopped short at the sight of something behind me. I didn't bother to turn around. I knew from her tentative smile exactly who it was.

"Am I interrupting?" Oliver asked.

"Not at all," Cameron said, standing. She picked up the tray of sloppily arranged appetizers next to us. "As it happens, I was just heading back out."

Oliver waited until she left before slowly circling the island situated between us. "Some turn out," he said. His tone was casual, but his gaze was probing. "Looks like everybody you've ever known is here."

"And then some," I said, busying myself stacking the dirty plates scattered about the tile countertop.

He smirked. "You're angry."

Stepping around him, I deposited the pile of dishes into the sink.

"She's just a friend."

I shrugged. "I'm really not interested."

"I invited her as a favor to my boss. You'd know that if you had answered my calls." He drew nearer, the corners of his mouth still turned up in amusement. "Then again, you are kind of cute when you're jealous."

I rolled my eyes, but put up no resistance when he reached for my elbow and tugged me to him.

Cradling me, he ran his hand along my bare shoulder, tracing its curve down my arm and around my waist until he was holding me so closely I couldn't tell our breaths apart. "There's no one else," he whispered, gently leaning in, his face inches away.

I felt a stab of momentary guilt knowing that I couldn't say the same thing, but the immediate proximity of his slowly approaching lips overrode the urge to confess everything that had happened while I was away. Tilting my chin upward, I closed my eyes just as his mouth was about to touch mine.

"Mack!" Cameron said, bursting in on us in a breathless tizzy. She took stock of me and Oliver intimately wrapped around each other and made an effort to reclaim herself. "Sorry." She shot me an anxious look and gave a little nod in the direction of the living room. "I think you should come out here."

"Can't it wait?" Olly asked.

Cameron, wired and fidgety, shook her head.

"What's wrong?" I asked, gently wriggling loose from Oliver's grasp. Forgoing words, she took hold of my wrist and dragged me through the kitchen archway.

Though still swarming with people, the party had gone ghostly quiet. Everyone's attention, I quickly realized, was focused on something near the door. My guests parted willingly as I made my way—with Cameron and Oliver close on my heels—across the hushed room, only to stop short with a soft gasp at the sight of Cooper Young standing in my foyer. I joined the others in stunned silence.

He smiled. "Hi."

"Hi." I smiled back. "What're you doing here?"

In one swift movement, he closed the gap between us, scooped me into a determined embrace and kissed me. It was eager and fervent and serenaded with a low rumbling chorus of stupefied murmurs from the throng of onlookers behind us.

I couldn't understand why it seemed so natural—how I could feel just as at home wrapped in Cooper's arms as I had been moments earlier cradled in Oliver's.

But it did. And I was.

"Is this OK?" Cooper asked once he'd pulled away. "Are you glad I'm here?"

There was no right answer. To welcome one was to automatically reject the other. It didn't matter that I wasn't prepared to choose. It made no difference that they both appealed to me in the exact same way for completely different reasons. Fate had forced my hand and someone would be hurt because of it.

"Of course," I said, looking over just in time to see Oliver maneuver around the rapt gathering, past me and Cooper and out of the front door.

Twenty-One

"This one's nice," Cooper said.

I nodded, distracted by the immense echo caused by my sandals hitting the freshly polished marble floors. We were standing in the domed antechamber of a penthouse condominium overlooking Lake Michigan. At 5,000 square feet, with six bedrooms, a gym, an indoor lap pool and round-the-clock butler and maid service, it was the nicest place I'd ever stepped foot in—save the four-story Greystone we'd viewed just an hour earlier. It came with an arcade and a two-lane bowling alley.

The Realtor, a prim woman with a stern manner and a sleek, gray bob guided us from one impeccably appointed room to the next. Clearly accustomed to presenting the finer things in life to those who could afford them, she made mention of the most impressive amenities with ennui.

Cooper nodded, unfazed by the master bath's majestic Papillion bathtub or the baronial den, which was attached to one of two fully-stocked libraries. Nor did he seem particularly moved by the mirror televisions hanging on every other wall or the custom kitchen furnished with sleek, imported appliances.

"It's a little big, don't you think?" I asked, taking in the view from the terrace one last time before I followed him back inside. "You're only one person.

How much space do you really need?"

He shrugged and plopped on a nearby sofa. "The bigger the better, right?"

"And to the discriminating renter," the Realtor added, aiming a condescending smirk my way, "worth every penny."

"Plus," Cooper said, reaching up and pulling me down next to him. "It's only a few minutes away from you."

A slow heat crept up my neck; I grinned.

Judicially, the Realtor averted her eyes, while he leaned in and slipped me a quick kiss. "Shall we have a look at the home's automation system?" she asked a moment later. "It's fully integrated and voice activated."

Cooper perked up, his attention piqued. "Lead the way."

"I'll wait here," I said as he stood.

"You sure?"

I nodded. We'd been touring properties since early that morning and they were all starting to blend into one big indecipherable maze of mind-boggling excess.

"We'll be right back," he said, following the Realtor, who had already started down a set of stairs that led to the smoking room—a dim hideaway that boasted a massive sandstone fireplace and leather floors.

Alone, I reclined against the cushioned back of the couch and gazed up at the lavish coffering of the living room's vaulted ceiling with an incredulous smirk.

The initial shock of Cooper's presence at the party had quickly given way to frenzied excitement. Within seconds, it seemed, we'd been swarmed by friends turned die-hard fans, all jockeying for an autograph or a photo op.

Her PR skills kicking into high gear, Cameron fished me and Cooper out of the bedlam, quarantined us in the kitchen and posted Gabe at the entrance to keep watch. Then, she set to work clearing the room.

I'd listened, with newfound respect, as she politely, but firmly ushered my guests out of the front door, while expertly evading their persistent questions and relentless pleas for the inside scoop.

"I didn't mean to cause a stampede," Cooper had said, biting his bottom lip apologetically as the distinct patter of dozens of retreating footsteps sounded from the other side of the wall.

I'd smiled, tickled by how out of place he looked standing beside my ancient stove. "I still can't believe you're here."

We hadn't really gotten an opportunity to talk. In the few stunned seconds that had followed his grand entrance—and preceded the resulting chaos—he'd only managed to tell me that he was in the city on business.

"A script crossed my desk," he said, sensing my curiosity. "For a second time actually. Initially, I passed it over because I was already committed to another project. But it turns out funding fell through and it was never green-lit." He shrugged. "Then yesterday, after you left, I got a call from the director of the other film asking me to reconsider the part. When I found out they'd be shooting in Chicago, I signed on and booked the first flight here."

"Just like that?" I asked, smiling. He made it sound so simple, but the more he told me, the longer my list of questions grew. How had he found me? When did filming start? Where would he be staying?

Drawing me close, Cooper buried his face in my newly lengthened hair and sighed. "My only consideration was us and making sure I didn't let you get away a second time."

I was about to ask him how long he'd be in town, but only minutes after sequestering us in the kitchen, Cameron had reappeared. "Coast is clear."

We emerged to find the living room empty save for a handful of people. A quick scan for Oliver had revealed that both he and Claire were gone. Only my family and Cameron had stayed. They were seated around the coffee table, a conflicting and unsettling combination of apprehension and wonder in their eyes.

"Everyone," I said, cautiously easing forward several steps. "This is my friend, Cooper. And Cooper," My grip on his hand tightened, "This is everyone. My mom, Mona; my two brothers, Gabe and Caleb; my sister, Danielle; and Cameron, one of my closest and oldest friends."

"Pleasure," Cooper said, his casual tone accompanied by a confident smile. "I've heard a lot about you all. It's nice to finally put faces to your names."

"Finally?" Danielle flashed a puckish grin. "Exactly how long have you two been friends?" she asked, suggestively punctuating the word friends with air quotes.

I tensed uncomfortably at her tactless taunt, but Cooper brushed it off with a husky chuckle. "We met a couple days ago in Los Angeles."

"Oh my gosh!" Cameron's eyes widened as she began to connect the puzzle, one incredible piece at a time. "*This* is the mysterious Prince Charming?" Her laugh was bursting, revelatory. "You weren't kidding about the gorgeous part."

Cooper bowed his head with a flattered smirk, while my face, mantled in embarrassment, grew a disturbing degree of hot.

"So, wait," Gabe said, confusion knitting his thick brows. "Were you part of the makeover?"

"Sorry?" Cooper asked.

"Nothing!" My interjection was loud and suspiciously insistent. They all stared at me in startled silence. Clearing my throat, I continued in a decidedly calmer tone. "We just happened to bump into each other at the gala and hit it off from there."

Cameron smirked, aware, I could tell, that whatever reason I'd given Cooper for being in L.A., had not involved *The Kitty Asher Show*. "So what brings you to Chicago?" she asked.

"Work," he said. "My next movie's being shot right here in the city."

Mom smiled. "Well, that's exciting."

Cooper glanced over at me, his eyes warm. "To tell you the truth, I'm more excited about the chance to spend time with Isabelle."

Caleb, who'd put himself through college moonlighting as an A.D., tilted his head questioningly. "I didn't think actors got a lot of downtime during filming."

Cooper nodded. "We don't, but principal photography doesn't start for another few weeks."

"So you flew out here early just to be with Mack?" Cameron pressed her hand to her chest and sighed. "That's kind of sweet."

"And a little nuts," my sister said.

"Danny." Mom's voice was stern, admonitory.

"No, she's right," Gabe said. "This whole thing is crazy." He turned in his seat to face me. "I mean, no offense, but let's be honest. It's moving sort of fast, don't you think?"

Chin set, I glared. "No."

He frowned. "You hardly know each other."

"We know enough."

"Like what?" Danielle challenged. "What's his family like? Where was he raised?"

Sacramento? San Francisco? Mentally sifting through the hours of information we'd exchanged the other night, I tried to recall the assorted details of his life, but they'd become one deep pool of murky facts.

"San Diego," Cooper offered. "With a protective older sister, two ornery cats, a lazy golden retriever, and a couple of loving parents, who just celebrated their thirty-eighth anniversary."

I hid my relief behind a smug grin.

"And your faith?" Gabe asked. "Are you saved?"

Smug relief instantly turned to clambering panic. One mention of Cooper's self-professed spiritualism was all they would need to tip the scales against us. I shot Cameron a desperate look in a silent plea for help.

"I think we might be getting ahead of ourselves," she said, her tone disarmingly buoyant. "It's not like she's picking out china patterns. They're just friends. What do you say we hold off on the interrogations until we know where this is actually leading?"

It was a provisional stand-down, but taking their cue from Cameron, Gabe and Danielle holstered their concerns, and the mounting tension in the room gradually dissipated into a civil, if not tenuous, ceasefire.

Cooper's charisma and Cameron's affability kept the conversation afloat over the next couple of hours. And I thought at one point, when he tentatively accepted Cooper's invitation to visit the movie set once filming started, that Gabe was warming to the idea of me and Cooper. But a short time later, after Cooper had already headed back to his hotel for the night and my family and

I were saying our good-byes, Gabe hugged me and with his mouth inches from my ear, whispered a warning that sent a shiver down my spine.

"Penny for your thoughts," Cooper said, snapping me back to the present with a start.

"Sorry, I didn't mean to scare you," he said, joining me, once more, on the couch.

"It's OK." Smiling, I placed a hand over my racing heart and returned my gaze to the breathtaking ceiling. "I was just enjoying the view."

"How much do you love this place?" he asked.

I shrugged. It was definitely striking, impressive—exactly the sort of home I imagined big Hollywood actors living in. But even with its floating stairs and wraparound terrace, the on-call chef and the round-the-clock butler, it didn't appeal to me. There was something lonely about it, a coldness that counter-manded its grandeur. It was neat to look at and fun to explore, but I was glad it didn't belong to me. "So, you think you've found the one, then?"

Cooper's gaze, brimming with meaning, met mine. "I do," he said. "And she's been worth every second of the wait."

I grinned. "Even after meeting my batty family?"

"I've survived worse," he said with a laugh.

"Are we really doing this?" I asked, my voice pitched with excitement. "Are we really giving this a shot?"

Scooting closer, Cooper reached for my hand. "All day, every day, I'm sur-rounded by people with agendas. And it's daunting. Before I became famous, I thought that success would open doors for me, but now I understand it just makes it harder to figure out which doors to open for yourself." He sighed. "I don't know who to trust anymore. Who's lying? Who's scheming? Who's angling for something in return? I'm constantly suspicious of others' motives, and I hate that. I don't want to be the guy who's always looking over his shoul-der. And with you, I'm not." Thoughtfully, he tilted his head. "You are the first honest thing that has happened to me in a very long time. When we're together, I feel different. I feel like the man I know I was meant to be. So, yes." He smiled. "I'm really doing this. I'm in—100 percent—if you are."

Strangely, I understood how he felt. I'd had an expectation of life, of God.

And those expectations, though they'd fallen flat, had cultured an immutable image of me. I was the churchgoing, Bible-reading, miracle-believing, prayer warrior; the non-drinking, non-cursing, uncompromising puritan. People knew me only in terms of that woman and they assumed I would always stay the same. It didn't matter that their perceptions were suffocating me. It made no difference that I'd outgrown the person I used to be. My role had long since been cast, and I played the part without trying. I played the part even though I couldn't identify with it anymore—even though it was nothing more than an act that made each day feel like more of a lie than the day before.

That's why Cooper was such a welcome interruption. He didn't have any preconceived notions of who I was or how I was supposed to be. When I was with him, I could do anything I wanted; I could say how I really felt. I could try on different versions of myself without worrying about drawing an unwarranted criticism or a disapproving frown. There was no contorting with him, no trying to fit inside of a box, no pretending. And I needed that. I needed the chance to be honest with myself, to figure out what I wanted independent of who everyone else thought I should be.

"I'm in," I said, nodding resolutely, even as I heard my brother's cautionary voice echo forebodingly in my head.

Careful, Mack. You're playing with fire.

Twenty-Two

"So this is the illustrious Au Bon Livre I've heard so much about," Cooper said as he maneuvered his rented SUV into one of the metered parking spaces lining the sidewalk. The truck—like everything else in his life, I was quickly learning—was big and top-of-the-line.

"That's it," I said, peering out of my window at the familiar quaint storefront.

After parting ways with Cooper's Realtor, we'd taken the short drive over to the bookstore at my behest. It had been a week since I'd been by and while the makeover and everything else that'd followed in its wake had served as a nice, unexpected vacation, I'd found myself missing my quaint little shop, which had become like a second home to me over the years.

Clear-skied and breezy, it was a typically gorgeous late-autumn day in Chicago. As far as the eye could see, people were out and about—jogging along North Beach, sunbathing in Grant Park, milling at Crown Fountain. I'd taken Cooper the scenic route down Lake Shore Drive hoping to point out some of the much-beloved sites we would pass along our way, but no sooner had he turned the key in the ignition than he was on his cell phone checking messages and returning calls.

I unfastened my seatbelt and watched with a smile as he jogged around the front of the truck to help me out. Strolling hand-in-hand, we crossed the cobbled crosswalk that led to the shop's gabled portico and entered through the chiming glass door.

Everything, as Cameron had assured me, was just as I'd left it. Scanning the mismatched sets of occupied sofas, chairs, and love seats situated haphazardly around the lounge area by the windows, I let out a comforted sigh. My eyes drifted to the message boards where customers could recommend a book or announce upcoming events, and then to the colorful potted flowers, and the vintage coffee tables and the funky, low-hanging lamps I'd happened upon in a small, sleepy town during a road trip with Cameron and Oliver several summers back.

"So, what d'ya think?" I asked, my arms spread wide, my grin proud, expectant.

"It's cute," he said, nodding slightly. Turning slowly in place, he took in the neat aisles of stocked bookcases ordered around us. "Cozy," he added with less enthusiasm than I would have liked.

When I'd first set up shop, the area had been a flourishing hub of local, family-owned businesses. There had been a couple of cafés, a dry cleaner, an organic market, several antique stores, and a few colorful boutiques. It may not have been Michigan Avenue, but it was the heart of the small community I'd grown to love and call my own.

We thought nothing of the empty lot that turned into a Barnie's Coffee seemingly overnight, or the Borders that was constructed beside it a few months later. But by the start of the next year, Target had popped up across the street several blocks away, then a Best Buy, The Home Depot, Whole Foods, and a DSW.

Within two years, nearly every small business that had helped make the neighborhood what it was, had moved—chased out by skyrocketing rent and astronomical property taxes, or convinced to sell to make room for the mega chain stores that had invaded inexplicably and without mercy.

I, like the rest of the small remnant of owners who'd managed to survive the tornado of big-box retail, prided myself as a keepsake of the neighborhood's original authenticity. But I couldn't expect Cooper, who was a staunch proponent of the bigger-is-better school of mind, to appreciate the nostalgia of it. "It's not fancy," I said, trying not to sound as disappointed as I felt by his lackluster reaction. "But that's part of the charm."

"I like it," he said, shrugging unconvincingly as we made our way past the colorful assortment of end caps lining the center aisle and to the front counter.

Iona, my senior sales clerk, was busy scanning and tagging a box of new releases. "Afternoon, folks," she said, waving distractedly in our general direction. "Just let me know if you need help finding anything."

"A week away and that's the best Welcome Home you can muster?" I teased.

"Oh my goodness," she gasped, looking up. Eyes wide and face flushed, she tossed down her tagging gun and ripped off the smock apron tied around her waist as she scurried from behind the counter.

Smiling, I readied myself for a deluge of raves and compliments similar to the ones I'd been fielding nonstop for the past few days. But as she neared, I realized that her giddy grin and gripped gaze were aimed at Cooper. Stopping just short of us, she clasped her hands behind her back and prodded me with an eager nod to make a formal introduction.

"Cooper, Iona. Iona, Cooper," I said, careful to keep my voice even and calm for fear that the slightest hint of excitement might trigger her discomposure, which, I could tell, was bubbling right below the surface.

"I can't believe you're actually standing here!" Iona gushed. "I love you! I'm a huge fan—*huge* fan."

Clearly accustomed to random bursts of adoration from complete strangers, Cooper responded with an easy smile. "Thanks, that means a lot."

"Do you think I can get an autograph?" she asked, already patting herself down for a pen and a scrap of paper.

"Sure," Cooper said.

"While you do that," I said, squeezing his arm as I veered toward the registers. "I just want to check on one thing."

Catching hold of my hand, he twirled me back around into his chest and delivered a playful kiss to my temple. "Take your time."

Iona's brow raised slowly, her interest intrigued. "I take it you had a nice vacation?" she asked, handing Cooper a marker and a blank piece of cardboard she yanked from a nearby box.

Nodding, I quickly busied myself shuffling through a zippered pouch bulging full of the past week's receipts. With no clue as to how much information Cameron and Oliver had shared about my sudden disappearance, and with Cooper still in the dark about my makeover, I was anything but eager to delve into the details of the last several days. "It was nice."

Iona smirked and cast a lingering glance at Cooper, who quickly scribbled something illegible without even bothering to look down. "I'll say."

Ignoring her suggestive tenor, I retrieved a calculator from the drawer beneath the scanners and tallied the sales slips. "Was it busy last week?" I asked, adding the receipts a second time. "These numbers seem really high."

"Oliver did some promotional thing," she said, seemingly too occupied by the movie star in the room to elaborate.

"What thing?" I urged.

She stopped batting her lashes at Cooper long enough to offer me a disinterested shrug. "Not sure, but he managed to get rid of most of the overstock in the back room."

"Really?" I smiled. An improperly filled out order form had stuck me with 40 boxes of bargain books. It was a hit I could not afford. I'd tried for weeks to sell them, even listing them on eBay at cost, but I'd had no takers. I mentioned the dilemma to Oliver in passing a while back, but I never imagined he would take it upon himself to mastermind a sales tactic that would solve the problem entirely.

The carking guilt that had been quietly plaguing me since last night when Oliver stormed out of the party only intensified at the realization that while I had spent my time away flagrantly disregarding his feelings, he'd spent it going out of his way to help me.

"So," Iona said, propping an elbow on the counter with a meddlesome slant of her eyes. "Are you guys, like, *together*?"

I glanced at Cooper, who only further aroused her prying suspicions with an inflammatory bounce of his brows. "We're friends," I said.

"Very good friends," he echoed.

"Yeah, I gathered that." She smirked. "Well, let me be the first to go on record as saying that you two make an adorable couple. Especially now that you went off and got all glammed up," she added, acknowledging my makeover for the first time since I'd entered the shop. "In my opinion, this is one look you should definitely keep."

"You mean to say she wasn't always the vision of loveliness we see before us?" Cooper joked.

"Are you kidding me?" Iona snorted. "For an entire week during last year's Christmas rush, she wore nothing but—"

"Can you ready the deposits before you leave tonight?" I asked, stuffing the receipts back into the zippered pouch and returning them to their designated cupboard. "That way I can run them to the bank first thing in the morning."

Despite the pleasant lilt in my voice, my words were crisp, terse. Iona readily caught my drift. "Sure," she said, her smile fading into a subdued moue. Retrieving the smock apron she'd discarded in her rush to meet Cooper, she slipped it over her head and joined me on the other side of the counter.

"Also, I need you to switch out the pocket displays before tomorrow's delivery."

"No problem," she said, reaching for the tagging gun.

"OK then, I think that's it." I looked up at Cooper. "You ready to go?"

He nodded. "Where to?"

"Are you hungry?" I asked, feeling my own empty stomach churning.

"Always," he said. "What's good around here?"

"You could take him to Duffy's," Iona suggested.

Duffy's was a unique little haunt just down the street that only served appetizers and desserts. Aside from the short walk, it offered a casual ambiance and an eclectic menu, both of which had, over the years, made it a staple of after-hours staff meetings among my handful of employees.

"That's actually not a bad idea," I said, rounding the counter toward Cooper who was waiting for me on the other side, his hand outstretched. Taking it, I smiled up at him. "Unless of course you have some sort of objection to killer lobster cocktails and the best Kobe beef sashimi this side of the city."

He laughed. "Definitely no objections here."

I turned to Iona, who was nosily following our exchange. "We're gonna head out. But I'll see you tomorrow."

I might as well have been air. "It was nice meeting you, Cooper," she said in a voice much softer and sweeter than her usual timbre.

His grin was humoring. "You too."

Only after we'd started to make our way back down the shop's center aisle did I notice the small pockets of people hovering between the rows of books. Some snapped pictures with their camera phones as we passed by; most just stared. The uninvited attention felt invasive to me, but Cooper kept an unruffled grin on his face, even rewarding those who worked up enough courage to wave hello with a cordial nod.

Outside, we received more of the same as unsuspecting passersby found themselves halting in stunned disbelief at the unexpected sight of Cooper Young strolling midday down a random Chicago sidewalk. The pointing and head-turning took on a snowball effect. The more people stopped to gawk, the more they incited others, who might've otherwise remained clueless, to do the same. By the time we neared the restaurant, the small gathering that'd started at the bookstore had turned into a tailing flock of spectators.

To her credit, the hostess at Duffy's made a valiant effort to contain her excitement as she greeted us at the door and escorted us to our table. But her cool demeanor lasted only as long as it took Cooper to thank her for the menu she handed him, at which point she abandoned all attempts at decorum and squealed her way through a barely intelligible request for a photo.

"They're like moths to a flame," I said, once I'd snapped a picture of the two of them on her cell phone and she'd floated happily back to the greeter's podium.

"Comes with the territory," he said with a shrug.

"Doesn't it drive you insane?" I asked, casting a paranoid glance over my shoulder. "It's like at any given moment, you could be mobbed."

He laughed. "My fans can be a little zealous at times. But without them, I wouldn't be where I am today."

"And where's that?" I asked. "Ducking crazed women in the back of a half-empty restaurant?"

"No." Shaking his head, he reached across the table and softly ran his thumb along the tips of my fingers. "On location in beautiful Chicago having lunch with a phenomenally phenomenal woman."

I smiled. "My dad used to call me that."

"Really?"

I nodded. "Every night, when I was a kid, he would read to me. And not your standard bedtime story fare either. We would read classics—*The Catcher in the Rye, The Grapes of Wrath, The Lord of the Flies*. It was sort of our special thing, quality time together—just the two of us—after my sister had disappeared into her room for the evening and Mom had managed to corral the boys and put them to bed.

"Sometimes, when we wanted to change it up a bit, we'd read poetry. He had this massive anthology of American poets. And we'd take turns flipping through it and one night, I flipped to Maya Angelou's 'Phenomenal Woman.' I loved it so much that I made him read it to me over and over again. He read it every night after that. No matter what other book we were working through, we always ended with that poem.

"When it was time to go to sleep, he would turn off the light, tuck me in, kiss my forehead, and whisper, 'Goodnight, my little phenomenally phenomenal woman.'"

Cooper smiled. "It's funny; I think that's the first thing you've ever told me about your father. How come you never talk about him?"

I shrugged and looked away, the old feelings of hurt and resentment curdling my stomach the way they often did when I thought about my dad for any great length of time. "Years later, he had an affair and left us."

Cooper frowned. "That's rough."

Rough didn't even begin to cover it. I'd returned home from my first summer at sleepaway camp to discover that my father had moved out. In his place were a host of family members intercepting phone calls and doting over my distraught mother, who seemed to have aged a decade in the two weeks I'd been gone. Shooed away every time we dared to go near her bedroom door, my brothers, sister, and I were left to find out weeks later, through the windstorm of whispers and hushed speculations circulating within our small community, that he had fathered a child with someone else.

When his indiscretion became public knowledge, he stepped down as senior pastor of the church he'd founded two decades earlier and moved clear across the country to California. I thought he was just lying low until the scandal blew over—that he'd be back as soon as he could to resume his rightful place as head of the Mackenzie household. But only months later, he married his mistress and they eventually had two more children together.

"Do you guys still talk?" Cooper asked.

I shook my head. For my sixteenth birthday, he sent me a card. That was the last time I ever heard from him. I'd tried many times over the years to throw it away, but despite my anger, I could never bring myself to get rid of it. Thus, it sat at the bottom of a shoebox full of keepsakes in my closet.

"It was a long time ago," I said, shrugging. "I'm not even sure where he lives now."

"You've never thought about trying to find him?"

Back when it first happened, finding my dad was all I thought about; the need to be a family again consumed me to the point that I would threaten daily to run away and go live with him and his new wife. But over time, once the reality of his abandonment had settled in and I understood that he was gone for good, I became embroiled in a different sort of search—one for comfort and love and acceptance.

Nothing I tried—not food or friends or feats—filled the hole left behind by my father like Jesus did. The more I pursued Him, the less alone I felt, the less confused. Through the lingering sadness, my faith blossomed and my soul healed until finally the longing for my earthly father was replaced by a desire for my heavenly One.

But I wasn't sure how to explain that to Cooper, who didn't know Christ and, thus, had no way of understanding the restorative power that came as a result of a personal relationship with Him. "I guess I just figure if he ever wants to talk, he'll find me."

"Well, if you ask me," Cooper said, "he was crazy to let you go at all."

"Thanks." I smiled and reached for my menu. "I like to think so, too."

Following suit, Cooper took a few minutes to peruse the glossy pages of appetizers and desserts. I took the opportunity to sneak peeks at him from across the table. "What're you having?" he asked.

I pretended to mull over my choices for a few moments longer. "I think I'm going to go with the shrimp shumai and the vegetable gyoza," I said, naming the same two dishes I ordered every time I went there. "How about you?"

"The coconut prawns sound really good, but I'm still debating over the dim sum and the edamame dumplings." His brow furrowed as he combed through the menu a second time. "Or, I could always just get both, right?"

I nodded, distracted by a peculiar flash of light. Like swaying glass held up to the sun, it fluttered, disappeared for several seconds, and then fluttered again. "What is that?" I asked, leaning closer to the window.

Cooper's gaze followed mine. "What?" he asked, surveying the seemingly normal scene outside. "I don't see anything."

Squinting, I searched for the flutter again. "There," I said, pointing at the neat row of median planting potters just as the light flashed again. "Is that?" I craned my neck, incredulous at what I thought I was seeing. "Is there a man hiding behind those flowers?"

Discovered, our intruder abandoned his hiding place and made his way across the street, camera in hand. Bending low, he snapped pictures of us from the sidewalk. "What's going on?" I asked.

Cooper sighed and shook his head. "I'm really sorry. It usually takes them at least a couple of days to find me."

"Paparazzi?" I asked, as we watched the man stop, swap out his camera lens for a bigger one, and resume taking pictures from several different angles.

"Just try your best to ignore him," Cooper said. "He'll go away eventually."

Returning his attention to the menu, Cooper asked something about the beef Wellington, but I couldn't concentrate long enough to answer him.

Outside, two couples strolling in either direction stopped, curious as to what had so thoroughly captured the paparazzo.

"No way!" one of the women exclaimed. Snatching off her sunglasses, she inched closer to the restaurant's window and motioned for her partner to come look.

Much like the scene that had unfolded on the short walk from the bookstore, her excitement attracted several more passing strollers, until what had started out as the imposition of one rogue photographer had turned into the irruption of a rabble of star-struck fans.

"Are you ready to order?" a quivering voice asked. I pried my eyes away from the mayhem brewing outside to find our waitress standing beside our table, a bundle of shy nerves.

"The beef Wellington," Cooper said, oblivious to the pen and pad vibrating in her shaking hands. "Can I get that served with a Bordelaise instead of a Madeira?"

The resulting pucker in her forehead made me question whether or not she even knew the difference between the two sauces. Still, she nodded and immediately began scribbling down his request.

"Great, then I'll have the Wellington and the coconut prawns," he said, closing his menu with a conclusive nod before sliding it her way.

She turned to me, prepared to take my order, but before I could get it out a spry teenager climbed into the flower beds lining the side of the building and tapped on the window. She smiled and waved. Cooper waved back.

My appetite gone, I shrugged. "I'll just have a pot of Oolong."

"You're having a horrible time," Cooper said, once the waitress had scampered off with our menus.

"No," I shook my head and tried my best not to glance outside at the mushrooming crowd watching our every move. "I'm just not very hungry, that's all."

"We can go," he said, leaning forward, his expression doleful. "I'll take you home."

It was a tempting offer, and I might have taken him up on it had I not been overcome with a swaying sense of pity. If his notoriety felt this harrowing to me, I couldn't even begin to imagine how difficult it must have been for him. I only had to experience the pandemonium in temporary spurts; he had to live it on a daily basis. "I don't want to go home," I said, meeting his concerned gaze with a reassuring smile. "I like being out with you."

The tightness in his jaw eased. "I know it can be overwhelming," he began.

I quieted his apologies with a shake of my head. "I'll adjust."

There was another tap at the window. We looked over to see two more girls in the flowerbeds. They held up a handwritten note to the glass. It read, "WE LOVE YOU!" in bright purple ink. Ever the sport, Cooper nodded his thanks and flashed them an ILY, to which they responded by jumping and screaming maniacally.

"Maybe not right away," I smirked and reached my hand across the table. "But I'm sure I'll get the hang of it eventually."

He smiled and laced his fingers with mine. "Take all the time you need."

The gathering held steady through our entire meal, but the more fixed my attention became on Cooper, the further into the background everything and everyone else faded. Between bites of perfectly crisped prawns and mouthwateringly moist tenderloin, he told me more about his upcoming project—the other actors who had signed on, which elements of the script had most attracted him, the scenes he anticipated would be the most challenging to play.

As he talked, I lost myself in long, elaborate fantasies of us holed up at my place surrounded by candles and carryout, laughing and flirting as we ran lines together. I liked the idea of it, the notion of being the one he wanted to go to—the person he chose to be with after the lights and the cameras had been turned off and he went back to being just a regular guy.

"I'm stuffed," Cooper said.

I surveyed the empty plate in front of him. "I told you you'd love it here."

"The food was good," he conceded with a nod. "But the company was even better."

I glanced away, embarrassed. "Did you save room for dessert?"

"There's no way." Patting his belly, the chiseled contours of which I could make out through his T-shirt, he grinned. "Which means we'll have to make plans to come back soon, I guess."

My smile met his. "Anytime."

"Can I get you something else?" our waitress asked. Despite her obvious nervousness, she'd done an uncannily efficient job of waiting on our table, appearing at the drop of a dime the very instant a glass was in need of refilling or a plate was in need of bussing. I'd been thoroughly impressed until I'd caught her sneaking peeks at us through the kitchen door's porthole and realized that she was no better than the nosy leeches watching us from outside.

"Just the check," Cooper said.

She nodded and piled our soiled plates and silverware into a neat stack that she promptly carried away.

Cooper tossed his napkin aside. "So what's next on the agenda?"

"I don't know. Did you have something in mind?" I asked.

"I was thinking we could take in a few of those amazing sites you're always going on about," he said.

My eyes darted to the window. Outside waiting for us to emerge, the paparazzi seemed to be multiplying like cockroaches. The thought of photographers hounding us at the Hancock Observatory or tailing us around Millennium Park took the appeal out of sightseeing altogether.

"I don't know," I hedged. "Maybe we could—"

"Mr. Young!" a deep voice bellowed from across the room. We turned to see a slickly dressed gentleman approaching. His stride was graceful, his stature imposing. "My name is Douglas Whitaker; I'm the owner," he said, tossing a disinterested glance in my vicinity after he'd offered Cooper a broad smile and a firm handshake. "Thought I'd come over and introduce myself. I trust everything was to your liking."

"Everything was great," Cooper said.

"Good, glad to hear it." He nodded his satisfaction. "Well, I just wanted to personally thank you for stopping in today. It was an honor, and as a token of our appreciation, your meal is on the house."

I'd been to Duffy's dozens of times over the years and I'd never once laid eyes on the owner, much less had him come to my table, introduce himself, and forgive my tab.

"That's really generous of you."

Douglas dismissed Cooper's thanks with a wave of one hand, while digging a camera out of his jacket pocket with the other. "Would you mind?" he asked, holding it up.

"Not at all," Cooper said, sliding out of the booth.

The hostess, who had clearly been instructed to stand by, rushed over and quickly snapped a picture of them. "We'll see you soon," Douglas said, giving Cooper a hearty pat on the shoulder as though they were old college buddies. "Don't be a stranger."

"We won't," Cooper promised as he turned to me. "Ready?"

Nodding, I stood and accepted his proffered elbow, a move that seemed to attract Douglas's attention. "You either, Darling," he said, his roving gaze straddling the thin line between admiring and lecherous. "Come back anytime."

The part of me that wasn't so darling wanted to inform him that I'd held my staff meetings in his restaurant the first Wednesday of every month for over two years, but then it hit me that everybody at Duffy's who knew me as a regular, knew me only as the mousy bookstore owner from down the street. The raven-haired Venus who'd strolled in with Cooper Young was every bit as new to them as she was to me.

Suddenly wary of being recognized by someone and outed as a former frump in front of Cooper, I resisted the urge to say something smart and nodded good-bye instead.

The relief I felt when we stepped out of the door and onto the sidewalk, though instant, lasted only as long as it took for the gathering waiting outside to swarm us. Cooper stopped for a few brief minutes to sign autographs and pose for photos with a few lucky fans. Then, fastening one arm securely around my waist, he drew me close and guided us through the scrum of jockeying photographers toward the car.

"Hey, Cooper," one of them called as he tread backward in front of us, a clicking camera butted up against his eye. I recognized him as the man who'd been hiding in the bushes. "How ya likin' the Windy City?"

"So far so good," Cooper said without breaking stride.

"You in town for work or just some R&R?"

Cooper smiled. "A little bit of both." Taking advantage of a green light, he maneuvered us off the curb and across the street. The farther we walked, the thinner the cloud of paparazzi around us became. One by one, I realized, they were tailing off, their pursuit for the perfect shot coming to an end.

"Who's your friend?" a lingering photographer asked.

I felt Cooper's grip tighten around the fabric of my dress, but he said nothing.

"Hey, Sweetheart," the nervy shutterbug beckoned, stepping toward me. "What's your name?"

Taking my cue from Cooper, I stayed quiet and kept moving. It seemed to work. The last of the photographers slowed their pace, loosening their ranks around us. "Take it easy, Coop," one of them called to our retreating backs as we rounded the corner out of their sight.

"You all right?" Cooper asked.

Nodding, I stopped to catch my breath. "That was bizarre."

"I know," he said, brushing my bangs aside. His concerned gaze searched my face. "I'm sorry. They can be real vultures."

"Are they like that all the time?"

"Sometimes worse," he confessed.

"And it doesn't upset you?" I asked, taking in his unruffled demeanor with a dubious slant of my eyes.

"I have my bad days like anybody else," he said as we resumed our walk to his truck. "But you get used to it. You teach yourself how to deal with it and just move on."

"So are those pictures of us going to end up in a magazine?" I asked, strolling in step with him.

He nodded. "Probably."

I considered the implications. "I hope they at least got my good angle."

Laughing, he draped his arm across my shoulders. "From what I can tell, all of your angles are beautiful."

The mayhem squarely behind us, we walked the rest of the way to his truck in comfortable silence. "Hey." He stopped just a few yards short of where we'd parked and pointed to the vacant building beside my shop. "What did that used to be?"

"More like what hasn't it been," I said, eyeing the structure's boarded windows and padlocked doors. "When Au Bon Livre first opened, it was a patisserie, but not even a year later, the owner—this batty old French woman from Seychelles—relocated to a lower-rent district on the city's Westside.

"Soon after, it became a hardware store. But that tanked as soon as The Home Depot went up. Eventually, someone turned it into a record store, which was my personal favorite. They sold mostly indie stuff—vintage albums and that sort of thing. But they were out of business within a couple of years.

"At one point the entire lot went into foreclosure and was scheduled to be auctioned. I'd thought about placing a bid on it—even went so far as to fill out the paperwork. But the bank ended up selling it to a private party. Rumor was the new owner planned to turn it into a day spa, but that never happened."

"What would you have done with it?" Cooper asked.

"Expanded the bookstore," I said, the thought instantly bringing a smile to my face. "That had been the plan from the very beginning. I'd always envisioned Au Bon Livre with a lounge and performance café, where young, up-and-coming artists could get on stage and debut their work."

"Sounds incredible," he said.

"Yeah, but I could never quite scrape together the startup capital I needed to make it happen." I sighed. "Just wasn't meant to be, I guess."

"I wouldn't say that." Escorting me to the passenger side of his rental, he waited for me to climb in and fasten my seatbelt before leaning in and kissing me. "You don't know what tomorrow will bring."

"No," I said, smiling giddily as he pulled away. "But, if today's been any indication, I can't wait to find out."

Twenty-Three

We made an earnest attempt to take in a few of the city's sights, but even with the bill of a Cub's cap we'd purchased at a corner convenience store pulled down low over his forehead and a pair of designer sunglasses masking his eyes, Cooper attracted mobs of people everywhere we went.

After causing utter pandemonium at the planetarium and then narrowly escaping an unruly crowd at the Field Museum, we wound up back at my place flipping through old photo albums and playing board games.

"Serves me right for challenging a bookworm to a Scrabble match," Cooper said, throwing up his hands in defeat after his third consecutive loss.

"Don't feel bad," I teased as I returned the lettered tiles to their velvet pouch. "Many before you have tried."

He laughed. "And how many have actually succeeded?"

"One," I said, the thought of Oliver hitting me with a wistful pang. "I haven't managed to beat him yet, but I always give him a run for his money."

"Well, my hat's off to him. He's a better man than me," Cooper said, yawning for the fourth time in as many minutes. He stood and stretched his arms overhead.

"You look exhausted. You should go home and get some rest."

He smirked. "Sick of me already?"

I felt a flicker of guilt. Sick, no. Tired, yes.

It'd been one week to the day since I'd wound up as a guest on *The Kitty Asher Show*—one week to the day since I'd had a moment to myself. Though, I'd spent a great deal of my time away considering all of the changes the makeover might bring, and though Cooper and every unlikely circumstance surrounding our relationship had exceeded even my wildest fantasies, I was surprised to discover, now that I was back, that I missed the simple things.

Sure, there was a certain allure in looking up and seeing Cooper Young standing beside the afghan my nana had knitted me for Christmas, but it didn't compare to the appeal of a hot bath, followed by a warm bed and a good book.

"Of course not," I said, putting away the rest of the game pieces and sticking the box back on the top shelf of the armoire. "But you have to admit, it's been a long day."

He rubbed his eyes, which were slanted sleepily. "I am kind of beat."

"You remember how to get back to the hotel, right?"

Nodding, he took my hand in his as I walked him to the door. "So, what time should I pick you up for breakfast?" he asked.

"I can't have breakfast with you tomorrow," I said. "Not unless you're planning to come over in the morning for a quick bowl of bran flakes."

He scrunched his nose.

I laughed. "Didn't think so."

"Well, how about lunch?"

"I would say yes, but you don't strike me as a tuna-salad-sandwich-in-the-break-room kind of guy."

"Then, when do I get to see you?"

I shrugged. "We close at six."

"In the evening?" he asked, his forehead wrinkled disapprovingly.

My smile was gentle. "I have a store to run."

"That's what Fiona's for," he argued.

"Iona," I corrected him. "And she's beside the point. I like to work."

"Nobody *likes* to work."

Standing on the tips of my toes, I folded my arms around his neck and gave him a hug goodnight. "Six o'clock will come before you know it."

"But you'll ruin the surprise," he said.

I pulled back, my curiosity piqued, and narrowed my eyes. "What kind of surprise?"

He smirked. "The kind of surprise that requires you to be free tomorrow afternoon."

"I can't just blow off work," I said, considering the possibility despite the insistence in my tone. "I haven't been there in a week."

"So you extend your vacation by one more day." He shrugged. "What's the big deal?"

The big deal was that I loved my shop and I missed being a part of its daily happenings. Tearing down displays and running bank deposits may not have been glamorous or even admirable, but they were two of the many seemingly insignificant responsibilities that formed the axis around which my world turned.

"OK, we'll compromise," I said. "I'll still go in, but I'll leave early."

"How early?"

"Two o'clock."

"Noon," he countered.

I considered my growing to-do list. It would be a tight fit. "Fine," I relented. "Noon."

His grin was broad, jubilant. "It'll be worth it," he promised, planting a wet kiss on my cheek. "I'll pick you up then."

Nodding, I waved and watched as he disappeared around the corner toward the elevators, before closing the door behind him with an unexpected sigh of relief.

Twenty-Four

"Turn to Channel 7!"

"Cam?" I called groggily into the receiver.

"Channel 7! Hurry up!" Cameron's insistent voice demanded loudly from the other end of the phone.

I rolled over and felt my nightstand for the alarm clock. "What time is it?"

"Just do it!" she shrieked.

"All right, all right." Sitting up, I grabbed the remote control and began flipping absently through the cable guide.

"Are you watching it yet?"

"I don't even know what I'm supposed to be looking for," I said just in time to see several images of me and Cooper flash across the screen. "Oh my gosh." I blinked. "Was that what I think it was?"

"You look good," Cameron said, a proud lilt to her voice.

After announcing that Cooper's camp had confirmed he was set to star in an as-yet-untitled movie scheduled to begin filming in the city later this month, the morning show's chipper host referred to me as "a mysterious beauty who is rumored to be a Chicago native."

Cameron chuckled. "You're eating this up, aren't you?"

"More like choking it down," I said, pointing at the still shots of me and Cooper leaving Duffy's. "You weren't there. That was a legitimately terrifying experience."

She laughed. "Nobody said playing the role of Cooper's arm candy would be easy."

"Is that what you think I'm doing?" I asked, my smile fading as I climbed out of bed. "Pretending to be something I'm not?"

"Well, no, but...," she sighed. "Come on, Mack. How long do you really think this is going to last?"

"You'll have to forgive me," I said, pacing agitatedly from one end of my room to the other. "I didn't know my relationship with Cooper had an expiration date."

"Relationship?" She chortled. "You met the guy three days ago."

I felt my pulse rise along with my defenses. "Need I remind you that he's in Chicago because of me?"

"He caught an earlier flight because of you," she said. "He's in Chicago to film a movie."

"What is your problem? Yesterday you were my biggest supporter. Today you're champing at the bit to see this fail."

"That's not true. Of course I want to see you happy. I'm just worried that you might be losing sight of what's important."

"Like what?"

"Well, for starters, Oliver. Whatever may or may not be happening between the two of you, he's still your best friend. And he's hurting and confused right now. But you're so preoccupied with Cooper that you've made absolutely no attempt to work things out or even check to see if he's OK."

My chest tightened at the memory of Oliver's pained expression the night of the party, when Cooper arrived unexpectedly and kissed me in front of all my guests. I'd wanted to call Olly a thousand times between then and now, but there was nothing I could say—nothing I could do—to make it better.

We'd encountered and endured almost every kind of challenge in our ten-year friendship, but this was one obstacle I didn't know how to hurdle, one mess I was helpless to fix.

"And let's not forget the bookstore," Cameron continued. "We all thought you'd be counting down the seconds until you were back at work. But yesterday, you completely blew off your responsibilities to go house hunting! That's not the you I know."

"You're lecturing me about responsibilities?" I balked, insulted. "You're responsible for nothing; you answer to no one. Your whole life you've pranced around oblivious, getting by on your looks and your parents' money, while I've worked myself ragged trying to create a legacy I can be proud of. And now that I'm having a little fun—now that I've decided to step back and actually enjoy the fruits of my labor—you have the nerve to question my priorities?"

"All I'm saying is that it's easy to get lost in the hype. This thing with Cooper is new and exciting and storybook perfect, but is it real? You should make sure before you toss aside your old life and everyone in it. Otherwise, when this little fantasy of yours finally runs its course, you just might find yourself sad and alone."

"I'm hanging up now," I said, my fierce grip on the receiver turning my knuckles white.

"Fine." She didn't sound the least bit fazed. "But don't forget, you were a whole person long before Cooper Young came along and you'll be a whole person long after."

Disconnecting the call with the push of a button, I tossed the phone onto my bed and, stifling a frustrated sigh, stalked to my bathroom to get ready for work. It proved to be far more time consuming than my old morning routine—a simple two-step process that had consisted of a speedy shower followed by a perfunctory change into my default uniform of loose khakis and a roomy polo.

The past week's unbelievable chain of events had brought with it an uncommon set of complications, the least of which was a daunting pressure to look ravishing at all times. If my day out with Cooper had taught me anything, it was that being with him automatically meant contending with looming paparazzi and awestruck fans, unsolicited stares, and constant recognition.

It meant that I could no longer waltz out of my front door sporting damp, scraggly ponytails and scuffed Crocs or wake up 20 minutes before it was time to head to work and thoughtlessly throw on the first thing I came across in my closet. Every word I spoke, every move I made, was now subject to public opinion and scrutiny. That understanding, coupled with the knowledge that I would be seeing Cooper in only a few short hours, compelled me to spend a considerable amount of time coordinating my look for the day.

Before the makeover, any such attempts to primp felt indulgent, while during the makeover, those very same efforts felt labored, foreign. But, as I slipped on the bangles I'd selected to accent my Chambray sheath, and stepped back to examine the finished result in my bathroom mirror, I realized that somewhere along the way, I'd not only started to enjoy investing time and energy into my appearance, but I'd also developed an increasing awareness of the dernier cri.

Stepping into my peep-toe booties, I took one last look at myself, and, with a satisfied thrill, headed to the kitchen, where I fixed a cup of coffee and spent the dwindling minutes before I had to head out channel surfing in a shameless search for another news broadcast about me and Cooper.

There wasn't one, nor did anybody, aside from the occasional passing businessman, seem to notice me on my short trek to work. I was surprised by my disappointment at the lack of fanfare, but the feeling quickly passed when I stepped through the shop door and was met immediately by Iona's teasing smile. "Is that the mysterious beauty?"

"I take it you saw the morning news," I said, making my way to the counter, where I swapped my purse for a smock apron.

"Are you kidding me? I saw it, recorded it, uploaded it, and emailed it to everyone in my address book."

I laughed. "Please tell me you're joking."

"What?" Her slanted brow was accompanied by a sheepish shrug. "It's not every day you get to say your boss is dating a movie star."

"I'm not even sure we're officially dating yet."

"Well, you better get your story straight," she said, reaching for the box cutter. "Because that's all those nosy reporters seemed to be interested in."

"Reporters?" I asked, my hand freezing over the scanner. "When?

Yesterday?"

She nodded. "And one this morning, just before you got here."

"What did you tell them?"

"Nothing," she said, slicing open a nearby case of books. "I kept my head down, played clueless, and eventually they left."

"I wonder how they knew where to find me."

She snorted. "My guess is they followed the trail of screaming fans."

"It's not like anyone's screaming for me, though. Cooper's the celebrity."

"But you're the latest flash of intrigue in the media-obsessed storm that's his life, which, by default, makes you important, too. Speaking of obsessed media...," she said, her eyes narrowing distrustfully at a figure entering through the chiming front door.

"How can you tell?"

"Tweed trousers," Iona noted, "weathered satchel, scoop-hungry glint of the eye."

Wielding an ingratiating smile, the approaching reporter came to a stop in front of the counter. "Just the woman I was hoping to find," she said, extending her hand in my direction. "It's Isabelle, right?"

Arms folded across my chest, I gave a curt nod.

"And you are?" Iona asked.

"Lee Dunham, the *Tribune*," she said, dismissing my snub with a shrug. "I'd like to sit down and talk with you, when you have the chance."

"Talk about what, exactly?"

The edges of her mouth rode up into a telling grin. "I spotted a little espresso bar not too far from here; we could grab a quick coffee, if now's good for you."

"It isn't," I said, motioning to the smattering of unopened boxes at my feet. "I'm busy."

"I can come back later," she offered.

My sigh was impatient. "Don't bother. I'm busy then, too."

"It'll only take a moment of your time. I just have a few questions," she persisted, fishing a digital recorder out of her bag. "Like, can you tell me anything about the nature of your relationship with Cooper Young?"

Ignoring her, I set to work neatly stacking the books that Iona had unboxed.

Lee waited in vain for a response. "OK." She pressed on with a determined purse of her lips. "How long have the two of you known each other?"

Again, silence. "Can you at least tell me where you met?"

Scanner in hand, I turned my attention to entering the new arrivals into inventory.

"Fine, I get it. Cooper's off limits," she said, her tone light and falsely familiar. "But that doesn't mean we can't talk about you, does it?"

"Listen, you're wasting your time—and mine," I added testily. "So, unless you plan on buying something, I think you should go."

Recorder still rolling, she meandered to a nearby display of discounted hardbacks and fingered several of their spines. "This is a great little shop you've got. How long have you been here?"

"Going on seven years," I said.

Iona's head snapped up in alarm. "Mack!"

"Mack," Lee echoed. Her eyes danced in such a way that told me she was pleased to have finessed this little nugget of information. "Is that a nickname?"

"Would you like me to ring that up for you?" I asked, nodding at the book in her hands.

She made a show of flipping through the pages, before setting it down. "I've never been much for reading, myself. But you studied comparative literature at Northwestern, right?"

"You tell me," I said. "Clearly, you've done your research."

She had the nerve to look flattered. "I make it my business to stay in the know," she said, sauntering back to the counter. "For instance, I know you were born and bred in the Midwest. Big family. Mom was a homemaker, dad was a pastor—well, until he ran off with his current wife, anyway." She paused to gauge my reaction. I didn't flinch.

"I know you're smart," she continued. "Earned a full ride to NU, graduated at the top of your class, started your own business. I know you make a habit of filing your taxes early, that you've never had so much as a parking ticket, that you donate to the same charities every year."

She tilted her head. "I know a lot of things. But what I can't figure out is how someone like you wound up crossing paths with the likes of Cooper Young."

"Are we done yet?"

"Almost—just one more question," she said, her gaze locking stubbornly onto mine. "How does it feel to be dating one of Hollywood's most coveted men?"

My smile was patronizing. "What's not to love? Psychotic fans, prowling photographers, guerilla journalists." I arched an accusatory brow. "It's a dream come true."

Stopping the recorder with the push of a button, she dropped it back in her bag and nodded her appreciation. "Mack, it's been a pleasure."

The knavish undercurrent of her tone sent an uncomfortable chill down my spine, but before I could challenge her or comment further, she disappeared into the maze of shelving and, moments later, breezed out of the store.

Twenty-Five

"This is for you," Cooper said.

Smirking curiously, I studied the delicate swirls of ornate tissue paper fanning exquisitely from the large gift bag dangling between us. "What is it?"

"If I told you, it wouldn't be a surprise, now would it?"

"But I thought you said you were taking me to the surprise," I said, drawing back one of the edges of the bag to get a peek inside.

Cooper shooed my hand away. "I am. That's for when we get there," he said, nodding down at the gift. "And this," he said, pulling a blindfold from his back pocket, "is for now."

I cast a dubious glance at the wrinkled handkerchief. "You can't be serious."

He responded with an amused shrug. "No blindfold, no surprise."

"OK, we'll play by your rules." My smile was buoyantly stern. "This time."

Cooper laughed. "You won't regret it," he said. "So are you ready to go?"

I had planned to tell him all about my unfortunate brush with the formidable Lee Dunham, but now, with one mysterious gift in hand and another just a blindfolded ride away, the need to relay the incident didn't seem quite so urgent.

Nodding, I searched the store for Iona, who'd made herself scarce when Cooper had arrived. "I'm heading out now," I called.

"Have a good time," she called back from somewhere within the labyrinth of towering bookcases.

I followed Cooper outside, where he led me to a sleek, sporty two-seater parked alongside a meter. "What happened to the truck?" I asked, as he opened the passenger side door for me.

"Weather like this was meant to be experienced in a convertible," he said, rounding the hood of the car in two easy bounds and sliding into the low, bucket seat beside me. I watched as he started the ignition and tinkered with the puzzle of buttons on the dash, causing the car's bulbous hardtop to retract and neatly store itself in the trunk.

I squinted up at a drifting mass of cottony clouds where the metal roof used to be. "Now that was cool."

"And we're only just getting started," he said, wagging the handkerchief inches from my nose.

Laughing, I shook my head. "But people will stare."

"Then I guess it's a good thing you won't be able to see them watching," he said, tying the swath of fabric around my eyes before I could protest further.

My stomach lurched as we sped away from the curb with a loud screech. Hair whipping in the wind, I clutched the gift bag in my lap and tried to temper the dizzying sensation of blind motion by focusing on the direction of the turns we took. I was pretty sure I'd charted our course north toward the Lake, but then Cooper abruptly veered and I lost my bearings.

"Almost there," he said, patting my hand reassuringly as he shifted gears.

The engine revved and my death grip on the center console tightened. After a few more harrowing minutes, our speed slowed and the sound of cars zooming past was replaced by the crunching of tires on gravel. Gradually, we bumped and bobbed our way to a stop.

"Stay there. I'll help you out."

"Can I take this off now?" I asked, pawing at the blindfold still fastened around my head.

"Not yet!"

I heard his rushed footsteps followed by the quiet groan of my door opening and the feel of his hand on my elbow. "Watch your step," he said, gently guiding me out of my seat. Proceeding cautiously, I submitted to his leading, stepping how and when he instructed. Eventually, the gravel beneath my heels gave way to concrete and the concrete to a steep wooden incline.

"OK," he said, situating me a few inches to the left, before releasing my arm. "You can look."

Yanking the handkerchief off with a grateful sigh, I discovered that we were standing on a pier and that docked directly in front of us was a massive yacht. *La Vita Bella* was scrawled in elegant script along its side.

"Surprise!" Cooper spread his arms wide.

"What's this?" I asked, managing a smile despite the gripping fear that he had, in his impetuousness, actually gone out and bought me a boat.

"I'm taking you sailing!"

My relief was palpable. "Sailing?"

"I know it's been hard adjusting to all of the attention," he said, placing a hand on either side of my waist and drawing me closer. "And how miserable yesterday was for you. So I thought we'd escape for the day—a peaceful, private afternoon on the water. Just you and me."

"Thank you." I closed the few inches between us and kissed him. "This is amazing."

Lacing our fingers, he helped me up the boarding ramp and onto the main deck, where we were met by a man who introduced himself as the captain. After welcoming us aboard, he handed us off to Eoghan, one of the yacht's tenders. We followed him down a carpeted staircase, past the salon and through a plexus of narrow corridors. As we walked, Eoghan shared interesting facts about the ship's history, including an impressive list of its many other notable passengers across the years. Cooper, whose attention oscillated between our private tour and his buzzing Blackberry, didn't seem especially impressed, but I found every aspect of the vessel utterly mesmerizing.

"And here we are." Eoghan slid open a set of paneled pocket doors. "The owner's suite."

"I've never seen anything like it," I said, entering the sprawling cabin, mouth agape. Bedecked with strikingly contemporary trappings and gorgeous white oak floors, the room boasted a crescent wall of windows that curved around the entire bow and offered a breathtaking view of the waters ahead. "I think this might be bigger than my entire condo."

"Can I get you anything?" Eoghan asked.

"We're fine for now," Cooper said, excusing him with a nod. Eoghan took his leave, dutifully closing the doors behind him.

Cooper watched, a satisfied grin playing at the edges of his mouth, as I circled the sumptuous space, captivated. "Beats hocking books all day, doesn't it?" he asked, flopping onto the tufted chaise beside the coffee table.

"Hands down," I said, cringing slightly at the sight of his shoes propped against the lounger's white leather. "I just wish I'd known this was where we were coming. I would have brought a change of clothes."

His smile was mischievous. "Then I guess now might be a good time for you to open your present."

Gnawing excitedly at my bottom lip, I retrieved the gift bag and carried it to the couch across from Cooper. He sat up and watched as I fished beneath the layers of tissue paper and retrieved two skimpy slivers of stretchy silver fabric. "Wow." I fingered the mesh lining. "It's..."

"A bikini!" he said.

Or pieces of one, I thought, unsure of how he expected me to cram what all I had into what little he'd given me. "I don't know what to say."

He smiled. "I knew it was you the instant I saw it," he said.

"Really?" I examined the suit's top. It looked like nothing more than a couple of flimsy triangles connected by floss. "You don't think it's kind of revealing?"

He shook his head. "If you've got it, flaunt it, right?"

I shrugged. *The more important question was, could I flaunt it without making it jiggle?*

186

"I'm going to leave you to get changed," he said, standing. "Meet you on the sundeck in fifteen?"

Nodding, I waited for him to leave before giving myself over to the panic of having more flesh than fabric to cover it. A second search of the bag uncovered a matching sarong and sunglasses, but nothing more. With time ticking down and Cooper waiting, I peeled off my dress and strapped on the scanty two-piece.

It fit better than I expected, but I still felt naked. My chest, which was pushed up and smushed together by the built-in underwire, spilled out of the sides. The bottom portion of the suit required a considerable amount of tugging and stretching before it managed to cover everything.

Afraid that glimpsing my reflection would flatten my already deflated confidence, I tied the sarong around my bare waist, slid on my new sunglasses and, bypassing the mirrored closets, headed to the upper deck.

Cooper, who'd changed into a pair of simple black swim trunks, was stretched out on a towel beside a glistening wading pool, hands clasped behind his head. "It's official," he said, rolling onto his side. "I'm the luckiest man in the world."

I simpered, his admiring gaze turning me self-conscious, and crossed my arms over my exposed midsection. "Thanks. From the looks of it, I didn't fare too poorly myself," I said, sneaking a peek at his rippled abs from behind my shades.

Cooper sat up and offered me a steadying hand as I climbed the set of shallow steps between us and joined him on the pool's platform. There I discovered platters of decoratively arranged fruit, iced water, and magazines. "You really thought of everything," I said, settling onto the empty towel beside his. Turning my face toward the city's disappearing skyline, I breathed in the warm, fresh air. "This is perfect. I could stay out here all day."

"Then you're definitely going to need some of this," he said, holding up a tube of sunscreen. "May I?"

I nodded and turned onto my stomach, but instantly regretted it when I felt the sides of my barely-there bikini ride up under my sarong. Scooting close, Cooper positioned himself over me and swept my hair aside. The lotion felt cool against my skin. He began massaging it into my shoulders, moving in slow methodical circles across my back.

The further down his hands traveled, the more uneasy I became. These were exactly the sorts of situations I'd worked hard to avoid throughout the years in a conscious effort to remain sexually pure. And while I might have been nursing a bourgeoning defiance toward my faith and its many parameters, this was one particular area I didn't feel compelled to challenge.

"That's plenty," I said, swiveling away just as his kneading fingers began to move down the back of my thighs. "Let me do you now."

Cooper assumed the position, lying on his stomach with his forehead resting on his crossed wrists. His bulging muscles felt firm under my palms. Applying the sunscreen in quick, mechanical strokes, I took care not to let my touch linger longer than necessary, but even in my rectitude, I felt like we were teetering on the edge of inappropriateness. "OK," I said, tapping his shoulder. "That should do it."

He flopped onto his back and gazed up at me with a content sigh. "I'm glad we did this."

"Me too," I said, turning to readjust my towel, which had folded in on itself in the breeze.

Before I realized what was happening, Cooper had hooked his arm around my waist, rolled me over his torso and pinned me beneath the weight of his body. "Meeting you at that gala turned out to be one of the best things that ever happened to me," he said, his hot breath tickling my nose.

Forcing a smile, I tried unsuccessfully to wriggle loose from his grip. "It's changed everything," I agreed.

Cooper lowered his lips to my neck and kissed it, causing a reflexive arch of my back. He grinned, pleased by the reaction, and planted a second kiss on the other side of my neck. "I feel so connected to you."

My laugh was strained. "Well, you are sort of lying on top of me."

"It's more than that," he said, shaking his head. "I can't explain it. You just take my breath away."

"You've left me pretty breathless too—literally," I joked, trying once more to squirm out from underneath him.

Running his hand up my leg, Cooper bent my knee and wrapped my calf around his hip. I felt his body flatten even more firmly against mine.

"Seriously, though," I said, pushing at his chest with the butt of my palms as he started in for another kiss. "I'm kind of uncomfortable."

"Do you hear that?" he asked, his ear abruptly turning toward the sky.

Sighing, I pushed harder against his chest. "I don't hear anything. Can you let me up?"

He shushed me with a wave of his hand. "It's getting closer."

"What is?" I asked, managing to untangle one of my legs.

"Listen," he whispered.

Momentarily abandoning my struggle, I trained my ear upward. Though it was faint, I could detect the whirring of spinning blades overhead. "It's probably just a news chopper covering rush hour traffic."

"We're on a yacht in the middle of Lake Michigan," he said. "There are no roads for miles. Trust me, it's not a news chopper."

Holding absolutely still, I searched the sky for movement, but I couldn't pinpoint which direction the noise was coming from.

"There," Cooper said, pointing. I followed his finger to an approaching aircraft in the distance. It circled twice before hovering low over the ship's bow.

Propping myself up on my elbows, I removed my shades and squinted past the glaring sun trying to get a clearer view. "Why are they so close?" I asked, my heart accelerating as my vision gradually came into focus. I could just make out the figure of a man, camera aimed, inside the copter's open hatch. "Oh my gosh!" I gasped, the reality of the situation finally sinking in. "He's taking pictures of us!"

"Don't freak out," Cooper said, his voice too low and calm for the present circumstance. "They'd love nothing more than to catch you making a scene."

His breath grazed my cheek, and in that moment, I was reminded of the compromising position we were in. "Get off!" I said, pushing him away with all of the might my arms could muster. This time, he moved. But the instant I lost him as a shield, my half-naked body was on complete display. "This is a nightmare!" I said, utterly mortified. Snatching the towel I'd been laying on, I wrapped it tightly around myself and retreated to the safety of the covered lower deck.

I could hear Cooper calling after me, but I kept moving down one narrow corridor after the next. My eyes stung with hot tears at the thought of where those photos would end up, or worse yet, who might see them.

"Will you hang on?" Cooper asked, jogging to catch me. He grabbed my shoulder. "Where are you going?"

"As far away from that thing as I can get," I said, pointing up at the paneled ceiling in the general direction of where the helicopter was no doubt still hovering.

"I really think you're overreacting. It's not that big of a deal."

"It's a huge deal!" I said. "How am I supposed to explain those photos to my family, my friends?"

His brow knitted confusedly, he shrugged. "What's there to explain? They know we're together."

"That's not the type of person I am. It's not the sort of woman I want to be perceived as," I said, shaking my head in frustration. It was like trying to explain the finer points of flying to an elephant. "I don't expect you to understand. You're not a Christian."

His expression hardened. "What does that have to do with anything?"

"Just forget it. It's my fault, anyway. I knew better than to be out there with you." My voice cracked. "And in this ridiculous bikini," I moaned, burying my face in my hands at the shame of it all.

He shoved his fists in the pockets of his swim trunks, clearly wounded. "You said you liked it."

"I was trying to play along," I confessed with an apologetic shrug. "You obviously went through a lot of trouble to make this happen and I didn't want to seem ungrateful. But the truth is, this isn't me."

He nodded, but said nothing.

"Maybe you should just take me home," I said, breaking the awkward silence that had settled between us.

The brooding set of his brow suddenly eased. He smiled. "I have a better idea."

———◆———

"Hey," Cooper called, gently shaking me awake. "We're here."

"Where?" I asked, blinking sleepily.

"The yacht club," he said. "We had to turn back. There's a storm headed this way."

I sat up and peered out of the porthole. The once calm crystalline waters were foamed with loud choppy waves and the tranquil pale blue sky had turned dusked and cloudy.

"Here." He handed me my clothes. "Just slip them over your bathing suit."

Already dressed, he commenced collecting our things, while I put on the sheath and booties I'd worn on board. Then, we headed to the boarding ramp, where we disembarked. Bypassing the main parking lot, which was packed with cars, Eoghan, wielding a large black umbrella, accompanied us into the club, down a long carpeted hallway lined with gold-framed portraits of pretentious looking men and straight into a private garage, where Cooper's sporty coupe was waiting for us.

The ride was quiet, but comfortable. Reclining in my seat, I smiled lazily up at Cooper as he took my hand in his and steered us back to my place.

Determined to diffuse the tension caused by the upset over the renegade helicopter, he'd returned me to the owner's suite, where he had gotten on the phone and called the ship's various quarters until he'd hunted down Eoghan in the galley and supplied him with a set of cryptic instructions.

Minutes later, another of the yacht's attendants had arrived and escorted us to a parlor on the lower deck. There, we were ushered into a cozy dimly lit room, outfitted with two tables dressed with crisp white linens. Lavender mist scented the air, while the calming trickle of water sounded from a pedestal fountain in the corner and the soothing melody of classical music wafted from the built-in speakers overhead.

"What's this?" I'd asked, once our guide had excused herself and we'd been left alone.

"My attempt to make up for this fiasco of an excursion," he said.

I shook my head. "You don't have to make up for anything."

"Yes, I do. When I planned today, I didn't stop to consider that this sort of thing might not be your style. And it's OK that it isn't," he rushed to add. "But I'd like another chance to get it right. I promise, if you're still having a miserable time after this, I'll take you straight home."

"OK." I nodded.

He smiled, relieved, and turned to the empty tables beside us. "I was thinking we might try a couple's massage. Or, we could lay out by the indoor pool," he suggested, when I didn't immediately respond. "Or, there's a media room. We could watch a movie."

I shrugged. "Which one do you want to do?"

"I don't care," he said, his tone earnest. "Just as long as I'm spending time with you."

We wound up doing it all, including a Fondue lunch in the sky lounge. It didn't take long for us to fall back into our easy rapport or for me to tune out the steady hum of the helicopter circling persistently above us. Still, Cooper's efforts to salvage the afternoon, while sweet and valiant, couldn't erase the memory of what had happened or shake the faint, but vexing doubt that had set in as a result.

"It's really starting to come down," he said, snapping me back to the present. We were parked a few blocks from my building. "Maybe we should wait for it to let up a little."

I frowned at the heavy sheets of rain pounding loudly against the windshield. "I think we should make a run for it."

"Can you run in those things?" he asked, smirking at my shoes.

My brow arched challengingly. "Fast enough to beat you."

"You're on," he said, throwing open his door just as I opened mine.

We were neck and neck until I skittered right into a puddle and splashed sooty water all over myself. "Are you OK?" Cooper asked, turning back when he saw me stop.

"There's something in my eye."

"Come here. Let me see." Using the edge of his soggy shirt, he gently wiped the dirt from my face. "Better?"

Looking up at him, I nodded.

He brushed my damp bangs from my forehead and smiled. "What do you say we call it a draw?"

"Afraid of losing to a girl in heels?" I teased.

"Well, there's that, of course," he said, laughing as he draped his arm across my shoulders. "And the fact that racing you isn't nearly as exciting as holding you close."

"Can't argue with that logic," I said, hooking my arm around his waist.

Oblivious of the rain, we strolled the rest of the way to my building and into the lobby. Cooper's sneakers squeaked loudly against the marble floors. Passing the smirking doorman, we boarded the vacant elevator and rode it up to my floor.

"I'll get you something to dry off with," I said, unlocking my door and flipping on the living room lights.

A dripping mess, Cooper kicked off his shoes and waited for me in the hallway. I grabbed a couple of towels from the linen closet and then made a beeline for my bedroom dresser. Pulling out the bottom drawer, I rummaged up the T-shirt and sweatpants Oliver had left behind the previous New Year's Eve, when he and Cameron had stayed the night.

I'd washed them the day after and had intended a dozen times since to give them back, but for some reason could never bring myself to part with them. Instead, I'd wound up stashing them in my room beneath some old sweaters.

Stacking them with the towels, I took the bundle to Cooper.

"Should I ask?" he said, nodding at the clothes.

I shrugged. "They're clean and they're dry. What more do you need to know?"

"OK." His grin was relenting.

"I've got to clean up," I said, pointing at my mud-streaked dress. "And you're welcome to do the same. The guest bath is just past the kitchen—first door on your left."

"I really enjoyed today," he said. "I know it started off kind of rough, but in the end, I have to confess, every day with you is better than the one before it."

I smiled. "And every day with you is an adventure."

"See you in a bit?" he asked.

I nodded and we both started down opposite ends of the hall. Back in my room, I closed the door behind me, peeled off my wet clothes—barely-there bikini and all—and headed to my bathroom, where I hopped into the shower. The water felt good as it pelted my skin and relaxed my muscles. Breathing in the billows of steam, I stood beneath the spray long after my hair had been scrubbed clean and the soap had rinsed away and the temperature had waned.

When I emerged, I was surprised by how much time had passed. The rain had stopped, the sun had set, and the street lights that lined the sidewalks outside were strewing shadows across my duvet. Aware that I had kept Cooper waiting longer than either of us had intended, I rushed to dry off and change. With my hair pulled back into a damp ponytail, my feet stuffed into warm slippers, and my soiled dress tucked beneath one arm, I made my way down the hall toward the living room.

The television was on and I could spot Cooper's wet jeans draped over the back of my love seat. "I'm so sorry," I began. But when I rounded the corner, I discovered Cooper fast asleep on the couch.

Gathering his pants and the rest of his clothes, I threw them along with mine into the wash. Then, I covered him with a quilt I retrieved from the front closet, switched off the table lamp and the television, and returned to my room to join him in peaceful slumber.

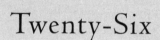

Twenty-Six

The phone rang, startling me awake.

"You're not watching the news, are you?" Cameron asked in an eerily similar start to the unpleasant conversation we'd had the morning before.

I groaned. "Is this going to become a habit?"

"Did you give any interviews?" she said, disregarding the edge in my voice. "Or speak to anyone off the record?"

"No." I rolled onto my back, slightly alerted by her worried tone. "Well, there was this one woman from the *Tribune* who came into the shop yesterday, but I handled her."

"What do you mean you handled her?" Cameron asked.

"I mean she came in sniffing around for a story and I sent her packing."

"So you didn't answer any of her questions?"

"Not really," I said.

"What do you mean 'not really'?"

My sigh was impatient. "I mean the exact details of the conversation are a bit murky at the moment."

"Then try harder to remember. This is important."

I sat up, stomach suddenly churning. "Cam, what's going on?"

"Think," she pressed. "Did you give her any information at all?"

"Well, she seemed pretty pleased when Iona let it slip that everyone calls me Mack," I said, scavenging my memory. "But all the other stuff, she already knew."

"What other stuff?"

"Everything from my driving record to my college major. She even knew about my father. The only thing she couldn't figure out, she said, was how Cooper and I met."

She was silent for a moment. "I'm coming over."

"Could you at least tell me what's wrong first?"

"I'm on my way," she said. "Just do me a favor and don't go near the television."

"What? Why?" I asked.

"I promise I'll explain everything as soon as I get there."

"Wait, hang on a sec," I said, throwing back the sheets and padding out of my room into the front hall. "I think someone's at the door."

"Don't answer it!" Cameron hissed.

Ignoring her, I continued to the living room, where everything was as I'd left it the evening before except for the empty couch.

There was another light rap. "He must have locked himself out," I said.

"Who?"

"Cooper."

"Cooper's there?"

"He spent the night," I said, not in the mood to explain. "It's a long story. Just let me call you back."

"No, wait," she protested. Pretending not to hear her, I hung up and rushed to let Cooper back in.

"How'd you wind up out there?" I asked, throwing open the door. Stunned,

196

I froze. "Oliver."

"I know." He bowed his head apologetically. "You hate it when I shirk the doorman, but I wasn't sure you'd let me up if I announced myself."

"What're you doing here?" I asked, craning my neck around him. Confused, I scanned the empty hall. If Cooper wasn't on the couch and he wasn't outside, where had he gone?

Oliver's face fell. He looked away. "I didn't know I needed a reason."

"You don't!" I said, instantly regretting the thoughtlessness of my words. "I'm surprised, that's all."

Slowly, he raised his eyes until they met mine again. "It's been a miserable couple of days," he said. "I missed your voice."

Resisting the overwhelming urge to hug him, I nodded. "I should have called."

"We've always been able to talk things out. It's one of the things I love most about us. And I don't want that to change, no matter what."

I took a step closer. "Me either."

His smile was slight, tired. "I was hoping you'd say that."

He motioned for me to wait, while he bent down and retrieved something he'd hidden just beyond the doorframe. When he straightened, seconds later, he was holding a bag from our favorite corner bakery and a cardboard carrier saddled with two lidded cups. "My first meeting's not for another couple of hours," he said. The unmistakable scents of fresh muffins and coffee mingled enticingly in the air. "I thought we could walk down to the park and have breakfast. Like old times."

"I'd love to—really I would," I said, my stomach knotting with guilt. "But now's not the best time."

"How come?"

Tossing a nervous glance over my shoulder, I searched the room, once more, for any signs of Cooper. "I'm kind of busy."

Oliver's frown was doubtful. "We can't just avoid each other, Mack. I want us to figure this thing out. But in order to do that you have to be willing to meet me halfway."

"Of course I'm willing."

"Then talk to me. Tell me what's going on."

"I can't, not right now," I said, nervously shifting my weight from one foot to the other. "But can we get together later? Maybe have dinner?"

He studied me for a moment, his gaze narrowed suspiciously as though he was trying to decide if my suggestion was sincere or a stall tactic disguised as a meaningful invitation. "What time?"

"Eight o'clock? I could make reservations at Topo Gigio," I said, proposing one of our regular haunts.

The tension in his brow slowly eased. "OK. Dinner it is."

I pointed at the breakfast in his hands. "Do I still get to keep those?"

Grinning, he handed me the bag and carrier.

"See you tonight?" I asked, my anxiety instantly waning at the sight of his smile.

Nodding, he started to leave, but suddenly stopped short, something behind me morphing his expression from confusion to realization to anger in a matter of seconds.

I turned to see a shirtless Cooper emerge from the kitchen palming a bowl of cereal. "Morning, Beautiful," he said, pausing briefly on his way back to the couch to shovel another spoonful of frosted wheat squares into his mouth.

"Well at least now I know what you were busy doing," Oliver said, backing out of the door with a disgusted shake of his head.

"Olly, wait!" I pleaded. Discarding the coffee and muffins on a nearby console table, I chased him down the hall to the elevators, where I found him furiously stabbing the call button with his finger. "It's not what you think. Let me explain."

Pacing frenziedly up and down the narrow gallery like a caged animal, he glared at me. "Are you sleeping with him?"

"No!" I balked. "How can you even ask me that? You know I wouldn't cross that line."

"I *should* know," he said, folding his arms across his chest. "But the truth is,

I'm not sure anymore. It's like you came back from this makeover a completely different person."

"Wasn't that sort of the point?" I asked.

The edges of his mouth slanted sadly. "I never wanted you to be anyone other than who Christ intended you to be."

I shrugged. "Well, what if this is who I intend to be?"

"Then, I obviously made a terrible mistake." The elevator arrived at my floor with a loud ping. Sighing, he stepped inside. "I guess next time around I'll have to be more careful about who I give my heart to."

"Olly, please wait," I called. The doors closed between us just as the second pair of elevator doors parted. Two stoic faces, one of which was unpleasantly familiar, greeted me.

"Adrienne, right?" I asked, swiping away tears I hadn't realized were there.

Her disapproving gaze traveled the length of my rumbled pajamas and back. "Where's Cooper?"

With Cooper's scowling manager and her briefcase-toting companion at my heels, I led the way to my condo. Brushing past me, Adrienne stalked the short distance to where Cooper was stretched out on the couch watching television and announced her presence by obnoxiously clearing her throat.

"Hey." He stood, his smile tentative. "What're you doing here?"

Adrienne surveyed the perimeter of my small cluttered living room, her nose turned up distastefully as though she was tempted to pose him the same question. "We have a problem, Coop."

My breath caught when Adrienne's mysterious cohort glimpsed my way.

Sweeping aside the quilt I'd given him, Cooper invited his two visitors to have a seat. "You remember Adrienne," he said, summoning me to join them.

I inched reluctantly to where the three of them were gathered. Adrienne acknowledged me with a purse of her lips, but said nothing. Cooper motioned to the second woman. "And this is Sue Giffin, my publicist."

She offered me a curt nod before primly lowering herself onto the worn leather couch cushion next to Adrienne.

"So what's going on?" Cooper asked, settling into the love seat alongside me.

Unlatching her briefcase, Sue retrieved a stack of magazines and tossed them onto the coffee table between us.

"It seems your friend here has been keeping secrets," Adrienne said.

Cooper and I both reached for one of the glossy publications. I was mortified to discover an old photo of myself occupying half of the cover. A full frontal aerial shot of me lounging in yesterday's string bikini graced the other side. The caption at the top read, "From Kitty's Pet to Cooper's Princess!"

"What is this?" Cooper asked, casting me a questioning glance.

I shook my head, unsure of what to say, where to start.

"She was a participant in one of those daytime makeovers," Sue explained in my stead.

"*The Kitty Asher Show*," Adrienne added in a tone that made it clear she found the whole matter tawdry.

My face grew hot as I watched Cooper flip through page after page of my most unflattering pictures. There were yearbook photos and family portraits, even stills from footage taken during the taping.

"So, you were in L.A. shooting a makeover?" he asked, swapping out the magazine in his hand for one of the dozen still strewn across the table.

"Not exactly." I could barely hear myself above the pounding rush of blood in my ears. "The show sent me afterward."

His brow wrinkled. "But you said you were on vacation."

My mind groped in vain for a reasonable explanation. "I..."

"The word you're searching for is 'lied,'" Adrienne said.

"And this is really you?" Cooper asked, holding up an incriminating two-page spread.

I grimaced at the center photo of me dressed in an ill-fitting khaki skirt and wrinkled button-down, my shoulder-length, mousy brown hair pulled back into a scrappy ponytail. "Not anymore," I whispered, looking away in shame.

We watched in silence as Cooper stood, fingers locked behind his neck, and walked the length of the room. "How bad is it?" he asked, his back to us.

"Given the widespread media coverage," Sue said, "The damage is considerable, but hardly beyond repair."

When Cooper turned around, his demanding stare was aimed directly at me. "Why didn't you just tell me?"

I shrugged, aware that there was no acceptable answer. "It all happened so fast. One minute I was sitting in a studio audience, the next I was toasting champagne with you in L.A. and the next we were saying our good-byes." I paused to swallow the sob swelling at the back of my throat. "I honestly never expected to see you again. And, when I did, I guess I hoped this sort of thing wouldn't matter to you."

"Oh, please," Adrienne droned with a bored roll of her eyes. "Of course it matters. First rule in showbiz," she said, her gaze searing, "Image is everything."

I waited for Cooper to speak up, to tell her she was wrong, but he remained silent.

"Luckily for you both," Sue continued, "The second rule is that no publicity is bad publicity. I think we have a real shot at spinning this in your favor."

"How?" he asked.

She shrugged and picked up a magazine. "At this very moment, millions of starry-eyed fans are identifying with the woman in these pictures. They're seeing themselves in her and nursing the hope that maybe, someday, they'll get their chance meeting with Cooper Young."

"It lends to the fantasy," Adrienne explained. "Makes you more accessible to your public."

"And what are we always telling you?" Sue asked.

"Accessibility is marketability."

Adrienne nodded, clearly pleased by his duteous response. "Leave it to us," she said. "By the time we're done, she'll be the envy of every dowdy housewife across America. And you'll be the coveted half of Hollywood's newest 'it' couple."

Cooper considered her guarantee. "OK," he said, rejoining me on the love seat, his brow set with concentration. "Where do we start?"

"First things first." Adrienne eyed me wearily. "We need to polish her image. There's a difference between plain and gawky."

"I agree," Sue said, opening her briefcase and withdrawing a pad of paper and a pen. "She's lacking a certain *je ne sais quoi.*"

"And then there's the issue of that ridiculous nickname." Adrienne frowned. "That absolutely has to go. It makes her sound like a trucker."

Sue nodded. "We need something classic, feminine," she said, simultaneously jotting down notes.

"Izzy?" Cooper offered.

Adrienne dismissed his suggestion with a shake of her head. "Bella," she said, her thin lips spreading into a slow grin.

Sue's eyes widened with approval. "I like that."

Cooper nodded. "Me, too."

It was frustrating, sitting idly by while they discussed me as if I wasn't in the room. But I didn't feel entitled to defend myself. I was the one, after all, who had committed the omission that was responsible for the unfolding media fiasco.

"Now," Adrienne said. Crossing her legs, she sat back and studied me. "The new look is passable, but still too common. We need to take it up a notch."

"I'm seeing New York sophisticate," Sue said, her gaze fixed upward as though the vision was unfolding before her very eyes.

"With a touch of boho couture," Adrienne added. "Think high-end, exclusive. The latest must-have handbags, designer shades, trendy scarves. We want her to epitomize simple style and elegance."

"In the meantime," Sue said, flipping to a clean sheet of paper. "We need to take advantage of her current visibility while we have it. The public is curious. This is the perfect opportunity to establish an airtight persona."

"Let's do a full launch," Adrienne said. "Print, television, the works."

Sue nodded. "I'll call around, see who's interested in an exclusive."

"We could have the interview here—invite America to get to know the real

Isabelle," Adrienne brainstormed. "At home with Bella Mackenzie."

"I don't know." Sue frowned and glanced around the room. "This place would need a total facelift."

Adrienne's eyes narrowed determinedly. "See if Nate's available."

"Berkus?" I gasped, before I could catch myself.

Both women glowered, irritated by the interruption.

"Sorry," I murmured, shrinking quietly back into my seat.

Adrienne's face softened as she turned her attention to Cooper. "If we play our cards right, we can use the media coverage to bolster publicity for your upcoming press tour."

Cooper smiled. "Brilliant."

"We still don't have a backstory, though," Sue said. "We need to figure out who she is, what she's all about."

"I think we should stick with the soft, introverted vibe she's already got going. It's sweet, likeable," Adrienne said, snarling even as she was offering me the closest thing to a compliment I would probably ever get from her. "People will respond to it."

Sue shrugged, seemingly satisfied with that approach. "And her shop?" she asked.

"It would make for a great meet-cute," Adrienne said. "Not to mention a credible setting for their first encounter. Think about it. Cooper's in town on business, he happens in looking for a good read. They lock eyes across an aisle and wham! Instant chemistry."

"I like it," Sue said. "Only potential hitch is that it's a Christian bookstore."

Adrienne let out a heavy sigh. "Wonderful."

I glanced between the three of them, confused by what they considered so obvious. "Why is that a bad thing?"

"Because," Sue said, rolling her eyes at my ignorance. "Religion is controversial and a nearly impossible subject to navigate without ruffling lots of feathers."

"Which isn't exactly advisable for someone trying to establish himself as the next big movie star of this generation," Adrienne added.

Sue nodded. "We've gone to great lengths to disassociate Cooper from any one faith."

"So we can't very well have him shopping at a Christian bookstore," Adrienne said, massaging the bridge of her nose. "Or dating the owner of one for that matter, can we?"

The room grew still as they attempted to devise a strategy around the dilemma, and I did my best to contend with the growing unrest stirring in my gut.

"What if we expand it?" Cooper asked, his voice slicing through the silence.

All heads, mine included, turned his way. "Go on," Adrienne said.

"The building directly next door is vacant. What if I buy it and we use the lot to build an addition? That way, we can broaden the inventory to include conventional titles, tack on a coffeehouse and an Internet café, maybe even add a lounge with a stage, where we can host live events. It'll be sleek and cutting edge—the latest wave in independent bookselling."

"That might actually work," Sue said. "We'll quietly make the transition from Christian to mainstream, while keeping the focus on community outreach—neighborhood revitalization, pro-literacy programs. It'll be fantastic PR."

"I love it!" Adrienne gushed in an uncharacteristic show of enthusiasm. There was a release of tension immediately followed by a burst of animated chatter. I listened, with mounting distress, as they discussed the many possibilities that lay ahead, and searched for the courage to intervene.

"I'm sorry," I said, my words escaping as a raspy whine. Clearing my throat, I sat up and tried again. "I'm sorry, but I don't think I can go through with this."

Their conversation came to an abrupt halt. "Why not?" Cooper asked.

The plan had seemed harmless enough when it revolved around a couple of designer bags and a handful of interviews. It had even been tolerable when they'd unilaterally decided to revamp my living space. But overhauling Au Bon

Livre was an entirely different matter altogether.

My store was a miraculous answer to prayer and the direct result of over a year of careful deliberation with the Lord. The vision He'd given me for the space had been so clear, so specific, as had its purpose, which was to use literature to spread the gospel of Jesus Christ to the city of Chicago.

How could I, then, extract God from the very thing He'd entrusted to me and use it to serve the world instead? The idea alone left me sick to my stomach. But there was no way of explaining that to Adrienne or Sue or even Cooper. Things like conviction and rectitude were of little consequence to them when it came to getting what they wanted. I shook my head. "It's too much."

"No." Adrienne glared. "It's pure genius."

Holding up his hand, Cooper motioned for her to hold on. "I don't get it," he said, his gaze soft and searching. "You told me yourself it's everything you hoped the bookstore would someday be."

"Yeah." I nodded. "Someday, but not right now. Not like this. I want to do it my own way, on my own terms."

"But this will be on your terms. I'll only be a silent investor. The day-to-day decisions, big and small, will be left to you. Then, sometime down the road, once the new and improved Au Bon Livre takes off—and it will," he added with a reassuring smile, "You can buy me out."

That cast another light entirely on their proposition. I wouldn't be throwing away one vision for another, but rather building on an existing desire. Meanwhile, Cooper would avoid ruffling any feathers and Adrienne and Sue would get their great PR. Everyone stood to win, and I, in turn, stood to gain the bookstore of my dreams.

"Picture it," Sue said. "Gourmet pastries behind the glass counter, the scent of espresso in the air, books as far as the eye can see, customers lounging in armchairs and lined up at the checkout counter, and you at the helm of it all."

Adrienne shrugged. "You'd be mad to pass up this kind of opportunity."

"So what do you say?" Cooper asked. The weight of their expectant gazes settled over me with jarring force. "Are you in?"

"Mack?" Cameron's voice, urgent and worried, beckoned me from behind the front door. "Mack, it's me," she said, pounding rowdily. "Open up."

Ignoring Adrienne's exasperated sigh, I excused myself and went to let her in.

"You didn't turn on the television, did you?" she asked, brushing past me.

I scurried after her as she breezed down the front hall. "No, but—"

"Just remember, it's not the end of the world." She turned the corner into the living room and flinched, the sight of Cooper, Adrienne, and Sue stopping her dead in her tracks. "Hello," she said, her tone hesitant.

"You remember Cooper, of course."

"Of course." She greeted him with a nod.

"And this is his manager, Adrienne, and Sue, his publicist," I said, gesturing toward the hostile strangers glowering up at her.

Cameron's smile was guarded. "Hi."

Adrienne sniffed disinterestedly. "Can we get back to business, please?"

"You know," Cameron said, glancing down at the magazines still strewn across the coffee table. She turned to me, her forehead wrinkled with concern.

Chin quivering, I bowed my head, unexpectedly moved by the sympathy in her voice.

She gave my arm a consoling squeeze. "I'm so sorry, Mack."

Adrienne cleared her throat. "Bella," she corrected.

Cameron frowned. "Excuse me?"

"In light of what's happened," I said, pulling her aside. "Sue and Adrienne thought it best that we formulate a plan—you know, damage control." Recoiling slightly at the furious glint in her eye, I motioned toward Sue's notes. "They've come up with some pretty good ideas so far."

Cameron's glare was penetrating. Moving with lightning speed, she darted the short distance to where Sue was seated, and snatched away the pad resting in her lap.

Neither Sue nor Adrienne made a move to stop her.

"Polish image: New York sophisticate with a touch of boho couture," she read aloud. "Establish persona: capitalize on visibility, full media launch. Overhaul condo: print exclusive, 'At Home With Bella.' Expand bookstore: convert from Christian to mainstream." She glanced over at me. "No more Mack."

"It's not as bad as it sounds," I said, unwilling to meet her gaze.

She tossed the notepad onto the table. "Have you lost your mind?"

"You don't understand. This is part of what it means to be with someone in the public eye."

Cameron shrugged. "Then don't be with him."

"That was certainly my first choice," Adrienne said, sneering.

Nostrils flaring and chest heaving, Cameron closed her eyes and took a moment to collect herself. "Will you excuse us?" she asked. Spinning on her heels, she disappeared into the kitchen. I followed and found her standing beside the sink, arms folded. "This has gone too far," she said.

"You're turning it into more than it is."

"They're trying to change you," she said, her tone pitched high with frustration. "And the scary part is you're letting them."

"So suddenly you're the only one who's allowed to make me over?"

She shook her head. "What're you talking about?"

"How is what they're doing any worse than volunteering me for *The Kitty Asher Show?*"

"We did that for you," she said. "They're doing this for themselves."

"Cooper's offered to invest in the bookstore. He wants to help me expand it—coffeehouse, reading lounge, Internet café, the works. Who's that for?"

"Still them," she said. "Don't you get it? They'll give you the world so long as you play the puppet and they hold the strings."

"This is a good thing, Cameron. They're offering me the chance of a lifetime."

"But at what cost?" she asked. "Everything has a price."

"Not this," I argued. "As soon as the new store's stable, he'll let me buy him out."

"Or he could wind up being a complete jerk, renege on all of his promises, and leave you high and dry without a buck or a business to your name; did you ever stop to think of that?"

I looked away, wounded by her discouragement. "Or maybe you're just jealous," I said. "Our whole lives, you've been the charmed one. You've been the pretty one, the fun one, the lucky one. And now the tables have turned. Fortune has finally shined on me and the only thing you can think to do is sabotage it."

"Charmed?" she asked, pressing her palm to her chest. "Is that what you think? That I've led a charmed life? I have spent twenty-eight years running from myself," she said. "Twenty-eight years stumbling and tumbling and making messes. Twenty-eight years trying to be more like you and failing miserably, each and every time, to come anywhere close.

"You did everything right," she said, fighting back tears. "You graduated from college, bought your own home, started your own business. Meanwhile, my greatest achievements include sleeping my way through half of Europe, getting disinherited by my parents, and settling for a job I hate, taking orders from a sleazy old man who only hired me because he thinks I have a nice rack."

"Cam." I shook my head. "I had no idea."

"How could you?" she asked. "You've been too busy envying what doesn't exist. That's always been your biggest problem, Mack. It's what keeps you searching for what you already have. And it's what's led you here. Those people," she said, pointing toward the living room, "They don't have loyalties. They're not in your corner. You are just an inconvenience that they've found a way to market. And when they're done with you," she warned, "when you've lost your novelty, and they've moved on to the next big thing, this will all have been a heartbreaking waste of your time."

We stood for a while, draped in weighty silence, neither of us sure how to proceed. "I understand why you have such strong reservations," I began, my words slow and measured. "The relationship is new and fast and totally out of character for me, which makes it especially unnerving. But the bottom line is, I like him a lot. He's a good guy, and we're good together, and I think if you just gave him a chance, you'd—"

She raised her hands in surrender. "You don't have to convince me. If this is what you've decided you want, I'm done trying to stop you."

"It's going to be OK." My nod was reassuring. "I know what I'm doing."

Her smile was small, pitying. "I hope you find what you're looking for," she said, edging toward the exit. "I really do."

I watched her disappear through the archway and listened with a pervading sense of regret as her fading footsteps disappeared behind the sound of the closing front door.

"Well, that's fifteen minutes of my life I'll never get back," Adrienne said when I emerged from the kitchen several moments later.

"Sorry." I reclaimed my spot next to Cooper on the love seat. "I didn't mean to keep you waiting."

"So, what have you decided?" Sue asked. "Are you in or aren't you?"

"I'm in," I said.

Adrienne offered one of her rare smiles. "Good."

Planting a kiss on my temple, Cooper wrapped his arms around my shoulders and pulled me into a tight hug. He sighed. "I'm so happy."

"Me too," I said, cringing, with some surprise, at the sound of my own voice.

PART T

Ciao, Bella

Twenty-Seven

"Are you busy?" Cooper asked.

I surveyed the neatly stacked piles of clothes organized on my bed. Sue and Adrienne had insisted that I vacate my condo for the rest of the week, while it was being refurbished. It was one of a list of instructions they'd given me over the course of the day, which they'd spent holed up in my living room, calling in favors, scheduling appointments, confirming appearances, and—when I asked too many questions—sending me on coffee runs.

"That depends," I said. "Where are Adrienne and Sue?"

He chuckled. "Most likely coasting along at twenty thousand feet somewhere over Nebraska. I dropped them off at the airport a couple hours ago."

I sighed, relieved.

"So what do you say? Can you spare some time?"

"Right now?" I asked, frowning at the mound of shoes at my feet. With the exception of my week-long makeover, I had never spent more than a couple days away from home. That fact made me a terrible traveler. Despite my most diligent efforts to sort accordingly, I was notorious for bringing things I didn't need, needing things I didn't take, and taking things I didn't use. "I'm trying to pack."

"You've got all night to do that," he said. "Come on, it won't take long. I can be there in five minutes."

"Where are we going?"

He tsked playfully into my ear. "When are you going to learn not to ask so many questions?"

I smiled. "Hopefully about the same time you learn not to keep so many secrets."

"OK," he relented. "I'll give you a hint. It involves sand, water, and, if we hurry, a breathtaking sunset."

I glanced out the window at a meandering tuft of clouds and then down at the tower of folded T-shirts threatening to topple onto the floor. A short break suddenly didn't seem like such a bad idea. "You win," I said. "I'll meet you downstairs."

His laugh was triumphant. "See you in a few."

———— • ————

Slipping off my sandals, I settled onto the blanket that Cooper had spread along the beach and watched as he lit the clusters of thoughtfully arranged candles he'd buried in the sand.

"Hope you're hungry," he said, trading his lighter for a bag of goodies he'd brought from nearby Fox & Obel.

I made room for him beside me. "That depends on what we're having."

"Well, I thought we'd start off with Oysters Rockefeller," he said unloading several containers. "Followed by caviar parfait and if there's any room left..." He granted me a quick peek at a plate of startlingly large chocolate-dipped strawberries. "A little dessert."

"You really went all out," I said, smiling as he popped the cork on a bottle of champagne. "What's the occasion?"

"Can't a man woo his woman without cause?" he asked, filling both of the flutes he'd brought and handing one to me.

I smiled. "By all means, woo away."

He shrugged. "I guess I just wanted to show my appreciation. Today wasn't the easiest. But you handled everything that came your way and you handled it with complete grace, which says a lot, not only about who you are, but also about your dedication to this, to us. And I know that Adrienne and Sue can be demanding," he continued.

I sipped my champagne. That was one word for it.

"But I want you to know that you can trust them and you can trust me when I tell you that they only have my best interest at heart."

Nodding, I forced a polite grin. I had every confidence they were watching out for Cooper. What had yet to be seen was who was watching out for me.

"The point is," he said, "I'm excited to be on this journey with you and I can't wait to find out where it takes us."

"Thanks." I reached for his hand. "I feel the same way."

He gazed for a moment at our laced fingers. "I'm glad to hear you say that because there's something I want to ask you."

"What is it?"

His laugh was bashful, nervous. "To be honest, I was hoping to get you loaded on a few more of those first," he said, nodding at my half-empty glass.

I smiled. "Well, if it's any consolation, the caviar and chocolate-covered strawberries are working in your favor."

He closed his eyes and took a steadying breath. "Will you come to Europe with me?"

It was my turn to breathe deeply. "What?"

"Come with me," he requested a second time. "I'm due in London for a premiere at the end of next week and I don't want to think about being away from you—not even for a few days. We could leave tomorrow—make a vacation out of it."

"But how?"

"All you have to do is say the word, and I'll take care of everything."

I shook my head. "I can't pick up and leave. I have a business to run."

"You and I both know the bookstore will be fine without you."

"It's not only that," I said, instantly thinking of Oliver and Cameron. Impetuously skipping the country with Cooper would only serve to further splinter my already fractured friendships. "There are people who love me. And I've disappointed them."

"If the first part of what you said is really true, then the second part doesn't matter."

I grinned. "You've got an answer for everything."

"And you're running out of excuses," he said, smirking.

I laughed. "This is insane."

"Why?" he asked. "You can't go back to your condo until after the remodel, anyway. You might as well enjoy yourself while you wait." Pulling me into his lap, he pointed our gazes toward the sprawling stretch of open water just beyond the shoreline. "Think about it. This time tomorrow, we could be anywhere in the world."

"Anywhere?" I asked.

He smiled. "Is that a yes?"

"I *have* always wanted to see the Colosseum," I said.

"Now's your chance." He nuzzled my ear. "But first, you have to say yes."

My sigh was waggish. "And I hear Nice is nice this time of year."

"Say yes," he ordered, reclining me so that my back was cradled in the crook of his arm. I looked up at him, his chiseled features set aglow by the soft candlelight.

"Just the two of us," I mused.

"Say it," he said, slowly leaning in.

"Yes," I whispered, smiling as he lowered his lips to mine.

Twenty-Eight

Packing was no longer my priority. I returned home later that evening. Trying to estimate how many pairs of socks I would need for the next several days fell a far second to breaking the news that I'd be spending those days in Europe with Cooper.

Cordless in hand, I curled up on the living room couch and debated who to tell first. I stared at the buttons for what felt like an eternity, mentally dialing numbers to the handful of people I couldn't find the strength to actually call.

Eventually, I worked up enough nerve to phone Iona. She was pleasantly supportive, even after I explained exactly to what degree her workload would increase in my absence. Dismissing my penitent promises to make amends for the sudden inconvenience, she pledged to look after the store as if it were her own and then fondly reminisced at length about her own travels across the pond.

By the time we hung up, my apprehension had given way to an encouraging, even if somewhat shaky, sense of optimism that the others might surprise me with an equally supportive response.

That hope was quickly extinguished, however, the instant I spoke with my sister, Danielle. For the better part of an hour, she methodically worked through a thorough list of every misstep I had already taken, only to spend another 20 minutes warning me of the many mistakes I would continue to make if I went through with the trip.

Similar conversations with my brothers followed. Gabe was most concerned with my witness. People would make certain assumptions, he argued. They would question Cooper's motives and my integrity and likely conclude that neither was pure. Caleb accused me of falling prey to the glitz and glamour of Hollywood. My mom expressed little more than deep disappointment, which wound up stinging worse than all the other reactions combined.

Sufficiently berated by my family, I was emotionally spent when I finally dialed Cameron's number. Eyes closed, I pressed the receiver to my ear and wearily braced myself for more of the same.

"I hear a 'Bon Voyage' is in order," she answered in lieu of, "Hello."

I halted, the carefully phrased opener I had prepared falling dead on my tongue. "Who told you?"

"Danielle. She called a while ago." Cameron chuckled. "Said you were getting ready to skip town with a potential axe murderer."

"That's funny; he was an escaped convict when she talked to me."

"Well, you know your sister." I could hear her smirking. "Convict, murderer, actor—they're all the same to her."

I laughed, grateful for the banter. "Cameron, listen," I began.

"It's OK. You don't have to explain," she said. "Just hurry home."

"I will," I promised.

She was quiet for a moment. "Hey, you know my friend Camilla from work?"

Keeping track of Cameron's colleagues was like trying to memorize the phonebook. "The one who ran the marathon?" I guessed.

"No, that was Kayla. Camilla's the one who got engaged last summer," she said. "Anyway, she's moving to Phoenix in a couple weeks with her fiancé, and yesterday we had a going away party for her at the office."

"OK," I said, curious as to where her story was leading.

"It was your standard send-off—cake, presents, a few lame speeches. And then Mr. Brenninger stood up and made a toast," she said, referencing their boss with her usual measure of disdain. "He told her what an asset she'd been to the company, assured her she would be missed, and then he wished her the best life had to offer.

"I'm not sure why then or there, but as we all raised our glasses, I understood with newfound clarity that for me the best of life has been you."

Touched, I smiled.

"I know you look at yourself, at how things have turned out, and you feel like you've been cheated out of the good stuff," she continued. "But Mack, for so many of us, you are the good stuff. And I think maybe if we had stopped to tell you that more along the way, this situation with Cooper would've played out differently."

"You still think I'm making a mistake," I said.

She sighed. "I do. But no matter what, you're my best friend, and if he's who you've chosen—if being Bella is what you want—then I'm happy for you both."

"If only it could be that simple with everyone else."

"And by everyone else, do you mean Oliver?"

"I can't figure out how this got so turned around," I said. "Being his friend used to be the one thing I was good at and now..."

"He's gone and complicated everything by falling in love."

"Did he say that?" I asked, my heart skipping a beat.

Her pause alarmed me. "Does it matter?"

"I just wish we could talk the way we used to. I miss his jokes, his advice."

"You should tell him that."

"I guess I haven't found the time," I said.

"A phone call only takes a few minutes."

"Then, I guess I haven't found the courage."

"What do you have to be flustered about? He's the one who's been humiliated," she said, a touch of accusation in her tone. "It's one thing to lose the woman you love; it's another thing entirely to lose her to a movie star."

"I never meant to embarrass anyone. You know that."

"Well, just be sure to go easy on him when you deliver this newest development. He's nursing some pretty serious wounds to his pride right now."

My stomach churned with guilt. "What should I tell him?"

"The truth," she said. "It won't be easy for him to hear, but at least he'll know that you still care enough to include him."

I gazed out of my window at the blinking city lights below and sighed. "Do you sometimes wish that none of this had ever happened?"

"You mean the makeover?" she asked.

"If I hadn't done the show, I wouldn't have gone to California and I never would have met Cooper."

"The thought definitely occurred to me," she confessed. "But I've been reading this book of morning devotions Olly gave me, and there's a chapter that talks about how God takes even the worst situations and creates something good from them, for everyone who belongs to Him. And if there's one thing I'm certain of," she said, "it's that you belong to Him.

"So I guess I'm kind of holding out hope that even if every decision that's led you to this point has been a mistake, He'll work it all out in the end."

"I'm sorry." I smiled. "Did you just say you've been having morning devotions?"

She laughed. "I know. I'm getting up early to spend time with God, and you're running off willy-nilly with some hot guy you just met. What's the world coming to?"

"Cameron, this is a big deal!" I squealed. "I'm really proud of you."

"I don't know why you sound so surprised. Twenty years of your incessant preaching... The truth was bound to take hold eventually."

"We'll have to go to church together," I said, realizing only after I'd offered that it was the first time in a really long time I truly wanted to go.

"Actually, I told Olly I'd go with him this Sunday."

"Oh." I felt suddenly left out. "OK."

"You're not upset, are you?"

"No, of course not. I just wish I could be there, that's all."

"We'll go when you get back."

"Definitely," I said, a false cheeriness to my tone. "I'm going to hold you to it."

The lull that followed told me our conversation had reached its end. "Well, I guess I'll let you go now. I know you have another call to make."

"Right." My sigh was heavy.

"Have a safe trip, Mack." She hesitated. "I mean, Bella."

"Don't you dare," I scolded. "I'll always be Mack to you."

But it was too late. She was gone.

I sat motionless for some time in the middle of my dark living room and considered the paradoxical nature of my current circumstances. In a few short hours, I would be embarking on the adventure of a lifetime with the man of every woman's dreams. And if that wasn't enough, after 30 years of blending into the background, I'd metamorphosed into a standout who turned heads nearly everywhere she went. I worked at my leisure, played at my whim, and was bound by nothing and no one, least of all my faith. In short, I had fashioned to a T the existence I'd convinced myself would be the antidote to my unhappiness, only to discover that the closer I got to what I wanted, the less appealing it seemed to be.

Carefree living had brought with it its own brand of disappointment and its own set of troubles and losses.

I glanced down at the phone resting in my lap, both comforted and saddened by the knowledge that Oliver was only a call away. Reaching him would be the easy part; figuring out what to say once I had him on the line was what kept me from dialing.

Cameron was right. I owed him an explanation. But the problem was, I didn't have one. Nothing I could say would change what had happened or make up for the hurt I'd caused.

I couldn't fix it.

So, I didn't try.

Instead, I returned to my room to finish packing. And the next morning, I boarded a private jet to France without offering Oliver so much as a good-bye.

Twenty-Nine

We touched down in Nice, France, Thursday evening after nearly ten hours of flying. Mere feet from the jet's steps, a white-gloved driver met us, and we were swiftly transferred, along with our things, to a waiting town car and whisked away to our suite at a nearby beachside resort.

I stared, mesmerized, and absorbed as much of the culture as I could from behind the sedan's tinted windows. There were hundreds of picturesque, mountainside homes packed neatly one beside the other, rows of colorful outdoor cafés, narrow streets congested with mopeds and cars so compact they looked like toys.

There were people, hordes of them, lying on the white pebbles of Ruhl Beach, strolling along the *Promenade Des Anglais*, purchasing gelato from the roaming street vendors.

And of course, there was the Mediterranean Sea—miles and miles of nothing but breathtakingly blue water. Set before a startlingly placid salmon sky, the scene overwhelmed my senses.

"It's almost hard to believe that places like this actually exist!" I said.

Cooper, who'd been fixated on his Blackberry since it had regained reception on the tarmac, looked up from his emails and smirked, seemingly amused by my childlike wonder. "Believe it."

"How can you fiddle around with that thing," I asked, nodding at his phone with a twinge of irritation, "when all of this is at your fingertips?"

Glancing absently out of the window, he shrugged. "Same city, different day, I guess," he said, his thumbs resuming their hurried dance across the device's miniature keyboard. Serenaded the rest of the way by the soft clicking of his typing, we arrived at the hotel to a flurry of readied attendants.

Despite Cooper's attempt to hide himself behind dark shades and a baggy sweatshirt, the hood of which was pulled over a long bill baseball cap, several guests milling in the lobby immediately recognized him. Their reactions, however, were far less brazen than anything I'd witnessed back in the States.

In lieu of unwanted snapshots and incessant demands for an autograph, they nodded discreetly and watched wordlessly as we were escorted past the check-in desk and directly to a private elevator.

The elegance of the Presidential Suite was understated, hidden in the straight, clean lines of the sparse, but chic decor. The suited manager, who'd met us at the car and accompanied us, along with two bellhops, up to our floor, insisted on giving us a tour of the sprawling two-level unit.

"It's OK?" he would ask once he'd finished pointing out all of the amenities in one room and was prepared to move on to the next. Taking my cues from Cooper, I followed politely behind and nodded approvingly even when his canorous accent muddled his words beyond what I could understand.

Only after ensuring our complete satisfaction did our solicitous host collect his dutiful attendants and, with a gallant bow and tip in hand, leave us to get settled.

"Long day," Cooper said, sinking into one of several sofas situated in the cavernous living room.

I eased down beside him and nodded. "Jet-setting's not as easy as it looks."

He smirked. "The trick is not to go to sleep. Otherwise, you'll never adjust to the time change."

I stifled a yawn. "So what should we do?"

"There's this great little discotheque not too far from here," he said, tossing his cap onto the large leather ottoman that sat where a coffee table would normally be. "It's got a live band, an energetic crowd, and the best chocolate martini you've never tasted."

Just the thought of loud music and sweaty bodies was exhausting. "I was hoping for something a little more low-key. Like maybe an early dinner and a stroll on the beach?"

His nose wrinkled disagreeably. "Maybe we should start with unpacking and play the rest by ear," he said, hoisting himself off the sofa before pulling me up after him. Instinctively, we both started toward the master suite, where the porters had presumptuously deposited both sets of luggage.

"Sorry." I stopped mid-step. We hadn't bothered to discuss sleeping arrangements. My cheeks grew warm. "I can take one of the other rooms."

"You should see your face right now," he teased. "It's a cross between panic and terror with a dash of mortification thrown in for good measure."

"Be quiet," I muttered, turning away.

"Hey," he grabbed my elbow and drew me back. "This trip is not about that. Don't get me wrong, I'm looking forward to when we get there. But no pressure. I'm a big believer that things happen naturally, when it's time."

I smiled and nodded even though I knew that the only natural time for me would be with my husband on our wedding night.

"You take this one." He pointed at the master. "I'll take the one upstairs."

"Are you sure?" I asked, aware that simply being there was gift enough. "I don't mind. You can have it."

"And deny you the killer view?" He shook his head. "Never."

Entering the room, he retrieved his bags and carried them out to the foyer, where he set them down at the foot of the stairs. "The hotel's got an amazing rooftop bistro—quaint, quiet, with Coq au Vin that melts in your mouth."

I nodded. "Sounds perfect."

"Good, then I'll leave you to..." His sentence tailed off. "What exactly do women do when left to their own devices?"

"Oh you know." I sighed. "Covert assassinations, hostile foreign market

225

takeovers—your basic attempts at world domination."

Laughing, he began his ascent to the second floor. "Well, dinner's at eight, so try to wrap up your diabolical scheming by then."

"I'll do my best," I said, smiling as I slid the door closed behind him.

Alone, I breathlessly explored my new room, with its silk-upholstered chairs and embroidered bed linens, custom walk-in closets, and imperially draped windows. Everything had been meticulously arranged, down to the handmade soaps artfully displayed atop the bathroom's double marble sinks.

Recalling Cooper's mention of the suite's spectacular view, I made my way over to a pair of sliding glass doors and let myself out onto the rambling veranda. In the time it had taken us to get situated, the sun had disappeared, darkening the sky and turning the azure sea into an indiscernible, inky mass. But the light gusts of warm air and the tranquil sound of cresting waves delivered a certain splendor all their own.

Stifling another yawn, I returned inside and changed into a comfy pair of drawstring leggings, a tank top, and my favorite hoodie. Too tired to unpack, I forwent Cooper's advice to stay awake and decided to sneak in a quick nap before I got ready for dinner.

I slipped between the bed's crisp, cool sheets and sunk into the neatly stacked rows of down pillows with a contented sigh. Exhaustion swiftly overtaking me, I switched off the tableside lamp. And the last thing I saw, before my eyes fell shut, were the curtains swaying gently in the evening breeze.

Thirty

I awoke, momentarily dazed by the whitewashed wood beams and the punkah fan swinging lazily from the ceiling above. To my left was a sliding shutter-door, to my right a private terrace that overlooked a brilliantly blue body of water.

Sitting up, I propped myself against the suede headboard and took in the soft white comforter wrapped around my body, the obtrusive television screen mounted to the wall directly ahead of me, and the gorgeous espresso floors gleaming beneath the tasteful furnishings.

Slowly, the puzzle came together one wondrous piece at a time. I was in Nice! Rolling out of bed, I bounded out to the veranda and took in the magnificent view of the beach below. The sun, golden and grand, gleamed luminously from its perch high in the halcyon sky. Eager to feel its warmth, I tugged off my sweatshirt and turned my face to its warm cascading rays.

The scents of the city—brine and café au lait, baking bread and oleander—mingled enticingly in the air. Breathing it in with a thrill, I smiled. But my exhilaration was abruptly cut short by the sudden realization that I'd accidently slept through the night.

Making my way back inside, I bypassed my suitcase, still resting unpacked on the luggage stand, scuttled through the sun-kissed parlor, and slid open the door to my suite. Standing quietly for several seconds, I listened for any sign of movement before tiptoeing across the foyer and up the stairs.

"Coop?" I called. Stopping at the top of the landing, I waited for a response, but was met by stillness. "Cooper?" I called again, rounding the corner to his room. The door was ajar.

I knocked. "Are you awake?"

There was no answer.

Poking my head in, I discovered his bed empty—sheets rumpled, pillows on the floor, a pair of jeans tossed carelessly across the love seat and a damp towel hanging from the post of his footboard.

"You in here?" I asked, creeping toward the bathroom. Aside from the stunningly extensive collection of hair and skin products cluttering the vanity, it too was deserted.

Retracing my steps downstairs, I ambled into the living room. There, lying on the couch was a large leather-bound binder. It was opened to the hotel's room service tab. And posted conspicuously across one of the embossed pages was a hand-scrawled note from Cooper that simply read, "Eat!"

Smiling, I sat down, kicked up my feet, and leisurely flipped through the entire menu before finally placing an order for sweet crepes with fresh berries and whipped cream.

Then, with food on the way and the Côte d'Azur beckoning just beyond my windows, I headed back outside to enjoy a quiet morning on the veranda.

Thirty-One

By the time Cooper returned a couple hours later, I had eaten, showered, dressed, and skimmed, cover to cover, a stack of brochures and guidebooks I'd discovered in one of the table drawers. Though it was a relatively small city, Nice was in no short supply of intriguing attractions. And I was champing at the bit to experience them all.

Of course, watching Cooper stride toward me, his shirtless torso glimmering with sweat, was proving to be something of an intriguing attraction as well.

"She lives," he said, kissing me hello, before easing into one of the armchairs.

My smile was apologetic. "You could have woken me."

"I didn't have the heart. You looked too peaceful." He shrugged. "I checked on you this morning, but you were still out cold. So, I had a quick breakfast and then went for a run."

"What'd you do yesterday?" I asked.

"I wound up going to a couple of casinos."

"Casinos," I said, unable to mask my distaste.

He nodded. "Played some Black Jack."

"I didn't know you gambled."

The reproach in my voice was lost on him. "I'm not a high roller or anything, but I do all right," he said, his head tilted humbly. "Anyway, I bumped into a couple of interesting guys. We ended up having a few drinks and then heading over to that discotheque I told you about."

"Wow." My smile was tight. "You had a busy night."

"I would have much rather spent it with you," he assured me.

"Well, maybe I can make it up to you."

Grinning, he leaned forward, elbows on his knees. "What'd you have in mind?"

"I've got the whole day mapped out." I felt my excitement return as I waved one of the glossy pamphlets I'd mercilessly dog-eared.

"Let's hear it," he said.

"I thought we might start at the MAMAC, work our way down to the Cathedrale Sainte Reparate, and then over to the Chapelle de la Miséricorde." Taking note of his sulky frown, I lowered my travel guide. "Or I could always pick out some other sites, if you've already seen all of these."

"No, it's not that." He sat back and sighed. "It's just, people typically come to Nice for the beaches, the shopping, the nightlife. Not to watch dirt grow in old, crusty ruins."

"I hardly think the Museum of Modern Art qualifies as a crusty ruin," I said.

He shrugged. "You know what I mean. We're here to relax."

"Well, can we at least take the walking tour of the Cours Saleya?"

"Walking tour," he echoed with audible eschewal.

My gaze was pleading. "For twenty euros, a guide will show us all around Vieux Nice."

"Is that what this is about?" he asked, his expression immediately softening. "Babe, you don't have to try to plan on a budget. You're with me now. We can afford to do the Riviera the way the Riviera was meant to be done."

I glared, unsure if I was more offended by his assumption that history was a pauper's pastime or by his accusation that I only wanted to take in the sites because I was too poor to know better.

"How about this," he said, standing. "I'll call down and reserve us a couple of lounges, while you go and change into that little two-piece I bought you. We'll hit the beach, soak up some rays, order a few cocktails. Then, later we can have a nice lunch, maybe browse the shops for a while. And, if afterward, it's not too late, we'll see about the tour. How does that sound?"

It sounded like a waste of a perfectly good afternoon. I could sip drinks and lie in the sun in Chicago. But while I was in Nice, I was eager to examine an original Matisse. I longed to explore a centuries-old chateau.

Cooper's attitude perplexed me. He could go anywhere, experience everything, and yet his favorite pastime, near as I could tell, was doing absolutely nothing.

I shrugged. "If that's what you want."

"You're upset," he said, crouching down in front of me, his wide eyes full of concern.

"No, I'm fine. Really," I said, my exasperation waning at the sight of his crestfallen expression. Nodding determinedly, I stood. "This'll be fun too."

His spirits just that easily restored, he smiled. "Meet you back here in ten?"

I cast one last languishing glance at the heap of brochures and guidebooks scattered across the sofa. "OK," I said, flinching as he sent me off to change with a stinging smack to my rear end.

Thirty-Two

Our outing to Ruhl Beach wasn't the insufferable ordeal I thought it would be, in large part because the chaise lounges that Cooper had reserved were located beneath a spacious marquee on the *premier ligne* of the Castel Plage, a private stretch of shoreline abutting the sea. It was an ideal setup, one that allowed us to drink in the atmosphere while shirking the noisy crowds, avoiding the blazing sun, and enjoying the cool Mediterranean breezes.

What was more, the marquee came equipped with two attendants who supplied us with absolutely anything we requested.

Though Cooper would have balked at the suggestion, the reality was that he had grown exceptionally accustomed to being waited on hand and foot. While the attentive stewards hustled back and forth in the sweltering heat fulfilling his frivolous requests for frosty beverages and extra towels, he thanklessly whiled away the time fiddling with his phone.

Watching his inconsiderate antics from my neighboring lounger, I likened him to someone who unknowingly grows accustomed to a strange aroma in an unfamiliar house. While uncomfortable at first, the odor, in time, becomes normal, undetectable. It's not that the potency of the scent changes or that it ever goes away, but rather that the person who enters, gradually and imperceptibly becomes a part of it.

Cooper's wealth had habituated him to luxury and in the process desensitized him to the inconveniences of others. And he, an unwitting convert, had been helpless to stop either. Or at least that's what I told myself to keep from berating him as the server he'd sent back twice for colder water returned, sweat dripping from his brow.

Gingerly, he placed a freshly filled decanter, along with a tall glass brimming with ice, onto the small birch table beside Cooper's chair.

Cooper, rapt by a text message he'd received, distractedly motioned for the waiting attendant to pour the water into the glass. He dutifully obliged.

"Merci," I said, dismissing the man with a smile and nod, while Cooper, laughing in response to something on his phone's miniature screen, promptly busied himself typing a reply.

"What's so funny?" I asked, leaning over my armrest to sneak a peek.

He tilted his phone away. "Just a dumb inside joke."

Intrigued, I waited for him to elaborate, but he only glanced up and shook his head. "You wouldn't get it."

"Who is it you're talking to?"

"Adrienne," he said, his phone chiming loudly with the arrival of a new message. "She says hello, by the way."

"Adrienne's texting you?" I could feel my dander rising. "In the middle of our vacation?"

"She's my manager," he said, a testiness to his tone.

"But I thought we agreed, no working on this trip."

"I can't just bury my head in the sand for a week. Part of what I do requires me to stay updated on the important stuff."

"Like dumb jokes," I muttered with a roll of my eyes.

Sighing, he lowered his phone and angled his body toward me. "Is this about the tour thing? Because I said we could go."

Actually, what he'd said was we would see about it—if there was any time left over after our long, tiring day of sunbathing and shopping. "It's not about the tour," I said. "It's about you being here. Present. With me."

"I'm here," he said. His Blackberry chimed with another message.

Glaring at it, I shook my head. "Only in body."

Cooper pressed a few more buttons on his phone, then turned to look at me again. But something over my shoulder caught his attention. I followed his gaze to two young women in the distance. Donning string bikinis even skimpier than the one Cooper had gifted me, they sauntered along the water's edge, hips swiveling flirtatiously as they drew near our marquee.

Had Cooper not been so engrossed in his digital dialogue with Adrienne, he would have known that it wasn't their first attempt to catch his eye. The coquettish duo had pranced by earlier, waving and giggling louder than necessary.

They were just two of many.

It seemed Cooper's morning run on the beach had tipped off the general public to his presence in the city. As a result, we'd been something of a live exhibit from the moment we'd stepped foot outdoors.

The hotel, with its discreet staff and diplomatic guests, had offered us a measure of anonymity. That particular community was too refined to make a spectacle over Cooper. Though their occasional stares may have betrayed a quiet curiosity, no one deigned to indulge the urge to acknowledge him with much else than a curt nod and a purse of the mouth. Anything more, I suspected, would have undermined the aloofness behind which they had erected their private, privileged existences.

But the beach was a different territory entirely. Squarely outside the hotel's decorous atmosphere, it was a place where shameless ogling and bawdy blandishments overrode decorum, and self-respect was an easy sacrifice for the chance to rub elbows with a dashing American movie star.

The two women slowed their pace as they passed us, taking care to toss a couple of saucy grins Cooper's way before continuing on. Captivated, he watched as they disappeared into the distance.

"You were saying?" I asked.

He turned back to me, a blank expression on his face as if he'd forgotten I was there. "Adrienne says you wouldn't recognize your place right now," he said, conveniently picking up where we hadn't left off. "The crew's already gutted the entire kitchen."

My muscles tensed at the news. "In one day?"

Cooper smiled. "She knows how to get things done."

He checked his phone for any straggling messages before setting it aside and reaching for his iced water, which had once again thawed in the searing heat. Tentatively taking several sips, he shook his head, piqued by its lukewarm temperature, and poured what remained onto the ground. Muttering to himself, he returned the glass to the birch table and reclined in his chaise with an exasperated sigh.

We sat in silence for some time and watched other beachgoers bob lazily in the sea. It might have been peaceful were it not so boring.

"Let's rent a paddle boat and cruise around the harbor," I said, desperate to do more than lie around. Nodding at the enormous yellow Water Sports sign flapping in the wind a few yards away, I smiled. "It'll be fun."

Cooper lifted his sunglasses and tossed a listless glance over his shoulder at the cabana, where adventurous visitors could lease everything from surfboards to rollerblades. "Maybe later," he said.

Annoyed, I turned my attention to the novel I'd brought. Halfway through the first chapter, Cooper's cell phone chimed and he resumed his usual routine of texting and chuckling.

"Pardon, Monsieur," someone beckoned cautiously from behind us.

Cooper and I both looked up to see the same attendant who'd spent the day fetching him ice standing just outside the marquee. What ensued was an accent-heavy invitation delivered in broken English on behalf of several "admirers" who had rented "Mr. Young and his companion" a jet ski for the afternoon.

"They would be delighted if you would honor them with your company," he said, pointing to a cluster of four bikini-clad women shyly huddling a few yards away.

Cooper removed his sunglasses and set them on top of his head. "You up for it?" he asked, bouncing his brows at me with newfound vigor.

Closing my book, I frowned. "You're going?"

He shrugged. "Might as well, they've already rented it. We don't want to be rude."

"Not even an hour ago, I asked you to go paddle boating with me and you refused."

"No. I said, maybe later." His stare was hard. "You said you wanted to cruise around the harbor, so let's go. What's the problem?"

The problem, I was starting to realize, was that Cooper and I had different ideas about how to make our trip memorable. It wasn't about romance for him. It wasn't about seeing the sites. It wasn't even really about getting to know each other better. It was about relaxing—about casting aside all thoughts and cares, all responsibilities and obligations—and going with the flow. Wherever that might take us.

Consequently, he had a way of making every decision, big or small, feel like it was part of the natural flow of a bigger picture, which meant that while I could differentiate between jet skiing with strangers and paddle boating with my significant other, Cooper saw it all as one big splash in the Mediterranean. To him, how we got to a point didn't matter nearly as much as being able to say we were there; whereas, to me, the journey was what made the destination worthwhile.

"Nothing." I shook my head. "It's fine."

Not one to keep his fans in suspense, he stood and offered me his hand.

"I think I'll pass," I said, holding up my book. "I'm just getting to the good part."

He sighed. "You're upset again."

"How can I be upset?" I asked. "I'm in paradise."

He studied me for several moments, uncertain, I could tell, if he would end up paying later for a wrong decision now.

"Go." I shooed him on. "I'll be fine."

Grudgingly, he capitulated. "OK, but if you change your mind, you know where to find me."

I nodded and watched him trot the short distance to his waiting admirers.

They scrambled, unabashedly, over one another, each one jockeying for her turn to give him the customary French greeting of a kiss on either cheek.

Cooper and his new friends made small talk for a little bit. Catching only broken portions of their conversation, I looked on with growing animosity as he flexed a bicep upon request, only to look away sheepishly when they all reached to touch it with a delighted squeal.

Eventually, the five of them migrated to a string of Sea-Doos idling in the shallow waters nearby and strapped on their life vests. Ever the gentleman, Cooper helped the women onto their crafts before nimbly straddling his own.

I waited to see if he would look back and wave, if he would offer any indication that I hadn't been that quickly forgotten. But to my chagrin, he simply gunned his engine and zipped away.

With his votaries in close pursuit, he disappeared, moments later, beyond the horizon. And I, not in the habit of being slighted for strangers, gathered my things, slid on my flip flops, and, casting one last glance at the rippling, iridescent blue water, headed back to the suite.

Thirty-Three

The winding, brick streets of Vieux Nice were a kaleidoscope of saffron, titian, and puce shops, churches, patisseries, and cafés. Though bustling with a steady flow of tourists, it still maintained a quaint, tranquil provinciality. The air, perfumed with jasmine sachets, lavender-scented soaps, *muguet* candles, patchouli oil, and other much-sought-after local specialties, possessed a vitality that could not be denied or ignored.

There were many charming squares to explore, hidden cathedrals to esteem, and outdoor markets to peruse. There were roaming vendors, street performers, and alfresco tables at any number of welcoming restaurants from which to leisurely observe the unremitting activity taking place all around.

There were hokey souvenir shops that peddled cheap knickknacks like refrigerator magnets and ceramic I-Heart-France mugs. Nestled between those were more selective boutiques boasting everything from hand-bound journals to crocodile purses. And in a tiny épicerie hidden away at the end of a cul-de-sac on a quiet, seemingly forgotten street, I discovered the most impressive selection of wines, pâtés, sea salts, chocolates, olive oils, and freshly baked breads.

Since abandoning Ruhl Beach, I had strolled Place Rosetti, enjoyed Saint Réparate Cathedral, checked out the Cours Saleya, ambled through the Albert

Ist Gardens, dined on a delectable *pain au chocolat,* and purchased a sinful number of gifts to take back home.

My legs were tired, my back was sore, and my arms throbbed from the sheer weight of my packages. Still, I wasn't ready to call it quits. There was too much left to see, so much more to do.

Flushed with energy, it was hard for me to imagine that only hours earlier I'd considered the day a wash. Sulking in my room after Cooper had sped away, I'd curled up with the novel I had started in the marquee. But I couldn't concentrate.

Instead, I'd found myself absently reading the same paragraph over and over, while my thoughts drifted to other things—namely the fact that my relationship with Cooper wasn't progressing as naturally or as seamlessly as the preceding days had led me to believe it would. Rather, the initial ease with which we'd connected was becoming quickly and soundly overshadowed by my bourgeoning understanding that he and I had very little in common.

On the flight over, my head had been swimming with fantasies of unforgettable visits to treasured landmarks, seaside candlelit dinners, romantic strolls along the beach, and long talks beneath the stars. Meanwhile, I never stopped to consider that the entire time he was seated next to me, Cooper was dreaming of Black Jack and discotheques.

Troubled by the possibility that the next six days might yield more of the same discord, I'd given up on the novel and relocated to the living room, hoping that a change of scenery would clear my mind. There, I had discovered the guidebooks and brochures I'd left lying open on the couch. Picking one up, I'd gazed longingly at the colorful pictures of places I would regretfully not get the chance to visit during our short stay.

But as I began to study the materials more closely, I realized that several of the sites I'd wanted to explore were within walking distance from the hotel. With each article I skimmed and every map that I studied, my mood heartened, as did my resolve to make the most of my time in Europe—even if that meant experiencing it without Cooper at my side.

And as I merrily tugged my shopping bags to a row of colorful boutiques in the distance, I was confident that I'd made the right decision.

The streets, like the businesses in Nice, were cramped, but with my body twisted at just the right angle and my newly purchased gifts pressed close by my sides, I managed to maneuver around the ambling locals and into one of the intriguing shops.

I browsed leisurely, making my way past racks of postcards and display tables of neatly arranged T-shirts. Toward the back of the store, I discovered unique pieces of jewelry—coral earrings, ivory anklets, and assorted gold baubles.

Leaning closer to examine the hand-beaded necklaces locked behind one of several glass cases lined against the far wall, my eyes caught sight of a Rasta tam hat, replete with faux dreadlocks, dangling from a hook in the corner.

Instantly I smiled as my mind swept me back to the best Spring Break of my life.

Thirty-Four

It was mid-March, my senior year in college. Though drearily gray, the weather was unseasonably warm, the campus unusually still. The week prior, the atmosphere had been infused with a subtle anxiousness. It was the same cabin fever that struck every year around that time. Itineraries were being finalized, deposits collected, swimsuits purchased, luggage packed.

With Christmas vacation a distant memory and summer more than two months away, students needed that week off during the spring to refuel, to finish the semester with their sanity intact.

And when it finally came—oh, when it came—they fled our small college town the way sailors abandon a sinking ship: quickly and without second thoughts.

I'd spent my first three years avoiding the hype and bedlam. Unlike Cameron, an only child whose parents were both dentists, or like Olly, whose education and living expenses were paid out of a generous trust that had been established in his name by his deceased grandfather, I couldn't afford extravagant tropical getaways.

My father had turned ducking child support payments into an art form, and my mother's small, home-based catering company barely grossed enough to keep the lights on and the mortgage paid.

We got by, but with the understanding that everyone had to pull his or her own weight. I worked, sometimes two jobs, and saved what I made to pay for expenses that my grants and student loans wouldn't cover. And though I tried my best, there were times when money fell short and I had to improvise. Like for the first few weeks of my sophomore year, when I'd been reduced to photocopying whole chapters from borrowed books. I quickly became an expert at strategically hitting up all the campus libraries in such a way that I wouldn't exceed the daily limit of free copies allowed per student, until a perceptive professor realized what was happening and pulled some strings to get the university to quietly gift me the texts I needed.

Gabe checked in from time to time to offer his support. As the eldest, he felt a sense of responsibility to step up and be the man our father hadn't. But on a modest teacher's salary, with his own student loans to pay, there was only so much he could do, so much he could give.

Being broke, like being on my own, was something I got used to. I learned to cut coupons, to scan the local paper for events that offered students free admission. I learned which restaurants were the cheapest, what coffee shops had two-for-one refills, which nightclubs waived cover charges.

Whereas my friends saw movies the weekend they opened, I rented them from the video store months later. Whereas they tossed their barely worn winter clothes into the donation receptacle outside of the student center, I took two buses and a train to the nearest Salvation Army in search of a down coat intact enough to keep the unrelenting wind at bay.

As hard as it was at times, I rarely felt sorry for myself. Even in my lack, I understood that there were people who managed to get by on much less. I simply learned to appreciate the challenge in finding creative ways to earn what others were given. And I kept my eyes fixed on the future, holding fast to the belief that fasting first meant I would feast later.

But my seemingly unbreakable spirits began to show signs of wear during my senior year. With my college days drawing to an end, I wanted just one extraordinary experience to take with me as I embarked into my new adult life in the real world—one perfect memory I could look back on and cherish always and forever.

So when Cameron, home for the holidays from whatever foreign country she'd been exploiting at the time, mentioned that she would be sojourning stateside for the next several months in order to accompany a group of her friends on their Spring Break to Jamaica, I asked if I could tag along. I had no idea how much a trip like that would cost, but split between eight people, I figured I could find a way to manage my share. Four years of moonlighting as a waitress had earned me a respectable little savings. And though most of that money was reserved for my move to the city after graduation, I was more than willing to part with a portion of it for the chance at a real adventure.

Over the course of the weeks to follow, Jamaica was all I could think about. When I wasn't attending lectures or studying, I was on the Internet scrolling through pictures of the island's bright green palm trees and sandy beaches or in the library poring over books about its warm weather, Caribbean cuisine, colorful locals, and warm customs.

The anticipation was bittersweet. Naturally, I found the months of waiting to be supremely torturous. But they also helped me understand the indubitable itch that descended upon campus like clockwork every year. They gave me the opportunity to experience, firsthand, the restlessness that caused legs to bounce anxiously and eyes to glaze over in class. And they allowed me, for once, to feel like a part of the collective student body, rather than just an outsider watching life unfold from the sidelines.

With an entrance exam and two interviews that would determine whether or not he got into law school scheduled right after midterms, Oliver was condemned to spend his Spring Break haunting the snow-covered sidewalks of our deserted campus. But that didn't stop him from listening untiringly and without complaint to my constant mention of my upcoming trip and all that I planned to do while I was away.

By mid-February, Cameron's friends had crunched the numbers and divvied the amounts and she, the common tie that bound us all, stopped by my dorm room one drizzling Saturday morning to deliver the bill. Scanning the breakdown, I skipped over the seemingly endless columns of fees and expenses, until my eyes settled on the grand total.

I blinked, horrified, by the number staring back at me in bold print from the bottom of the page.

After spending their last Spring Break in Cancun getting pawed by random guys and dodging vomit at a hotel that had been overrun with rambunctious students, Cameron explained, the group had decided to rent a villa. "You know how the party thing wears thin after the first few days," she said. "This way we'll be able to get away when we want and relax."

While it sounded amazing, that sort of convenience obviously didn't come cheap. Studying the itemized summary more closely, I was humiliated to discover that the money I had so proudly set aside was barely enough to cover the airfare and taxes.

My expression must have betrayed my shock, because Cameron looked away, embarrassed. "I can always go back and see if any of the other girls would be willing to cover some additional costs."

"Are you kidding me?" I shook my head and prayed that the tears pooling at the base of my eyelids wouldn't spill down my cheeks. "This is even less than I was expecting."

Her relief was palpable. Smiling radiantly, she threw her arms around my neck and squealed. "This is going to be the best Spring Break ever!"

Not one to give up without a fight, I spent the next several days brainstorming ways to come up with my share. But even if I spent nothing, doubled the amount I had initially planned to drain from my savings, and pulled double shifts at the restaurant where I waitressed every weekend until the day they left, I wouldn't have enough.

My only hope was to ask for help.

I felt unconscionably selfish as I dialed my mom's number. She had her own worries, her own financial burdens. And, like the rest of us, she had long since grown accustomed to getting by on just the necessities.

Still, there were months when her catering business did unexpectedly well. More often than not, what extra income she made went to catching up on the endless rotation of past due bills. But every now and then, when she could, she would mail me a little something tucked inside a card with a note expressing her love.

She listened intently while I laid out my well-organized arguments for why I wanted to go and never once questioned my firm assurances that I would start to pay her back the instant I found a place in Chicago and got a job. Eyes pinched shut, I was confident as I waited through the long silence that followed my breathy plea, that she would provide the answer I was looking for. She would do what mothers did and magically make everything better.

But when she finally spoke, it was to tell me that the station wagon had broken down again, and that after paying for the repairs, she'd been forced to borrow money from Gabe for groceries.

"Honey, I'm so sorry," she said, her voice riddled with guilt. If there was anything worse than learning that she couldn't help me, it was hearing how badly she felt about it. Shamed by her shame, I pretended to seriously consider her suggestion that I call Gabe, Caleb, and Danielle to see if, between the three of them, they would be able to scrape together the amount I was short. But the instant we hung up, I tossed the printout Cameron had given me into the trashcan, wiped my desk clean of every map and reference book, and stowed the swimsuit and canvas tote I'd purchased on clearance weeks earlier in the back of my closet.

I mentioned nothing of my misfortune to Cameron or Oliver. Whether it was pride or denial or a paralyzing combination of both, I just couldn't bring myself to tell them that I couldn't afford to go. Instead, I spent the next two weeks continuing to chew Olly's ear off about the approaching trip and playing along when Cam called, with increasing frequency, to finalize last-minute details.

It's not that I meant to be untruthful. In fact, I hated keeping secrets. But I didn't hate it nearly as much as I hated the idea of returning to my place on the sidelines.

February eventually turned into March and an excited Cameron showed up one evening on her way to the travel agency to collect my deposit. Caught off guard by her request, I stammered through a painfully long lie about an internship I'd nabbed at a local paper after the applicant they'd previously selected had backed out. It was an excuse I'd been considering for the occasion, but hadn't quite gotten around to perfecting—and it showed.

Crushed, Cameron's countenance fell. "I didn't know you'd even applied for an internship."

I snuck a nervous glance at Oliver, who was watching me curiously from his spot on the floor, where he'd been writing a term paper. "It was over the summer...way back. I didn't tell anyone because, well, you know." I shrugged. "It seemed like a long shot at the time."

Cameron frowned. "And they won't let you start after Spring Break?"

"I asked," I said, shaking my head. "But they told me they'd be forced to give the position to someone else."

We went back and forth for some time. I was surprised by how easily the lies rolled off of my tongue, how believable I sounded. "There'll be other trips," I promised after she'd exhausted all of her rebuttals and had reluctantly accepted the inevitable. "You'll just have to have enough fun for the both of us on this one."

She nodded, her chin trembling with disappointment, and left.

Even though I could feel his questioning gaze glued to me, I refused to acknowledge Oliver as I closed the door behind her and returned to my desk.

"So it's going to be just the two of us," he said.

Unable to find my voice, I buried my nose in my textbook and nodded.

He didn't probe further. But as he turned back to his work, I heard him say, "Looking forward to it."

———— • • ————

The day before Spring Break officially began, Oliver and I found ourselves on the rooftop of his apartment building. Technically, it was a restricted area, but students had long since defaced the warning signs, pried off the lock to the access hatch, and set up chairs and tables they had pilfered, piece by piece, from the commons when security wasn't around.

That evening, with midterms safely behind us, we ordered a pizza and snuck up to the deserted hideaway, where we knew we would be safe from the sheer madness that was brewing below.

"Can you believe people are having pre-Spring Break parties?" I asked, tossing my half-eaten crust into the open box between us. "Who throws a party to celebrate partying?"

Olly laughed and took a swig of his soda. "People who really like to party?"

I wiped the grease from my hands on a napkin and shrugged. In the month since I'd been forced to back out of the trip, my dejection had hardened into snarky bitterness. "Well, I'll be glad to see them gone come Monday."

"Don't be such a grouch," he chided. "If it weren't for your new job you'd be heading to Jamaica to carouse with the best of them."

Wrapping myself in the blanket we'd brought along, I forced a smile. "Right."

The internship I'd concocted was turning out not to be such a brilliant idea. Like most lies, it required me to tell more lies. And I was running out of reasons why I was always on campus and never at work.

"You know what I like most about being your best friend? It's easy," Olly said, draining his soda and discarding the bottle at his feet. "Sometimes, when I'm with the guys, there's a pressure to be someone I'm not. And some of the girls I meet." He shook his head. "I'm on pins and needles from hello to good-bye. But with you, I'm free to be me, no shields or pretenses, no secrets. I can tell you anything. I can show you every side—good, bad, and ugly—and know that you'll love me anyway."

My grin was feeble. "I'm glad."

"Do you have the same confidence in me?" he asked, holding out his hand.

Taking it, I nodded. "Of course."

"Good." His expression was tender. "So, then, tell me about this internship."

"What do you want to know?" I asked, turning my head as the tears dripped off my chin.

He reached across the armrest and, cupping the side of my face, turned it toward his until our gazes met. "The truth."

Sighing, I closed my eyes and confessed. "There is no internship. I couldn't afford to go to Jamaica and I was too embarrassed to tell anyone."

"Even me?"

"It's not like you didn't already know," I said, my tears spilling down his fingers.

Using the edge of his sleeve, he dried my damp cheeks. "You want to talk about it?"

With a shuddering gasp, I released the squall I'd been holding in and shrugged. "It's just not fair."

Tugging me out of my chair and onto his lap, Olly cradled me as I cried. My charade exposed, I explained, between choking sobs, how I had grossly underestimated the cost of the trip; how I had called home and asked for help to no avail; even how I had blown a week's worth of tips on a swimsuit and a canvas tote I would never get the chance to use.

Holding me closely, he listened and rocked me until the wave passed.

"You know what's weird?" I asked, sniffling. "I think I was looking forward to seeing the ocean most of all."

"That's not weird," he said.

"And the palm trees," I added.

He smirked. "OK, *that's* a little weird."

Despite myself, I laughed.

Snuggled together in one chair, we talked for what felt like hours. The conversation eventually turned to other things. We discussed our plans after graduation, his upcoming interviews, my search for the perfect apartment. But the topic of Jamaica didn't come up again. Having admitted my wrongs and lamented my dashed hopes, the trip and the many exhausting emotions surrounding it became immediate and inconsequential parts of my past.

With the idea of an exotic tropical getaway finally put to rest, I was able to focus instead on an enjoyable Spring Break with Olly. We made plans to visit the Lincoln Park Zoo and the Adler Planetarium, the Museum of Science and Industry, and the Botanical Gardens. We talked about using our student discounts to catch a play at the Ford Center, mapping out a day trip to Lake Geneva, and even taking an overnight hike in the Indiana Dunes.

By the time we finally decided to pack it in for the evening, I was so excited about the week to come that I'd completely forgotten why I had ever wanted to leave home at all.

When Monday arrived, I slept in, ate a leisurely breakfast at the desolate dining hall and then took the scenic route back to my dorm, where Oliver and I had planned to spend some time doing dry runs in preparation for his interviews before catching a movie and grabbing a bite to eat.

But when I returned to my room, I found in Olly's stead, a note tacked to my message board requesting that I go to his place. Armed with the index cards of practice questions he'd given me the day before, I obligingly set out across the abandoned campus to his apartment. There, taped to his door, I found a second note instructing me to meet him on the roof.

My footsteps echoed along the concrete walls of the stairwell as I climbed the five flights to the top of his low-rise. Pushing open the heavy metal access hatch, I clambered over the protective railing and stepped into a most surprising and spectacular scene.

The ground, ordinarily a black mass of peeling tar was covered with golden sand. Seashells lay scattered about a low-sitting kiddy pool brimming with water, and in the two farthest corners of the roof, massive inflated palm trees, wrapped in blinking Christmas lights and tethered to the roof vent pipes, swayed slightly in the breeze.

Courtesy of a jumbled mass of extension cords, space heaters, of every size and make imaginable, were plugged into the outlets located around the roof's low-sitting walls. Strategically situated, they oscillated to create a warm crosscurrent that warded off the mid-March chill.

And lounging in one of two frayed beach chaises at the heart of it all was Oliver. Sporting orange and white Bermuda shorts and a faded green T-shirt, he stood and ushered me over with a broad smile.

"What's all this?" I asked, stepping around a parasol and over a beach ball to reach him.

"It's our own private tropical oasis." He spread his arms wide. "What do you think?"

I smirked. It looked like he had robbed a dollar store. "Very authentic."

Holding up his hand, he motioned for me to stay where I was, while he got into character. Briefly turning his back to me, he slipped on a pair of sunglasses and a motley Rasta tam adorned with faux dreadlocks. "Let me give you a tour of the island," he said with a newly acquired Jamaican accent.

Laughing, I allowed him to lead me to the first of several stations. "Over here, we have the bar." He gestured toward a lopsided card table cluttered with a blender, a bowl of half-melted ice, and a thorough assortment of sodas and juices.

"And over here our five-star beachfront grill," he said, escorting me to the neighboring stand on which he'd set up the hot plate, portable propane stove, and Dutch oven we often used on overnight camp stays.

I smirked. "Classy."

"Across the way, you'll notice our VIP lounge." He positioned me so that I was facing the pair of rickety beach chaises situated in the center of our rooftop escape. A "Reserved" sign, fashioned from the flap of a cardboard box and bearing my name, was propped against the seat next to the one he'd been occupying.

"But the real *pièce de résistance*," he said, pausing dramatically for effect, before pointing down at the round, inflatable pool, "is our spectacular ocean view."

My grin was dubious.

He shrugged. "OK, so it's not the ocean. But feel the water."

Bending, I dipped my fingers in. It was warm.

"And..." He dashed the few steps to a boom box resting nearby in the sand. With the push of a button, crashing waves and squawking seagulls sounded from its speakers. Oliver smiled. "If you close your eyes, it almost feels like you're there."

Turning slowly, I surveyed his handiwork and laughed. God only knew where he'd found so much sand or, even more mystifyingly, how he had managed to get it six stories above the ground. And there was no telling where he'd located the wading pool and inflatable palm tree or who he'd borrowed the space heaters from or when he had found the time to hunt down a soundtrack of beach noises. But the understanding that he had done it all for me, swelled my heart.

"It's perfect," I said, thrusting myself into his arms.

He returned my hug. "There's one more surprise."

252

Reluctantly, I let go and watched as he reached beneath one of the chairs and produced the canvas tote I had relegated to the back of my closet. "Open it," he said.

I complied. Inside was my new bathing suit, price tag still dangling from the strap, flip-flops, sunblock, a disposable camera, and other odds and ends. "How did you get this?" I asked, holding up the purple one-piece.

He smirked. "I have my ways."

"But I saw it in my room just this morning." I shook my head, nonplussed. "When could you have possibly taken it?"

Handing me his keys, he spun me around and started me toward the open hatch. "The only thing you need to concern yourself with is getting changed."

My smile faltered. "Into what?"

"Your bathing suit."

"But it's barely sixty degrees outside!"

He shrugged and pointed to the space heaters oscillating behind us. "We've got warm breezes."

Obediently, albeit questioningly, I made the trek back downstairs to his apartment, where I slipped out of my clothes and into my swimwear. Upon further inspection of the bag, I found a pair of blue jean shorts. After tugging those on, I pilfered a T-shirt from Oliver's dresser drawer and then hurried to rejoin him on the roof.

In my absence, Olly had replaced the crashing waves and squawking seagulls with smooth reggae, applied a white slathering of zinc oxide to his nose and blended us a batch of colorful-looking cocktails.

"Here, put these on," he said, handing me a pair of sunglasses and a tam, both identical to his.

Laughing, I shook my head. "I'm not wearing those."

"No dreads, no tropical paradise," he said, snatching back the cup he'd given me with a menacing smile.

Feigning disgust, I rolled my eyes, but promptly slid on the retro shades and stuffed my hair into the cheesy hat. "Happy?"

Nodding, Olly returned my drink. "Yah, Mon."

Walking the few steps from the bar to the reserved VIP seating area, we eased into our loungers and dipped our feet into the warm ocean.

"So..." Olly gazed at me, his brows arched expectantly. "Is Jamaica everything you hoped it would be?"

"Nope," I said, sipping my cocktail. Lying back, I closed my eyes and let out a contented sigh. "It's even better."

———◆———

For the rest of the week, our secret oasis became a home away from home. When Oliver wasn't off interviewing or we weren't out exploring Chicago's many wondrous attractions, we were relaxing without a care beneath the clear blue sky. And on the one evening that it rained, Oliver, not to be outdone by Mother Nature, schlepped our chaises down to his living room, where we gorged ourselves on jerk chicken and watched movies in our tams and bathing suits into the wee hours of the morning.

By the time students started trickling in from their respective vacations, Cameron and the villa in Jamaica seemed like a foggy memory. And when, upon her arrival, Cameron could do nothing but complain about Montego Bay's inclement weather and bad food, Olly and I, holding tight to our secret, merely exchanged faint smiles and quietly basked in memories too precious for words.

———◆———

"I'll let you have it for ten."

"Sorry?" Dazed, I looked over at the woman whose voice had jerked me back to the present.

"Ten euros," she said, pointing to the tam I hadn't realized I was gripping. "It's a bargain."

"No. Thank you." With an unsteady hand, I returned the hat to the hook on the wall. "I'm just looking."

"All right, eight," she said, hungry for a sell.

"Really." I backed away, bumping into strangers with my packages as I went. "I don't need anything."

"They make great gifts," she called after me.

"I know," I murmured, stepping out of the shop and onto the street. Momentary relief gave way to inexplicable loneliness. "I used to have one just like it."

Thirty-Five

The suite was dark, save for the strips of soft moonlight shimmering through the barren windows of the empty living room. I stood motionless for several tenuous moments—my ear aimed toward the staircase—and listened for any movement from the second floor.

Cooper wasn't there.

Grateful for the solitude, I carried my bags across the vestibule and deposited them beside the coffee table in the master parlor. Switching on the lamp next to the couch, I maneuvered, feet aching, around the battery of shoes I had left lying about the floor earlier that morning and lumbered to my bed, where I was met by a note from Cooper.

In it, he explained that he and his new friends from the beach had met up with the friend he'd made the night before at the casino. After waiting for me until the last possible minute, they had all headed downstairs to catch the hotel's burlesque show. Dinner was to follow and then drinks at a popular bar in nearby Old Nice. My ticket was at Will Call. *Can't wait to see your face,* he'd signed it. *Missing you like crazy.*

With a shake of my head, I crumpled the paper into a tight ball and tossed it into the trashcan. I had no desire, whatsoever, to waste away the remainder of my evening watching complete strangers fawn over Cooper. And I was even less interested in spending the next two hours gazing up at half-naked women flouncing about on stage.

But what I could use—the thing I really wanted—was the sound of a familiar voice.

Rummaging through my purse, I pulled out my wallet and retrieved the calling card I'd purchased earlier that afternoon. From the hotel phone, I carefully dialed the string of numbers printed on the back along with Cameron's direct extension at work, where I knew she would be, thanks to the seven-hour time difference. Holding the handset to my ear, I listened to the ringing on the other end and willed her to answer.

"Snyder & Smith. This is Cameron," she said just as I was about to give up.

"Hey, it's me."

"Bella!"

I frowned. "I wish you wouldn't call me that."

"I see someone still hasn't warmed to her new alter ego," she said with a laugh.

"As it is, I haven't warmed to much of anything—or anyone," I added ruefully.

"Uh-oh." She tsked. "Trouble in paradise already?"

"If by trouble you mean we've spent more time apart than we have together, then yes, there's trouble already."

"Well, what happened?" she asked.

I sighed. "I don't know, when we got here I—"

"Wait, hang on a second. I have to take this other call," Cameron said. Before I could respond, she'd placed me on hold. Classical music filled the dead space on the other end until she returned several minutes later. "OK, sorry about that. You were saying?"

"Just that it's not what I thought it to be."

"What isn't?" she asked.

"This," I said, waving my arm around the room, despite knowing that she couldn't see me. "The private jets and fancy hotels and chauffeured cars. It's not what I expected."

"Which was what exactly?"

Reclining against the mound of pillows neatly arranged along the headboard, I took a moment to consider her question. "I guess I assumed it would be my life, only better. Kind of like going from black and white to Technicolor. But instead it's—"

"I have to put you on hold," she said, abruptly interrupting again. "Save that thought."

Rolling onto my side, I sighed as classical music filtered, once more, through the receiver. A day rarely went by when Cameron, bored and antsy, didn't call me from work. Though I was almost always otherwise engaged, she would occupy me, without interruption, in drawn out conversations over trivial matters like what shade of nail polish she was contemplating for her next manicure or her ever-changing list of top five celebrity crushes. But now, when I actually needed her, she was too busy to talk.

"OK, I'm back," she said, sounding a tad flustered.

"I can call you later, if this is a bad time."

"No, it's fine. I'm just a little swamped at the moment is all. We've got two major campaigns launching this week, and I volunteered to finalize the press kits for both."

"You volunteered?"

She chuckled. "You could at least pretend not to be so surprised."

"Well, I wouldn't be," I said, "If I didn't personally know you as someone who runs away screaming from anything that even remotely resembles responsibility. Now, you're suddenly asking for more of it?"

"I know. I never thought I'd see the day either. But I went to Bible study last night."

"*You* went to Bible study?"

She laughed. "OK, stop doing that."

"Sorry," I said, shaking my head. "I'll try to reel quietly."

She continued. "The discussion was on the Spirit of Excellence and how we should approach everything we do as if it's been assigned to us directly by our Creator. Like, for instance, would you complain about having to go home and cook dinner for your husband after a long day, if your husband was the Almighty Himself?"

Relishing her simple sincerity, I smiled. "Definitely not."

"Exactly!" she said. "Anyway, before we left, one of the study members challenged us to treat a specific area in our lives as though it was a personal service to the Lord for the next thirty days and note the improvements. And that got me to thinking; maybe if I started looking at my job as an opportunity to honor God rather than a tedious chore, I'd stop hating it.

"So this morning, when I realized one of the account supervisors was shorthanded, I offered to fact-check the backgrounders, and the next thing I knew, both teams were asking me to take over their press kits. Which is kind of a big deal," she added, "because they usually only let senior staff handle media relations."

"How exciting!"

"I know," she said. I could hear her smiling. "When I told Olly, he joked that it was only a matter of time before I *was* senior staff."

"You talked to Oliver?"

She hesitated briefly before answering. "About an hour ago."

"How is he?" I asked.

"You would know," she said, a sudden chilliness to her tone, "if you had bothered to call him."

Guiltily, I bit my lip. "You're angry."

"I've been prouder."

"Cam, there was just no way to tell him. I tried."

"No, you didn't," she challenged. "All you had to do was be honest, but instead you ran. To another country. With another guy. Like a big fat coward. None of which, by the way, has added up in your favor."

By that, I knew she meant Oliver was upset. "How bad is it?"

"He's really hurt and a little lost," she said, her words coming haltingly.

Stomach churning, I sat up. "What aren't you telling me?"

The sound of her nervous swallow left a dull aching in my chest. "You've got to figure this out, Mack. And soon." Her tone was pleading. "I used to be so certain that nothing could tear the two of you apart, but your friendship with Oliver is at its breaking point, and if you don't do something, it's liable to crumble under the pressure."

"Did he say something?" I asked. "About us?"

I sensed her reluctance to speak freely. In my absence she'd clearly developed a loyalty to Oliver that would not easily allow her to betray his confidence. "He's got some major decisions ahead of him," she hesitantly divulged. "And I would hate to see him choose the wrong path because it took you too long to realize that you chose the wrong guy."

Hers wasn't, by any stretch, the first warning I'd received about Cooper. Nearly everyone I knew had attempted to discourage the relationship at some point within the past week. But I had refused to believe that something so magical, so sweetly serendipitous, could be a mistake. Instead, I'd chalked up their concerns to the bodings of well-intentioned loved ones who would rather see me sorry and safe than heedless and happy.

Two days in Europe with Cooper, though, had begun to lend credence to their misgivings. He and I were fundamentally different people with radically different interests and markedly different values. Initially, I'd found our distinctness exciting, our compatibility rare. But as time wore on, the two were proving inversely proportional; the more contrarieties I uncovered, the less fitting we seemed. And now, as it were, I was left with little else than Cameron's ominous caution and a sinking sense of dread.

"What would you do?" I asked.

"Find a way to get back to basics," she said. "How to just be Mack and Olly again."

The mere idea made me smile. "Hey, do you remember the last Spring Break before Olly and I graduated?" I asked. "The year you and a bunch of friends decided to go to Montego Bay?"

She groaned as she always did at any mention of the calamitous trip. "What

261

on earth made you think of that?"

"There was this woman selling Rasta tams earlier today," I said. "You know, those hideous hats Olly and I wore everywhere we went that summer. The colorful ones with the dreadlocks attached."

Her second groan was louder than her first. "I forgot all about those ugly things."

"Me, too," I said wistfully. "I wonder whatever happened to mine. I held onto it for years, but it eventually disappeared." Vainly, I tried to recall the last place I'd seen it. "I think I lost it during one of my moves."

Cameron laughed. "It's not lost—unfortunately."

"What do you mean?"

"Oliver has it. He has them both. He told me once they were his most prized possessions." An urgent beep sounded on her end. "Listen, that's my other line." Her tone was apologetic. "I should really get back."

"OK." My sigh was one of disappointment. "Maybe I'll call again in another couple of days."

"You better," she gently ordered. "And don't forget what we talked about."

"I won't," I promised, just before the line went dead.

Returning the receiver to its base, I glanced at the clock on the table beside the lamp. Cooper wouldn't be back for hours, which meant that the rest of the night was mine to do with what I pleased—if only I knew what that was.

I wasn't sleepy, nor did I have much of an appetite. Television was a turnoff because all of the stations aired in French, and the novel I'd been working on had a thin plot and stock characters that hadn't yet managed to hold my interest for more than a few pages.

Having spent most of the day outside sweating beneath the hot sun, I considered christening the clawfoot tub in my bathroom. But I quickly realized that there was something else I wanted to do more.

Hopping off the bed, I made the short trip to my suitcase and unzipped the top pocket. Inside, I felt my way past a curling iron, a bottle of vitamins, my emergency stick of deodorant, and a tube of lotion until I grasped what I was searching for. Steadying myself against the luggage stand, I drew out the pocket Bible I had packed at the last minute.

With a startling thrill, I carried it to the adjoining sitting room and curled up on the couch. The Book, worn from years of use, fell open to Psalms. Carefully, I moved the satin ribbon marker neatly tucked into its centerfold, flipped to the nearest chapter and, for the first time in more weeks than I cared to count, began to read the Word.

Thirty-Six

My eyelids fluttered open with a start. Blinking groggily, I gazed around the sunny room and then down at the chiseled frame perched at the end of my bed.

"I didn't wake you, did I?" Cooper asked. He pointed to a small gift bag on the dresser. "I snuck in to drop that off, but you looked so stunning just lying there, I wound up watching you sleep instead."

My shrug was awkward. I didn't exactly feel stunning with my hair braided into dowdy plaits and my rumpled pajamas twisted around my ripe body. "What time is it?"

"Just after ten," he said.

I nodded and sat up, aware, as I worked to flatten my tousled bangs with the butt of my palm, that he was studying my every movement. Self-consciously, I tucked my knees to my chest and pulled the comforter to my chin. "What's in the bag?" I asked.

"A little something to show you how sorry I am for yesterday." He glanced down at his feet and shrugged. "I should have just gone on the stupid tour."

It wasn't exactly a heartfelt apology, but I appreciated the attempt. "I think things worked out for the best," I said. "I ended up having a great time on my own."

"Right." Frowning dubiously, he eyed the open Bible and loose pages of notes scattered about beside me. "It looks like your evening was real entertaining."

I smiled. "Actually, it was." After devouring the Book of Psalms in one veracious sitting, I'd changed out of my clothes and climbed into bed, where I wound up revisiting my favorite Old Testament stories well through the night and into the wee hours of the morning. I was amazed by the details I'd forgotten, the new lessons I unearthed. Though I fully understood that Scripture was an inspired work of God and that, as such, it had an unparalleled ability to resonate with the Holy Spirit inside of me, I didn't expect to find myself chuckling so earnestly at Adam and Eve's adventures in the Garden of Eden or repeatedly choking up while reading David's trying journey from shepherd to sovereign. "I couldn't tear myself away."

He shook his head. "I just think the Bible's too antiquated to have real relevance anymore."

"But it's not," I assured him. Fervidly, I leaned forward. "Some things never change, no matter how much time passes. Take the prodigal son for instance. Who hasn't screwed up royally at one point or another and desperately needed to be forgiven? Or look at Noah; he reminds us that sometimes, in order to do what's right, we have to find the courage to seem crazy to others. Then there's Moses—perhaps the best example ever that there's a leader in everyone. And don't forget the Messiah Himself! His birth, life, death, and resurrection are proof positive that the best gifts come in the most unassuming packages."

"Speaking of gifts," Cooper said, briskly cutting me off. "Aren't you curious what I got you?"

I sat back, stung by his blatant dismissal. "I guess."

Oblivious to my affront, he retrieved the bag from the dresser and handed it to me. "You'll need them for later," he said, smiling.

"Why, what's later?"

He demurred. "You have to wait and see."

I held in a sigh. Cooper's flashy, overly elaborate surprises were proving to be more stressful than they were enjoyable.

"Trust me; you'll like this," he said, reading my slumped shoulders and long face with a hurt tilt of his head. "I think I may have finally figured out a way to mesh both of our interests."

"How?" I asked.

He pointed at the bag in my lap. "Consider that your first clue."

Humoring him, I reached inside and extracted a wide black case. At Cooper's prodding, I opened it and discovered a clownishly large pair of bejeweled sunglasses tucked neatly beneath a protective velvet cloth.

"They're Salvatores!" he exclaimed in response to my blank expression. "An early sample from his fall collection."

My indifference was thinly veiled. "No kidding."

"Technically, those aren't even on the market yet," he said, his chest poked out proudly. "I know a lot of women who would gladly swim the English Channel to get their hands on a pair."

Not as gladly as I would swim it to get rid of them, I thought, examining the farcical shades with a grimace. "You shouldn't have, but thank you."

Bending down, Cooper planted a kiss on my temple. "There's more to come."

My smile was taut.

"You should probably start getting ready," he said, rounding the corner out of the room. Moments later, I heard the door close. But not before he casually declared, "We're due at the airport in less than an hour."

Thirty-Seven

Waiting for us at the Côte d'Azur International Airport was a helicopter—blades spinning, hatch open, pilot primed and ready to go.

Exiting the car that had shuttled us to the helipad, I used one hand to grip my cardigan and the other to try to subdue my hair, which was swirling wildly in the strong winds that were being stirred up by the enormous aircraft. "What's going on?" I shouted over the noise.

"I'm taking you to Monte Carlo!" Cooper said, smiling as he ushered me toward the idling five-seater.

A waiting steward helped us climb up and buckle in, then handed us both headsets equipped with boom microphones that allowed us to communicate with each other and the pilot, who welcomed us on board.

Fixated by how his hands glided expertly across the control panels, I watched him push buttons, flip switches, and turn knobs until finally the helicopter rose with a gentle jerk. Weightlessly, it hovered for several seconds before beginning its ascent into the sky.

If I thought Nice was a sight to behold from the ground, the aerial view was nothing short of celestial. It became abundantly clear, as we made our way across the densely inhabited mountains and over the shimmering Mediterranean

Sea, why Cooper had given me sunglasses. As we traveled, bright sunbeams reflected off the radiant white clouds and into the windows, flooding the tiny cabin with light.

Removing my new Salvatores from their case, I hurriedly slipped them on and returned my gaze to the picturesque panorama below. It was a spectacle of snaking shoreline and gracefully gliding sailboats, terracotta rooftops, and narrow calanques.

I'd always assumed that when the time came for me to travel the world, I would do it with Oliver at my side. Fresh out of college with little more than each other and impermeable idealism to fuel our hopes, we'd spent many a countless hour planning the places we would one day go, the exotic trips we would someday take.

Over the years, though, our talks of hiking the Himalayas and scuba diving in the Indian Ocean were replaced with complaints of conference calls and deadlines, depositions and quarterly reports, meager pay and evil bosses. Until eventually, we stopped dreaming altogether.

Watching as a caravan of kayaks dawdled across the water toward a secluded inlet, I smiled. If Oliver, an active outdoor-lover, were sitting next to me, he would insist we find where to rent our own set of paddle boats and then map out a gumptious excursion around the entire south of France. Eyes closed, I could almost see his cheery face—almost hear his animated voice going on and on about the earth's stupefying vastness and the splendor of God's creation.

Meanwhile, Cooper's adventurous spirit was dependent on five-star resorts and first-class service, his appreciation for the wonders of nature limited to what quick glimpses he bothered to spare from behind the tinted windows of big yachts and fancy cars.

I looked over at him. Blackberry clutched in his hand, he glanced down at the diamond-encrusted watch strapped to his wrist and anxiously bounced a knee. Sighing, I rested my forehead against the metal pane.

"Takes your breath away, doesn't it?" Cooper asked, his tinny voice filtering through my headset.

My gaze trained outside, I nodded. "When I consider your heavens, the work of your fingers, the moon and the stars which you have set in place, I wonder what is man that You are mindful of him?"

"What's that, a poem?"

I smiled. "Sort of. It's part of a Psalm—one of my favorites actually. I sometimes forget how infinitesimal we are in the grand scheme of the universe. But being up here is an awesome reminder of just how small we really are, how insignificant and undeserving."

When he didn't respond, I turned to look at him. The muscles in his jaw tensed. "What's with you today? Why are you so preachy?"

"Sorry?" I asked, taken aback by his obvious irritation.

"Earlier, you were going on about life lessons and Bible characters and now it's talk of being inferior and feeling unworthy." He shook his head. "Can't you just try to enjoy this?"

It took me a moment to find my voice. "That's what I thought I was doing."

His shoulders eased. "I didn't mean for it to come out like that," he said, reaching for my hand. "I just think you need to learn how to lighten up a little. You people are always so doom-and-gloom."

"You people?"

"You know what I mean." He shrugged. "The problem with religion is that the more you believe in God, the less able you are to appreciate what He's supposedly created."

"Are you saying you think I'd be better off without my faith?"

He sighed. "I'm saying there's a time and place for everything, including God. And the sooner you recognize that, the happier we'll both be."

I nodded, uncertain how else to respond, and lowered my eyes from his face to our fingers entwined on the seat between us. They were misaligned. And in that instant, I understood with unsettling certainty just how stuck between two worlds I had become.

———•———

Less than ten minutes after we'd taken off in Nice, we landed in Monaco.

And, as was Cooper's custom, he'd arranged for a car to meet us upon arrival.

To my delight, Monte Carlo was a series of steep rolling hills flanked by pristinely-lined trees, closely-packed homes, and tiers of staggered mid-, high-, and low-rises butted against a boat-filled port and back-dropped by the gorgeous snowcapped Maritime Alps.

Like Nice, there was a plethora of shops and restaurants to tease the senses and an ever-bustling crowd of festive vacationers to keep them filled.

Though I wasn't expecting to visit Monaco and didn't know a great deal about it, I did recognize its legendary Yacht Basin as we cruised past it en route to a destination that Cooper, despite my persistent pestering, would not divulge.

In time, we came to a stop on the Avenue des Beaux-Arts in front of a quiet area that I would later come to know as, "The Golden Circle"—a notoriously exclusive section of town containing only the haute-couture boutiques of the world's most coveted designers and premier jewelers.

Exiting the car, I followed Cooper as he led us along a winding maze of cobblestone paths with a certainty that told me he'd walked them many times before. Eventually, we came to a brightly landscaped courtyard bordered by stately sets of glass doors. Each ostentatiously boasted the well-known moniker of a different high-end clothier.

"Almost there," Cooper said, heading past the collection of swanky stores toward an inconspicuous boutique at the farthest end of the square. Unlike the surrounding shops, it bore only a blank black awning over its open door.

The soles of Cooper's tennis shoes squeaked sharply against the gleaming marble floors as he strode in. Without hesitation, he breezed through the empty lobby, bypassed the unmanned reception desk, and crossed under an ornate stone archway that gave entry to an empty room.

My suspicions rose as I took in the angled armchairs, the readied rack of tape measures and weighted clips, the shallow steps leading to a circular platform in front of an enormous, three-way mirror.

"Hello?" he called into the stillness. "Anyone home?"

"You're late," a voice said, seconds before the statuesque woman who belonged to it emerged from a wall of heavy velvet drapes I hadn't realized was there. I studied her as she floated to Cooper, her arms spread wide for an embrace.

She was older, though her years were subtle—visible only in the dark spots speckling her wrinkled hands and the faint lines that delicately framed her eyes and mouth. There was a manner of importance about her, a sureness in her demeanor. Airily, she turned to me with a toss of her hair and, propping her spindly fingers against her slim hips, waited for Cooper to make our acquaintance.

"Genevieve, this is Bella," he said. Something about his swaggering tone and sweeping arm made me feel more like an item being presented than a person being introduced.

"Pleasure," I said, extending a hand.

Promptly ignoring it, she grabbed me by the shoulders and planted a kiss on both of my cheeks. Unlike the disingenuous air kisses I'd received from others over the last few days, Genevieve's leathery lips made contact with skin. Despite myself, I cringed at the wet rings of saliva left to dry on my face after she'd pulled away.

"Welcome. I've been looking forward to working with you ever since I got Cooper's call," she said with a viscous accent that made her difficult to understand.

"I'm sure I would say the same." I looked at Cooper, who seemed to have forgotten that he still hadn't told me where we were or what we were doing. "If I knew why I was here."

Cooper thrust his eyes to the ceiling and shook his head, as though to suggest that anyone with a little ingenuity and a bit of common sense would have figured it out by now. "Genevieve tailor-makes all of my suits," he explained. "She usually only holds private fittings for, you know…" Letting his sentence trail, he tucked his square chin to his muscular chest and raised an evocative brow.

I did know. She, like everyone else in his small, privileged world, only bent backward for significant people—people who could afford to pay what it cost to be fawned over like the gods they'd convinced themselves they were.

"But when I explained the situation and who you are to me," he continued, "she graciously agreed to help you select a dress for the premiere in London."

My stomach curdled with disappointment. It was our last day in France and we had just traveled by helicopter to one of the most beautiful, most frequented cities in all of Europe. There were streets to stroll, foods to sample, attractions to visit, but instead, I was stuck shopping.

Even more frustrating, I already had a gown to wear to the premiere. It was the same dress I had worn to the gala in L.A.—the night Cooper and I first met. I'd packed it thinking it held sentimental value for us both. But that was clearly a foolish assumption. If my trip with Cooper had taught me anything so far, it was that he wasn't sentimental and he didn't value much beyond his own immediate wishes.

Their gazes fixed on me, Cooper and Genevieve quietly awaited my response. And not just any response, I could tell. They were waiting for me to express my profound appreciation, to acknowledge the magnitude of their favor with a befitting display of gratitude.

"Thank you." I bowed my head. "This is really generous of you both."

Cooper nodded in agreement, while Genevieve, arms folded and lips pursed, began to circle me like a vulture sizing up its prey. "Great figure," she finally said. "Nice posture. Very good proportions. I think we can do a lot."

Pleased, Cooper smiled. "Then, I'll leave you ladies to it." He turned toward the nearby bank of empty chairs, while Genevieve and I disappeared behind the curtained wall.

On the other side was a sprawling studio, brightly lit and outfitted with nothing but racks of clothes and rows of shoes. At Genevieve's command, I waited up front, while she nimbly navigated the cramped makeshift aisles, pulling the items she wanted to try first.

"I like this color for you," she said, thrusting a plum slip-dress at me upon her return. "It compliments your warm skin tone."

We stood facing each other for several uncertain seconds. "Well, come on," she urged. Her sigh was impatient. "Put it on so I can see."

"Here?" I asked, aghast.

The corners of her mouth turned up into an amused smirk. "Believe me; you don't have anything I haven't seen a thousand times before."

I tightened my grip on my cardigan and silently begged to differ.

"Here, let me help you," she said, her tolerance for my modesty spent. Positioning my arms above my head, she undressed me like a mother would a child. Cold and naked, save for my underwear, I waited—knees turned inward, arms crossed over my bare chest—for her to gather the dress and slip it over my head.

It was short—very short. And it only felt shorter after I'd stepped into the sky-high heels she placed in front of me. "I like it," she said, examining my reflection in the mirror. "It's sophisticated, yet flirtatious."

"Maybe a little too flirtatious," I said, crossing my ankles to shut out the air drafting between my thighs.

Her glare was icy. "Why not let Cooper decide?"

Teetering behind her, I retraced our steps to the waiting area where we'd left Cooper. Predictably, he was slouched in one of the armchairs typing on his Blackberry. His thumbs paused midair when he looked up. "Where have you been hiding those legs?" he asked.

"She doesn't like it," Genevieve rushed to announce.

Cooper sat back. "Why not?"

Avoiding Genevieve's unrelenting stare, I shrugged. "I didn't say I didn't like it. I just think it's kind of short."

"I can take out the hem," Genevieve said, her tone disapproving. "But that would ruin the silhouette."

Cooper took a moment to consider the options. "Let's see her in something a little longer," he said.

Her instructions clear, Genevieve returned me to the studio, where she promptly stripped me down and zipped me into a different dress. This one, a silver halter-gown, dragged the floor. It also had no back to speak of and a neckline that plunged to my navel. I might have liked it, were I not convinced it was one piece of double-stick tape away from being a wardrobe malfunction.

"See how it accentuates your shoulders?" she asked, lifting my hair off my neck and turning me sideways so I could better appreciate the view.

My lesson learned the first time around, I nodded and suggested that we go show Cooper. To my relief, his nose crinkled. "Too sparkly," he said, dismissing the dress, but not before stealing a lingering glance at the cleft of bare skin between my breasts. "Something simpler."

Genevieve nodded and we retreated, once more, behind the curtain wall.

As a woman, I'd spent my fair share of days shopping—more than my fair share, if I included the countless afternoons I'd fallen victim to Cameron's compulsive spending. And yet, I was not prepared for the intense energy, the prolonged, focused concentration and effort that would be required of me to search for one measly dress.

As two hours turned to three and three to five, my world became a pastiche of cuts and fabrics I never knew existed. Notch bodices and ruche satin, silk organza and scalloped lace, tulle underlay, taffeta trim, crepe lining, corkscrew hems, chiffon ruffles, bugle beading, accordion pleats. It was enough to give me a migraine.

Still, Cooper managed to find something wrong with absolutely everything I modeled for him. Some were too poofy, a few were too bland; a couple didn't show enough skin, while several didn't leave enough to the imagination. One was too bright, another simply unflattering. And a number of them, he'd seen on fellow actors at past premieres. To all of the others, he simply shrugged disinterestedly between text messages and said, "Not it."

By the tenth dress, I was ready to settle on anything. In fact, I would have gone to the premiere in a burlap sack, if it meant parting ways with Genevieve and spending what was left of the day enjoying the city before we were forced to head back to Nice.

But my hope of taking in a few sites eventually sank with the sun, which began its descent behind Monaco's golden mountains around the same time I ambled out in the black jersey sheath that Genevieve had paired with red pumps and an alligator belt.

"Too casual," Cooper said, shooting down the outfit before I'd even managed to climb the shallow steps to the carpeted platform. "I don't want you to feel underdressed."

Wordlessly, I returned to the studio, where Genevieve was waiting for his verdict. I shook my head. "Too casual."

She sighed. The hours had bonded us in common misery.

Kicking off my pumps, I joined her beside the racks of dresses we hadn't yet searched. An entire afternoon of catering to Cooper's very particular fashion sense had given us a fairly good idea of which garments were entirely out of the question, but every once in a while, we lucked across something we thought was worth a shot.

"How about this one?" I asked, holding up a delicate-looking dress I'd found tucked between a hideous tiered jumper and the sequined bolero that had been made to go with it.

Genevieve shrugged. "Why not?"

Carrying it over to the mirror, she helped me put it on. The silk felt cool against my skin. "It's a little big on you," she said, swiftly pinching and pinning fabric until it draped flawlessly. "But you wear it well."

Fingering the crumb-catcher bodice, I turned to one side to appreciate the low, V-cut back and then to the other to admire the playful slit that flashed just the right amount of leg when I moved.

Sliding into a simple pair of sling-backs, I crossed my fingers, took a deep breath, and made the well-worn trip back to the waiting area. When Cooper saw me, his cell phone fell to his lap, and I knew we had finally done it.

"That's the one!" he said.

They were the words I'd been waiting all day to hear. But I soon discovered that finding what we came for did little in the way of getting us out of the boutique. The selection of the dress, it turned out, was just the first step in a series of many. It had to be steamed, then marked for tailoring, then registered, then purchased. Then, arrangements had to be made to have it shipped to the hotel in London where we would be staying for the premiere.

By the time we exchanged kisses with Genevieve and made the winding trek back to the car, the harbor had been set aglow by the soft twinkling of the city lights and the lush mountainsides had been devoured by the atramentous sky.

Unbeknownst to me, Cooper had arranged an intimate dinner for the two of us. Sitting beneath the stars at one of Monte Carlo's famed waterfront restaurants, we sampled cundiun, barbagiuan, and other Monégasque delicacies.

And afterward, when he suggested an evening stroll through Fontvieille Park, I willingly agreed.

The car ride to the heliport was marked by a calm serenity, as was our return flight to Nice. We talked easily and steadily on the short trip back to the resort, and when he took my hand in the elevator, I didn't pull away. Nor did I deny him a kiss in the suite's vestibule, where we eventually said goodnight.

It wasn't until I was alone in my room that I finally gave in to the numbing uneasiness gnawing at me. And it wasn't until I climbed into bed and turned off the lights that I realized just how ready I was to go home.

Thirty-Eight

"You're being ridiculous," Cooper said, tossing his half-eaten toast down on his plate.

I sipped my orange juice, unmoved by his outburst. "Why is it ridiculous?"

"Because this place is world-renowned. And they bent over backward to clear a slot for us, when people usually have to make appointments months in advance."

"So go, then," I said. "You don't need me to be there."

"But it's a couple's massage," he argued. "They're expecting both of us."

Pushing my chair back from the table, I shrugged. "I'm sure they'll manage."

"I don't get it," he said, following me inside from the villa's patio, where we'd taken a late breakfast. "Most women would love a day at the spa."

"Well, not this woman." Sighing, I flopped onto the couch. "What's the problem? I thought we talked about this."

Determined not to have a repeat of our stint in Nice, I'd explained to Cooper before we ever left for Italy that I would be taking a different approach to our trip from that point on. There would be no more seaside lounging or all-day spending sprees—not for me, anyway. I was going to take full advantage of the rest of our week in Europe and I was going to do it on my terms—even if that meant we'd have to spend some of our time apart.

He'd said he understood, but no sooner had we unpacked our bags in Milan, than he started secretly masterminding ways for us to spend every waking moment together. It might not have been quite so irritating if only he had planned activities that we would've both enjoyed. But as it was, I'd wasted one afternoon grudgingly lounging by the pool and the other watching him buy clothes.

"You said you'd be fine with us taking time apart from each other to do our own thing," I said. "But it's our last day here before we leave for London and I still haven't done one thing I want to do."

"That's not true. What do you call what we did yesterday?"

I frowned. "Shopping—cleverly disguised as sightseeing."

After announcing that I'd booked a guided tram tour of the city, Cooper informed me that he had already arranged to take me to Via Monte Napoleone. He'd promised beautiful buildings, treasured landmarks, and a healthy dose of Milanese culture. But I quickly discovered, once we got there, that Via Monte Napoleone was the equivalent of Nice's Avenue des Beaux-Arts. It was where the trendsetters went to drop insane amounts of money on designer threads. And while there was a whimsical little café that served amazing espresso and an eyeful of classical Italian architecture to keep me intermittently occupied, the rest of my cultural immersion began with Dolce and ended in Gabana.

"How about this," he said, easing into the chair adjacent to me. "We'll keep our appointment and immediately afterward, we'll have a car take us straight to the train station."

I shook my head. I'd already done my research, purchased my Metro ticket, marked my map, and charged my camera. There was no way he was talking me out of my daytrip to Stresa. "I'm not going to the spa, Cooper. And that's final."

He sat back, defeated by the stubborn glint in my eye. "So I don't get to see you at all today. Is that what you're saying?"

"You could come with me," I said, certain he would decline my offer. Public transportation, long hikes, and historical monuments—or "crusty ruins" as he'd so dimly dubbed them in Nice—weren't his ideas of a good time.

"Fine." His sigh was resigned.

"What do you mean, fine?" I asked, my pulse spiking in response to my consternation.

He shrugged. "You win. I'll skip the spa and go to Stresa like you want."

"I didn't say I *wanted* you to go." Wounded, his chin jerked back. I instantly regretted my brusqueness. "What I mean is, you shouldn't feel like you have to come with me. I was just offering as, sort of, a last resort. If you'd rather get a massage, that's what you should do."

"I'd rather be with you," he said, moving to the sofa. "Tomorrow we're off to London and after that, home. This may be one of our last opportunities to be alone—just the two of us."

"Just the two of us," I echoed. It didn't have quite the same ring as when I'd said it on the beach in Chicago—before we'd actually embarked on our transcontinental adventure. I had no way of knowing then that Cooper was so trying, his temperament so high-maintenance.

Among its many advantages, my day-trip to Stresa was supposed to give me a badly needed break from his relentless beleaguering. But now, faced with the possibility of being stuck together for the rest of the day, I was seriously considering rethinking my plans.

"I know. Hard to believe it'll all be over soon," Cooper said, clearly misinterpreting my dread for nostalgia. "Or that two people could make each other this happy." Scooting closer, he cupped my face in his hands and slowly leaned in for a kiss.

Reflexively, my muscles tensed. Ever since our second night in Nice, my attraction toward him had been gradually, yet steadily waning. Outwardly, he was the same guy who'd approached me at the gala in Los Angeles—the same Adonis whose smoldering eyes and come-to-bed smile made men jealous and women swoon. But inwardly, I was changing.

Whether it was because of the conversation I'd had with Cameron or the fact that I had begun to rekindle my relationship with Christ or simply that the more I grew to know Cooper, the less I grew to like him, I wasn't sure. But somewhere along the way, my feelings for him had shifted.

Meanwhile, I was having rich Bible studies and deep prayer times, the bulk of which revolved around how to fix the many mistakes I'd made while running amiss.

When I was a child, while on one of our annual family trips to the beach, I fell asleep in my inner tube. With four rambunctious kids and a husband who tended to play more than he supervised, my mother didn't notice as the gentle current slowly pushed me out to sea. By the time I woke, the shore was gone, the sun was fading, and I was surrounded by nothing but an inky blue mass. Sheer terror gripped me as I bobbed helplessly in open waters. My imagination turned every lapping wave, every gust of wind, into a circling shark or a hungry killer whale. Searching the distance for land to no avail, I began to cry. I was convinced that I was too lost—too far gone—and that even if people were aware that I was missing, they would never be able to find me.

Spiritually, I'd fallen asleep and been set astray in a similar way. I didn't know, at the time, how soundly I'd been dozing or how far I was allowing myself to drift from God. But I felt like, after weeks of floating aimlessly, I'd awakened to a false version of myself...trapped in a foreign country...with a man I hardly knew. It was unnerving, but not nearly as distressing as the thought that my negligence may have cost me my best friend.

Suddenly, every step I took toward Cooper seemed like a step away from Oliver. Every touch of Cooper's hand, every brush of his lips, felt like an insult to God.

Not long after I'd found myself adrift in my inner tube, beach patrol came to my rescue. Hoisting me onto their boat, the two officers wrapped me in a blanket, rushed me back to shore, and reunited me with my relieved family. Over the next several months and, eventually, years, the ordeal faded from a harrowing experience into a cautionary tale. But it forever left me with a haunting understanding of the grave consequences of human peccability, as well as a sincere appreciation for the redemptive nature of second chances.

God's mercy I had received upon repentance, but I wouldn't know until I got back home if everyone else I'd disappointed would be as willing to forgive and forget. In the interim, I was firm in my decision not to do anything that might further hurt the people I loved or damage the life I'd so foolishly discarded.

"We'd better get going, if we want to make the next train," I said, turning my cheek to Cooper just before his mouth met mine. Wriggling free from his hold, I stood and grabbed the small purse I'd readied with maps, euros, a Metro pass, and my camera. "You're sure you want to do this?"

His forehead rippled suspiciously, and for a moment I thought he was going to question my standoffishness, but to my relief he simply joined me with a smile and said, "Stresa, here we come."

We got as far as the sidewalk before Cooper started to complain.

First he carried on about the crowds, then, once seated on the subway, he bemoaned the scent of the car. Granted, both did possess a rather pungent bouquet of body odor and bad breath, but neither merited the fuss he made for the better part of six stops and two transfers.

"What was the point of that again?" he asked as we stepped out of the Metro and onto the platform.

"We had to get to the train station somehow." Pausing, I consulted the signs posted along the wall before navigating us toward the exit. "This was the fastest, easiest option."

"How was that easier than taking the car and driver I hired?" he asked, following me through the maze of underground tunnels.

Mounting the stairs out of the Metro, we emerged on a busy street corner. "This is how you really get to know a city," I said, retrieving the PopOut map I'd tucked into my pocket.

He rolled his eyes as I shook it open. "Could you be any more of a tourist?"

"How else do you propose we find our way?"

"A taxi," he said.

Pinpointing our location, I quickly figured out the route to our destination. "No need. The Milano Centrale is just a few blocks up."

Sighing, he plodded alongside me, dragging his feet like an ornery child. We arrived minutes later. And, after buying Cooper a snack and finding him a place to sit, I hunted down the booking booths and bought our tickets.

There was a peaceful stretch of silence while Cooper ate his chocolate bigne and we leisurely made our way to our platform. But that ended the instant he took the last swig of his water and promptly began questioning how much longer it would be until the train came.

"You're not going to believe this," I said, making a show of rifling through my purse. "But I forgot to bring an extra set of batteries."

He shrugged. "We'll buy some when we get there."

"But my camera's dead and I really wanted to take pictures of the countryside on the way up."

He used the back of his hand to wipe the sweat from his forehead. "Well, what do you want me to do about it?"

"I think I saw a gift shop by the main entrance. Would you mind getting me a couple packs of Double A's?" I asked. "And maybe you should grab another bottle of water while you're at it. You look hot."

"Yeah, that's probably not a bad idea," he said standing. "I'll be back in a few."

I nodded and watched with a grateful sigh as he maneuvered through the turnstile and disappeared into the crowd.

Thirty-Nine

"I think it's just up here a little ways," I said, pointing over the hill ahead of us.

Cooper groaned. "You said that ten minutes ago."

I turned to see him trudging several paces behind me. His T-shirt collar was stained with sweat, and his bottle of water—the third he'd guzzled since we'd arrived in Stresa—was empty.

"Do you want to take another rest?"

"Where?" Throwing his arms out to the side, he revealed two wet rings beneath his armpits.

I looked around at the gorgeous hydrangeas and rose bushes abloom with a profusion of colorful bulbs, the boundless stretch of meticulously manicured lawns, the tranquil waters of Lake Maggiore. There was an abundance of natural beauty, but nowhere for Cooper to sit.

"We've only got two options at this point," I said. "We can either push on or turn back."

"And do what?" he asked. "The train to Milan doesn't come for hours."

I shrugged. "We passed a couple of really nice cafés by the lakefront. You could grab a bite to eat and escape the heat, while I go ride the cableway."

He shook his head, clearly no more satisfied by the prospect of being left behind than he was about continuing on. "I told you this trip was a bad idea."

"I'm sorry," I said. "I had no idea you…" *were such a prima donna,* seemed unduly harsh. "Would have such a horrible time."

"Who wouldn't?" he asked. "There are a million people and it's a thousand degrees outside. Not to mention all of the hills. You can't walk twenty yards without climbing Mount Kilimanjaro."

I glanced at the gentle slope in the distance and smirked. "Dramatic much?"

"My point is, if you had listened to me, we could be at a topnotch spa right now receiving the royal treatment. But instead we're here, melting in the middle of nowhere."

Indignant, I folded my arms. "How is it you can't handle a little sun and the occasional knoll, but you somehow manage to work out three hours a day?"

"One word," he said. "Air conditioning."

"That's two words." I glared. "Not like it matters. Either way, it's more words than I plan to waste on any more of this conversation." Spinning on my heels, I resumed my trek toward the cableway.

I'd woken up that morning with serious thoughts of going home early. Cooper was becoming less appealing, while I was becoming more discom- posed, and, with the exception of my rogue excursion in Nice, our trip had been reduced to a veritable rotation of eating, shopping, and lounging.

Though I would've had to pay through the nose to book a flight on such short notice, and while I only had a different set of troubles waiting for me back in Chicago, I had nearly talked myself into making the arrangements. But then I thought of my witness to Cooper.

For most of the short time that we'd known each other, I had behaved like a woman with no scruples. Within hours of our meeting, we had kissed, within hours of that we had spent an entire night alone with each other, and within days of that we had flown halfway around the world together. And to make matters worse, I'd done it all while blowing off my work obligations and alienating my friends and family.

I couldn't bear to leave Cooper with that impression of me. Or, more crucially, leave him with such a misleading example of Christ at work in someone's life.

Convicted, I sighed and slowed my pace. During my devotional, I had vowed to use the remainder of our time in Europe to be a living example of God's love for Cooper. I was off to a poor start.

Turning around, I retraced my steps and followed the path back over the hill, where I spotted Cooper sulking beneath a tree. "Speak through me, Father," I quietly prayed.

He kept his eyes down as I drew near and joined him in the shade. "I don't want to fight," I said, lowering myself on the ground next to him.

Absently flicking a blade of grass, he shrugged. "Could have fooled me."

"I know. I'm sorry. I let my frustration get the better of me."

"I don't see why you're frustrated. I'm the one who got dragged out here against my wishes."

That wasn't true. In actuality I'd offered—practically begged—for him to keep his spa appointment. But pointing out that I hadn't wanted him to come in the first place would only add insult to his injury.

Gently, I bumped my shoulder against his. "I hate that you hate this. And if there was any way I could get us back to Milan sooner, I would. But like you said, the next train doesn't come for another few hours. So the only thing I know to do is to try to make the best of it.

"You're hot, I'm hungry, and according to this," I said, unfolding the map of Stresa I'd plucked from the information desk at the depot, "we're less than a half-mile's walk to the cableway." His gaze shadowed my index finger as it traced the short journey from Point A to Point B.

"The view on the way up is supposed to be breathtaking," I continued. "And the brochures I read mentioned a restaurant at the mid-stop. I'd love it if you would ride to the top and have lunch with me." Straightening my back in a posture of sincerity, I gave him my best attempt at the scout's honor. "I promise to be on my best behavior."

Grinning, he nodded at my spread fingers. "That's the Vulcan salute from Star Trek."

"I'm not sure which is worse," I said, frowning at the faulty gesture. "The fact that I didn't know the difference or the fact that you did."

He laughed. "It's pretty sad either way."

Tilting my head, I smiled. "So what do you say? Can we keep going?"

Standing, he wiped the grass from his pants and offered me his hand. I took it and together we continued to walk.

If Cooper had any more complaints, he kept them to himself. I, in the meantime, made a point of keeping our pace easy and our conversation light. The tension between us broken, we made it to the cableway a short while later without any further upsets. Once there, we bought our tickets, purchased a couple of bottled waters from a lone vending machine planted by the restrooms, and then climbed the several flights of stairs that separated us from the loading pier.

"This is kind of cool," Cooper conceded as we watched the yellow cable car slowly approach. It ended its descent down the mountain with a soft lurch in front of the crowded platform. The doors slid open and the driver emerged, microphone in hand. After dispensing a litany of instructions—in several different languages—he collected our passes and invited us onboard.

Cooper and I piled in along with everyone else, and shuffled our way to the back of the coach, where we were fortunate enough to get two spots beside one of the windows. The air in the car was thick and hinted of the same unpleasant aroma as the Metro. Instinctively, I braced for another of Cooper's snide comments. But he only coughed and turned an attentive eye to the conductor, who promptly began to pelt us with interesting facts about the city's history.

The ride was slow and jerky, but inspiring. Suspended hundreds of feet in the air, it felt like we were flying. With my camera poised, I captured the picturesque splendor: Lakes Maggiore and Orta, the classic majesty of the Swiss Alps, and the elegant sublimity of Monte Rosa, as well as some of the simpler, more unexpected scenes we came upon. I was especially taken with a small village situated between a knot of gently rolling hills. The cluster of cottages seemed to dangle precariously from the mountainside, while bearded goats roamed the wild meadows and white linens pinned to clotheslines flapped languidly in the wind. The setting belonged on a postcard.

Before we were ready, the driver announced that we had reached Alpino— the mid-point between Stresa and Mottarone. As the cable car came to a stop and the doors slid open, he informed us that another coach would arrive in an hour to take us up the remainder of the way. Encouraged to use the time to explore the area, Cooper and I opted to take the short hike to the nearby Botanical Gardens Alpinia before we ate lunch.

But only a few paces past the first bend, he got spooked by the wasps hovering in the tall grass covering the overgrown path. "I don't think I can do this," he said, swatting at imaginary bugs.

I was tempted to be irritated by what I perceived as his lack of effort, but I was quickly learning that patience was my greatest weapon and my only defense against Cooper's exhausting personality.

"You want to head back to the restaurant instead?" I asked.

On his nod, we aborted our hike and mere minutes later we were being seated at a table inside a charming rustic cabin.

"This isn't so bad," he said, settling into one of the hand-carved chairs.

I nodded and cast a longing gaze out of the window at a couple heading up the trail we'd just come down. "I'm glad you like it."

"I feel like such a jerk." Sighing, he watched with me as the man and woman disappeared behind a hill. "Clearly, you're really into all this stuff and I'm ruining it for you."

I smiled. "I wouldn't say it's ruined, so much as drastically altered."

Chuckling, he shook his head. "I bet you wished you'd come alone."

"Not alone," I said, instantly thinking of Olly. "But these sorts of things are definitely a lot more enjoyable if everyone involved likes nature."

"We can give the Botanical Gardens another shot if you want."

"That's sweet," I said, my smile appreciative. "But I don't know that you'd be quite so solicitous if you knew the real reason why I wanted to come up here."

His eyes narrowed. "Try me."

"Mottarone has these hiking paths," I explained. "They're legendary. And there are guides that hike groups up and down the mountain."

"And you wanted to hike down," he said.

I shrugged. "It just seemed like one of those once-in-a-lifetime opportunities that I shouldn't let pass me by."

There was a brief lull as he sipped his water. "Then, we should do it."

"What?" Laughing, I shook my head. "No offense, but if you couldn't make it a quarter of a mile to the Gardens, you certainly won't make it down Monte Mattorone."

Feigning despair, he gripped his chest. "You doubt my ability to see it through?"

I grinned. "Not so much as your ability to see it through in one piece."

"I deserved that. I haven't exactly shown you anything to suggest otherwise," he said. "I don't know what it is. I've just never been a big fan of the outdoors."

"I didn't used to be, either," I confessed. "But in college, my best friend got me into hiking and then camping and before I knew it, I was hooked."

"Why? What's so great about it?"

I shrugged. "For the most part, it's therapeutic. There's something healing about disconnecting for a while and escaping to a quiet space. Years back, I was part of a Bible study that took monthly hikes at Sag Valley. We'd start out in a group, but eventually break off along the way and find our own private spots to commune with God. I used to love to bring my Bible with me and read how He made the earth, while I was actually holding pieces of it in my hand.

"I guess that's what's so great about it," I said. "I never feel as close to my Creator as when I'm surrounded by His raw creation."

Cooper's gaze was hard as he sat back in his chair with a disgusted sigh. "Why do you have to do that? Why do you have to turn everything into a lecture about God?"

"I wasn't lecturing. You asked me a question."

"About camping," he said, his words clipped with anger. "And you, for some reason, took that as an opportunity to try to shove Jesus down my throat—again."

I shook my head, nonplussed. "Am I missing something?"

"You're like a broken record lately, and frankly, I'm sick of it. We can't go anywhere or do anything without you bringing up your faith."

"That's because my faith is a huge part of who I am. It colors the way I see my world."

"Well, it doesn't color the way I see mine," he said. "I wish you would just keep all of that religious nonsense to yourself."

"First off, it's not nonsense. And second, why should I have to censor myself?"

"You don't hear me pumping you full of my beliefs."

"What beliefs?" I scoffed. "Your unerring trust in the cosmos?"

"It's better than your blind hope in a dead guy."

"That's where you're wrong," I said, shaking my head. My tone was calm, sure. "He's very much alive. I feel Him everywhere I go. I witness Him in everything I see. And I'm sorry that offends you. But I don't know another way to be. I don't know how to change it, and honestly, I wouldn't want to even if I could.

"I am who I am," I said. "And maybe the more important issue here isn't whether or not I'm right, but whether or not I'm right for you. Maybe the bigger truth in all of this is that you and I just aren't meant to be." Tossing my napkin onto my empty plate, I reached for my purse.

"Bella, wait." He placed his hand over mine. "Where are you going? We haven't even ordered yet."

I shook loose of his grip. "I'm not hungry."

"Well, what about the hike down?" he asked, a hint of pleading in his voice.

"I'm not up for it anymore," I said. The legs of my chair scraped loudly against the floor as I pushed it away from the table.

"Don't you at least want to visit the Gardens while we're here?"

"There's nothing I want that you can give me." Standing to leave, I met his gaze with a small, but resolute shake of my head. "I'm done."

———•———

Sighing, I squinted at the television and tried, once more, to make sense of the episode of *Un Posto al Sole* I'd been watching for the better part of an hour. Every time I thought I had the popular Italian soap opera figured out, a new character would appear and throw a wrench into my carefully contrived theories.

It wasn't exactly the way I'd expected to spend my last night in Italy, but it was better than crying over my disastrous afternoon with Cooper—which, incidentally, was what I did on the entire train ride back to Milan.

After walking out of the restaurant, I'd caught the next departing cable car from Alpino and returned to Stresa alone. Hungry and upset, with hours still to kill, I wound up treating myself to lunch at a small osteria I discovered tucked between two shops at the corner of a dead-end street. Then, stomach full, I caught a water taxi to Isola Bella, where I whiled away the remaining time taking an audio tour of the sprawling palace, roaming the Baroque terraced gardens, and snapping pictures of the regal albino peacocks as they strutted by.

If Cooper was on the train home, I didn't see him. Curled up in the window seat of an empty row, I cried quietly until we pulled into the Milano Centrale an hour later. With the help of my map, I found my way to Metra and finally to the villa, where I'd been barricaded in my room ever since.

"Bella?" Cooper's muffled voice called from behind the door. He knocked twice. "Can I come in?"

Using the remote control, I muted the television. "Sure," I said, sitting up.

Hair ruffled and eyes ringed with purple shadows, he looked tired as he entered. "What're you watching?"

"Soap opera."

He grinned. "And you understand it?"

"For the most part." I pointed to the actors flashing across the screen. "I'm pretty sure those guys were best friends until they both fell for the brunette. But she's already engaged to that guy, who's been cheating on her the whole time with the leggy blonde."

"Sordid," he said.

I smiled. "Indeed."

"Do you think we can talk for a sec?" he asked, inching closer.

Nodding, I turned off the television and waited for him to speak.

"I've been aimlessly roaming the streets for hours," he began. "Thinking about everything you said. But mostly trying to understand why it cut so deeply."

"That's not what I wanted."

He shook his head. "You were just saying what you felt. And, for what it's worth, you were right. There was no reason for me to react like that—no good one, in any case."

"Then, why did you?" I asked.

"I think it's because, deep down, your faith in God terrifies me." His sigh was heavy. "My formula for success over the years has been pretty basic. Work hard, stay humble, do unto others, and the universe will eventually do unto you. It was as good a philosophy as the next, I thought. And it seemed to be serving me well."

He shrugged. "I lead a pretty charmed life. Great career, lots of money, tons of fans. I'm the guy who's got everything. But then you come along with your talk of sin and Christ and love and redemption. And suddenly, I turn into the guy who's got everything and nothing at all. I don't know how to wrap my head around it. Some days, I'm not sure that I even want to. But you speak about Him with such certainty—more certainty than I've ever felt about anything—and it worries me. I don't want to reach the end only to find out that the entire time I was missing the bigger picture."

"You don't have to," I said. "And you don't have to take my word for it, either. He'll come running, if you just seek Him."

"Seek Him how?"

"Why don't you start by talking to Him? It doesn't have to be fancy or public or even long. It could be as simple as telling Him about your day." I smiled. "Trust me; He'll respond."

Cooper nodded. "I do trust you, and I'm going to give it a shot. But, I want you to give something a shot, too."

"What's that?" I asked.

His gaze met mine. "Us."

"Cooper," I began with a sigh.

He shook his head. "I know the way I acted today, the things I said—it's no wonder you're questioning whether or not we're right for each other. But I'm asking you to stick this out with me, anyway. I'm asking you to see me for the man I can someday be, instead of the man I am now.

"There are no scripts here, Bella. There's no special lighting, no clever edits, no second takes. Just a guy in love trying to figure it out as he goes. I'm not asking you to give me an answer tonight, but promise me you'll think about it. OK?"

I nodded.

Gingerly leaning over my bed, he planted a tender kiss on my forehead. "Get some rest," he said. "We fly to London first thing in the morning."

Eyes closed, I listened as he slipped through the door and quietly closed it behind him. Then, alone in the stillness, I released a breath I hadn't realized I was holding. And with tears streaming down my face, I pulled the covers to my chin and cried myself to sleep.

Forty

"Nervous?" Cooper asked.

Resting a sweaty palm against my churning stomach, I nodded. "A little."

"Don't be. You look gorgeous."

Glancing up at him, I smiled. "Thanks."

"If it makes you feel any better," he said, "my first premiere was a disaster. I tripped twice, forgot the name of the film I was there to promote, and wound up sneaking out early after I hurled all over my tuxedo in the men's room."

I laughed. "That's a terrible story."

"But one with a happy ending." He grinned. "Because now I'm here, sitting next to the woman of my dreams, getting ready to show her off to the entire world."

Bashfully, I looked away. "I think you just made me more nervous. If that's even possible."

Chuckling, he reached for my hand—ostensibly to hold it—but at the last minute raised it to his lips and softly kissed the back of it instead. "You'll be fine," he said. "I promise."

The faint screams of manic fans could be heard in the distance as the limo neared the venue. From our spot amidst the line of chauffeured cars crawling along the heavily guarded street, I spotted hordes of people quarantined behind metal barricades and gangling stretches of velvet ropes. Posted every few yards, uniformed policemen acted as added enforcement, and at the heart of all the mayhem was a star-studded red carpet.

Cooper straightened his jacket, tugging at his sleeves and then his lapels, before giving my knee a reassuring squeeze. "Ready?" he asked.

Breathing deeply, I nodded just as the car slowed to a stop and his door swung open.

He stepped out, in what seemed like slow motion, to an ear-shattering symphony of shrieks and cheers and desperate pleas from love-struck teenage girls flying homemade signs to jockeying paparazzo aiming imposing cameras alike. Cooper gave a cordial wave to no one in particular and then reached back inside to assist me.

I couldn't be sure if it was my nerves, the limo's low bucket seats, the height of my heels, the length of my gown, or an unwieldy combination of the four. But to my complete horror, I toppled out with an ogreish grunt.

"You all right?" Cooper asked, catching me before I hit the ground.

Using my hair to hide my face from the crowd, I nodded. "Just slowly dying from humiliation," I said.

Laughing, he consoled me with a kiss to the temple. "Remember, as soon as you find yourself in the bathroom with vomit on your dress, that's our cue to leave."

Despite myself, I smiled.

At the beckoning of one of the frenzied assistant coordinators, we cleared the way for the attendees arriving behind us and began our walk to the first journalist, who was waiting, microphone poised.

Draped across Cooper's arm, I felt every bit the glamorous accessory and I hoped, as I returned the reporter's warm smile, that my words would prove less clumsy than my feet had. But just before we reached her, someone caught hold of my elbow and tugged me around the bank of filming camera crews and through a discreet set of side doors.

It was Sue. Wearing a satin pantsuit and a laminated press pass, she listened, with a haggard expression, to the message being relayed through her headset. "I'm on it," she said, scribbling a note across one of the sheets of paper cradled in her arm.

Decidedly friendlier than when we'd last met, she smiled at me as she capped her pen and offered me a stiff hug. "You clean up nicely."

The muffled voice on the other end of her earpiece spoke before I could. Sue's eyebrows furrowed. "No, tell them ten minutes," she ordered in a tone that assured me she meant business. "Listen, I've got to get back." She motioned for me to make myself comfortable in one of the empty chairs lined against the wall. "As soon as Cooper is done with his interviews, I'll come and get you."

Nodding, I watched as she scurried out of the door and back into the mayhem.

There were a handful of women already lingering in the sparsely furnished holding room. Dresses sparkling and hair flowing, they all looked like slightly varying versions of one another. I couldn't help but wonder, with an inward shudder, if, to an outside observer, my appearance possessed the same fabricated quality.

No one spoke or even made eye contact as we waited like checked furs for our handlers to reclaim us. Three more dates were ushered in and another out before Sue appeared, as promised, to escort me to the theater, where Cooper was already seated.

His face brightening at the sight of me, he stood and waited patiently as I stepped over couture shoes and designer purses to reach him in the center of the row. "How're you hanging in there?" he asked. "Sue didn't torture you too badly, did she?"

Shaking my head, I eased into the chair beside his. "She was great," I said. "But I wish you would've told me ahead of time about the checkroom for dates."

His frown was apologetic. "I'm sorry about that. Red carpets can be kind of tricky. I never really know until I get there if they'll ask me to fly solo."

I shrugged. "It was probably for the best. Odds are I would've just tripped again."

He laughed. "I'm sure no one noticed."

"That's sweet." I smiled. "Even if it is a complete lie."

"Look at it this way," he said. "The hard part's over. Now all you have to do is sit back, relax, and enjoy the movie."

I glanced up at the giant screen before us and sighed. "So this is it? This is what all the fuss was about?"

He nodded. "Pretty anticlimactic, right?"

"Totally," I said. "I much prefer the regular approach to moviegoing—the kind that involves more popcorn and less eveningwear."

He grinned. "You and me both."

We chatted cordially with our neighbors as the theater slowly filled. Eventually, the house lights flickered and a bearded gentleman, who introduced himself as the director, gave a short speech about the inspiration for the film we were about to see.

Two hours later, the audience applauded as the ending credits rolled. The lights came back up, another short speech was given, and we were wished a good night.

"You did it," Cooper said, ushering me through the lobby toward the limo-lined curb. "You survived your first premiere."

"I feel strangely accomplished," I said, taking his proffered arm.

"Well, what do you say we reward your accomplishment with a little dinner before we head back to the hotel to pack?"

Smiling, I nodded. "I say that sounds like a perfect ending to one unforgettable trip."

PART IV

Back to Basics

Forty-One

My pulse quickened at the sight of Cameron seated at our usual table in the rotunda of the Grande Luxe Café. She stood when she saw me rushing toward her and easily caught me as I threw myself into her open arms.

Reluctantly releasing her, I took in her smart black blazer, matching pencil skirt, and simple leather pumps. "You look incredible!" I said, not entirely sure why I was surprised that she could pull off a tailored suit just as well as she could a micromini.

"Thank you," she said with a prim nod. Tilting her head, she scanned my unruly hair, wrinkled cardigan, and baggy jeans. "You look tired."

"Be nice," I cautioned as we slid into our opposite ends of the booth. "I spent eight turbulent hours flying home to discover that my condo's been hideously remodeled."

Cameron smirked. "How hideously?"

"Let's just put it this way: I am officially in Pottery Barn hell."

She laughed. Cameron, of all people, knew how much I despised pristine catalogue houses that looked like no one had ever lived in them.

"It's completely impractical," I said, thinking of the immaculate white sofa

301

sitting where my worn, leather couch used to be. "And on top of that, I can't find anything."

Adrienne, in addition to replacing my furniture, had taken it upon herself to rearrange everything from my CDs to my silverware. She'd also, despite my explicit instructions to the contrary, emptied my closet of nearly all of my pre-makeover clothes.

"The important thing is that you're back," Cam said, reaching across the table for my hand. "I missed you."

"I feel like I haven't seen you in forever," I said. "And it doesn't help that you waited until I was gone to go and get all grown-up." With an approving nod, I admired the classic pearl studs gracing either of her earlobes and the natural, understated tones of her makeup. "I don't think I've ever seen you look so sophisticated."

"Well, I'm glad you like it, because you'll be seeing me in stuff like this a lot more from now on."

"Why?" I asked, leaning forward intently.

Her smile was broad. "I got a promotion."

"Cam, that's fantastic!" I shook my head. "But I thought you said the offer was a lateral move."

"That's when I was up for lead coordinator," she said, proudly poking out her chest. "But you are looking at Snyder & Smith's newest account manager."

"What?" I blinked, stunned. "How did that happen?"

"There was a mix-up with a huge potential client," she said. "A couple of their suits flew in from New York for this big presentation, but the project lead had taken a personal day. Turns out her secretary had scheduled the meeting for the wrong week. No one on her team could find her and no one wanted to cover for her. Meanwhile, the execs are twiddling their thumbs in our boardroom. So I offer to take them to lunch—just to stall. And the next thing I know, I'm pitching ideas over prime rib at Morton's. By the time their car arrived to take them back to the airport, the ink was drying on their contract."

"So you saved the day," I said.

She gave a modest shrug. "When Mr. Brenninger heard what happened, he offered me account manager on the spot. He said I have a personality that will go far in PR."

"And anywhere else in life you want to go," I said.

Just then, our waitress appeared tableside and took our orders. "And to drink?" she asked, her pencil poised above her pad.

I flashed Cameron a naughty grin. "Let's get mimosas to celebrate."

"It's barely noon," she said with a slight frown.

I hesitated, unsure of what to make of her newfound propriety. "When has the time of day ever been a prerequisite to your drinking?"

"Actually, I've stopped drinking altogether. I decided it's not a habit I want to keep moving forward. But don't let me ruin your fun. Get whatever you like. I'll just have water, no ice, with an extra lemon wedge on the side," she said, glancing up at our server.

Feeling slightly flattened by Cameron's rebuff, I shrugged. "Water for me as well."

"So, I'm dying to hear all about Europe," she said, once the waitress had walked off with our menus. "Tell me everything."

I sighed. "Well, there were some good parts, but a lot of rough parts, too." Before I could tell her about either, her purse began to ring.

"Sorry," she said, digging through its front pocket.

I was horrified when, in lieu of her beloved pink flip phone, she pulled out a Blackberry identical to Cooper's. "This is Cameron," she sang in her most professional tone.

"Are you busy?" a deep, familiar voice asked from the other end. It was Oliver. Cameron lowered the volume with several discreet presses to one of the side buttons.

"Sort of," she said, casting a nervous glance in my direction. "Why, what's up?"

She listened quietly for several moments and then laughed. "Well, I told you not to do it," she said. "That's what you get for being hardheaded."

There was an ease to their exchange that, not so very long ago, hadn't existed. And I envied it. In the span of one week, it seemed, I had become a stranger in my own world. I hardly recognized my home, my oldest friend was wearing a suit and brandishing a Blackberry, and now Olly—my Olly—was calling midday to shoot the breeze with her instead of me. For as long as the three of us had known each other, I had been the common link, the glue that held us together. But in my absence, they'd formed a new bond—one that didn't include me—and I could do nothing but sit by and watch.

Sighing involuntarily, I sank into my seat as Cameron laughed, once again, at something he said.

She took me in from across the table with obvious pity. "Listen, I have to go. But I'll call you later."

Disconnecting the call with the push of a button, she returned the phone to her purse. "Sorry," she said. "I probably should have let that one go to voicemail."

"It's fine." I forced a smile. "I'm glad he has you."

A brief, but awkward silence fell between us. "Have you talked to him yet?" she finally asked.

Looking away, I shook my head. "I think maybe I'll give him some space and let him call me when he's ready."

Cameron's eyebrows furrowed with concern. "Mack, this is not Oliver's mistake to fix. He doesn't owe you the first move. And frankly, I don't think he has any intention of making it. If you want this friendship back, you're going to have to swallow your pride, roll up your sleeves, and work for it."

"I know. You're right. I just have no idea where to even start."

"I think I might," she said, her grin cunning. "There's this overnight camping trip he organized through a community center on the Southside. And the co-counselor he lined up fell through at the last minute. He's been scrambling all week to find a substitute, but no one could do it on such short notice. I felt sorry for him, so I said I would go, but it turns out I have a thing."

I narrowed my eyes suspiciously. "A thing?"

"Yes, a thing."

"What kind of thing?"

Cameron smirked. "A work thing."

"A work thing," I echoed, my tone skeptical.

"What difference does it make?" she asked. "The point is, I can't go and I nominate you to replace me."

"That'll never work," I said, shaking my head. "He won't believe it. I don't even believe it."

She shrugged. "He doesn't have to. The only thing that matters is that there are nine campers signed up and he has to have one adult per every five children. If he doesn't want to cancel the trip, he'll have to take you—whether he believes us or not."

"I don't know," I said, my stomach knotting as I began to consider the possibility in earnest. "This could end up making things worse than they already are."

"Maybe at first," she conceded. "But he can't stay mad at you forever."

"Why not? It's not like I wouldn't deserve it."

"Because he's still in love with you."

I swallowed back the hopeful swell in my throat. "How can you be so sure?"

"I just am," she said. "But it doesn't do you any good to keep taking my word for it. It's time for you, Isabelle Mackenzie, to gather your courage, face Oliver, and find out for yourself."

Forty-Two

Oliver, dressed in jeans, a sweater, and a down vest, was standing in the parking lot beside the open door of an idling van. Smiling, he slowly sipped coffee from the topless cup in his hand and nodded engagingly in response to the conversation he was having with a huddle of milling parents.

It was the first time I'd seen him since the morning he'd shown up unannounced at my condo and discovered that Cooper had spent the night. Cowardice gripped me in a wave of nausea as I stood paralyzed and grappled with the temptation to gun my engine and speed away.

Cameron had called before I left to rehearse the plan one last time and give me a much-needed pep talk. Drawing what strength I could from her echoing words of encouragement, I climbed out of my car. But with every step I took toward Oliver, her reassurances grew fainter, drowned out by the sound of my pounding heart.

Oliver shook hands with one of the departing couples, waved good-bye to several others, and took another slow sip of coffee before turning to see me standing a few feet away.

Any lingering hope I had that he would be glad I'd come was quickly put to rest by the shadow that crossed his face. Tossing his cup into a nearby trashcan, he stuffed his hands into his pockets and grudgingly made his way over to me. "What're you doing here?" he asked. His cold tone and callous stare were disheartening reminders that second chances were given solely at the discretion of the scorned.

"Cameron couldn't make it," I said, an imperceptible quake in my voice. "She had a thing."

"A thing?" he asked, his skepticism plain.

"I know. That was pretty much my reaction too," I said, braving a small grin.

He glared. "So she bailed on me?"

"Not exactly. She sent me to fill in."

Oliver's sneer was searing. "No thanks." Shaking his head, he started to back away. "I'll figure something else out."

"Olly, don't," I pleaded. "You can't just—"

"What? I can't just what?" he barked.

I flinched, startled by the anger I hadn't realized was bubbling so close to the surface.

"Say it," he ordered. "Please, I have to know exactly what it is you think you have the right to tell me I can't do."

There was a challenge in his stance, a ravening hunger for me to give him one last reason to push me away for good.

I chose my next words carefully. "You've got to have a second counselor in order to go. Why chance cancelling the trip when you don't have to? This weekend is about the kids, not us. I'm only here to help."

Sighing, Oliver closed his eyes and massaged the bridge of his nose, while he considered his limited options. Unaware of how much I'd missed him, I took the opportunity to rememorize his features.

Abruptly, he looked up and caught me staring. His expression hardened. "You're with group two. We leave in twenty minutes."

Nodding, I watched him make his way to the van, but halfway there, he turned and stalked back. "And just for the record, you're right. This weekend isn't about us," he said with a defiant thrust of his chin. "Because there is no us."

———•———

The kids were understandably excited as we pulled out of the parking lot and onto the highway for the three-hour drive to Wisconsin's Lake Kegonsa State Park. Ranging in age from eight to fourteen, most of them had never left the city's Southside, much less Illinois.

Olly was masterful with them, leading sing-alongs, making up silly games, telling corny jokes; he commanded both their adoration and respect without even trying.

I kept my distance and sat by a window in the back.

His last words to me still rang loudly in my ears. If I believed him, it was too late; our friendship was already over and he had only agreed to let me come because Cameron and I had pinned him against a wall.

But I didn't believe him. Though I had no doubt that I had hurt Oliver or that his hurt, over time, had rankled into seething malice, I was equally confident that same malice was cause for hope. In a strange, backward way, Oliver's anger meant he still cared. It meant somehow, beneath the blustering and blaring, I still mattered. And when it came to Olly, I would rather matter in a backward way than in no way at all.

We arrived at Kegonsa around noon, and with daylight burning and a campsite to reach before dark, immediately began the five-mile hike. It was an easy trail, not too steep and well tread, but for children who were accustomed to walking as far as the corner bus stop, it proved challenging.

Thunderstorms earlier in the day had left behind cumbersome quagmires in the natural dips and crevices of the rugged terrain. That, too, proved challenging for our little group of city slickers, who, thanks to Oliver's charm and finesse, had been gifted with brand-new hiking boots from his law firm's Charitable Contributions Fund. Determined to preserve their new shoes as best they knew how, they wasted valuable time and energy trying to delicately navigate around every mud slick and murky puddle in our path. And to top it off, thick cloud cover blotted out what small measure of warmth we might have received from the sun, while unseasonably gusty winds left fingers numb and noses red.

As the co-counselor, it was my job to keep my group of four girls motivated, and most importantly, together. But that was difficult considering that I was having an even harder time keeping up than they were.

Working against a running clock and a closet that had been purged of all things practical—including my trail hikers—I'd been forced to make do with what few articles Adrienne had left me. That was why instead of sturdy, waterproof boots that hugged my feet and laced to my ankles, I was wearing the shearling mukluks Cameron had gotten me for Christmas.

Oliver had on more than one occasion jokingly referred to them as glorified house slippers. His assessment, it turned out, wasn't far off. Though they looked built for hiking in the rugged outdoors with their wool lining and lugged soles, they were actually best suited for far less demanding activities. Like short strolls from the couch to the kitchen.

They provided no traction and no protection against the elements, which meant that several missteps into a few deceptively deep pools of water early into the hike had saturated my shoes and turned my socks soggy.

Banding together in an impressive display of teamwork, the girls in my group helped push and tug me up the inclines I would have been otherwise helpless to climb.

Oliver offered no assistance, opting instead to stay a good distance ahead with the rest of the pack. Seemingly, it made no difference to him whether I made it to the site or got left behind in the dense woods. And as my body began to tire and my emotions began to wear, I began to wonder if it had been a mistake to come. I began to question if what once was would ever be again.

Then, I slipped. Hitting the ground with a forceful thud, I shrieked. And Oliver stopped. He stopped and waited for me to get up, brush the soot from my hands and knees, and collect the canteen that had dislodged itself from my backpack, before turning and continuing on.

And just like that, my doubts were silenced.

———◆———

Near the halfway mark, we reached a clearing that offered stumps as makeshift seats and a rousing view of the lake below. Olly announced that we would take a 15-minute break and encouraged both groups to explore. Two hours of tramping up a dirt trail had soundly relieved them of their fear of getting soiled. And they wasted no time excitedly roaming about, their natural curiosity leading the way.

I claimed the trunk of a tree that had been presumably knocked over in the recent storms and took in the golden bed of leaves at my feet, the towering oaks at my side, and the majestic clouds overhead with a humble sigh.

In that moment, it seemed preposterous that I could have ever—even for an instant—questioned God's existence. His Spirit was alive and well in me, His sovereignty apparent in everything I saw. Like a dam breaking, I was flooded with memories of the many blessings and mercies He had gifted me throughout my walk with Him. All of the lessons He had tenderly taught. All of the patience He had untiringly granted. All of the joy He had willingly supplied. And I was overwhelmed with breathtaking gratitude.

Though my knees were already beginning to ache from my fall, my wet feet had grown numb with cold, and I had absolutely no idea how I was going to make it through the second half of our hike, I closed my eyes, tuned out the noise around me, cast my face to the sky, and gave the Lord praise.

I thanked Him for His unconditional love and unfailing goodness. I honored His dominion and worshiped His righteousness. I exalted Him as the faithful and just Father, King, and Savior He always had been, was, and would be. And then, with my heart contrite and my spirit meek, I repented.

Consumed with remorse, I confessed the countless selfish choices and wrong decisions I'd made in willful disobedience over the past several months. I asked His forgiveness for my contemptuous behavior and unappreciative attitude. I invited Him to resume His rightful place at the center of my life. And lastly, I beseeched Him to unknot the tangled mess I'd made of my relationship with Oliver.

My conscience felt light as a feather and my soul free as a bird as I thanked Him for hearing my prayer. Softly, I began to hum the first few bars of my favorite hymn.

"I don't get it," someone said. I opened my eyes to discover Oliver standing over me. He nodded down at my waterlogged mukluks. "Is this some sort of exercise in self-torture?"

"I'm fine," I said, shrugging.

He studied me for a long, silent moment, his gaze keen and searching, before kneeling down in front of me with a sigh. "I know you know these aren't real boots."

I only nodded.

"Then why did you wear them?" he asked. "Where are the trail hikers?"

I could have explained how they'd fallen victim to a decorating coup orchestrated by Cooper's agent, but something told me that Cooper's name would be best left unmentioned on this trip. "I couldn't find them," I said.

He narrowed his eyes, aware that I was holding back, but opted not to press the subject further. Instead he turned his attention to his backpack. After a few moments of digging, he pulled out a pair of socks—the kind that would wick away water. Using scissors he'd retrieved from the first aid kit strapped to a side pouch, he sliced them open from ankle to toe. "You don't have to do this," I said, gazing guiltily at his polyester liners.

"The temperatures are going to keep dropping," he said, resting one of my legs on his thigh. "And the trail just gets steeper from here. You'll never make it like this." Gently, he slid off my boot and turned it upside down. Water trickled out and he laughed. "Honestly, I don't know how you made it this far."

Wordlessly, I watched him insulate the bottoms and sides of my mukluk with the strips of fabric he'd created. Peeling my wet sock from my foot, he replaced it with a dry cotton one, over which he slipped a thick, wool knee-high. The effect was instantaneous. My toes ached and prickled as the warmth gradually returned to them.

"That should help," he said, repeating the same steps on my other foot, before lowering it to the ground with a satisfied pat.

I nodded my appreciation. "Thanks."

"You're welcome," he said, repacking his tools. His mission accomplished, I expected him to walk away; but he sat down, unscrewed the cap to his canteen, and took a swig of water. "Want some?" he asked, pointing it at me.

I took a sip and handed it back.

Quietly, we watched the kids frolic around us. Some chased each other with

312

sticks and leaves they'd found in the brushwood, others snacked on granola bars and juice boxes as they rested and talked. The mood was relaxed, peaceful.

"You could have told me, you know," Olly said. He kept his eyes forward and his voice even. "That you were leaving."

"I should have," I said, counting that failure chief among the many mistakes I'd made in recent weeks. "I should have done a lot of things."

He didn't respond, nor did I ask him to, and silence, compromising, but comfortable, settled once more between us.

———•———

With the back end of our hike still ahead, Olly wrangled the kids, did a head count, and then announced that we would, moving forward, be traveling as one, large group. "It's going to get a little tougher from here on out," he warned as he made eye contact with each of the attentive faces staring up at him. "Let's be sure to stick together. And if anyone needs a rest, don't be afraid to say so."

With newly padded boots and warm feet, I resumed our trek refreshed. Stepping confidently, I easily kept pace with everyone and even had to fall back for a couple of kids who had started to lag behind. But a mile in, we hit an especially muddy stretch of trail for which my pseudo-boots were no match. Holding out my arms to either side for balance, I attempted to scale an incline, but quickly lost my footing and began to fall.

Reflexively, my group lunged to my rescue, but it was Oliver who caught me. "I got her," he said, tightening his grip. Assured that I was in good hands, the girls rushed ahead to rejoin the rest of the clan.

Draping my arm around his neck and wrapping his arm around my waist, Oliver pointed at a bed of rocks to our immediate left. "Step there," he said, steadying me as I obeyed. "And now there." His finger was aimed at a thatch of leaves and broken twigs. As I followed his directions, I realized that the roughage underfoot was creating the traction that my soles lacked.

Slowly, we made it to the top. With the ground level once more, I could keep pace again. I managed sufficiently on my own, but Oliver stayed close enough to reach out a sure, supportive hand whenever he thought I might need it.

The sun, which had come out of hiding only long enough to begin its descent behind the horizon, was nearly gone by the time we reached the campsite. I helped the kids pitch their tents, while Olly and a couple of the older boys went in search of firewood.

Our dinner of baked beans and hot dogs, followed by a messy dessert of gooey s'mores, was a crowd-pleaser. Bellies full, we abandoned the log benches provided by the park and lay, instead, on the ground. Using each other for pillows, we quietly stared up at the sky and marveled at the twinkling spectacle to which we city dwellers weren't customarily privileged.

"Will you tell us a story?" a small voice called out into the stillness.

Smiling, I waited for Oliver to launch into one of the epic campfire yarns he'd become known for spinning amongst our camping buddies in our college days. But when I propped myself on my elbows and peered around, I was surprised to see that the little girl who'd made the request was looking at me.

I sat up and examined the rest of the group, faces set aglow by the flames flickering at the center of our huddle, waiting for me to answer. Nervously, I glanced at Oliver, who only smirked. "OK." I nodded. "Sure."

While they all got resituated on the logs, I mentally ransacked my limited arsenal of tall tales. Finally settling on a spooky one that could be easily curbed or embellished depending on their reactions, I commandeered a nearby flashlight, lifted it to my chin, and began.

It happened to be the story told by a friend to me and Oliver on our very first camping trip together. Listening alongside the others, his gaze was sentimental, his smile affectionate.

As any narrator worth her salt would, I made sure to give all of the characters distinct voices and pause for effect during the suspenseful parts. While Oliver, on occasion, provided the requisite soundtrack of heavy footsteps and creaking doors.

I was tickled to see that even the older kids, who'd clearly fancied themselves cynics, were growing increasingly jumpy as the tale reached its end. But noting one of the youngest campers timorously snuggled against her big brother's arm, I omitted the grisly climax and left our heroine lost in the haunted forest, never to be seen or heard from again.

There was a beat of silence, followed by a collective sigh of relief and then an unexpected torrent of pleas for more.

Laughing, I shook my head. "That's all I've got."

"And it's past your bedtimes," Oliver said, intervening. "We agreed lights out by ten. So scat!"

Grumbling, they collected their lanterns and dispersed to their designated tents.

In my desperation to tag along, I hadn't considered sleeping arrangements or the possibility that not bringing a tent of my own might pose a problem. My dilemma was not lost on Oliver.

"Come on," he said, pointing to his. "We can share."

"It's OK," I demurred. "I'll just..."

"What? Freeze out here in your sleeping bag?"

I shrugged. He had a point. The Midwest's autumn chill was a stark contrast to the balmy temperatures I'd experienced in Europe.

"Don't be a brat." He held back the rain fly. "Just get inside."

With my backpack in tow, I crawled to the farthest corner of the double-wall shelter. The space was cozy, intimate. Entering behind me, Oliver zipped us in.

Removing his down vest and crewneck, he replaced them with a hooded sweatshirt, bearing the name of our alma mater, layered over a Henley. Even though his long johns kept the moment perfectly innocent, I turned my head away as he tugged off his jeans and slid into a pair of track pants. "Aren't you going to change?" he asked, rolling his dirty clothes into neat bundles and storing them in the plastic grocery bag he'd brought.

I shrugged. "I'm good."

The corners of his mouth turned up into an amused grin. "You did bring something to sleep in, didn't you?"

I had. But not the heavy flannel pajamas needed to make it through a nippy night outside. Those, like my trail hikers, had fallen victim to Adrienne's less than practical fashion sense. In their place, she'd left a drawer full of nighties and satin drawstring pajamas. I'd brought a set of the latter hoping that the weather would be mild, but as I listened to the wind whir around us, I knew I'd be better off sleeping in my clothes. "These will be warmer," I said, pointing at my mud-stained khakis.

Olly shook his head. "They're wet. You'll catch a cold." He pulled a spare sweatshirt from his backpack and handed it to me. "Here, just put this on over whatever you brought."

While I faced one direction to change, he faced the other and busied himself arranging our sleeping bags into one large palette. Teeth chattering, I scampered beneath the top layer of blankets.

"All set?" he asked, reclining next to me.

I nodded and rested my head against the tent's padded floor as he put out the lantern. The darkness only seemed to magnify the chill. Closing my eyes, I tucked my knees to my chest in an attempt to warm myself.

"Do you feel that?" Oliver asked. I traced his silhouette in the shadows as he sat up and leaned toward me. "Mack, you're shaking."

"I'm OK," I said.

Ignoring me, he scooted closer and gathered me into his arms. Grateful, I pressed my shivering frame against his torso and buried my raw nose into his sweatshirt. Rubbing my back with quick, rhythmic strokes, he helped to speed my thaw.

Wistfully, I breathed him in. Unlike Cooper, who smelled of a different cologne every day, Olly's scent was familiar, comforting.

"Better?" he asked after a while.

"Much," I said, my sigh content. For a fleeting second, I feared he would use my answer as an excuse to pull away, but he only rested his chin against the crown of my head and let out a contented sigh of his own.

Eventually, his hand traveled from my back to my hair. The gentle caress of his fingers against my scalp, coupled with the steady rise and fall of his chest proved tranquilizing.

"Don't these annoy you?" he asked. I felt him finger several of the extensions that Sergio had added as part of my makeover. Oddly, that entire experience seemed like it had taken place a lifetime ago.

"You kind of forget they're there after a while," I said, my eyelids growing heavy. Tilting my neck, I positioned my forehead so that it rested in the soft crook between his jaw and shoulder.

He responded by hugging me closer. "I liked it better the old way."

I smiled. "Short and boring?"

"Simple and natural," he said.

There, lying against him, I felt a palpable shift in the mood. The uncertainty in the air dissipated, his guard fell and we were free to be us again—if only for a little while.

"Are you still mad at me?" I asked.

"Yes," he answered, though not immediately.

My swallow was audible. "I'm sorry. For what it's worth."

Shifting his weight, Oliver leaned away enough for us to look at each other. I could faintly make out the contours of his nose and mouth. "I guess I don't understand why," he confessed. "Why you did what you did."

I wasn't sure if he was referring to my decision to run away to Europe or my choice to pursue a relationship with Cooper instead of him. In the end, it didn't really matter. My reason for both was the same. "I think I felt I had to see what it would be like. I wanted to know what it was all about."

"And?" he asked.

Reaching up, I swept my hand along his lashes, down his cheek and jaw and across his lips. "None of it compares to you."

Breath mingling and noses touching, we hovered like that for some time. A gentle tilt of either of our faces and we would have kissed. But he didn't make a move. Something was holding him back. Resting his forehead against mine, he sighed. "I don't know anymore," he whispered. "I'm not sure I still feel the same."

The news struck me like a jab to the gut. "I understand," I said, turning my hips to roll away.

He stopped me with a firm press of his palm to the small of my back. "I just need some time to think things through."

Timidly, I returned my head to his shoulder. Gingerly, he resumed stroking my hair.

It didn't take long for exhaustion to overtake me. "I miss you," I murmured into his chest. Moments later, I grudgingly gave myself over to sleep.

But not before I heard him whisper, "I miss you, too."

Forty-Three

"Hey, time to get up."

My eyes fluttered open to see Oliver kneeling over me. Tenderly, he brushed the bangs from my forehead. "Good morning," he said.

Groggy and disoriented, my gaze searched the domed tent and then Olly's fresh sweater and jeans. I sat up. "You're already dressed?"

He nodded. "How'd you sleep?"

"Really well, actually."

"That would explain the snoring." He smirked.

"Whatever," I said, dismissing the accusation with a shake of my head. "I don't snore." Peering at him curiously, I bit my lip. "Do I?"

"Like a bear." He deadpanned. "With a sinus infection."

I laughed. "Be nice to me. I just woke up."

"I know, which is why I brought you this." He produced a tin cup of piping hot coffee.

"You know me too well," I said, accepting it with a grateful smile. He watched as I took several tentative sips. "What?" I asked, raising a brow at his

319

strange expression.

"Nothing." Shrugging, he glanced away, but quickly returned his gaze. "I just forgot how beautiful you look in the morning."

I simpered and took another sip of coffee. He was flirting.

"You should probably get dressed," he said, grinning at my grin. "The kids are finishing up breakfast and we'll start breaking down camp soon."

Nodding, I waited for him to leave and lower the rain fly behind him. Then, alone and brimming with giddiness, I set my cup down, threw my arms overhead, kicked my feet in the air, and gleefully tossed my head from side to side.

"Did I leave my wallet in there?" Oliver asked, popping back in without warning. Catching me in the throes of celebration, he smirked.

Nimbly, I crossed my legs Indian-style and breezily combed my fingers through my hair in a futile effort to play it cool.

"Never mind," he said, his eyes flickering with amusement. "See you out there."

Cheeks flushed, I buried my face in my hands as I listened to the sound of his fading laughter. When I had recovered enough to move, I brushed my teeth and took a quick bird bath using a bottle of water and a bar of soap. Changing into a clean pair of pants and a long-sleeve shirt, I tamed my hair into manageable pigtails, slipped on my damp mukluks, and joined Olly and the kids for the last half of breakfast.

After we'd all eaten our fill of bacon and eggs and Oliver and I had finished off an entire pot of coffee, we packed everything up and prepared for the four-hour hike back.

To my delight and great relief, the return journey was much easier. It was due in part to the fact that the pesky inclines we'd encountered on our way up had turned to navigable slopes on our way down. And it also helped that the frosty overnight temperatures had hardened the mud patches that had brought me to my knees the day before. But the best change—the difference that really mattered—was Oliver.

Walking in step with me the entire trek, he found reasons to stay near. Occasionally, he would lean in closer than necessary to point out roaming wildlife in the distance. At other times, he would graze his fingertips against mine as he turned to whisper something into my ear. Each touch and every look made my heart flutter and my head spin.

I was disappointed when we rounded the final bend to see the van waiting for us at the pick-up point. Oliver and I had reclaimed a piece of our old affection in the solitude of the woods and I wasn't sure what returning to the real world, with all of its uncertainties and complications, would mean for us.

We sat together on the ride home. His knee rested against mine as we sang silly songs with the kids, who were running high off of their sense of accomplishment.

As the van exited the highway and turned down the familiar potholed roads that led to the community center, Oliver slipped his hand in mine. "Come over tonight," he said, his breath tickling my ear. "I'll make dinner."

I smiled through the butterflies in my stomach and nodded. "OK."

Holding my gaze, he cupped my jaw and, caressing my cheek with his thumb, gently drew my face closer. The commotion taking place around us seemed to disappear as I tilted my chin and closed my eyes.

"Look!" someone shouted. "It's Channel 7!"

I heard Olly sigh as his hand dropped. The moment sufficiently broken, I followed the trail of pointing fingers to a news truck idling amidst a gaggle of waiting parents.

"How much you wanna bet somebody got shot?" one of the kids asked as the van came to a shuddering halt. I spotted Cooper's rented sports coupe amidst the rows of parked cars and instantly knew that the only thing in jeopardy of being fatally wounded was my relationship with Oliver. He and I were the last to debark.

Rushing over, Cooper swept me up and planted a sloppy kiss on my lips as a news camera rolled nearby.

"What're you doing here?" I asked, wriggling out of his arms the instant he pulled away. Self-consciously, I glanced at the crowd watching our every move.

"We wrapped early today so I thought I'd surprise you."

"With a camera crew?" I asked.

"They tailed me here. You know how it is." He shrugged. "What's the matter? Aren't you happy to see me?"

I didn't get the opportunity to respond. Having had ample opportunity to dig up scraps of paper, the kids bum-rushed us in their quest for an autograph from Cooper. Laughing, Cooper borrowed a pen from one of the starstruck mothers and began scrawling his signature.

With her cameraman in hot pursuit, the eager reporter who'd followed Cooper all the way out to South Deering muscled her way through the huddle of children with a polite, but determined smile. "Mr. Young," she said, flicking a strand of hair over her shoulder, "Can you tell us about your work with the community center?"

Still scribbling his name, Cooper glanced distractedly at the microphone hovering inches from his face. "I love kids," he said. "And I've always believed in doing whatever I can to invest in their futures."

I shook my head and glared. The scene was completely wrong. Oliver was the one they should have been thanking. He's the one who deserved their praise. Backing away from Cooper, who had moved on from signing autographs to shamelessly pumping his upcoming flick, I searched the lot for Olly.

Unable to find him, I checked the van, the building, and the playground behind it. There was nothing. He was nowhere. Panic set in as I retraced my steps outside, where the swarm around Cooper only appeared to have grown.

Angered by how easily their allegiance had been swayed, I considered marching over there and giving them all a piece of my mind. But my thoughts were cut short, my disgust sidetracked, as I watched Oliver's SUV pull out of its parking space behind the news truck and drive away.

Forty-Four

Costumed in a silk fishtail gown and dripping in diamonds, I stood in front of my closet mirror and studied my reflection. The dress and jewels had been couriered to my condo earlier in the day, along with an engraved invitation from Cooper to a glitzy black-tie event.

It's not the way I'd hoped to be spending my evenings after my camping trip with Oliver. But my countless phone calls to him had gone unanswered, every desperate message left unreturned. Meanwhile, Adrienne and Sue's calls to me wouldn't stop. They had spent the week Cooper and I had been in Europe masterfully coordinating Bella's grand unveiling in an exclusive they'd wheedled with some high-profile magazine.

From what I could gather through their emails and constant texts, the impending days were going to be a whirlwind of wardrobe fittings and photo shoots. I was tired of being fashioned and I didn't want to be debuted, but my protests to that effect were casually dismissed as last-minute jitters.

The choice to reclaim my life was mine. I knew that. At any given moment I could say the word. I could end things with Cooper and simply walk away. But every time I worked up enough nerve to do it—each time I picked up the phone to make the call—I was gripped by paralyzing doubt.

What if I was too late? What if Oliver still wouldn't forgive me once I left Cooper? What if after all of the upsets and tumults, the missteps and blunders, the remorse and amends, I wound up alone?

Fear was a pathetic reason to stay in a relationship with a man I had concluded I could never love. Cooper wasn't God's choice for me. And if the preceding weeks had taught me anything, it was that I was better off by myself for the right reasons than with somebody else for the wrong ones. But those nuggets of wisdom offered very little comfort in the wake of how carelessly I had handled Oliver's heart.

As things were, I had no assurances when it came to our future, only the sound knowledge that if he and I were meant to be, the Lord would bring us back together in His own way in His own time. And the horrifying understanding that if we weren't, I stood the chance of losing him forever.

My phone rang and I rushed to answer it, hopeful, as I waited for a reply, that I would hear Olly's voice on the other end.

But it was just the doorman calling to let me know that the car Cooper sent for me had arrived.

The tent that had been erected to host the affair in Millennium Park was enormous and heavily guarded.

Gloriously lit, we spotted it some distance away at the security checkpoint, where my chauffeur pulled to a stop and flashed my invitation. We were waved through and I was driven to the entrance, where a white-gloved attendant opened my door and welcomed me with a formal bow as I stepped out.

Thanking him, I tucked my clutch beneath my arm, smoothed the creases from my gown, and followed the blue carpet that led up a shallow set of steps and into the soiree taking place on the other side of canopied walls.

The dimly lit space was teeming with guests festooned in their finest, all talking and drinking and sampling hors d'oeuvres. I spotted many recognizable faces, from the mayor and his wife to a cast member from my favorite reality show, as I compassed the room in search of Cooper.

"Champagne?" one of the passing servers asked. Smoothly, he lowered his tray of flutes.

"No, thank you. But is there anywhere I can get a glass of water?"

He aimed me toward the bar, where I spotted Cooper carrying on a conversation with an older gentleman and his much younger date. He looked comfortable and confident with one hand tucked into the pocket of his tuxedo and the other holding what looked like a snifter of cognac.

I headed in his direction, intermittently excusing myself as I steered around and skirted between milling parties.

He glanced at me as I approached, but disinterestedly looked away when I waved. It wasn't until I came to a stop beside him that his eyes narrowed with recognition.

"Sorry I'm late," I said, nodding to the couple opposite him as I joined their circle.

Cooper's frown was disapproving. "What happened to your hair?" he asked, looking behind me as though he might find the rest of it there.

After two days of crying on Cameron's shoulder over how disastrously my weekend with Oliver had ended, I decided it was time to stop lamenting the current state of my circumstances and start making the necessary moves to change them. My first appointment was with my pastor to arrange weekly counseling. And the second was with a salon to have my extensions removed.

Natural and simple was what I'd told the hairdresser when she sat me in her chair and asked if I knew what sort of style I wanted. We decided to keep the side-swept bang, but whittled the rest down to an asymmetrical bob that fell just past my chin.

"Nothing happened," I said. "I got it cut."

He shook his head. "Not very well."

The rail-thin blonde standing next to me gave my forearm a sympathetic squeeze. "Don't worry about it. Just the other month, I went in for a trim and my girl lopped off three inches." She rolled her eyes in a show of kindred commiseration. "I could have strangled her. Fortunately, even the worst haircuts grow out with time."

Cooper sipped his drink. "Let's hope this one's no exception."

Ignoring his quip, I extended my hand. "Isabelle Mackenzie," I said, introducing myself. The couple, Bob and Sheila, I learned, owned the production company that was producing Cooper's current project.

"We were just telling Coop about our trip to Vail."

"Do you ski?" Sheila asked.

"No." Shaking my head, I shrugged. "Never came across the opportunity."

Bob smiled. "You won't be able to say that for much longer."

"They've invited us to join them at their chalet next weekend," Cooper explained.

Glancing up at him, I was barely able to mask my indignation. "And *we* said yes?"

"Oh, you'll love it," Sheila assured me. "It's got shopping like you wouldn't believe, great spas, amazing restaurants."

"Hunting," Bob interjected with a manly grunt.

"Plus, we've found it's the perfect little couple's hideaway," she said. Her grin was suggestive as she snuggled against Bob's chest. "We've been going there for years to keep the spark alive."

"How long have you been married?" I asked.

Sheila smirked. Bob laughed. "We're not married—never will be, if we can help it," he said. "Trust us when we tell you that's the other key to keeping the spark alive. Soon as you get that piece of paper, it's all downhill."

Chuckling, Cooper placed a hand on my hip and reeled me closer. I tensed, but didn't resist. "We'll be sure to keep that in mind," he said.

Just then, our MC for the night took his place behind the microphone and prompted us to find our seats. "We'll begin shortly," he promised.

"Shall we?" Bob asked, stepping aside so that Cooper and I could lead the way into the sea of tables.

"Actually, you guys go ahead," I said, tossing my thumb over my shoulder in the direction of the bar. "I'm going to get something to drink."

Holding up his empty snifter, Cooper nodded. "I think I'll get a refresher too," he said. "We'll catch up to you."

Watching, I waited for them to saunter out of earshot, before aiming an angry scowl in Cooper's direction. "How dare you commit me to go to Colorado," I hissed.

His forehead puckered. "Did I miss something?"

"I have a life here, Cooper. I have friends and family and a business to run. You can't assume that I'll always be at your beck and call." Huffing, I folded my arms. "You need to start asking me if I *want* to do things."

"Fine." His tone was curt, his gaze stony. "Bella, do you *want* to go to Vail with me next weekend?"

"No!" I glared. "And would you please stop calling me that?"

He studied me intently for several moments. "OK, what is this really about?"

"It's about you making plans *for* me instead of *with* me."

"No, it's bigger than that," he said. "Ever since we got back from London it's like I can't do anything right. Why?"

Suddenly exhausted, I felt the fight drain out of me. "Forget it," I said, turning to walk away.

"Hey, hang on a second." Gently, he grabbed my elbow and pulled me back. "Talk to me, Bella." There was a pause as his eyes, wide and sincere, met mine. "Mack," he amended. "Tell me what's going on?"

Sighing, I lowered my gaze with a shake of my head. "I don't think I can do this anymore," I confessed. "I know I promised to give us a shot and you're a great guy, but this isn't me. I don't belong here." Summoning my last bit of courage, I peered up at him. "I don't belong with you."

He stood silently for a brief while, before taking my hand in his and nodding. "I know."

I stared, stunned. "Why didn't you say something?"

"Well, I wasn't just going to let you go. You're too rare a catch for that." He smiled. "I guess I hoped over time I could make you fall for me the way I fell for you."

"I don't think it works that way," I said.

He shrugged. "A guy's got to dream, right?"

"I really am sorry, Cooper."

"Me, too. But at least I'm walking away with one good thing."

"A killer tan?" I joked.

He laughed. "That. And I talk to God now—every morning, in fact." His eyes flickered with pride. "I think it may be the beginning of a beautiful friendship."

"The best one you'll ever have," I promised.

A poignant lull settled over us as we stood facing each other, neither of us certain what to do next. "The night's still young," Cooper said, gazing over my shoulder at the roomful of people still trying to find their tables. "Will you stay? Have dinner with me?"

"I can't. There's something I have to do."

His nod was understanding. Wrapping his arms around me, he drew me in for a long hug. "Take care of yourself, Mack. And don't be a stranger."

"You either," I said, giving his hand one last squeeze before turning toward the exit.

Outside the evening air was cool, liberating. I bypassed the bank of parked town cars and limousines and headed straight for the row of taxis. Hopping into the nearest one, I gave the driver Oliver's address and guaranteed him a generous tip if he stepped on it. Then, I fished my cell phone out of my clutch and called Cameron.

"I did it!" I shrieked the instant she picked up. "I ended things with Cooper."

"I'm proud of you," she said. "You sound different already."

Sighing, I leaned back against my seat. "I feel different."

"So where are you now?"

"On my way to Oliver's," I said. "I have to fix things with him or at least try."

"I'm not sure that's such a good idea." There was an anxious edge to her voice that made me sit up.

"Why, what's wrong?"

Her sigh was preceded by a long silence. "I begged him to tell you, Mack. I really did."

"Tell me what?" I asked, straining to keep my dread from turning to full-blown panic.

"A couple of weeks ago, Oliver was offered a senior associate position at his firm's San Francisco office." The pause that followed was ominous. "He accepted."

"So he's leaving?"

"No, Honey," she said softly. "He's already gone."

Tears, stinging and uncontrollable, sprung to my eyes and streamed down my face. "There's got to be some sort of misunderstanding." Swallowing back a sob, I swiped at my damp cheeks. "I was just with him last weekend. He asked me to come over for dinner. Why would he do that if he was planning to move?"

"I wish I had more answers for you," she said, her own voice cracking in response to my distress. "All I know is that he wasn't supposed to leave for another few days, but he decided last minute to catch a red-eye out tonight."

I sniffled. "Tonight?"

"Yes," she said. "And I only know that much because I happened to call him while he was at his gate."

"How long ago was that?" I asked.

"I don't know. Ten, maybe twenty minutes."

"Did he happen to say what airline he was flying?"

"AmeriWest, I think. Why?" She gasped. "You're not going to do anything stupid, are you?"

"Which airport?"

"Mack, don't," she pleaded. "The flight leaves in an hour. You'll never make it anyway."

"Midway or O'Hare?" I asked.

"Listen, give it some time. Let him have his space. Who knows? Maybe in a few weeks, he'll be ready to sit down and—"

"Cameron!" My grip around the phone was so tight my knuckles ached. "Midway or O'Hare?"

The answer came quietly and with audible reluctance.

Thanking her, I hung up and banged on the Plexiglas partition. "Change of plans," I said to the driver. "I need you to get me to O'Hare as fast as you can."

Forty-Five

Running mascara and a ball gown serve as an automatic pass to the front of a line. I discovered that as I pleaded with a winding procession of AmeriWest customers for permission to cut in front of them. Of the scads of passengers waiting to check-in, not one said no.

The booking agent whose request for the next person in line yielded me looked unsure, as though she was teetering between offering her condolences and calling security. "I need a ticket," I said.

Her nod was slow, her mouth pursed with suspicion. "To anywhere in particular?"

"San Francisco. There's a flight leaving tonight."

Fingers dancing across the keyboard at her station, she squinted at something on the computer screen and frowned. "I'm afraid that flight is unavailable. Tickets have to be purchased at least two hours before departure. This plane is scheduled to push back in twenty minutes."

"Then, I'll take the next flight," I said, my anxiety mounting with every second I wasted talking and not running to catch Oliver. The details printed on my boarding pass were inconsequential. I just needed something—anything—to get me past security and through to the main terminal.

She punched more keys and consulted her screen. Another frown. "Our next flight to San Francisco leaves tomorrow morning."

"OK, fine," I said, retrieving my ID and credit card from my purse. I slid them across the counter. "Book it."

She studied me for several moments, a glint of sympathy in her eye, before leaning closer. "It won't do you any good," she said, her voice hushed, conspiratorial. "In order to get to the concourses, you have to have a boarding pass for a flight that departs tonight."

Chin trembling, I nodded.

"You might consider a trip to Miami instead," the agent said with a telling raise of her brow. "It's supposed to be beautiful this time of year and it leaves in just a few hours."

My smile was weak, but grateful. "Miami, then."

She worked quickly and efficiently, understanding, if nothing else, that I was up against the challenge of trying to catch a flight that would be taking off in mere minutes. "Good luck," she said, offering a supportive wink as she handed me my refundable ticket.

I thanked her and rushed to security, where I tearfully convinced the befuddled guard manning the nonexistent, first-class line to make an exception and let me through his detector.

Once on the other side, I consulted the wall of television monitors that listed all scheduled arrivals and departures. Oliver's plane was leaving in eight minutes from Gate C29. I didn't know what I would do when I got there, how I would explain myself, who I would have to convince in order to get on the plane. But I filed those details under Bridges to Cross When Reached, removed my heels, hiked my gown, and made a dash for it.

Parrying the stares of curious travelers, I sprinted down the series of moving walkways, dodging rolling luggage and strolling seniors, passing retail merchants and fast food chains. I kept moving, even though the gates came slowly. I kept stepping, despite the ache in my calves and the burning in my lungs.

As I ran, I assured myself that I would make it on time, that everything would turn out all right—not because I deserved it or because he owed me another chance, but because ours was a love worth saving.

Nearing his gate, I slowed to a trot—C26…C27…C28.

C29 was deserted save for the AmeriWest attendant behind the ticketing counter. The boarding doors next to her were closed and from the large picture windows facing the tarmac, I could see that there was no plane parked outside. The information scrolling across the electronic sign above the kiosk was for a flight departing to Boston.

"Excuse me," I said, jogging up to the woman.

She took me in from windblown head to bare toe. "Yes?"

"Isn't there supposed to be a flight to San Francisco leaving from this gate?"

She nodded. "It's taxiing now."

Yanking my cell phone from my clutch, I checked the time. "But it's not supposed to leave for another two minutes," I said, holding it out to her as proof.

"Yes." She nodded again. "But all confirmed passengers were onboard so they were cleared for an early takeoff."

I stared blankly at the empty runway, my hope evaporating. "This can't be happening," I said, the words coming out as a whisper.

"Would you like me to see if I can get you a seat on the next flight?" she asked.

Unable to speak, I shook my head, and with a quiet shuddering sob, finally, helplessly surrendered to the truth.

I was simply too late.

Forty-Six

The cab ride home was quiet. I thought my emotions would be reeling, my mind processing, but I was strangely subdued as I stared at the familiar blur of twinkling city lights just beyond my window. It was as if my subconscious knew that I could take no more. The evening's happenings had eviscerated me. And all that remained was a crushed spirit and a broken heart. Tomorrow, I would seek comfort in my heavenly Father. I would crawl into His arms and search the reasons why as I cried the first of many tears. But tonight, I would sleep. Not to rest, not to dream, but to forget.

I arrived at my building well after midnight. The lobby was empty save for the doorman, who tipped his hat and wished me a good evening. I smirked resentfully at the well-intentioned pleasantry. It was going to be a long time before the word *good* would be used to describe anything in my world again.

Riding in the elevator, I steadied myself against the mirrored wall and tried to take solace in the thought of a hot shower and my warm bed.

My eyes flew open with the sudden realization that *my* bed was gone. It had been replaced with some froufrou wrought-iron contraption of Adrienne's choosing that creaked when I sat on it. A loud, bitter laugh escaped my lips as the doors parted and I stepped onto my floor.

"Fun night?" Oliver asked.

I froze at the sight of him standing in the carpeted hallway.

His eyes trailed the length of my evening gown, stopping at the red-soled stilettos dangling from my fingertips, before finally settling on my shocked face. "You look nice." He pointed at his own hair in reference to mine. "I like the new do."

"It's not what it looks like," I said.

He shoved his hands in his pockets. "What does it look like?"

Like I was stumbling in after a late night out with Cooper. Like the camping trip had meant nothing. Like I was a liar.

"I've been at the airport for hours," I said.

"Because of me?"

My chin trembled. "I thought you'd left."

"Without telling you?"

I nodded.

Sighing, he lowered his gaze. "I thought about it," he confessed. His jaw flexed with unspoken resentment. "You made it look so easy."

Sniffling, I braced myself for a fresh wave of tears. If only he knew what I would give for a chance to turn back time and right every wrong decision, every rash mistake.

"But I couldn't," he said. His shrug was accepting, his smile faint. "I owe you this. If nothing else."

That was the answer to the question I'd been desperately wondering, but too afraid to ask. He hadn't come to tell me that he'd rethought the promotion or that he'd changed his plans. He wasn't standing in my hallway to grant forgiveness or mend fences. He'd come to say good-bye.

"Please don't go," I begged, my voice cracking. "Don't go, Olly." It wasn't the time to reserve judgment, to mince words or save face. I was operating on borrowed time, and I was prepared to use every last second of it pleading with Oliver to stay in Chicago. To stay with me.

He shook his head. "I have to."

336

"You don't!" I said. "You have a choice." A wail, choking and guttural, fought its way from my chest to my throat. "Choose me."

"Don't cry," he said. His expression was tender as he reached out for me.

Pushing his hand, I stepped back. I didn't want to be held, not by him. Not when his eyes told me that he was still leaving.

"I'll visit. We'll see each other," he promised.

"I love you." The words came out as a whisper. "I'm *in* love with you, and I want us to be together."

His brow wrinkled with emotion as he looked away. "I love you, too."

"Then, where are you going? Why are you giving up?"

"Because it's not enough anymore," he said, his lashes moist. "They offered me this position at the end of last year. Did you know that?"

I shook my head.

"And again just a few months ago." He sighed. "But I kept stalling. I kept putting them off because of how I felt about us. I didn't want to do anything that might jeopardize my chance to be with you. And for a brief window there, I thought it might actually happen. But then Cooper Young, of all people, blew in and swept you off your feet."

"Only because I was too blind to see what I had right in front of me."

"It doesn't matter," he said. His smile was kind. "The point is I have to stop staking my fulfillment in other people, including you. This promotion is a huge opportunity—one I feel the Lord leading me to take." Wiping his wet chin on his sleeve, he reset his shoulders with newfound determination. "It's time to start focusing on what's best for me. And right now what's best for me is San Francisco."

It was a fork-in-the-road moment; the sort of seminal juncture that would not only determine his ultimate decision, but also influence everything that came after it.

Despite his arguments to the contrary, Oliver was not resigned in his resolve to move. I could see the uncertainty in his wavering gaze; I could hear the hesitation in his every faltering word. He would sacrifice the promotion, if I begged long and hard enough. If I pressured him to reconsider, he would stay.

But I'd made a wrong turn myself not so long ago. And it'd led me down a dark, frustrating road—one that had been exponentially more difficult to journey out of than it had to venture into. I didn't want that for him. In his own gentle way, Oliver was trying to help me understand that his happiness hinged on my heartbreak. Because he knew, as well as I did, that in the end, the choice was mine to make.

Smiling feebly, I shrugged. "Then you should go to San Francisco."

The tension in his stance eased as he received the permission he'd been seeking. "You're going to be fine," he said, closing the distance between us. Cupping my face in the palm of his hand, he held my gaze with his. "We both are."

I nodded, though the throbbing in my chest suggested otherwise.

Grazing his thumb across my cheek, he leaned in, chin lowered. I closed my eyes and waited somberly for our lips to meet. But at the last minute, he tilted my neck downward and planted a soft kiss on my forehead.

It felt strange, empty.

He pressed the call button and, seconds later, offered me a small wave as the lift arrived. The metal doors parted with a familiar ding. "I'll see ya," he said.

Words failing me, I nodded.

And just like that, Oliver strode onto my elevator and out of my life.

Forty-Seven

"I forgot how good these were," Cameron said. She picked up the miniature sauce bowl on the table between us and dredged her shrimp toast along the sides in an effort to scrape off the remnants of spicy mustard. Popping the last bite into her mouth, she sighed. "Heaven."

I laughed. "Would you like to lick the plate? I see a couple of crumbs you missed."

"Hey, back off," she said, smirking as she chased her lunch down with a sip of water. "This is the first thing I've had to eat all day."

"That's because they've got you running eighty miles an hour over there lately." I shook my head. "Pretty soon you're going to have to start scheduling bathroom breaks."

It turned out Cameron really did have the personality for PR. In the short time since she'd been made account manager, she had signed on two more clients, one of which had flown her to Hawaii for a week to oversee the marketing campaign she had spearheaded.

"It's a little insane right now," she admitted. "But I start interviewing second assistants next week."

I grinned. "I never thought I'd hear you utter those words."

"Me either." She shrugged. "Just goes to show what God can do when we surrender ourselves to Him, right?"

I nodded. The only thing more incredible than Cameron's burgeoning career was her blossoming faith. Shortly after she began attending Sunday services with one of the members of her small group, she prayed to receive Christ. It marked the beginning of one of the most passionate chases after the Lord I'd ever seen. Her fervor was inspiring, and I treasured the deeper level of intimacy it brought to our friendship, especially as I worked to get my own walk back on track.

It wasn't as easy as I'd anticipated or as simple as I had hoped. Though I was confident in God's love for me and resolved in my renewed devotion to Him, I found myself still plagued by the anger and doubt that had led me astray in the first place. Weekly counseling sessions with my pastor slowly unearthed the root of both as my longstanding resentment toward my father, while rich daily devotionals helped me retain my joy and secure my peace through the painful healing process.

As I began to gain my footing, I made intentional efforts to surround myself with other believers. I joined my church's praise and prayer teams. I plugged into the singles' ministry and volunteered for weekend service projects. And at Cameron's behest, I hosted a now-thriving women's Bible study that she and I co-taught. There were still moments when heaviness set in, still spells when I wasn't sure where I'd find the strength to get out of bed and face the world, but my hope was secure in Christ; and as I took my steps of faith, one day to the next, I found that the good weeks were finally starting to outweigh the bad ones.

"That's right." My grin widened into a smile. "You are walking proof that God specializes in miracles."

"And fresh starts," she said, a familiar pestering glint in her eye.

Tossing my napkin on the table, I shook my head. "Don't."

"He asks about you all the time."

I braced myself for the pang, the same piercing stab that followed every mention of Oliver. He'd been gone for six months. Initially, his calls came regularly, even though our talks were forced and awkward, plagued with long silences we seemed helpless to fill. Alone in an unfamiliar city, with a new demanding job and few friends, he needed me. And with time and a little persistence, we eventually found our long-distance stride.

But as the weeks passed, our conversations began to change. I heard less of what he missed about Chicago and more of what he loved about his new home. The streets were cleaner, the weather was warmer, the restaurants were better, and the people were friendlier. Gradually, our phone calls were postponed—put on hold in favor of a game with the guys or an evening run in the park—until finally, they were forgotten altogether.

The more he acclimated to his life in San Francisco, the less I could bear to hear his voice. To my riddled conscience, it served as a daily reminder of what we were. And of what we were never going to be.

My decision not to talk to him anymore wasn't one I took lightly or made easily. It was preceded by many sleepless nights of prayer and a string of tearful afternoons on my pastor's sofa weighing the potential consequences. But in the end, I understood with utter clarity that I wouldn't be able to fully move on until I let Oliver go.

I issued him no warnings and offered no explanations; I simply stopped picking up the phone when I saw his number on my Caller ID.

His first letter arrived within a week. I slipped it, unopened, into my nightstand. But another came soon after, and another soon after that. In a month's time, I had a drawer full of envelopes holding his thoughts, possibly his feelings. But to read them would have been to rip open the wounds associated with our failed relationship. And no matter how stubborn my curiosity, I couldn't chance returning to that dark space.

Cameron, not yet aware of my decision to distance myself from Oliver, let it slip that he would be in town for Thanksgiving. I packed my things and headed to my brother's for the weekend. She made the same announcement about his Christmas plans, and I extended my visit home through New Year's.

His efforts petered out after a while, but he still sent the occasional message through Cameron, who made no qualms about her belief that Oliver and I were meant for each other.

"I thought we agreed you wouldn't do this."

"Do what?" she asked, her eyes wide and innocent.

"Play Cupid."

"Cupid makes people fall in love," she pointed out with a glib shrug. "You two are already in love. So technically, I'm in compliance."

I shook my head. "Clever."

"All I'm saying is that you can't keep going like this. Moping is not healing."

Maybe it wasn't. But who I was, the person I'd become over the resulting weeks and months, was my natural state of being in Olly's absence. Some days, I felt like the equivalent of a patient who'd lost her breasts to cancer or a soldier who'd returned home without a leg. Though they'd be forever changed, forever impaired, they learned to operate in a new normal.

It's not what they would have wished for themselves; it certainly wasn't easy. But they figured out how to work around it, how to smile in spite of it, how to persevere because of it. And so it was with me.

"Where'd you steal that from?" I asked. "A fortune cookie?"

"Dr. Phil," she said, smirking.

I laughed. "Well, I appreciate the concern, but I'm fine. Really."

"Good." She studied me for a quiet moment. "Because I have something to tell you."

Sipping my iced tea, I waited for her to go on.

"I was picked to head up the Nakamura launch," she said.

I felt the tension in my shoulders ease. "That's good, right?"

"Amazing, actually. They're one of our biggest accounts."

"What an honor," I said, feeling every bit the proud best friend.

"I know. I was shocked. It's a huge job." She bit her lip before hesitantly adding, "And it's in New York."

"So you're leaving me," I said, smiling despite the roiling in my stomach.

"Only for a few weeks. But I'll call every day, and we'll do something special when I get back—just the two of us."

I nodded. "Looking forward to it."

Flipping her wrist, she glanced at her watch and grimaced. "You know I'd love to stay longer."

"But you've got to go," I said.

"I have a meeting across town in half an hour," she said, pulling out her wallet.

"This one's on me."

"Are you sure?" she asked.

I smiled. "Call it a congratulations for landing your first big account."

Scooting out of the booth, she bent down and gave me a quick hug. "I'll call you later," she said, slipping on her trench coat before rushing into the brisk March afternoon.

I watched her trot down the street and around the corner before summoning our waitress and asking for the check.

She was the very same woman who'd served me and Cooper the time I'd brought him to Duffy's, though she offered no indication that she remembered me. It could have been my hair, which I now maintained in a bob, or simply that she had only noticed Cooper that day, but either way, I was glad to be a stranger—to be anonymous.

The morning after the gala, I'd received a call from Adrienne. She was insulting and irate, as though she was the one who'd been dumped the night before. Her breathless diatribe included a threat to come and get all of the new furniture in my condo—to turn my place back into the "tasteless dump" it used to be.

I'd welcomed her to do just that, a move that had only provoked another profanity-laced tirade. The most hurtful of her accusations was her assertion that I had used Cooper for his money. She claimed that I had no regard for his feelings or for the time and effort he'd stupidly invested in being with me, and insisted that I'd masterminded our meeting in California with the specific intention of "milking him for every quarter, dime, and nickel" I could get.

And though Cooper and I had never slept together, she called me a floozy, and informed me that I would be hearing from his lawyers concerning repayment of everything I'd fraudulently taken in our sham of a relationship.

Admittedly intimidated, I'd considered consulting an attorney of my own. But the following afternoon, I received an elaborate flower arrangement from Cooper at the bookstore. When I called to thank him, he informed me that his offer stood. If I wanted to expand Au Bon Livre, he was still willing to invest.

I turned him down. Though I was emotionally and mentally spent in the wake of Oliver's move, I had the wherewithal to know that a business partnership between me and Cooper was bound to be ill-fated. Any lingering fantasies I might have entertained were soundly put to rest just a few mornings later, when I arrived at work to discover a red "sold" sign on the boarded building next door.

A month after our breakup, rumors of a budding romance between Cooper and his newest costar surfaced along with rather convincing photos of the pair on vacation in Saint Tropez.

I shouldn't have been hurt and I had no right to be jealous. But I was. Cooper had a new leading lady; Oliver had his new life in San Francisco; Cameron had her new career. And I was still stuck, still waiting for my turn to arrive.

During one of our sessions, my pastor asked me if I would have chosen differently had I known in advance what the end result was going to be. Would I have settled for Cooper if only I'd been aware that leaving him wouldn't make Oliver stay?

The answer was no. Though the outcome had proven wholly unsatisfying and completely unfair, my choice had been the right one. And knowing that, I hoped, would someday be enough.

"There you go," the waitress said. Laying the billfold on the table, she briskly collected the soiled dishes and glasses cluttering the table and carried them away.

After checking the total, I placed the cash inside, slid out of the booth, and slammed right into Oliver.

"Whoa." He grabbed hold of both my arms to keep me from toppling over. "Are you OK?"

Moving the only part of my body that seemed to be working at the moment, I blinked.

He released me and took a small step back. "Iona told me you were at lunch," he said, pointing across the street in the direction of my bookstore.

I blinked again.

Anxiously, he rubbed his hands against his jeans and motioned toward the booth. "Can we sit?"

That time I managed a blink and a nod.

"You're just the same." Under the table, his foot touched mine. "Maybe a little quieter," he added with a nervous simper.

I decided to try my voice. "You look good." It was true. He'd grown out his hair and put on a little weight.

He smiled. "Thanks."

"You just missed Cameron," I said, attempting to fill the lull. "She's heading to New York soon—landed her first big account."

His forehead wrinkled. "I saw her yesterday. She didn't mention it."

It was my turn to look confused.

His shrug was weighted with guilt. "I've been here for a few days. Don't blame Cam," he rushed to add. "I swore her to secrecy."

"Why?" I asked, suddenly curious as to what else they'd been keeping from me.

"I wanted to surprise you myself." Narrowing his eyes, he grinned. "Plus, every time she tells you I'm coming, you skip town."

He was trying to keep the mood light, to recreate earlier, simpler times. But I couldn't. Somewhere in all of the hurt and confusion, the upset and disappointment, I'd lost my will to pretend. "What do you want, Olly?"

Shifting uncomfortably in his seat, he looked away. "I've been checking out real estate." He cleared his throat. "Commercial real estate."

Quietly, I waited for him to continue.

"For my own practice." His gaze met mine again. "Here in the city."

"So what're you saying?" I asked. "You're moving back?"

He nodded.

Six months ago, that was all I'd wanted to hear. Now, broken and exhausted, I wasn't so sure that I cared. "But you love San Francisco."

"No." He shook his head. "I love you."

I was surprised by the laugh, bursting and savage, that gurgled up from my gut, as well as the tears that sprung to my eyes.

"You don't believe me," he said, visibly wounded.

"I don't know." Dabbing at my cheeks with the back of my hand, I shrugged. "I'm not sure I know much of anything anymore."

"You know me," he said, his tone certain. "You know us."

Joining me on my side of the booth, Oliver swept my bangs from my forehead and angled my chin so that our gazes were level. "I haven't just been checking out buildings. I bought one," he said. "Next door to your shop."

"What?" I asked with a gasp and a bewildered tilt of my head. "Why? How?".

"Well, as to the how," he said grinning, "it was just a matter of contacting the owner. Turns out he's some big Hollywood actor with a soft spot for beautiful bookstore owners. As soon as I explained who I was and my motivation for the purchase, he offered it to me at a steal. And as to the why..." His eyes searched my face with an intensity that left me breathless. "Because I want to be the one who gets to make all of your dreams come true."

"But what happened to San Francisco, to focusing on what's best?"

He smiled. "Funny thing is, the longer I was away, the more I realized that what's best for me is you."

"Are you sure?" I asked.

"I've never been more certain of anything," he whispered.

In the wee morning hours of my thirtieth birthday, Oliver had kissed me. I was clueless, helpless to know that through his impulse God would set into motion a string of random and rocky events that would ultimately grant me everything I'd always thought I wanted, only to show me that what I wanted could never compare to what I already had.

"Come here," he said, gently drawing me closer as my tears ran down his hand.

The kiss that followed was every bit as sweet as the first, his touch every bit as soft as I remembered. He tasted of happiness and promise, hope and fulfillment, purpose and possibility. Even after we pulled apart, I could feel the tingle of forever on my lips.

"What now?" I asked, my adoring grin mirroring his.

"Anything," he said. "Everything."

And I knew he was right.

About Ryan M. Phillips

Ryan M. Phillips lives in Orlando, Florida. She is the communications specialist for The Ephraim Project, Inc. and the author of three previous novels. Other books include *Saving Grace, After the Fall,* and *Fall From Grace.* Ryan is currently working on her fifth novel, while pursuing a master of arts in English. Visit her Website at www.ryanmphillips.com.